DIRE THREADS

W9-COO-735

DIRE THREADS

JANET BOLIN

**WHEELER
CHIVERS**

This Large Print edition is published by Wheeler Publishing, Waterville, Maine, USA and by AudioGO Ltd, Bath, England.
Wheeler Publishing, a part of Gale, Cengage Learning.
Copyright © 2011 by Janet Bolin.
The moral right of the author has been asserted.
A Threadville Mystery.

LIBRARY OF CONGRESS CATALOGING-IN-PUBLICATION DATA

Bolin, Janet.
  Dire threads / by Janet Bolin. — Large print ed.
    p. cm. — (A Threadville mystery) (Wheeler Publishing large print cozy mystery)
  ISBN-13: 978-1-4104-4162-1 (pbk.)
  ISBN-10: 1-4104-4162-8 (pbk.)
    1. Embroidery—Fiction. 2. Murder—Investigation—Fiction. 3. Large type books. I. Title.
PS3602.O6534D57 2011
813'.6—dc22   2011028242

BRITISH LIBRARY CATALOGUING-IN-PUBLICATION DATA AVAILABLE

Published in 2011 in the U.S. by arrangement with The Berkley Publishing Group, a member of Penguin Group (USA) Inc.
Published in 2012 in the U.K. by arrangement with the author.

U.K. Hardcover: 978 1 445 87098 4 (Chivers Large Print)
U.K. Softcover: 978 1 445 87099 1 (Camden Large Print)

Printed in the United States of America
1 2 3 4 5 6 7 15 14 13 12 11

To the original Edna
and the original Naomi,
who loved creating with thread.

ACKNOWLEDGMENTS

Many thanks to my supportive critique partners, Krista Davis, who writes the Domestic Diva Mysteries, and Avery Aames, who writes the Cheese Shop Mysteries. I couldn't have done this without you.

I really appreciate the enthusiasm of my first agent, Jacky Sach, then at BookEnds, and my acquiring editor, Sandy Harding, then at Berkley Prime Crime. Jessica Faust of BookEnds never ceases to amaze me for the time she's willing to devote to my projects. Faith Black, my editor at Berkley Prime Crime, took my manuscript and turned it into a *book*. Thanks to all of the people at Berkley who helped her, particularly Robin Moline, who created the beautiful painting for the cover, Annette Fiore Defex, the cover designer, and Tiffany Estreicher, the interior text designer, who added touches that make the book even more special.

I also have to thank Bill Richardson and Shelagh Rogers of CBC radio for their encouragement over the years and for understanding my humor and making it funnier in the way they read my stories aloud on their radio programs.

Sisters in Crime, especially the Guppies Chapter, have been very helpful, including Lorna Barrett, Sandra Parshall, and Annette Dashofy. I loved hanging out with other members of the New York/Tri-State Chapter when I lived in New York. Those dinners in Greenwich Village made me feel like a real writer. Besides, I learned important things like the mechanics of getting published, and that authors, agents, and editors are approachable. Also that shouting, "Let's kill him!" in a restaurant can get one some funny looks. And no, I wasn't the one who did the shouting.

Thanks to all my friends at www.Killer Characters.com, where the characters of our books carry on a dialogue (and just plain carry on). Thanks to Avery Aames, Lorna Barrett, Krista Davis, Betty Hechtman, and Mary Jane Maffini for taking time to read my manuscript and comment.

And thanks to my friends and family for engaging in some rather peculiar conversations about murder and how to solve it.

We're nice people — really!

Last but not least, thanks to my readers. You're the greatest.

1

For the first time, my new boutique, In Stitches, was officially part of the Threadville tour, which was both exhilarating and daunting. What if the ladies from today's tour avoided my shop, or worse, hated it?

But the first person to enter In Stitches on its opening day was a man. Mike Krawbach was gorgeous, if you liked icy blue eyes and an underfed look that made a certain type of woman want to take him home and fatten him up. I didn't trust him. He always talked to me like I was two years old, for one thing. He tossed an envelope onto a bistro table displaying my embroidered white linen tablecloth. "Here you go, Willow. My decision on your application to renovate that *shed* at the back of your property."

Shed? Blueberry Cottage was a Victorian confection of curlicues and gingerbread trim. Small, made of wood, and quaint. Definitely not a shed. Renting it to others would help ensure my financial survival, but it needed work. "You mean Blueberry Cottage."

Mike stretched his neck up as if to make himself taller and remind me that he was the village's zoning commissioner, and I wasn't. "It's been called that grandiose name since my granddad was a boy. It's a shed, and it's on a flood plain, too close to the river for us to allow a building permit. You can paint it, inside and out, but you can't do anything structural, like replace leaky plumbing. Or leaky windows."

I resisted the urge to peek at his feet. He was tall, but even standing on his tippy toes, he wouldn't be able to loom over me as much as he might like. I argued, "The hiking trail is between it and the river, and that trail is wide. The Elderberry River couldn't rise that far."

Mike shrugged. "The decision is final. Take it or leave it."

That was a choice? He strode out, leaving me seething. In Stitches hadn't had a customer yet, and I was almost ready to return to investment counseling in Manhattan.

Almost, but not quite. Outside, the Threadville tour bus arrived, and ladies streamed from it. Their handmade hats, coats, mittens, and scarves outshone ice crystals dancing in the pale February sunshine. Women disappeared into The Stash, Batty About Quilts, Tell a Yarn, and Buttons and Bows.

Threadville's real name was Elderberry Bay. The village had been heading toward ghost town status until my best friend, Haylee, had fled Manhattan, opened The Stash, and inveigled other people to open other textile arts boutiques. Now, crafty women flocked to this small village on the Pennsylvania shore of Lake Erie to browse, take courses, find inspiration, and spend money.

I was a little stunned when about twenty of them poured into my shop. Their coats were decorated with every form of embellishment known to woman, except one — machine embroidery. They were coming to me to round out their education, and I had optimistically put five chairs around the table holding my computer and sewing machine.

A woman frowned at the logo I had embroidered on a suede vest trimmed with fun faux fur. The logo was my own design, a stylized weeping willow. Uh-oh. Didn't she like my work? The willow was supposed to help new students remember my name. "Tut, tut," she said. "Willow for sorrow."

The name Rosemary was emblazoned in sequins across the front of her sweater.

Rosemary for remembrance, I thought. "Willow's my name." I'd been Willow all my life and had never known sorrow. Except, perhaps, during Mike's visit a few minutes before. But I wasn't going to let Mike Krawbach ruin my first business day in my new shop.

"Maybe your sorrow will be trying to stay willowy all your life. You're doing a good job, so far." She lowered her voice to an ominous murmur. "Luckily, you can get away with wearing poufy fun furs, especially with your long legs and those tight jeans, but wait until you hit thirty and middle-aged spread. And you don't even color your hair, you lucky girl."

Choking down a laugh at all these personal comments from a stranger, I touched my hair. It was fine and straight, flyaway with static electricity at this time of year. "How do you know I don't color it?"

"No one would dye their hair that mous—" she began. Flushing, she attempted to pull her foot out of her mouth. "People with light brown hair usually choose a more vibrant color. But the brown goes so nicely with your blue eyes."

Without admitting that I was already a

14

couple of years beyond thirty and suddenly tempted to color my hair, I retrieved more chairs from my storeroom and set them up. My students crowded around the wood-stove, warmed themselves with mugs of hot cider, and eyed my embroidery boutique.

It looked great, and I was proud of it. A hundred years before, this building had been a brand-new home. Recently, someone had converted it into a store, and Haylee had called to tell me I had to come and see it. Someday, I hoped to meet whoever had done the renovations and built the store's oak cabinets and shelving, which perfectly matched the building's original Arts and Crafts style. The shop was charming, especially the antique walnut floor and wainscoting, which together were probably worth more than my mortgage.

The merchandise I offered for sale was appealing, too. Sleek new sewing and embroidery machines would make mouths water and pocketbooks open. Bolts of natural fabrics brightened one corner of the shop, while my classroom area occupied another. My notions were specific to embroidery — stabilizers, spray-on adhesives, hoops, and scissors with funny, curved blades. My favorite displays, the ones I always lingered over, were the racks of embroidery threads. Gleaming in nearly every color imaginable, machine embroidery thread came in shining metallics, lustrous rayon and silk, sparkling polyester, and subtle, rich cotton.

If my customers or I needed anything else, all we had to do was meander across the street to the other boutiques. I loved Threadville, and I loved my new life in it. Except for Mike Krawbach, of course. There had to be a way around his high-handed decision.

Students left the woodstove to examine samples of my work. Rosemary pointed at one of my favorite projects, a patchwork backpack embroidered with mythical beasts. "That's what I want to make."

I unfolded the last chair. "We'll get there." Judging from the clothing these women had sewn for themselves, we'd get there quickly.

With a gentle tinkling of sea glass and driftwood chimes, the front door opened enough for a thin woman to sidle into the shop. Pulling her coat tightly around herself, she perched on a chair in the back row. She was dressed all in black, her gray hair hung limply, and her face was lined with sadness. I hid a shiver. She should be the one wearing the willow.

16

I opened my mouth to begin the day's lesson.

Behind me, the glass in my chimes clashed, and the front door banged open.

"Ladies," a man called out in a rich, deep voice. "Good morning."

I turned around. Of all the gall. Mike Krawbach was back. I glared at him.

He beamed as if he were bringing these ladies a long-awaited treat. "You all adore Threadville, right?" he asked.

My students nodded and shouted their agreement, except for the sorrowful woman, who must have dropped something. She bent over and scrabbled her hands over the floor.

Mike displayed his teeth in a smile gauged to make each of the ladies think it was meant personally for her. "Then you'll want to sign this petition to show Threadville how much you love it. Your husbands will want to come here, too, and will drive you here. Often."

What a throwback, acting like women couldn't drive. I suspected that many of the Threadville tourists chose the bus because they reveled in their all-day outings with other textile enthusiasts.

"Ooh," one woman breathed. "That would be great."

"Ha!" another said with scorn. "I couldn't buy a yard of fabric or a skein of yarn with hubby looking over my shoulder."

Mike gave her a special smile. "If you sign my petition, he'll be too busy to look over your shoulder, I promise you." In a boyish gesture that looked calculated to me, he pushed a lock of hair off his forehead. There was something furtive in the way he set a sheaf of papers and a handful of pens on my embroidered tablecloth, as if he hoped I wouldn't notice and my students would.

Rosemary leaped up to defend my handi-work. "Ink can stain this sumptuous white linen." She moved the pens and papers to my measuring and cutting table.

Making a mental note to clean that table before I unrolled fabric on it, I studied Mike's expression of affected innocence. What was he planning, a bar where hus-bands played pool and watched TV while their wives shopped? Why would that require a petition? He winked at my students in a way that made me more uneasy than ever, then marched out, wide shoulders, narrow hips, and all. Working in his vineyard had given him a physique that any man might envy.

I heard several sighs. Nostalgia? Many of the women were old enough to be Mike's

18

mother, maybe his grandmother.

I reclaimed my students' attention by asking them when they had first become interested in embroidery. Like me, most of them had been given a simple embroidery project as soon as their fingers could hang on to a needle.

One woman, dressed head to toe in mauve, summarized it. "I worked my way up from satin and cross stitches to needle weaving and cutwork, but —"

Rosemary laughed. "Hand embroidery is beautiful but life's too short."

I held up a stitched portrait of a long-haired tortoiseshell kitten. "How long would this take by hand?" I asked.

"Weeks," the lady in mauve said.

Rosemary groaned. "Decades."

Everybody laughed. "The actual stitching," I said, "was done in about an hour." I patted my computer monitor. "I started with a digital photo that the kitten's owner e-mailed me. My software transformed it to an embroidery design. The most time-consuming part was changing the thread for each new color."

Rosemary shouted, "I want one of those machines!"

The class was off to a perfect start. However, I had to tell them they could have fun

19

with machine embroidery without purchasing a shiny new machine. "Today, I'll show you how to embroider with your sewing machine, even if all it does is straight stitches." I hoped that, after a few lessons from me, many of my students would discover they *needed* embroidery machines and would purchase them from me. I distributed pens containing water-soluble ink and asked my students to draw something with straight lines, like a building, on squares of felt.

A few of them copied the Blueberry Cottage design I had embroidered on towels. The woman in mauve stationed herself at the back window. With a few simple lines, she sketched an elegant version of the cottage. These classes were going to be wonderful. I would learn at least as much as I would teach.

I demonstrated how to load felt, backed by stabilizer to support it and prevent it from puckering, into the kind of embroidery hoops our ancestors might have used, golden brown oak laminated in concentric circles.

Rosemary looked skeptical. "Don't we need special hoops for machine embroidery?"

"Not for freehand embroidery." I thumped

a finger on the felt in the hoop. "Tighten the hoop, but don't stretch the felt, and don't tear it."

The women laughed and nudged each other, welcoming me into their jovial community. We had all experimented with threads and fabrics. We knew how adding one more layer to our creativity could lead to instant disaster.

I held up a spool of thin nylon thread. "If the stitching on the back won't be seen, you can save money by using lingerie thread in your bobbin instead of embroidery thread."

I touched the little teeth below my sewing machine's needle and presser foot. "These are called feed dogs. Usually, they move the fabric. Today, we're the ones deciding which direction the fabric should go, so we have to lower them out of the way." With the machine I was using, it was easy. I pushed a button.

"They don't lower out of the way on my machine at home," a woman in a be-ribboned sweatshirt commented.

I beckoned her closer and popped my stitch plate out. "You can remove your feed dogs, but be careful. Don't lose the screws."

She smiled happily. "I've got enough loose screws already." When the laughter died down, she added, "Now I'm certain I need a new machine."

I snapped a spring-loaded presser foot especially suited to embroidery onto my machine, and everyone wanted to know where to purchase one.

"From me," I said. "Tell me your sewing machine's model, and I'll look for one or a method of adapting one."

I chose an ornamental stitch from my machine's many possibilities. Five more women began murmuring about new machines.

My students watched me guide the hooped felt so that the needle followed the lines I'd drawn. After a few changes of thread color and lots of stitches, the drawing became an embroidered motif.

Enthusiastically, the women took turns at machines around In Stitches. The thin, sallow woman in black said nothing except to demur quietly when I asked her if she wanted to try, too.

"Another time, then," I said, in a hurry to help everyone finish before the group's lunch at Pier 42, a restaurant overlooking Elderberry Bay's broad, sandy beach.

Chattering, the women donned coats and lined up to buy a surprisingly large amount of supplies so they could do their homework, creating an embroidered flower by stitching over floral fabric, carefully matching colors and contours. Many admitted that they probably had just the right fabric at home but would shop at The Stash before they left town for some of the lovely fabrics Haylee had on sale. Tomorrow morning's class, when these ladies brought their homework back, should be fun. I'd heard that most of the same women came Tuesday through Saturday on the Threadville tour bus. The women could shop, attend classes, or both. Like the other Threadville proprietors, I offered a repeat of each morning's class in the afternoon for those who had been attending other workshops or browsing elsewhere.

After my customers went to lunch, I had to tell Haylee about my successful morning. I hung my *Back in Five Minutes* sign — red cross-stitches on white canvas — on my glass front door. It wasn't that I had to surround myself with embroidery, it was only that I loved to create new designs and couldn't help embroidering them on anything that stood still long enough.

The other four Threadville boutiques were across Elderberry Bay's main thoroughfare, Lake Street, in a perfectly maintained two-story Victorian edifice with apartments above the stores. Unlike buildings of a

23

similar vintage in Manhattan, this one's red-brick facade and carved limestone decorations had stayed clean and bright all these years in this village surrounded by forest and farmland on three sides and Lake Erie on the fourth. Haylee's shop faced one of my next-door neighbors, the General Store, recently purchased by a couple I had not yet met. Opal's Tell a Yarn was directly across from In Stitches. Edna's Buttons and Bows faced my other neighbor, The Iron-monger. Naomi's Batty About Quilts was across from a vacant building beyond the hardware store.

Hugging myself in the cold air, I dashed to Haylee's store. For anyone who loved to sew, entering The Stash was like coming home. The fragrance of new fabrics made me yearn to design and create. Dark wintry wools, corduroys, and fleeces beckoned, but I couldn't help touching luscious spring cottons, especially the floral prints I'd asked Haylee to show my students. I loved the quality, sheen, and heft of Haylee's fashion fabrics. They would drape beautifully. I wanted them all.

Haylee wasn't among the rolls of silks, satins, velvets, veiling, and lace for wedding and formal gowns, and I didn't see her where faux furs and novelty fabrics made a playful display. She wasn't paging through pattern books in one of the comfy chairs near the window, either.

"Haylee?" I called.

She charged out of her classroom, her long blond hair flying. Fury had replaced her usual calm amusement. "Willow! I was texting you." She grabbed a fistful of paper from beside her cash register. "Did you see this?"

"What?" I faltered, remembering my students studying Mike's petition almost as raptly as they'd studied him. I'd been too busy ringing up sales to look at the pages he'd left in my store.

"That sleazeball, Mike Krawbach, tricked ladies from the Threadville tour into signing some stupid petition while I was teaching them how to create burnout velvet. Why on earth would women from Erie want an ATV track to go through Elderberry Bay?"

So their husbands would be glad to come here, too, Mike had said.

Wait a second. An ATV track . . . "Let me see," I said.

Sure enough, Mike the sleazeball was petitioning the village to lift the ban on motorized vehicles on the riverbank trail, the one that ran behind Blueberry Cottage. My quiet life above the Elderberry River would be shattered by roaring engines and stinking fumes.

Worse, he wanted Elderberry Bay to condemn Blueberry Cottage and appropriate the land it sat on for public restrooms.

Mike wanted to bulldoze my cottage and steal my land so he could erect outhouses on it.

Outhouses!

Ten of Haylee's students had signed the petition. Haylee and I looked at each other and raced outside.

In Stitches was centered on its lot, with side yards sloping down to the back. The Arts and Crafts front porch and deep eaves made my store look especially welcoming and comfy. For once, I barely had time to admire it all. Haylee and I barreled inside.

I grabbed the petition Mike had left in my shop. Nineteen of my students had signed, probably without reading it. They'd been swayed by Mike's blue eyes.

My eyes must have turned red at that moment, because that's what I saw. I tore up Mike's petition and threw the bits into the wastebasket behind the cash register.

Haylee's mouth dropped open. We'd known each other for years, and even at the most stressful of times — blowing the whistle on our boss, a corrupt, embezzling

26

financial manager, and testifying against him in Manhattan — I'd been pretty easy-going.

To my immense gratification, Haylee scrunched her petition into a tight ball and jettisoned it as well.

An ancient red car spluttered past, driven by a woman so small that I couldn't see much of her besides gray hair straggling out from underneath her wide-brimmed hat. I recognized her, anyway.

"What's she doing here?" Haylee asked.

"She came to my class, didn't socialize with the other women and didn't want to try the embroidery exercise. Do you know her?"

Haylee shook her head. "Not really, but there can't be two cars like that around here. She's the one Mike nearly ran off the road the one — and only — time I went out with him. She owns a farm east of the vil-lage. She hardly ever ventures into town."

I couldn't help laughing. "Maybe she's embarrassed about not giving you a ride into town after you slammed yourself out of Mike's truck."

Haylee sighed in exaggerated dismay. "Ten miles of country roads. One pair of shoes totally wrecked. They were brand new." She faked a shiver. "It was pitch-black out, besides." She cocked her head. "What's that noise? Your dogs?"

Sad whining came from downstairs. I'd taken my pair of one-year-old pups on a long walk before I opened In Stitches that morning, but I'd left them alone in my apartment for two entire hours. "Tally-Ho. And his sister is probably happily shredding her bed." Only a week ago, I had rescued the dogs, who had more border collie heritage than was probably good for them, or for me, from a pound. We still had a lot to learn about each other. "I'd better take them out."

"And I should get back to The Stash." Coatless and petitionless, Haylee jogged across the street.

Leaving the door between the store and the stairway open so I could listen for customers who finished lunch early, I went down to my apartment. Sally-Forth had not shredded anything, but Tally-Ho was cuddling my white parka as if he were about to begin his own version of cutwork embroidery, without the embroidery. Both dogs wriggled with joy when they saw me.

My building was on a hill, giving In Stitches and my apartment plenty of natural light from back windows. Like the shop, the apartment had been renovated exactly as I would have done it. The kitchen and living area offered great views of my backyard. My bedroom looked out on one side yard, while my guest room looked out on the other. En suite baths, large walk-in closets, and a small laundry room were sandwiched between the bedrooms. Mostly above ground and decorated in white, the apartment did not seem like a basement.

Naturally, I'd embroidered everything possible. The bedroom curtains were white with machine hemstitching along the bottoms. I'd gone a little wilder with my linens and throw pillows. Actually, I'd gone a lot wilder, but I could change everything with the seasons or my latest whim.

I had not yet decided whether to curtain the vast windows across the back. The view was calming. Dense rows of cedars lined both sides of my backyard, leading the eye to Blueberry Cottage, a pretty little building with teal siding and dark red trim. Above the cottage, branches traced charcoal lace against the sky. The hiking trail ran between the cottage and the river, where ice chunks bobbed along like merry little boats. Trees covered the far bank. It was all so beautiful that the only reason to add draperies to my back windows would be for the sake of embroidering more yardage.

I made certain that the dogs noticed me sticking a handful of treats into my coat pocket, and opened the door leading outside from my open-concept great room and kitchen. Before I'd adopted Sally and Tally, I'd had a sturdy chain-link fence built around the property, with a gate near the front yard and another at the foot of the hill, beyond the cottage, giving us a shortcut to the hiking trail. The pups chased and wrestled in their large, safely enclosed space. Whenever they returned to me, they got a treat. Before long, we were all inside again, munching on peanut butter sandwiches.

The chimes clashed together again. With Sally and Tally at my heels, I ran upstairs.

Mike Krawbach was snooping around my fabric cutting table. My usually friendly Tally growled and barked. Above the din, I thought I heard Mike say into his cell phone, "Here she is."

I grabbed the dogs' collars, pulled them to the stairway leading down to the apartment, and closed the door.

Dropping his pens and cell phone into his shirt pocket, Mike tossed me one of his phony smiles, pretending he wanted my friendship when he really wanted my land.

For his and hers outhouses, of all things.

His smile became an accusing sneer. "Where did you put my petition?"

2

Chin up, fingers tensed at my sides, I evaded Mike's question. "I didn't say you could leave a petition in my store."

"Then give it back. I just talked to the ladies in the restaurant. They said they signed it." Those blue eyes seemed to cut through me.

"Most of those women don't live here. Their signatures don't count." I sounded as fierce as I felt.

Haylee, her mother Opal, and Opal's two best friends burst into the store. Throwing her arms around me, Opal smothered me in the bulky depths of her hand-knit sweater. "Congratulations, Willow! Your store was full of customers."

Opal was as tall as her daughter, not much older, and every bit as exuberant. I eased away so I could breathe. I liked Opal's sweater, but I wasn't sure about the slacks she'd knitted to match. Cables ran every which way over both garments.

Naomi, in one of her amazing quilted jackets, patted my shoulder. "So glad you're up and running, and one of *us*."

Behind the women, Mike fumed. Let him.

Edna shook her head ominously. "I still don't like the name you chose, Willow. In Stitches! Know what it sounds like?"

Winking at me over Edna's bright orange curls, Opal guessed, "An embroidery boutique?"

I tried, "Stand-up comedy?"

"No," Edna said. "A hospital."

I asked, "What should I have called it?"

"Embroidery Room."

"ER for short," Haylee quipped. "Great idea."

Edna covered her mouth with her hand but rallied quickly. "The rest of you are just as bad at naming your stores. I don't know why you chose The Stash, Haylee. It sounds like a drug dealer's emporium, not a fabric boutique. And Naomi, what must customers conclude about a woman who names her shop Batty About Quilts and runs around in padded jackets? And Tell a Yarn, Opal? What were you *thinking?*"

"That I was opening a yarn store," Opal answered drily. "And planning sessions of storytelling and needlework."

Thirty-three years ago, when Haylee was born, Naomi and Edna had teamed up to help their teenaged friend, Opal, raise her fatherless baby. They had juggled childcare with degrees and professions. Then, after Haylee became disillusioned with the financial world and told them about the row of Victorian shops for sale in Elderberry Bay, they'd abandoned their careers and joined Haylee to convert their hobbies to businesses, and Threadville was born. The three women claimed they were having the time of their life. None of them had quite reached fifty. They jokingly referred to themselves as The Three Weird Sisters.

Haylee, of course, called them The Three Weird Mothers.

The moment I moved to Elderberry Bay, Haylee's mothers had adopted me, too, and I was certain they had scurried to my store just now to protect me from Mike Krawbach. I didn't like the smug smile that appeared on his face as they teased each other, though.

Edna smoothed her jacket, decorated with ribbons and rhinestones from her notions boutique. "At least when they come to Buttons and Bows, they know what —" She was interrupted by an odd cacophony coming from outside.

Elderberry Bay had only one police cruiser, so old that its siren mooed, which went well with the sheeplike bleating of its horn. The farmyard noises ended when the banged-up vehicle halted in front of In Stitches.

Everybody around, from toddlers to ninety-year-olds, called the village's only police officer Uncle Allen. He'd been christened Uncle way back in kindergarten because of the way he always looked after everybody else. Nearly sixty years later, he had not lost the nickname. He unfolded himself from the driver's seat and lumbered toward In Stitches.

Mike must have been talking to Uncle Allen when I came upstairs with the dogs. Mike had called the police.

Haylee inched past her mothers until she was with me behind my counter.

Uncle Allen wended his way through the phalanx of protective proprietors. "What's up, kiddo?" he asked Mike.

Mike pointed at me. "That woman stole my property."

He was a fine one to talk, with his designs on my cottage. I argued, "His 'property' was only a petition he left here without my permission."

Mike puffed out his muscular chest.

35

"Then give it back."

I tried my hardest not to glance toward the wastebasket at my feet. "I can't. I don't have it."

Uncle Allen figured it out. Leather gun holsters creaking, he lurched forward and pulled Haylee's crumpled petition out of the wastebasket. He handed it to Mike. "This your property?"

"Hey, you can't do that," Haylee objected. "Where's your search warrant?"

"Don't need one," Uncle Allen said. "Been the law here for over twenty years."

Haylee opened her eyes to their widest, and I could tell she was thinking the same thing I was. Manhattan and our lawless boss there might have been more civilized than this Wild West type of policing in Elderberry Bay.

Mike straightened the petition. "This isn't the petition I meant." He pointed at Haylee with his whole hand, palm slanted upward, all of his fingers except the middle one slightly curled inwards, a gesture he must have practiced to make its rudeness appear, especially to Uncle Allen, accidental. "This is the petition I left in *her* store." He could not have sounded more derogatory. "I penciled your lot numbers on each petition." The gathering now included the tour

36

bus ladies, who must have run out of Pier 42 before they finished their dessert. Opal, Naomi, and Edna wore defiant expressions that should have made Mike apologize and slink out of the store. Instead, he threatened, "All you shopkeepers, you just better make certain I get my petition back in one piece."

That must have given Uncle Allen an idea. He leaned over and peered into my wastebasket. "There's your other petition, Mike," he said. "She tore it up and threw it away."

"Did she?" Mike's attempt at a purr held a scissorlike edge. "Then I'll just make another copy of the petition" — he grabbed my guest book from beside the cash register and ripped the first pages out of it, the signed ones — "and staple these to it."

I reached for the pages. "No!"

Mike moved them away from my outstretched hand and turned toward the door.

The artistic lady in mauve from this morning's class fell into step behind him. "Taking those pages is theft! I signed her guest book. I live here in Elderberry Bay, and I have no intention of signing your petition." Her enunciation was careful and clear.

We all crowded out the door behind her and Mike. Cold stabbed through my turtleneck, jeans, and fun fur-trimmed vest.

Rosemary yelled, "I didn't sign the petition, either." Nudging me, she murmured, "We come here to get away from them." I guessed she meant men. Threadville had become a haven for shopaholic and fabriholic women. Did it bother Mike that the men around Elderberry Bay were becoming outnumbered?

I called after Mike, "You can't just say my cottage is blighted and steal the land it's on."

Mike whipped around to face the crowd. "It's encroaching on village property."

"That's impossible." I tried to lower my suddenly shrill voice. "I have a survey."

Mike's smirk became self-righteous. "Your survey's outdated. Ice jams cause floods during every thaw. Last year, ice knocked your shed an inch onto village property, and then you went and built your fence right on the trail. They both have to come down."

I could have the fence moved, I supposed, but bulldozing Blueberry Cottage because it encroached a whole inch? I thought of myself as a nice, law-abiding citizen. Mike was carrying the law a little too far, and I couldn't help wondering what his real agenda was. Besides, wouldn't ice push the cottage away from the river, not toward it?

Sam Fedders, the octogenarian who owned the hardware store next to In

Stitches, shouted out, "The river very seldom comes up that high, Mike Krawbach, and you know it." Around him, retired farmers who spent their winter days around the potbellied stove in Sam's store nodded their heads.

His eyes colder than ever, Mike glared at the crowd milling in the street and on both sidewalks. "If anybody wants to argue with the decisions of the zoning board, just go right ahead, and if you ever want permits to renovate your own properties, I'll make certain you have a fight on your hands you won't soon forget."

"Mike, Mike, Mike," Sam cautioned softly. "Don't you be threatening us, now."

Haylee spoke up. "The hiking trail will be ruined if motorized vehicles are allowed on it."

Mike shot back, "Members of the ATV club won't agree. They'll love it. They bring more money into this town than a trickle of birdwatchers and dog walkers."

How, by buying gas?

"You want to destroy Threadville," Haylee accused.

That was too much for Mike. "And you want to destroy everything."

Haylee laughed, the old farmers snickered, and warmth finally came into Mike's eyes.

Heat, actually. Anger flamed in them.

He obviously guessed that nearly everyone in the village knew about Haylee's high-heeled hike home from his pickup truck that time, and that she had refused subsequent dates.

The Threadville tourists must have seen the flare in Mike's eyes. Murmuring, the women crowded around Haylee, Opal, Naomi, Edna, and me. No one could be more protective than sisters-in-thread.

"Give us Haylee's petition," they demanded. "We want to remove our names."

The woman in mauve raised her voice only slightly, but her words could be heard all up and down Lake Street. "Return Willow's guest book pages to her."

I turned in frustration to the cop. "He stole those pages from me. Either make him give them back or arrest him." Arrest? Maybe I was getting a little too steamed up. Or not steamed up enough. I was about to freeze.

"C'mon, kiddo," Uncle Allen finally said, taking Mike's arm and escorting him toward the cruiser. To arrest him?

Uncle Allen merely let Mike help him into the driver's seat, then drove away, his siren beginning its slow, sad mooing.

Mike swaggered to a black pickup truck

and got into it. He still had the petition Haylee had crumpled up and the pages he'd torn from my guest book.

I imagined horrible, smelly restrooms at the foot of my backyard instead of a charming cottage. "If he knocks Blueberry Cottage down, I'll kill him." I didn't realize I'd said it aloud until Haylee elbowed me. *Kill* him? I didn't usually let anger get the best of me.

As if to rescue me from the crowd, which now included men wearing ATV club patches on their baseball caps, Opal looked at her watch and acted surprised. "We're late for our classes."

The women who attended my afternoon lesson were as attentive and enthusiastic as the morning's students. Afterward, the Threadville tourists had time to browse before their bus was scheduled to leave. I demonstrated machines to potential customers, and one woman bought a top-of-the-line sewing machine to lug home on the bus. Judging by the competitive light in her friends' eyes, I would soon sell more machines.

The tour bus left shortly after five. While the pups sniffed, ran, and wrestled in my backyard, I checked on Mike's allegations that Blueberry Cottage encroached on

41

municipal land. The board and batten siding stuck out about an inch beyond the foundation in front, but in back, the siding was even with the foundation's edge. Maybe the cottage had been built that way in the first place, and Mike had made a wrong assumption. If he was right, though, my fence encroached more than the cottage did.

Erected between the trail and Blueberry Cottage, the fence had been good at keeping the dogs in but hadn't been as successful at keeping vandals out. Sometime during the past twenty-four hours, someone had thrown about a half gallon of paint over the fence and onto Blueberry Cottage's front porch, and now a thick and ugly aqua blob marred the porch's gray floorboards. I wondered where they'd thrown the can. Not in the river, I hoped. I planned to repaint the entire cottage after the renovations. First, I would have to find a way of overturning Mike's zoning decision.

Far away, up the river, dogs barked.

Sally and Tally were no longer snuffling in the underbrush.

Worse, the gate separating my yard from the trail was wide open.

I panicked. "Tally-Ho! Sally-Forth!" Did they know their names yet? Calling, whistling, and rattling treats in my pocket, I sprinted upriver, the direction the barking had come from. I'd been warned that if the two littermates ever got away, they'd feel secure with each other and might not realize they were lost until too late and they could no longer find their way home to me. That probably explained how they became strays in the first place, something I never wanted to happen to them again. They had looked at me with their matching amber eyes, trusting me completely, and I had given those two darlings my heart.

And then someone opened my gate and let them escape.

It had to be Mike or one of his buddies from the ATV club. Mike had driven away early in the afternoon, but he wouldn't have needed to go far to sneak back to the trail behind my place. He was the one who supposedly knew my property so well that he could tell when ice pushed my cottage an inch onto public land.

He could be miles away by now. So could my two innocent little dogs. "I'll kill him," I repeated, startling a pair of hikers. "Someone opened my gate and let my dogs out," I explained.

The hikers hadn't seen my dogs, but a flock of birders had. This time, my accusation was more specific. "Mike Krawbach helped my dogs escape from my yard."

"Are your dogs wearing tags?" a woman asked.

"Yes, and my address is on their collars, so if you find them . . ."

"The poor dears." She wiped at her eyes. "If we see them, we'll bring them back." Elderberry Bay had its share of sympathetic citizens.

But what if the dogs lost their collars? Or some horrible person like Mike Krawbach took them home and didn't pamper them?

It was too dark to see. Telling myself that Sally and Tally could have returned home, and also telling myself not to think about the treacherous ice patches in the river, I jogged back. I'd left my gate open so the dogs could come in. I called them, but all I heard was my shop phone ringing. I ran up the hill and answered the extension in my apartment. Nobody. No messages, either.

Where were Sally-Forth and Tally-Ho? Staring out into the darkness toward the river, I kicked myself over and over.

I should have padlocked my gates. I didn't dare leave to buy locks right now, though. The dogs might return, find they couldn't come inside, and blithely run off.

Upstairs in my shop, the doorbell rang.

3

I charged up the stairs at a breakneck pace.

Sally and Tally pressed their noses against the glass of my front door. Breathless with relief, I threw the door open. They galloped inside, towing a man behind them. Without a glance at the man, I knelt and buried my face in cool fur, first Sally's, then Tally's. The wriggly pups whimpered and kissed me until my cheeks were wet from more than their kisses.

I forgot the man until the door latched, closing him and the dogs inside my shop with me. "I take it these two scamps belong to you," he said.

I rose from my emotional greeting with my pups and blushed. Not because the man's warm brown eyes radiated kindness and concern, but because I'd neglected to thank him for bringing the inquisitive pooches home. He knelt to cuddle the dogs. Luckily, he didn't seem to mind being slobbered over.

A red pickup truck with white lettering on the door was parked underneath a streetlight outside. I stammered my thanks, adding, "I hope they didn't track too much mud into your truck."

"They were good. It was hard to see over the two of them, though. They sat on my lap." He stood. I'm tall, but he had to look down to see into my face. His teasing grin made me wonder if he was telling the truth. If he was, my dogs had good taste in men. He untangled a rope looped through both collars, then held out his right hand. "Clay Fraser."

I let his warm hand engulf mine. "Willow Vanderling."

"You're freezing." He frowned toward the back of the room. "Your woodstove's nearly out."

So it was. I turned on lights, strode to the stove, and tossed in a piece of firewood. The cider on the stove's soapstone top still radiated heat. "Want some cider?"

"Sounds good."

I poured us each a mug and passed him a plate of molasses cookies, my favorite recipe.

"Your shop looks great," he said, chowing down. "You've arranged everything the way I pictured it."

The way he *pictured* it? Understanding beginning to dawn, I dodged past bolts of cloth for a better look through my huge front windows at the words on his truck. *Fraser Construction.* "Did you have anything to do with the renovations here?" I asked.

"Haylee described what you wanted, and I carried it out."

I had to admire Haylee's nerve. The first time I ever heard about this building was *after* it had been renovated, when Haylee told me I had to fly up from New York to see this store that had just come on the market. I arrived the next day, and as Haylee must have planned, I'd known immediately that I'd needed to open the embroidery boutique I'd always dreamed of owning.

In Threadville.

I'd fallen in love with the empty store and with my dogs at first sight. I sternly told myself I wasn't about to fall in love with any man at first sight.

However, if I ever changed that rule, this might be the man I'd want to catch sight of. It was too late for first sight, I supposed, but I could fake it.

Standing near this obviously strong and capable man, I felt brave enough to tackle anything. "Would you be interested in

47

renovating my cottage, the one beside the hiking trail?"

"Blueberry Cottage? Sure, if the inside's anything like the outside."

"Falling into disrepair?" I prompted.

"Architecturally important. It's a great example of carpenter gothic."

Important, Blueberry Cottage? How dare Mike Krawbach deny me that building permit!

Apparently, Clay knew about that, too. "I'll help wangle permits. Krawbach gave Pete DeGlazier, Uncle Allen's brother, a permit to build a gazebo upstream. That gazebo is on the flood plain. It's also closer to the river than Blueberry Cottage is."

That figured. Mike's real reason for rejecting my application had been to commandeer some of my land for outhouses.

"We'll go over Krawbach's head," Clay said.

"You can do that?" No wonder Haylee kept this man a secret.

"Mike was appointed zoning commissioner by the mayor, Irv Oslington. We'll tell Irv about Mike's favoritism."

I shoved the plate of cookies at Clay.

He polished off the cookies and let the dogs lick his hands. "How did these two escape?"

"Someone opened my gate." My voice became hard. "Mike Krawbach, probably. I wish the hardware store wasn't closed for the night. I need padlocks so he can't let my dogs out again."

"In the evenings, the hardware store is more like a men's club, but you can buy things. I'll come with you."

I wasn't used to leaning on anyone and would have to be very stern with myself about relying on Clay Fraser. "Okay," I said, planning to be stern with myself later, like maybe tomorrow. I locked the dogs into my apartment and zipped my parka. "Did you renovate the downstairs apartment, too?" I suspected I knew the answer.

Clay tilted his head like he was trying to figure something out. "Haylee relayed your instructions, and I followed them. Do you like it?" He opened the front door and held it for me.

"It's gorgeous, all that white and natural light." I was going to have to talk to Haylee about how she had "just happened" to find a shop and apartment I was sure to love.

The hardware store was so old that the sign above its door was made of wrought iron and said *The Ironmonger.* Inside, nothing besides merchandise seemed to have changed in a century. Even the lighting was dim, as if whoever had installed the bulbs had decided that anything brighter than the original gas lanterns might be too luxurious. The effect was cozy, giving the natural woodwork a charming patina. As in my shop, the floor was black walnut. The walls were lined with oak drawers, each with a handle above a small metal square framing a slip of paper with the drawer's contents handwritten on it.

Several of the men sitting around the potbellied stove had witnessed my lunchtime fight with Mike. Two much younger men, Irv Oslington, the mayor, and Herb Gunthrie, our hunky postman, had now joined them. Herb waved his good arm and threw me one of his heart-stopping, devil-may-care grins.

Haylee's three mothers, who usually ate dinner together, taking turns in each other's apartments, scooted into the hardware store right behind us. They were very protective of Haylee and, as I'd seen this afternoon when they streamed into my shop in my defense, had decided to protect me, too. Having seen Haylee roll her eyes at their lack of subtlety, I grinned to myself. Who or what were they trying to guard me from now?

I told Sam I needed two padlocks.

"Betcha I can find you a pair that use the same key, so's you'll only need to carry one. They stamp secret codes on the packages. Here, I'll show you."

Apparently, he'd owned The Ironmonger for so long he didn't need much light to find his stock. He hauled packages of padlocks from a deep drawer underneath the counter and held one up where I could see it. "See this four digit number printed up here in this corner? All's we have to do is find two packages with matching numbers and eureka! The locks will have matching keys." He dumped packages of locks on a table near the old-timers and Irv and Herb. They immediately started shuffling through the packages and shouting numbers at each other.

Clay poked around in barrels of nuts and bolts.

Opal hugged me. "I guess we showed that Krawbach creature, didn't we?" I wasn't so sure. She looked me up and down. "Have you made an appointment with Dr. Wrinkle-sides yet?"

"Why?" I asked, startled. Had my anger at Mike turned my face permanently purple?

"He's got lots of experience. He's so good the coroner calls on him for assistance."

How reassuring. With any luck, I wouldn't

51

need a doctor.

Edna sidled up to me. The top of her bright orange head came almost to my shoulder. "We were discussing you over cocktails," she whispered. "You're too thin. Like Haylee. You're both wasting away. You could have an eating disorder."

If I did, it was the same as Edna's and Opal's — being too fond of food.

Naomi, the bony one, edged between us. "Haylee and Willow both look great."

Clay had moved on to spools of twine, chain, and wire. He had his back to us but must have heard every word. His shoulders shook. I wanted to laugh, too. The urge came out as a huge smile, which undoubtedly would have encouraged the three women to continue with their nagging if they hadn't been distracted by the arrival of a tall, muscular, blue-eyed blond man.

"Ooh," Opal whispered. "Now Willow really will have to go see Dr. Wrinklesides."

"Why?" Edna asked.

Opal elbowed her. "She's about to break out in hives."

Edna looked bewildered, but Naomi giggled. Shielding her mouth with her hand, she stage-whispered, "It's that beekeeper, the one who's sweeter than his honey." The three women gathered around me and a carton of windshield scrapers.

Throwing an apologetic glance at my fierce chaperones, the beekeeper spoke to me over Edna's head. "I'm sorry about my cousin. He doesn't have any manners."

Edna's lips thinned. "You're that Mike Krawbach's cousin?"

"Smythe bought his hat and gloves at my store," Opal said. "They look great, Smythe."

The hat was a whimsical stocking cap, knit in yellow and black stripes, complete with a hand-knit stinger at the crown. "Smythe Castor," he introduced himself, removing his yellow and black striped gloves and looking deep into my eyes. "Haylee told me all about you." Trust Haylee to know all the handsomest men in the county.

"What're you doing here, Smythe?" Herb yelled. "I thought you were in Erie."

Smythe smiled. "I'm on my way there this very minute."

"And you said to hold your mail for three days?" Herb asked.

"That's right." Smythe's yellow parka perfectly matched the yellow stripes in his hat and gloves.

Herb's grin grew. "And what's the name of the conference where you're speaking?"

Smythe looked adorable when he blushed.

"The Honey Makers' Conference."

Herb smacked his thigh with his good hand. "Looks like he's trying to make some honey right here and now."

The men around the stove guffawed.

Opal nudged me and murmured, "Mmmm."

His face scarlet, Smythe ran out of the hardware store.

Sam called out, "Okay, Willow, we found two matching packages."

I paid for my padlocks. Clay left with me, and so did Opal, Naomi, and Edna, presumably to finish their interrupted cocktails.

Clay opened his truck door. "I'll call you tomorrow so we can set up a time to go through Blueberry Cottage together."

"Okay," I managed, at my loquacious best.

After I was inside my shop, Mike Krawbach strode past, squinting toward In Stitches as if he were trying to see inside. I stayed very still. He climbed into his pickup and peeled away. Had he gone to The Ironmonger after we left, or had he been in my backyard, gloating over land he was planning to steal for outhouses?

I went outside, fastened my new padlocks to the gates, and made certain they were locked before I let the dogs join me. They did their usual mad dashes. If they were tracking a trespasser, it wasn't obvious where the trespasser had gone. On the other hand, I wouldn't put it past Mike to zigzag erratically all over my yard. I took the dogs inside.

Sally and Tally each had a bed embroidered with their names and, thanks to my computer and software, very realistic embroidered portraits of their faces, but tonight they cuddled together on Tally's bed, probably to dream of running unfettered along the river trail. I would dream of having Mike's zoning decision quashed so I could renovate Blueberry Cottage and rent it out. Or maybe of doing so well in my embroidery shop that I would never regret leaving a lucrative career in Manhattan. I would not, of course, consider dreaming about Elderberry Bay's heartthrobs, Clay Fraser, Smythe Castor, and Herb Gunthrie.

Dreaming about heartthrobs would have been better than the nightmare about the roaring menace bearing down on me. Barking madly, the dogs woke me up. An engine roared behind Blueberry Cottage. No one should be driving there, especially at four in the morning. The noisy engine stopped suddenly, as if someone had shut it off.

Still groggy, I pulled my embroidered duvet over my ears. The dogs added whining and pawing at the back door to their entreaties. I buried my head underneath the pillow and tried to go back to sleep. The dogs' barking became frantic.

Mike Krawbach could be out there wrecking Blueberry Cottage so he could replace it with outhouses. I eased out of bed and tiptoed to the windows.

Blueberry Cottage was a dark blur. It was fine.

Tally revved up his whimpering until he sounded more like a goose than a dog. Clumsy with adrenaline-interrupted sleep, I patted around in the dark for my jeans, sweater, boots, coat, scarf, hat, and mittens. Putting them on seemed to take forever, especially to my impatient dogs. I opened the door.

The night was like a wall of darkness. Cold needled my lungs and pasted my nostrils shut. Yipping, the dogs bounded down the hill toward the river. That gate had to be locked, had to. The dogs stopped short, barking at bushes. I could barely make out Tally's white plume of a tail and Sally's white fur cape. Had I bundled up at this hour so they could corner a rabbit and then be afraid to chase it into its lair?

A dark vehicle was parked on the trail. Nervously, I turned on my flashlight. I might have known. An ATV.

No one stirred, and the trailside gate was locked. I had an eerie feeling that someone was watching me from inside Blueberry Cottage. Was the odor of gasoline coming from the ATV, or had someone poured gas around Blueberry Cottage? I shined my light on the structure. The door of the lean-to where I kept my canoe, lawnmower, and garden tools swung open, creaking in breezes so slight I could barely feel them on my frozen face. Last I knew, that door had been padlocked.

Whimpering, Tally nudged my mittened hand. I looked down. He turned his head to stare at his sister. She nosed at something on the ground.

Mike Krawbach lay sprawled on his back.

4

Mike groaned. He didn't move.

I did. Breathlessly, I called my dogs. We flew up the hill to my apartment. I shut them in with me and dialed 911.

The dispatcher said she'd alert the doctor, ambulance, and police, and I should stay on the line with her while I unlocked my gates and attended to the victim.

Clamping the phone to my ear with the help of my shoulder, I shut the dogs in the apartment, went around to the front gate, and fumbled with the new padlock. My thick mittens didn't help, but I couldn't bear taking them off. My hands shook.

A car door slammed. A portly gentleman walked toward me more briskly than I would have expected for someone his size and age. He carried an old-fashioned doctor bag and wore an ankle-length black wool coat. A hand-knit white scarf was wrapped around his neck and lower face so many times I couldn't help thinking of the word "muffler." Someone had stitched furry earflaps to his fedora, and they were folded down over his ears. I'd read in books of men tipping their hats, but this was the first time I'd seen one do it. He breathed out an icy cloud. "I'm Dr. Wrinklesides." He reached over the gate for my phone. "You got 911 on the line?"

Relinquishing the phone to Dr. Wrinklesides, I babbled, "Mike Krawbach is out cold by the riverside trail." Cold? More like half frozen. "He moaned," I added lamely, finally undoing the padlock and opening the gate.

Dr. Wrinklesides patted my shoulder. "It will be okay," he shouted.

I led him to Mike.

Dr. Wrinklesides took one look at Mike and boomed into my phone, "Where's that danged fool with the ambulance?" He muttered, "You'd think the way this village is growing, they could park the thing less than ten miles away."

Uncle Allen's police cruiser mooed and bleated its way toward us. I climbed the hill and met him at the front gate. Lights went on in apartments above The Stash, Batty About Quilts, Buttons and Bows, and Tell a Yarn.

Its tires loud against the pavement in the otherwise still night, a dark pickup drove slowly up Lake Street from the direction of the beach, turned onto Cayuga, and went out of sight.

"Who was that?" I asked Uncle Allen.

"Kids. They use the beach as lovers' lane. Is that why you called?"

Impatiently, I shook my head and told him that Mike was lying at the foot of my yard.

"I'll drive down there." He stumped to his cruiser and drove noisily down Lake Street toward the beginning of the trail. I ran back down the hill to unlock the gate nearest Mike. Uncle Allen didn't seem to know how to turn his siren off, but why did he keep pounding on the horn? Its racket banged into my skull like a sledge hammer.

Waiting at the trailside gate for him, I shivered, not only from the cold. The blank windows of Blueberry Cottage seemed to stare at my back.

"Willow, Willow, where are you?" With wild yoo-hooing and shining of flashlights into bare, witchy treetops, Haylee and The Three Weird Mothers stormed down through my yard. Haylee wore a parka, snow pants, and boots, like she was dressed for skiing. Opal's hand-knit hat was stretched over huge curlers. Naomi's face was covered

60

in green goo. Beribboned flounces of Edna's flannel nightie stuck out below her coat over jeans tucked into boots.

"What's wrong?" Opal asked.

Judging by their hastily thrown-together outfits, I could have asked the same thing. Instead, I explained as succinctly as I could.

"Drunk." Edna could be even more succinct.

Dr. Wrinklesides bellowed at Uncle Allen, who was right beside him, "Head injuries. It looks like he was beaten by that canoe paddle. It's one of those old wooden ones. Weighs a ton."

"That must be my paddle," I said. "But it wasn't anywhere near Mike when the dogs and I found him. Last I knew, it was in my lean-to." I pointed. The door to the lean-to still gaped.

"You must be mistaken," Uncle Allen growled. "Or you and your dogs moved it."

"We didn't do that," I said hotly.

"I feel queasy," Naomi faltered.

"You look it," Edna agreed. "What's that green stuff all over your face?"

Naomi covered her cheeks with her hands. "Oh! I forgot! What must I look like?"

Haylee covered her mouth, but her eyes gleamed with silent laughter.

"Oh, no, you don't," Opal scolded, shaking a finger. "You girls aren't going into one of your laugh-'til-you-cry fits again. This is serious." She pointed at Mike.

As if on cue, he moaned again.

Uncle Allen bent over him until his ear was nearly in Mike's mouth.

Opal put her finger to her lips to shush us, but we had all tensed as if the cold had solidified our muscles. The night became suddenly darker. Had one of Elderberry Bay's streetlights blinked out?

Mike mumbled.

Slowly, Uncle Allen stood. He blinded me with his flashlight.

I shielded my eyes. "Would you check Blueberry Cottage? Whoever did this might be in there."

Uncle Allen only glared.

Flashlight in hand, Haylee started toward Blueberry Cottage.

Opal called her back. "No one should go in there."

Edna nodded her scarf-swathed head toward Uncle Allen. "Except *him*."

Dr. Wrinklesides hollered, "C'mon, young fella, you can do it!"

I expected to see him help Mike stand up. He pressed his stethoscope several places on Mike's chest, listened for long minutes, then slowly got to his feet. "He's gone," he said, not shouting for once.

Haylee turned away as if she didn't want anyone to see her expression.

Opal quietly repeated, "Gone?"

"Dead?" Edna asked.

"Deceased?" echoed Naomi, her eyes round in her ghoulish green mask.

I felt frozen, inside and out, and unable to speak. Mike, who only this afternoon had swaggered around carrying the pages he'd ripped out of my guest book, who only moments ago had groaned and mumbled, was dead? As in permanently . . . gone?

Uncle Allen stalked with exaggerated menace toward me and the other four women. He rested his fists on his hips, which placed his hands dangerously close to his guns. "Mike Krawbach is dead. *Dead.*" He let that sink in for one brittle moment, then added, "And his last words were, 'That woman did it. Get her.' "

5

Opal put her arm around Haylee. Haylee buried her face in her mother's shoulder but lifted her head almost immediately. By the glow of our flashlights, her eyes appeared fearful. Edna and Naomi closed around the other two, leaving me to face Uncle Allen by myself until Opal reached out and pulled me to her. We shrank toward each other and away from the policeman.

In the darkness beside Mike's prone body, Dr. Wrinklesides shouted, "Uncle Allen!"

Uncle Allen's shoulders drooped, and instead of resembling a dangerous predator, he became a tired man who had just lost a friend.

I had disliked Mike and what he wanted to do to my cottage, but I wouldn't wish a beating on anyone, much less a beating in the dark of what was possibly the coldest night of the year.

Edna sniffed. "I smell gasoline."

I'd become accustomed to the odor and had forgotten it. I shined my light past the cottage. "Mike's ATV is out on the trail."

Haylee focused her flashlight on a dull orange shape up the hill from Blueberry Cottage. "What's that?"

I tiptoed to it. An uncapped gas can lay on its side. It reeked of gasoline. I called out in a voice squeezed by outrage, "Mike came here to torch Blueberry Cottage."

Haylee and her mothers turned their backs on the men and whipped their lights upward to illuminate their faces. Naomi looked horrified. Haylee shook her head. Edna frowned. Opal's forehead furrowed.

They were right. I had cleverly broadcast a great motive for me to have attacked Mike.

Uncle Allen bore down on me. "Or he found *you* about to destroy your cottage for the insurance money, and was going to inform on you. And you stopped him."

My whole body went rigid. "I did no such thing. He's the one who wanted to get rid of my cottage. I didn't know about the gas can until right now. He must have brought it." I returned to Haylee and the other women.

"What did you say his last words were?" Opal asked Uncle Allen.

"That woman did this. Get her."

65

"What woman?" I asked. Hadn't he reported before that Mike said, "did it," not "did this"? A little part of my mind said *unreliable witness.* What was I doing, preparing my own defense? I'd physically fled Manhattan and the stresses related to working in a company after Haylee and I successfully testified against our boss. He had funneled funds from his clients — and ours — to his own accounts. Mentally fleeing was more difficult. Was I always going to automatically defend myself, justify my actions and my words? Plan my testimony? This time, I thought with a jolt of panic, I could be the one being tried. For murder.

Edna asked, "Mike accused some woman of doing something? Who, and what was it?"

Uncle Allen pointed at me. "Her. Mike said she beat him up. I can believe it. Yesterday, a bunch of witnesses reported to me that she threatened to kill him."

"I didn't mean it that way!" My vocal chords frayed like worn thread.

Uncle Allen ignored me. "This is her property, and she already admitted that the murder weapon is her canoe paddle."

By now, Dr. Wrinklesides stood beside the other old man. "Uncle Allen." It would have been a gentle reminder if Dr. Wrinklesides hadn't shouted.

Uncle Allen glowered at him. "You don't have to yell. I'm right here."

Dr. Wrinklesides reached a hand toward Uncle Allen. "Don't jump to conclusions."

Naomi crowded into me. I put an arm around her and hoped she wouldn't rub her green facial masque against the white snowman I'd embroidered on my parka.

The corners of Uncle Allen's mouth turned down, like he was playing bad cop. It looked more like sad cop. "All of you women are now murder suspects. I have to question you all."

"Now?" I asked. "What about that pickup truck we saw when you arrived? Shouldn't you go after them?"

"They could be anywhere by now."

My point, exactly.

"And besides," he went on, "half the village drives trucks like that. I'll get to them. First, I need to question you women. Separately." He singled me out with a sour look. "You first. The rest of you, go wait in different corners of her yard, and do not speak to each other until I'm done with all of you."

"It's too cold to stand out here," Haylee objected. "We're not dressed for it."

I wasn't sure anyone could dress for this cold. Pressed against me, Naomi and Opal were trembling so much I couldn't be

67

certain whether or not I was shivering, too.

An ambulance chugged along the riverside trail and stopped behind Uncle Allen's cruiser. Paramedics leaped out.

"Go tell them what to do, Doc," Uncle Allen ordered.

"Don't stay out in the cold any longer than you have to, Uncle Allen," Dr. Wrinkle-sides retorted. Standing vigil, the doctor began to sing, a dirge from an opera, I guessed. He had a good voice, warm and deep.

He was bundled up, but Uncle Allen risked frostbite by wearing neither a hat nor a scarf.

I suggested, "Why don't we all go inside, if we promise not to talk to each other?"

Uncle Allen must have been as cold as he looked. He agreed.

Sally and Tally were overjoyed at receiving company so early in the morning. I turned on the lights in my great room.

Naomi looked at my shoulder and gasped. "I'm sorry about your jacket, Willow. I hope my facial masque doesn't stain."

Opal, staring at my right sleeve, kicked her in the ankle. Naomi covered her mouth and turned around. "Your kitchen is lovely, Willow." Her voice shook. It had to be obvious she was changing the subject.

68

The shoulder of my pale gray parka was smudged in green matching Naomi's face.

The sleeve, however, had a reddish brown streak down it.

"Take off your coat, Willow," Opal ordered. "We should rinse that makeup out right away. In cold water." Shooting meaningful looks at her friends, she emphasized the last two words. They would know that cold water had the best chance of preventing blood from staining.

Unfortunately, Uncle Allen understood, too. "That blood proves she's the killer. Give me your coat for evidence. Do you have a plastic bag —"

Edna corrected him. "It should be paper, for —"

Opal kicked her in the ankle, too. If this kept up, The Three Weird Mothers were going to be The Three Limping Mothers.

Edna raised her rounded little chin and stared at Uncle Allen. "Blood on her jacket doesn't prove a thing. She found him."

I hadn't touched Mike. My dogs must have transferred his blood to me, but I wasn't about to mention it. Defending myself would be less heart-wrenching than defending my two sweet, innocent dogs against charges of murder.

I folded my jacket into a plastic garbage

bag and handed it to Uncle Allen.

"Your beautiful jacket," Naomi wailed.

"I make more coats than I can wear," I admitted. In addition to embroidering everything in sight, I suffered from sew-too-much syndrome.

Haylee and the mothers nodded their heads. All of us usually had more than one project on the go and made most of our own clothing.

Uncle Allen looked around unhappily. "There's no space in here to isolate everyone."

I didn't want anyone to have to spend more time outside. We worked it out that Haylee would go upstairs to In Stitches, Opal would wait in my bedroom, Naomi would hide in the guest room, and Edna would barricade herself in the laundry room. It was an odd arrangement, but at least we were warm and farther from the sad scene at the foot of my backyard.

Uncle Allen sat at my dining table and swept aside a white linen placemat, hemstitched and embroidered tone on tone with sprigs of thyme. I perched on a chair across from him, with Sally and Tally curled around my feet. Uncle Allen searched through his wallet until he found a yellowed piece of paper. He fumbled to unfold it.

"I'm to read you your rights."

My rights? I'd seen such things on TV and in movies, but didn't know for sure what it meant. Surely, he couldn't be arresting me.

I told myself to calm down. Maybe Uncle Allen had to read me my rights simply to ask me questions. Besides, he was an unreliable witness.

He was unreliable at more than witnessing. He took off his glasses, rubbed his eyes, and put his glasses back on. "I can't read the thing. You'll have to read it to yourself." He handed it to me.

Rights? These looked more like wrongs.

"Read it out loud," he demanded.

Hadn't he just said to read it to myself? "Carrots," I said haltingly. "Onions, potatoes. Milk." Helplessly, I looked up at him.

Not surprisingly, he was staring at me like I hadn't a clue what I was doing. He grabbed the scrap of paper and pried at its edges with cracked and dirty nails. He shoved the paper back at me. "It's still folded. You have to finish unfolding it."

I managed to open the small square of paper. It was creased, and the handwriting was tiny, faded and blurred.

"Read that," he directed. "So's I can hear it."

I tried. "You have the right to something

71

something."

"Remain silent," he barked.

I clamped my mouth shut.

"Go on," he said.

"You said to remain silent."

He took a deep breath. "It says you have the right to remain silent. And . . . what else does it say?"

That I have the right to throw you out of my apartment, I considered snapping, but I didn't think he'd go for that. This afternoon, he had displayed a strong disregard for search warrants. "It says, 'anything something something can something something something the right to an attorney something something —"

Edna popped out of the laundry room. "The right to an attorney! You can't question us without our attorneys present!"

Haylee clattered down the stairs from my shop, and Opal and Naomi flew out of their assigned bedrooms. Barking, the dogs danced around, jumping on everyone except Naomi, whose green face apparently made them wary, and Uncle Allen, who looked dumbfounded at the incursion of noisy women and dogs into his interview.

"I'm only asking questions," he said. "I need answers now, while everything is fresh in your minds." His lower lip trembled.

"Someone killed a young man I've known since he was a baby, and I would think that any good citizen would want to help me put that person behind bars."

Opal, Naomi, and Edna examined each other's faces, then mine and Haylee's. They raised and lowered eyebrows, cocked heads, and puffed cheeks in a language that only they understood.

They must have reached a consensus. Opal said, "Of course we'll help every way we can. C'mon girls, back to our hidey holes." She seemed to be enjoying herself a little too much.

They scampered away, leaving me bewildered. But not Mirandized, which may have been their plan. If the attending policeman didn't read us our rights properly, perhaps nothing could be used against us in court.

I didn't have much to tell Uncle Allen, anyway. "Mike must have been riding his ATV on the trail. The noise woke me up. The dogs barked, and we went outside. Both of my gates were padlocked, but Mike was lying in my bushes. I called 911, and Dr. Wrinklesides came first, then you. While I was gone, my canoe paddle appeared beside Mike's head. Then, when you arrived, we saw that pickup truck." Uncle Allen made me recite it all about a hundred times, probably in hopes of tripping me up, then sent me upstairs to trade places with Haylee.

I didn't bother closing the door at the top of the stairway. Despite the dogs panting and tap dancing beside me, I heard everything the other four women said, and it was all the same. Uncle Allen's siren woke them up. They came to my place to find out what was wrong, and he knew the rest.

When he was finished, I went downstairs. The dogs got there first.

Opal and Edna kissed me good night.

Edna whispered to me, "Don't worry about the blood on the jacket. He put it in a plastic bag. Plastic compromises organic compounds." She was already thinking up ways my mythical defense attorney could have me acquitted?

Naomi hugged me.

Haylee, obviously having trouble controlling new giggles about the green smudge Naomi had just added to my sweatshirt, kept her head turned away from Uncle Allen.

I threw on another of the coats I'd made, a burgundy wool one. Before assembling it, I had embroidered the collar and cuffs with a simple burgundy design in varying widths of satin stitch. Maybe I had a tendency to embroider everything possible, but I did occasionally restrain myself.

All of us, except for two dejected dogs, who would have welcomed any excuse for an outing, went outside. Calling quiet good-byes, the women went uphill toward the street. Uncle Allen's flashlight hadn't become any brighter in the warmth of my apartment. I guessed Elderberry Bay's law enforcement budget didn't allow for an adequate supply of batteries. Shining my light ahead of us, I let him lean on my arm while we negotiated our way down the hill. The ambulance was gone.

I pointed toward the dark woods on the other side of the river. "What's over there?"

"Trees."

Helpful. "Who owns them?"

"It's a state forest."

"So Mike's attacker could have crossed the river and escaped through the state forest?" And would be far away by now.

Uncle Allen let out an exasperated sigh. "No one can cross that river. They'd be crushed by shifting ice or fall in. They'd drown."

It wouldn't be easy to cross all that moving ice, but it was possible, especially for a desperate risk-taker like the person who had assaulted Mike. I asked, "What are you going to do about Mike's ATV?"

"I'll go over that in daylight. It's close to dawn already."

I held out my flashlight. "Take mine and go over it now."

"That wouldn't be enough. And don't forget I need to go check up on every dark pickup truck in the county."

Most of the time, Elderberry Bay was probably fine with only one police officer, but tonight he needed backup. I suggested, "The state police could send investigators and check up on everyone around here who owns dark pickup trucks. I think it was black."

"It was too dark to be sure."

He was right. I offered, "I could help you guard the crime scene until state troopers arrive." They shouldn't take long, should they?

"You are to stay away from the crime scene. Stay out of your backyard. Don't touch anything on your way inside."

I asked, "Do you have some of that yellow police tape in your cruiser?"

"I'll bring some." He shuffled to the ATV and held something up. "Got the key."

Taking the key might keep someone from driving off on Mike's ATV. It wouldn't keep anyone from tampering with evidence.

Uncle Allen shut himself into his cruiser and started it. His horn began honking again, as if he couldn't turn it off. With any luck, it would wear itself out like the siren, which was now only moaning. That cruiser needed some serious repairs. He backed slowly down the trail to a wide spot. Holding my breath for fear he would skid down the bank into the river, I watched him turn around. He headed uphill toward Lake Street. The cruiser's barnyard sounds passed the front of In Stitches, then whooped off into the icy distance.

Relocking my gate, I couldn't help glancing into the bushes where Mike had died. How had I missed seeing my canoe paddle underneath those bushes when the dogs and I first found Mike? I hadn't let Sally and Tally out of my sight after we discovered him until I locked them in my apartment, so I knew they hadn't moved it. I hadn't, either. How had it suddenly appeared near Mike?

I shuddered from lack of sleep, creeping horror, and freezing temperatures. My quaint little Blueberry Cottage had become frightening and forbidding. Maybe I would have it bulldozed, after all. As if being chased by a million murderers, I ran up to the other gate, locked it, then dashed back to the apartment.

Cuddled together in Sally's bed, the dogs barely lifted an eyelid.

Why did Mike Krawbach drive his ATV to my place and climb over my fence? Maybe he had attempted to torch the cottage, became giddy from gasoline fumes, tried to climb out of my yard, fell off my fence, and sustained terminal injuries. Or my canoe paddle failed as a pole vault.

Beaten, Dr. Wrinklesides concluded in the cold, moonless night.

What if someone had been trying to murder me, had come into my dark yard, and had attacked the wrong person?

Would he return to make another attempt on my life?

6

Had the murderer seen Mike in the dark and mistaken him for me? Mike was almost as tall as I was. Maybe, in a bulky winter coat, he could have passed for a woman. It wasn't a pretty thought.

Besides, who would want to kill me? The only person I could think of was Haylee's and my former boss, Jasper, now incarcerated in a white-collar detention center for his financial crimes.

Two hours had passed since Mike's ATV had awakened me. It was only six, but there was no point in trying to sleep. Uncle Allen had said to stay out of my yard, and I had no desire to venture into it, but he hadn't said I should stay off the trail. Maybe, before Uncle Allen could return with a team of investigators, I'd see something in the pre-dawn that hadn't been noticeable in the dark. I slipped my flashlight and digital camera into pockets, leashed the dogs, took them outside through In Stitches, and walked them down Lake Street to where the trail met the sidewalk. The ATV had been parked facing upriver and had probably crossed this sidewalk, but I couldn't see tracks from ATV tires on the sidewalk or in the street.

The pickup truck that Uncle Allen and I had seen creeping around the corner could have come from this spot or from the beach, at the foot of Lake Street. The only vehicle in sight was my car, parked halfway to the beach. Though tempted to dash to it, I walked the dogs to the trail and turned toward Blueberry Cottage. I searched for ATV tracks, but the ground was frozen solid and I couldn't see any tracks, not even from Uncle Allen's cruiser.

I peered over my locked gate. The door of my shed still hung open, and the gas can and my canoe paddle hadn't moved. How had that paddle ended up near Mike while the dogs and I were inside calling for help? Maybe Mike had leaned the paddle against branches, and it had fallen. I photographed everything as well as I could from my vantage point, which wasn't easy with two dogs pulling at leashes looped over my wrist. I didn't let the dogs anywhere near the ATV, and I stayed away from it, too.

I hurried the dogs back along the trail and up to Lake Street. I felt paralyzed, not only from the cold. I didn't know which direction Mike's attacker had come from or where he might have gone.

He knew where I lived, and although he might not have planned to kill me in the first place, he might think I'd seen him, and he would come after me. Perhaps he was lurking around even now. Didn't they say that criminals sometimes returned to the scene of the crime?

And there was my car, a half block away on Lake Street, near the beach. I could be a moving target instead of a stationary one, which was hardly reassuring.

At least I wouldn't have to drive around aimlessly. Recently, I'd been commissioned to embroider a rural scene on a large piece of linen, and I hadn't yet taken the photos for it. This morning's snowless dawn would be perfect. I'd gotten the job through my website, where I offered my designs for sale and also advertised my custom work, like the kitten portrait I'd shown my students yesterday. Custom work could be the most fun — and the most challenging. My software would translate my digital photos to embroidery designs.

Sally and Tally didn't mind running with

me the rest of the way to the car and jumping into the backseat. They curled up and covered their noses with their fluffy tails.

Checking my mirrors for pursuers, I drove out of the village and east on Shore Road. The sky in front of me began to pale. Vehicles, most of them black pickups, were parked in driveways, but no one else was on the road. I meandered along, searching for the sort of scene my client wanted.

And fighting to shut my memories of the night into a less accessible part of my brain.

Embroidery. Focus on embroidery . . .

Unlike most of my clients, who wanted portraits of their pets, homes, and cottages, my latest client wanted me to design the entire thing, and also wanted the wall hanging to resemble stumpwork, a centuries-old technique, similar to appliqué, of layering embroidery over stuffing or wood. Lately, machine embroiderers had copied stumpwork by using thin, dense foam for the stuffing. They called this method puff embroidery or three-dimensional embroidery. I preferred the antique sound of stumpwork.

Traditional stumpwork also incorporated flexible, narrow-gauge wires into smaller embroidered pieces that would represent objects like leaves, petals, or animal ears, and would be fastened to the original design for the third dimension. Starting with a photo would give the design realistic light and shading. I would need to devise a way for my embroidery machine to stitch wires into place reliably without breaking needles.

I'd driven farther than I'd planned, almost ten miles. Curving, the road emerged from a small wood. The perfect panorama for my project opened before me. A field, tan with last summer's broken cornstalks, was in the foreground, in front of hazy, gray blue woods, all of it underneath a pink-tinged sky. A hunter wearing a camouflage jacket and a neon orange hat added a speck of color to the woods. I pulled off the road and snapped picture after picture.

When I could no longer see the hat among the trees, I drove on. The sky in the south brightened from pale apricot to delicate azure. The road ran along bluffs above Lake Erie, covered with ice resembling a quilt stitched together from patches of peach, periwinkle, and lime. I parked again and got out. Some of the photos I took showed the lake as if no human had ever touched it, but when I aimed the camera in another direction, I captured images of ice fishing huts dotted over the frozen bay. Smoke swirled from the chimney of one. An ATV was parked beside it.

Boom!

I dove to the ground beside the driver's door. Had the murderer followed me out of the village to take potshots at me?

The noise rocketed out onto the lake, too prolonged for a gunshot. The thick lake ice must have developed a sudden, and very long, crack. I had to admire one thing about ATV club members. Riding an ATV onto that ice took courage. Or, perhaps, a blithe disregard for danger.

If the lake was going to scare me half to death every few minutes, I was done taking pictures. I opened the door, slipped into the car, drove back to Elderberry Bay, and parked near the beach again.

I hesitated on my shop's front porch. In Stitches usually felt like home, but I didn't relish being alone, and my customers weren't due for at least an hour.

I turned around and surveyed the windows of the apartments above the shops across the street. Could I barge in on Haylee or one of her mothers?

Haylee came out of The Stash and beckoned. I lifted a hand to show I'd be there in a minute, put the dogs into the stairway leading down to my apartment, locked my shop, and ran across the street.

Haylee met me in the doorway. "Come

84

for breakfast," she said.

I needed no further encouragement. We could talk and talk about last night and never completely get the horror out of our systems, but we could try.

The last time I had been in her store, less than twenty-four hours before, Mike was alive and we were both angry at him and his arrogance. My anger had evaporated, but it was strange seeing those same fabrics displayed on racks as if nothing had happened.

Haylee's store was the largest in town, with rooms and rooms of beautiful fabrics, and her apartment above the store was huge, loft style, with arched windows, vast open spaces, light hardwood floors, and high ceilings. Her furniture was spare, comfortable with no fussy decorations. I loved the look, but her mothers often suggested she should add their unique sorts of embellishments, and I usually teased that she needed embroidered touches. At the moment, I didn't feel like teasing.

She led me to her minimalist, uncluttered kitchen and handed me a knife, a small onion, and a red pepper. "You chop those while I beat the eggs," she said. "Let's make as much noise as we can."

I raised an eyebrow at her. "Noise?"

She shrugged. "Whatever. Noise. Activity. Pounding, chopping. To help us cope with . . . earlier this morning."

"Did you sleep," I asked. "After?"

"Not much. Did you?"

Tearing seeds and white membranes from the pepper, I told her about my explorations.

"You should have asked me to come with you. Or any of my mothers."

"Maybe they managed to sleep."

She banged her whisk through the eggs and against the sides of her stainless steel bowl. "We should have all . . . gotten together to sew or something, instead of going back to our own apartments and lying awake."

"I didn't like him," I said. It wasn't a change of subject.

She agreed. "No, he was full of himself and he had a mean streak. But . . ."

"There was no reason to kill the guy," I finished for her.

"As Opal would say, 'live and let live.'" Haylee called the women who raised her, including Opal, her birth mother, by their first names. "Who would have done such a thing?"

"Uncle Allen suspects me."

Haylee snorted. "He doesn't know you."

I waved my knife in the air. "I did say, in front of half the village, that I'd kill Mike if he bulldozed my cottage. And I have the impression that Uncle Allen is looking for revenge, not justice. I'm an outsider, a convenient scapegoat."

"My mothers and I are outsiders, too."

"Great," I said. "Uncle Allen probably suspects us all."

"Me, especially." She poured the beaten eggs into an omelet pan. "Everyone knows I refused to go out with Mike a second time." She shuddered.

"You know where he lived, right?"

"Yes." She made an exaggeratedly stern face. "But this isn't like when we lived in Manhattan and needed evidence to convince the police that Jasper had been stealing from clients. This time, the police know there was a crime. We'll have to let them do the investigating."

I slid the pepper and onions into the omelet. "Do you think Uncle Allen will do a decent job?"

"I'm not sure he *can*." She grated cheddar over the veggies and eggs. "But you and I would *never* go snooping where we shouldn't, right?"

I loaded two slices of her yummy home-made bread into her toaster. "Never. In

87

New York, we had a perfect right to work late at night when no one else was around. And we didn't have to break into Jasper's office, either." Our boss had been so sure he could get away with his crimes that he hadn't bothered locking his office.

Haylee gazed out the window toward her car in the parking lot behind her mothers' shops. "Mike showed me where he kept a key to his back door. And he said I was welcome to use it anytime. As if I would have wanted to visit him unannounced or go out with him again! You wouldn't believe the rage he got into simply because that woman in the red car drove too slowly in a no-passing zone."

"No wonder she hid her face when Mike barged into my shop."

"When he did pass her, I was afraid he'd force her into a ditch. He had a sudden and horrible temper."

"I'm guessing that someone else has a worse one," I said. "Maybe someone who drives a black pickup."

Haylee challenged, "What if Uncle Allen fails to follow up on that truck?"

"Then we'll . . . do something."

Haylee only laughed. We carried our omelets and toast to her great room and sat in simple yet comfortable armchairs. She pressed a button, and flames leaped from a stainless steel slot in the hearth. This latest version of a gas fireplace would have amazed the first people who had installed gas heating and lights in this Victorian apartment.

The omelet was delicious. I asked Haylee, "Did you hear or see anything unusual when you came outside early this morning? People? Vehicles?"

"Only my mothers, who are unusual at the best of times. We were awakened by the siren, if you can call it that. We saw Uncle Allen's cruiser in front of your place, so we all came outside."

"How did you manage to arrive at the same time? Phone each other first?"

"My mothers have been best friends since they were in first grade, and they all raised me, so it's not surprising when we all do approximately the same thing. My mothers are all wacky, but they're always supportive."

I spread grape jelly on my toast. "I really like them. You're lucky."

She looked down at her plate. "I know. They can cramp my style, but it's great having them nearby."

How many other people would invite their mothers to move to a sleepy village and help change it to a lively one where people could buy and make every sort of textile imaginable?

Haylee raised her head and the affection for her mothers in her smile lit the room. "Like anybody, I know which parent to go to for what. If I need enthusiasm for a project, I go to Opal. If I want someone one to tell me I'm perfect, I ask Naomi. And I can always count on Edna to say what she thinks. No set of parents could have loved me more."

"That's pretty obvious," I said. Even before I met Haylee's mothers, I'd been able to tell she'd been raised by loving parents.

She swept her hair off her shoulders. Her blue eyes twinkled with mischief. "They have their quirks, especially now that they own textile arts shops. They feel duty-bound to make the most creative garments possible, and actually wear them."

I had to grin. Now that I had time to embroider almost everything, only a few of my outfits escaped touches of embroidery. I could be heading toward quirky dressing, myself. I defended her mothers and me. "We all need to advertise our stores and our talents, even you, with your expert tailoring. Your clothes look very expensive. That could be considered eccentric at our age."

"Pooh. If anyone wants to think it, let 'em."

"See?" I teased. "You're getting as quirky as your mothers."

"Maybe that's not a bad thing." She sat up straighter in her chair. "They're strong. And tough."

Haylee had acquired the same traits.

Had I? My mother was strong and tough, but she had never had time to belong to me the way Haylee's three mothers belonged to her. My mother was a physician who had turned to politics.

Unlike Haylee, I knew my father. He was an inventor, seldom seen outside the carriage house behind my parents' home, where he tinkered and invented. I'd lost count of the number of patents he had, but I wouldn't categorize him as either strong or tough like our mothers were. My parents had never come to visit me in Manhattan and were even less likely to stir from South Carolina to the northwestern corner of Pennsylvania.

We finished breakfast. Haylee put our dishes into the dishwasher. "Any time you need to, call or come see me," she offered. "Or my mothers." She gave me a big hug.

Feeling less anxious and alone, I left her bright apartment. I couldn't help touching fabrics as I passed them on my way out of The Stash. As always, the feel of cotton calmed and comforted.

I expected to see several law enforcement vehicles outside In Stitches when I returned, but the only cars and trucks seemed to belong to early-morning shoppers. I gave the dogs another short outing, started a fire in my woodstove, and put a pot of cider on its top.

Turning the cross-stitched sign in my door to *Welcome* may have been a mistake. Uncle Allen tromped in. "Your front gate's locked," he complained. "Give me the key."

That didn't seem like a good idea, so I went outside and unlocked it for him. "Are you going to need to get into my cottage?" I asked. "Somebody took my canoe paddle out of the lean-to and left the door open."

"Is there a way from that lean-to into your cottage?"

"No."

"And the cottage is locked?"

"Yes. The door facing the river bolts from the inside." I pointed down toward the cottage. "I have a key for the door we can see from here." I hadn't decided whether that door or the one facing the river should be called the front door.

"Well, you can't come into the crime scene to unlock it for me, now can you?"

Not as long as he told me I couldn't.

"What's in your cottage?"

"Nothing. It's vacant."

"Okay, you can either give me the key now or wait until I get a search warrant and give it to me then."

"I have nothing to hide, and I'd like you to find Mike's murderer and arrest him as soon as possible." A good citizen, I gave him the key. "When are the other investigators coming?"

He turned his back to me, flapped a hand in dismissal, and marched down toward where I'd found Mike early this morning.

Back inside the shop, the fragrance of cider, orange zest, cinnamon, and cloves warmed me. I'd be safe from Mike's attacker now that a policeman was in my backyard, wouldn't I?

Tally, a dreamy sort, whimpered on the other side of the apartment door. Sally, the practical, heavy-footed one, clumped down the stairs, probably to claim the choicest napping spot on Tally's bed. Or on mine.

Cooing at Tally through the closed door, I downloaded pictures from my camera to the computer. I cropped the photo of the man disappearing into the woods beyond the field of dead cornstalks, then launched my embroidery software, loaded the photo into it, and clicked on the appropriate icon. The software began generating stitches that mimicked the photo.

Suddenly, everything glowed red.

The ancient red car that Mike had attempted to railroad into a ditch came to a halt outside in the bright morning sunshine. The quiet woman inched her driver's door open, looked left and right, then scurried toward In Stitches like she was hoping no one would see her.

She slipped sideways into In Stitches. Her bulging cloth bag was almost bigger than she was.

"Help yourself to cider," I called.

She shook her head. I left her to browse.

The next thing I knew, she was peeking over my shoulder. "How do you do that?" she asked.

I showed her the photo I'd started with, and the embroidery software's amazingly true-to-life depiction of how the design would look when stitched on cloth. "I need to adjust it here and there to force it into my vision." I would also need to add varying thicknesses of foam to some of the trees, and maybe to the man, too. Seventeenth-century embroiderers often ignored things like scale, and a man could be bigger than a horse or a castle. Or a tree. Creating that stumpwork look was going to be fun.

"That's what you'll be teaching?" Her voice was reedy, her question tentative.

"We'll work up to it, get used to the machines and the software in small steps." I smiled. "I don't want to give away all my tricks in the second lesson."

My attempt to put her at ease failed. She stared at my gleaming walnut floor. "No, of course not." She turned back toward the front windows. "Your boutique is lovely." Tapping her index finger against her lips, she frowned toward the woodstove. Finally, she tiptoed to the fabric cutting table. "May I show you something?"

"Of course." I followed her.

She turned her bag upside down and shook placemats and napkins out of it. Like any true fabriholic, I couldn't help touching them. They were obviously hand woven, of natural fabrics, in beautiful shades. "These are gorgeous," I burst out. Her purple hat was also hand woven, as were her black coat and emptied bag. "Did you do the weaving?"

"Yes. Do you really like them?" Gazing down as if saying a reluctant farewell, she ran quivering fingers across the placemats and napkins.

"They're fabulous." I wasn't gushing. They were.

95

"Do you think you could sell them in your store?" She didn't look up at me.

"They'd sell anywhere, but I'd be afraid to sell them here for fear someone would take a notion to embroider things on them. They're beautiful the way they are."

"That wouldn't matter." Even her voice trembled.

Was she desperate for funds? I shouldn't have problems selling these gorgeous hand-woven linens, but I'd have to prevent myself from buying them, because no matter how many times I told myself they didn't need embellishment, sooner or later I'd stretch them into hoops and let my machines have their way with them. "Okay," I agreed. "Let's talk about prices and my mark-up and how I'll display . . ."

"I'm sure you'll do it all just right."

How could she be so trusting? "No," I said firmly. "Let's sit down and discuss this."

She sat, but she wouldn't take off her coat.

I suggested prices.

Gasping, she clapped both hands to her cheeks.

"Not enough?" I asked.

She quavered, "Too much?"

I shook my head. "Definitely not."

She pulled a scrap of paper from a pocket. "Here's my address. If you sell anything, send me the check? And . . ." She fiddled with the paper. "Would you mind coming out to my studio to pick up new pieces? That is, if you ever want more."

"I'd love to see your studio and your work." Once a fabriholic, always a fabriholic. Besides, looms fascinated me.

"I hate coming to town." She appeared to hold her breath in hopes I wouldn't question her about it.

Not that I could have. My sea glass chimes jangled. She shoved the paper at me. *Dawn Langford, Weaver,* I read.

Sam came halfway in. "Hey, Willow, how'd those padlocks work out for you?"

"Fine," I answered over Dawn's lowered head. "Thanks for thinking of matching ones."

Dawn bent farther forward. Her face was inches from her knees.

"Y'know," he called out, "the guys who hang out in The Ironmonger and I were talking, and we all thought what you did to Mike Krawbach was perfect."

My hair was too long to stand on end all over my head, but that's what it felt like it was doing. "What *I* did to Mike Krawbach?" Did everyone in town think I'd murdered Mike? And they were applauding me for it?

Sam nodded several times. "Stood up to

97

him, you did. Yesterday afternoon in the street. Throws his weight around too much, that boy. Always has."

Dawn seemed to crumble into herself. Sam didn't seem to know that Mike was dead. Did Dawn?

Uncle Allen pushed his way into the store past Sam. "Stood up to Mike, my foot. Murdered him, more likely."

Pot lights in my ceiling reflected onto Sam's bald head, giving it a jaunty look, like he'd pasted fat white sequins on it. Sam examined Uncle Allen's truculent expression. Sam's smile disintegrated. "Uncle Allen, my boy, you're not serious, now, are you?"

"Serious as all get-out. We found Mike beaten up at the foot of *her* backyard last night." He jabbed a thumb toward me. "He died there."

Dawn Langford tumbled off her chair and onto the floor.

7

Strangely, it was the hardware store owner, not the policeman, who ran to the fallen woman. He hollered, "Uncle Allen, get on your radio and call for help!"

If Uncle Allen had a radio, would it work?

We weren't about to find out. Uncle Allen shaped his hand like a revolver and pointed the barrel at me. "Now she's gone and killed another one."

His accusations were becoming tedious. Besides, Dawn didn't appear to be dead, much less murdered. Her color was returning. I knelt beside her. Her lips moved.

Uncle Allen shuffled to us. Dawn's lids fluttered open, revealing dazed and wobbly pale gray eyes. She focused on the two men above her, then scuttled crabwise away from them. I was probably the only one to hear her whisper, "Don't let them touch me."

I murmured, paying no attention to what I was saying, trying to calm and soothe.

I took her hand in mine. Her skin felt dry and calloused. Her muscles, presumably from all that weaving, were like steel cables. She nearly crushed my hand.

As if sensing her unusual strength, Sam backed away, taking Uncle Allen with him.

The door opened, admitting a blast of cold air. And Naomi, who apparently had invisible, trouble-seeking antennae. "What's wrong?" she shouted.

"Nothing," I said.

"Nothing," Dawn repeated. She whispered, "Don't let her near me, either."

My mouth dropped open. Naomi was one of the sweetest people on earth. "It's okay," I told Dawn, extricating my hand and flexing my fingers. They seemed to work.

Naomi asked, "Should we call Dr. Wrinklesides?"

Dawn sat up. "No!" Her face was a healthy pink.

"She's fine," I said. "She slipped off her chair."

"Bring that chair over to The Ironmonger," Sam offered. "I'll have a look at it."

I flashed him an appreciative smile. He probably knew as well as I did that the chair was fine.

Naomi tiptoed closer. "Oh, the poor dear." She had removed the green goo from

100

her face, but Dawn shrank from her anyway.

Naomi turned toward the window. "Our local students, Georgina and Susannah, are going into my store." She left.

I supposed that, under the circumstances, I should be glad I didn't have customers, only a thin wraith of a woman given to swooning, an angry cop given to accusing me of murder, and a kindly ironmonger given to tripping over his feet in his rush to return to his hardware store so he could tell his cronies about Uncle Allen accusing me of murder.

Maybe instead of running a business, I should take my cue from Dawn and hide under chairs.

Uncle Allen marched outside and turned toward The Ironmonger as if he wanted to deliver his version of the news to the old-timers hanging around the potbellied stove.

I couldn't help picturing all those retired farmers sitting in a jury and weighing evidence against me, putting me in jail where I would . . . design and embroider gorgeous motifs all over everyone's orange jumpsuits?

I shook myself back to reality. It wouldn't happen. Uncle Allen would call in reinforcements, and they'd find out who attacked Mike.

I helped Dawn stand. "Maybe you should see a doctor." During my short time in Threadville, I'd picked up some questionable hinting skills from Haylee's mothers.

Dawn looked about as energetic as the bag she'd brought her weavings in. "I'd rather die."

I couldn't think of anything to say. Besides, if I pressed her about visiting a doctor she was obviously afraid of, she might swoon again, and I would never get her off my floor.

She leaned toward me. "Don't you let them be accusing you of murdering that Mike Krawbach. Lots of people wanted to murder him."

Including her?

"The first place to look is his friends," she said. "When they were boys, they were a nasty bunch. Uncle Allen called what they did mischief, but it was downright vandalism. They came around my place at night knocking on my doors and windows and hollering for me to come out and stop them. They threw paint over my porch furniture. Wicker. I had to repaint it."

And someone threw paint on my porch.

"And that wasn't all," she confided in whispers. "Somebody burned down my outbuildings. Three Halloweens in a row.

102

Chicken coop, smokehouse, corncrib, all burned to the ground. No one believed me that the culprits were Mike and his gang, and their parents claimed their kids were home watching TV."

How many years had she waited to tell this to someone? I had to keep her talking. "Do the other members of Mike's gang still live around Elderberry Bay?"

"Most of them. One's none other than our sainted mayor, Irv Oslington. Who would vote for him? And Herb Gunthrie, the postman everyone loves so much. I don't trust that guy to deliver the mail without checking the envelope for things he might want."

"Did Smythe Castor run around with Mike and his buddies?" I asked.

"I may have seen him with them once or twice. I think he's younger than the ringleaders."

"What about Clay Fraser? Was he one of Mike's gang?"

"I can't remember. There were so many of them. Different ones at different times. But always Mike spurring them on." She seemed to fold in on herself. "You be careful around all of them, and don't let them blame you for things they did. And that includes Uncle Allen DeGlazier. He's wilier than he looks."

"You be careful, too." I tried to keep doubt from my face. Was she warning me against Mike's friends for my sake or to deflect suspicion from herself?

Looking satisfied at accomplishing her mission, whatever it was, she sidled out. Was agreeing to sell her weavings a mistake? If fear was contagious, I might catch it. But the linens were beautiful. I didn't want to display them near the front windows where they might fade. I moved the bistro table farther back. Dawn's colorful work contrasted nicely with the heritage designs I'd stitched on the white tablecloth.

The Threadville tour bus trundled past. Minutes later, my morning students charged into my shop.

"What happened? Why is that cop car outside again?" Rosemary asked.

"A man died in my backyard early this morning."

Yesterday's artistic woman, the one who'd said she lived in Elderberry Bay and had drawn a picture of Blueberry Cottage in a few deft strokes, was dressed head to toe in chocolate brown today. She raised her chin. "I heard it was that snirp —"

Rosemary interrupted. "What's a snirp?"

"You know, a twerp in a snit, like that Mike Krawbach who was in here yesterday trying to pack a petition with illegal signatures. If anyone was asking to be killed —"

"Now, Georgina," the woman beside her scolded. Susannah, the other local?

The somber mood lightened as everyone poured themselves cider and showed off their homework. Following the instructions I'd given them yesterday, they had bought floral fabrics at The Stash and had hooped fabric and stabilizer together, but any resemblance to each others' work ended there. They'd chosen a variety of fabrics, colors, and stitches, and had ended up with deliciously different embroidered flowers.

In addition to flaunting unique designs, each student made it her mission to describe how she planned to use her completed homework. Several motifs were destined to be sewn onto babies' and children's clothes. Some would decorate quilts. One woman was going to use hers to patch a sheet that had suffered an unfortunate clash with a sofa bed. Another planned to use hers to beautify an apron for her mother. Two women pranced around in vests, one quilted pink twill, the other black velvet, both embellished with their homework. These women were a traveling fashion show.

Rosemary cut their show-and-tell short. "What are we making today, Willow?"

I held up an embroidery hoop that fit one of my embroidery machines. I had loaded it with stabilizer and a square of sage green felt. "We're going to embroider with machines."

They cheered.

Grinning at the enthusiasm the women must have fanned into flames during their bus ride from Erie, I showed them a small memory card. "In addition to pretty designs, this contains several fonts." They gathered around while I inserted the card into the attachment and demonstrated choosing letters, resizing them, and centering them in the hoop.

I started the machine. It wrote *Willow* in — what else? — willowy script. My students loved it.

Georgina asked, "What about those threads between letters? They show."

They did, barely. "You can clip them. Very carefully."

"Won't your name unravel?" Susannah asked.

"Not if you don't cut the threads on the back of the design," I answered.

They dispersed to machines around the shop. Judging from their chatter and triumphant yelps, they had a wonderful time, especially Rosemary, Georgina, and Susannah, working together in a back corner of the store. Their laughter drew the rest of us to them.

"We're making mottos," Georgina explained. "Mine's for my sewing room." She eased away so we could see what she'd stitched. *So Many Fabrics, So Little Time.*

"I'm putting mine above the bed." Susannah showed us bright red felt, cross-stitched in eye-zapping royal blue. *She Who Hoards The Most Fabrics Wins.* I couldn't blame her for substituting "hoards" for the usual "dies with."

Rosemary gestured like a game show host and declaimed, "Mine's going over hubby's widescreen TV in the living room. Now he won't have to ask why I spend my days in Threadville." With a flourish, she revealed, *What Does "Need" Have To Do With Buying Fabric?*

Fabriholics had to be among the happiest addicts around. Not that any of us saw it as an addiction. By the time they left for lunch at Pier 42, everyone had stitched their names *and* a motto.

As I ate my own lunch, Clay phoned, wanting to know if this evening would be a good time to tour Blueberry Cottage and discuss renovating it.

I gripped the phone so hard my nails bit

into my palms. "We can't. My whole back-yard, including Blueberry Cottage, is a crime scene. We're not allowed in it."

Silence. Then, "You're kidding."

"I wish I were. Mike Krawbach somehow managed to get himself beaten up near Blueberry Cottage last night, and now he's dead, and Uncle Allen thinks I did it." I was probably coming across as hysterical.

"I'll come right over," he said.

And he did. He parked his truck in front of Tell a Yarn, got out, and stopped dead, staring toward my front gate. Seconds later, he was inside In Stitches. "Are you okay, Willow?" He looked so concerned and ready to console that I was tempted to say I wasn't.

Haylee hurtled through the front door. "Clay!" They slapped palms. She looked about to explode in mirth. "Did you notice — ?"

His shoulders shook. "Yes, I did."

Haylee collapsed in my chair in a fit of hysterics.

"What's so funny?" I demanded like a whiny little kid around her big sister and her big sister's boyfriend and their mysterious secret society.

"She hasn't seen it yet, has she?" Haylee gasped.

108

"I guess not," Clay answered.

"Come outside," Haylee demanded. "Close your eyes."

8

I wasn't sure that closing my eyes was a great plan, but I obeyed. Haylee and Clay helped me down the wide front porch steps and turned me right. I felt the relative smoothness of concrete under my shoes. We had to be on the path leading toward the gate between my front and side yards.

"Open your eyes," Haylee ordered.

My expression, which must have been startled to say the least, threw her into another fit of giggles.

Uncle Allen had festooned my fence and gate with yellow police tape. He had woven it in and out, through chain links and around gateposts. Apparently, he'd had to cut the tape to open the gate so he could leave my property. He'd made up for it by draping several more layers of tape around the cut ends. Where was he, at home eating his lunch? Waiting for a team of investigators to arrive and help him? All this tape would impress them, no doubt.

I leaned over the gate. Because of the tall cedars parading down both sides of my yard, I couldn't see all of my fence. What I could see of it, and of the gate at the foot of the hill, was covered in tape.

"It's a work of art," Haylee managed.

"Maybe Uncle Allen really wants to retire and take textile arts courses from the Threadville shopkeepers," Clay suggested.

Haylee checked her watch. "I'd better finish preparing for this afternoon's class." She dashed through my front yard and across the street.

Clay came into In Stitches with me, opened the stove, threw in a chunk of wood, then poured each of us a mug of warm cider. "I'm used to making myself at home," he said. "I worked here for so long that I sometimes forget it's not my place."

"Anytime," I said with more conviction than I wanted him to hear if he and Haylee were as close as they appeared to be. I covered it with a quick, "Like some cookies?"

Tally whined from the top of the apartment steps on the other side of the door.

"Maybe we should take your dogs out first," Clay suggested.

I let the pups into the shop, snapped

leashes on them, and put on my burgundy jacket. Clay took Tally, and I took Sally. While the dogs sniffed at the yellow tape woven through my fence, I told Clay about Mike's death. I didn't tell him what Mike's purported last words were. For one thing, Uncle Allen changed them every time he repeated them. I concluded, "So, because Mike died in my yard and my canoe paddle and an empty gas can were near him, Uncle Allen is going around saying that Mike found me about to burn my own cottage down and I killed him so he wouldn't report me to my insurance company."

"Even Uncle Allen must know that's a stretch. He hasn't arrested you." Clay frowned toward two large white trucks parked near the vacant store. "What's with the trucks?"

"I don't know." I was beginning to suspect everyone and everything, including mysterious unmarked trucks, of murder.

Clay bent down and scratched Tally's head. "Maybe the vacant building on the other side of The Ironmonger is finally being renovated. Usually, I hear about things like that. Those trucks don't belong to any construction company around here."

The dogs seemed more than willing to help investigate. They tugged us past the

112

hardware store. I wondered what allegations about my connection with Mike's death were swirling around that potbellied stove.

The vacant building had been constructed from early twentieth-century concrete blocks, the ones cast with bumps to resemble stone. Once ubiquitous, these buildings were becoming rare and had a certain antique charm. Newspapers were taped in the large front windows, so we couldn't see inside, where hammers pounded, saws whined, and a radio blared. Clay handed me Tally's leash, strode to the door, and knocked. No one answered. Clay tried the knob. Locked. He returned to the dogs and me.

Tally pulled him to the next building, a brand-new one with Victorian gingerbread styling, wide porches, glassed-in balconies, and many huge windows. "This is going to be a restaurant," Clay told me. "It's supposed to open this spring."

The restaurant would have a fabulous view of the village park, which included the beach, the mouth of the river, and the end of the riverside trail where I'd searched unsuccessfully this morning for tracks from Mike's ATV.

Pier 42, where the Threadville tourists were eating lunch, boasted a similar view, but from the other side of Lake Street, so it didn't overlook the river. At the rate the Threadville boutiques were drawing tourists besides the usual summer sun lovers, the village would soon easily support two year-round restaurants.

Clay helped me convince the dogs to go back to In Stitches, where we all feasted on peanut butter cookies, made without sugar for the dogs and with plenty of rich brown sugar for us. Clay stared at the corner of my shop where I kept my computer, beside the door to my apartment. "If you had a pen for the dogs here, at the top of the stairs, they could stay near you in your store, and you could leave your door open for them to wander to and from your apartment when-ever they wanted to."

I loved the idea. "And Tally wouldn't have to whine and whimper so much. Could I hire you to build it?"

"You could."

We spent the next five minutes gobbling cookies, mapping out the penned area, and designing a gate for it. We agreed that Clay would build it on Monday, the day the Threadville shops were closed.

Clay fished a card from the inner chest pocket of his jacket. "Here's my number. I don't live far away, and I'm building new houses up the river. If this place gives you problems, call me anytime, day or night."

I asked, "How did you know my phone number to call me just now?"

He grinned. "The dogs told me. It's on their tags."

And he'd made a note of it. Thorough.

He knelt to tell the dogs good-bye. Unabashedly, they gave him more than his share of kisses, then rewarded me with reproachful looks for letting him leave. To add insult to injury, I closed them into the apartment.

Halfway through the afternoon class, my students and I heard Uncle Allen's police cruiser. We watched it lead a flatbed truck up Lake Street. The truck carried an ATV. It had to be Mike's. Originally, it must have been black. Now, dust and road salt made it appear gray.

It was after five and getting dark when the tour bus left. I began tidying the store. My sea glass chime jingled.

Uncle Allen. "I've taken your canoe paddle and gas can as evidence, and Mike's ATV. Do you have anything to say for yourself?"

I walked close to Uncle Allen so I could tower over him. "It wasn't my gas can. And Mike was —" I almost said *hateful.* "He had a way of making enemies."

"Only you and your friends with your silly hobbies. Why did you all have to invade our peaceful village and start murdering folks?" He backed into a rack of sparkly embroidery threads. Spools bounced and rolled over my black walnut floor.

I gathered errant spools of thread. "None of us harmed him. None of us would hurt anyone." I poked spools back into their places in their rack.

Widening his stance and placing his fists on his hips, he endangered my rack of low-gloss cotton embroidery thread. "Mike told me you women killed him." Uncle Allen seemed determined to change — or forget — Mike's last words. "Only a woman would use a canoe paddle to kill someone."

It was such a cockeyed accusation that I wondered if Uncle Allen had planned it first, then attacked Mike with my canoe paddle. Uncle Allen was big, but perhaps not coordinated enough to do real damage with a canoe paddle, even one made of good, sturdy hardwood like the one that had come with Blueberry Cottage.

I put my favorite scissors into their drawer. "That doesn't make sense."

"Sure it does. Men have guns and knives. What do women have? Rolling pins and . . .

and canoe paddles."

Scissors, too. I slammed the drawer. "Besides, my gate was locked when I found Mike. If someone threw him over the fence, it had to be someone strong. A man."

"No one had to throw Mike. Maybe you left your gate unlocked last night."

"I don't dare leave my gates unlocked. Mi— *someone* opened one and let my dogs out."

"Aha!" Uncle Allen raised an index finger. "I heard that you blamed Mike for letting your dogs escape."

I fought to control a guilty expression. Last night, I'd told people on the trail that Mike had let my dogs out of my yard. I may even have uttered a death threat. I'd undoubtedly looked murderous. My sweet little Sally-Forth and Tally-Ho could have been lost, injured, or killed.

"I'm sure he did open my gate. I got the dogs back, bought padlocks, and locked my gates, so I had no reason to harm him."

He grunted in scorn. "Your gate started out locked last night, then *someone* unlocked it, let Mike into your yard, beat him up, and locked the gate. Who would that be?" The finger pointed at me. "That'd be you. The woman who threatened to kill him."

"I didn't mean it that way. I spoke in anger." I was digging a bigger hole for myself. "I admit I shouldn't have spoken like that, but it was just words. Besides, I was the one who called for help when he was injured."

He jutted his chin, which he probably hoped made him look dangerous, but really only stretched his wattles. "You didn't *mean* your words. Maybe you didn't *mean* to kill him, either, but when you saw how badly you'd injured him, you got scared, and called 911."

"I didn't even know he was in my backyard. I never touched him, never hurt him, never would have!" I told myself to ratchet down the anxiety before it manifested itself in twitches or blushes. "Have you checked up on everybody around here who owns a dark pickup truck?"

"Check up, how?"

I held my hands out, palms up. "To see if any of them had grudges against Mike. Or —" I tripped over my words. "Wouldn't Mike have fought his attacker? Maybe someone went to the emergency room with strange wounds last night. Or visited a doctor."

"If they did, I'd hear about it."

I wasn't so sure. "I never saw that gas can

before, or touched it. Someone brought it to my place. Why don't you dust it and the canoe paddle for prints? The paddle came with the property, and I may have touched it, but I'm sure you'll find someone else's prints on it. More recent prints than mine. That'll be your man."

"Woman," he jumped in. "And she . . . you . . . wore gloves. I already dusted them."

Everyone wore gloves or mittens last night. Overcoming my panic was becoming increasingly difficult. On the other hand, Uncle Allen seemed more interested in taunting me than arresting me. I asked, "Why haven't the state police sent teams to help you investigate?"

Uncle Allen puffed out his chest. "I haven't asked them, and they can't go butting into my jurisdiction. What would they know about Elderberry Bay? This case I'm solving myself. In all my years of policing this village, nothing like this has ever happened before."

All the more reason to ask for help. "They could take some of the burden. You'll be putting in hours of overtime."

Somewhere among the chins and wattles, Uncle Allen had jaw muscles he could clench. His teeth made a horrible grinding noise. "I watched Mike and all the other

119

young folks around here grow up. Whenever they had a problem, they always knew they could come to me. I was about to retire. Mike trusted me. I owe it to him to stay on until his killer is nailed."

Maybe he believed that being denied a building permit was a motive for murder, but I knew a better one. "Who inherits Mike's vineyard?"

Uncle Allen backed away as if hoping I wouldn't recognize the grief in his eyes. "His parents are dead and he had no sisters or brothers or wife or children. He struggled with that vineyard all by himself, had to mortgage everything after a couple of disastrous winters killed his grapevines. The poor boy had nothing besides debts. He was about to get on his feet."

He turned and shambled toward the door.

"When can I use my backyard again?"

Pushing my door open, he called over his shoulder, "I'll let you know."

Seething at Uncle Allen's stubborn belief that I had to be a killer, I hung my embroidered *Closed* sign in the door, then called Haylee and asked her to come for a walk with me and the dogs. She came out and took Sally's leash from me. As we strolled together through Threadville, it was apparent that her mothers had not yet begun their supper. Opal was inside Tell a Yarn, stocking her shelves — diamond-shaped niches — with yarns in spring colors. The pine shelving, walls, and ceiling gave the shop a warm glow. Next door, Edna was vacuuming. Buttons and Bows was mostly white inside, a background for Edna's sparkling, floor-to-ceiling displays of buttons and trims. The front room of Naomi's shop, Batty About Quilts, was an art gallery showcasing gorgeous quilts. We caught glimpses of Naomi bustling around in the brightly lit shop behind the gallery.

Although all different, the shops shared a fresh, clean style. "Did Clay renovate all of the Threadville shops?" I asked Haylee.

"Yep. He did a great job, didn't he?"

I let Tally pull me down the hill toward the beach. "He said you told him what I wanted."

"Did he?"

"Haylee, when you called me to come see the shop and apartment below it, they were already finished."

"I was right, then. He did renovate it perfectly for you."

"Yes, but —" I spluttered. "You tricked me."

We ventured onto the sandy beach. "I wanted to do you a favor. You'd been dreaming of leaving that stressful job in Manhattan and opening your own shop where you could play with embroidery to your heart's content, right?"

"Right." And I did love living and working in Threadville. How could I not? Waves thundering onto the beach, adorable dogs that I would not have subjected to apartment life in Manhattan, a wonderfully warm and fun set of friends and customers, and fabrics, fabrics, fabrics. And embroidery.

"How do you like Clay?" she asked, with a teasing lilt.

"He's very nice."

"Is that all you can say? I practically throw you two together, and . . ."

"Um, Haylee, don't you have first dibs on the guy?"

"Clay? I like him. Really like him. He's a friend. But he would be perfect for you." Sally pulled Haylee away from the breaking waves.

Tally, of course, pulled me toward them, so I had to shout. "If he's perfect for me, why wouldn't he be perfect for you?" Maybe she had her eye on someone else. Hauling Tally back to Haylee and Sally-Forth, I hinted, "Your mothers seem to adore Smythe Castor."

The wind whipped her hair over her face.

She pulled the hair away. "Everyone says he's as sweet as the honey his bees make. But . . . right now, I'm only looking."

"Me, too," I said firmly, turning Tally toward home.

Behind me, Haylee snickered.

We all jogged up the hill. In the street between our shops, I took Sally's leash from Haylee. "You're right about only window shopping for now, Haylee. Until Mike's murderer is behind bars, both of us need to be cautious about *all* of the bachelors around Elderberry Bay."

She retorted, "You sound like my mothers. But I'll be careful."

"Promise?"

"Promise. I saw Uncle Allen at your place a while ago. How's his investigation going?"

I groaned. "He's still ignoring any evidence that doesn't point to me as Mike's murderer."

"Maybe we should drive out to Mike's place and see if Uncle Allen has put police tape around it."

"And if he has?"

"We'll respect it and stay out."

"And if he hasn't?"

9

Haylee looked off into the distance. "Someone needs to keep an eye on Mike's place."

"Maybe we should head out there now."

She shook her head. "Too many people up and around."

"How about midnight? Meet you at my car."

"Done. See you then." She crossed the street toward The Stash.

I took the dogs inside and gave them treats. Before Haylee and I involved ourselves in something we knew we shouldn't, I would give law enforcement one more chance. I dialed the Erie detachment of the Pennsylvania State Police.

A woman with a soft voice introduced herself as Trooper Smallwood. I explained that a suspicious death had occurred in Elderberry Bay. "And we only have one policeman. He needs help solving the murder."

Trooper Smallwood sounded very nice and caring. "If he needs help, he'll ask us."

I wasn't so sure. "I don't think he should be the only investigator." The line became quiet. "Are you still there?" I tried not to whine.

"I'm here," she reassured me. "And I understand your concerns. I don't believe Elderberry Bay has requested our assistance recently. I'll check."

Before she could hang up, I blurted, "I called 911 last night when I found the victim. He was still alive. The dispatcher sent Unc . . . er, Officer DeGlazier. If he hadn't been available, wouldn't the dispatcher have contacted you? It would have been your case from the beginning."

"It's not that simple. I'm sorry. I know this must be very difficult for you. Frustrating. I'll see what I can do." She clicked off.

I was relieved at finding a sympathetic listener. Maybe she would pack a posse of investigators into a van and bring them to Elderberry Bay. Tonight.

Meanwhile, there were other people I should talk to before Haylee and I snuck off to Mike's. I called Dr. Wrinklesides.

The woman who answered told me his evening walk-in clinic would stay open for me.

125

"I don't want to keep him late. I just want to speak to him. It's not about my health." Well, in a way it was, if his answers could keep me out of jail.

"He stays late every night. He doesn't do phone consultations."

I locked up and stepped off my front porch. A couple with three children, all of them singing, climbed out of a minivan and filed into the General Store. Lights were on in Naomi's apartment, where Opal, Edna, and Naomi were having supper. The Iron-monger had its usual lamp-lit ambience, with men talking around the potbellied stove near the back of the store. Pickup trucks, most of them black, were parked all up and down Lake Street. I walked around the corner from Lake Street to Cayuga. Calling cheerful greetings to each other, diners converged on Pier 42 and opened the door. Chatter and laughter spilled from the restaurant. The library, bakery, bank, and post office were closed for the night, and the hamburger and ice cream stands wouldn't open again until spring.

Dr. Wrinklesides's street, Jefferson Avenue, was mainly residential, lined with Victorian houses, Arts and Crafts–style bungalows, and newer ranch homes. Lights were on inside and drapes were not yet closed. Living rooms looked inviting with art on the walls, books on the shelves, and children nestled together in overstuffed sofas. Susannah was setting a table in what must be her home. Next door to her, a family ate supper by candlelight. I looked for Georgina in other houses on the street, but didn't see her. Aromas of wood smoke and cooking seemed to warm the evening.

Dr. Wrinklesides's office was in a converted ranch home. The waiting room was warm, which was nice, and full of patients, which wasn't so nice, since they all probably had communicable diseases. A young woman behind the reception desk gave me a friendly smile. Her nametag read Dr. Eaversleigh. It was reassuring that the elderly Dr. Wrinklesides had a colleague. She looked about to say something, but a printer behind her spewed paper and squeaked, drowning out whatever she might have wanted to say. *Eejee weejee, eejee weejee, eejee weejee.* With a good-humored shrug, she gestured toward chairs lining the waiting-room walls.

I sat down and picked up a magazine about quilting.

In the next room, Dr. Wrinklesides boomed, "Open your mouth! Wider. I want to look right through you to your shoes."

His young patient wailed.

Fluorescent tubes flickered, buzzed, and gave off a greenish light that made everyone in the waiting room look sick. *Eejee weejee, eejee weejee, eejee weejee.* I flipped a page, from Drunkard's Path to Monkey Wrench. The foremothers who named these quilt patterns had interesting senses of whimsy.

Apparently, Dr. Wrinklesides had more than one examination room. A man yelled, "I was hurt —"

Eejee weejee, eejee weejee, eejee weejee.

Was interference from that screeching printer Dr. Wrinklesides's version of patient-doctor confidentiality?

Uncle Allen had claimed that no one had gone to the hospital with wounds that Mike might have inflicted. What if Mike's attacker hadn't needed a hospital but went to Dr. Wrinklesides instead? Had the man consulting Dr. Wrinklesides been hurt fighting with Mike?

Bent over a gnarled walking stick, the injured patient limped out of the building. I didn't catch a glimpse of his downturned face.

An aria burst from one of the examination rooms. Knowing very little about opera, and even less about Italian, I didn't know what Dr. Wrinklesides was singing, but it brimmed with heartfelt pathos. The singing broke off. Sounding quite jolly, Dr. Wrinklesides bellowed at his next patient, "*You're* still alive?"

Maybe Dr. Eaversleigh could be my doctor if I ever needed one. All professional competence, she ushered me into an examination room and left me alone to wait for Dr. Wrinklesides.

I heard the outer door open and the low murmur of new arrivals.

Dr. Wrinklesides bounced into my room. He looked smaller without the long coat, earflapped fedora, and enormous hand-knit muffler, but he was still a huge man, and his face was red, as if he'd suffered an extreme case of frostbite early that morning in my backyard. His white lab coat barely met over his wide middle. He flipped a folder open to reveal a blank sheet of paper. "Okay, young lady," he yelled. "What seems to be your problem?"

I could almost hear the patients in the waiting room next door creaking forward in their seats to listen to my answer.

Where was that printer when I needed it?

I reminded Dr. Wrinklesides, "You were at my place last night —"

"Sure," he hollered. "I remember last

night. We didn't have the best time of it, did we?"

What did the other patients think of that?

"Well," he went on, "I suppose you expect counseling."

"No, I —"

He didn't seem to notice that I'd shaken my head. He thundered, "The counseling I give people like you who believe they've endured trauma is, 'Time heals all hurts.' You just wait, young lady, and you'll discover I'm right." He unlooped his stethoscope from his neck.

I warded him off with upraised palms. "I'm fine. I just wanted to ask you a question."

He cupped his hand behind his ear. "What's that?"

The last thing I wanted to do was shout the question. Hoping that printer would magically start its *eejee weejee*ing, I said loudly, "You were with . . . um . . . *that man* when he spoke last night."

It took several repetitions for him to get the gist of that. "Uncle Allen DeGlazier?" he asked. "The cop?"

"No. The other one."

"Oh!" he shouted. "Mike Krawbach!"

The printer remained stubbornly silent.

I enunciated carefully, "What did he say?"

"Something about a woman doing something?" Dr. Wrinklesides's eyes shined with cheer.

"Do you remember his exact words?" Having given up on both the printer and any sort of discretion, I was now yelling, too.

"Uncle Allen's?"

"No! The other man's."

"Mike's? Nah. He mumbled something, but I couldn't make heads nor tails of it. My hearing's not what it used to be." Benevolence beamed from his faded blue eyes.

His revelation stunned me into silence. Maybe if I'd gotten enough sleep last night, I'd have figured out that Dr. Wrinklesides shouted so much because he didn't hear well.

The implications hit me.

Only Uncle Allen and Dr. Wrinklesides had been close enough to make sense of Mike's mumbling. Uncle Allen had to know about the doctor's hearing problems and could have invented Mike's last words.

He would have done that for only one reason — to hide the real murderer by throwing suspicion on someone else. Unfortunately, I happened to be the most convenient scapegoat. Was Uncle Allen protecting himself? Or someone else?

While all this flitted through my mind, Dr. Wrinklesides watched me as if he were considering which vile medications to prescribe for me. I squirmed out of my chair. He grabbed my hands and turned them over as if he couldn't help checking for diseases. "How'd you get that bruise?" he hollered.

Bruise? The slight, purplish stain on the heel of my hand looked more like a smudge. Rubbing at it only made it more noticeable. "I fell." I didn't want to admit that I'd hit the pavement after being frightened by ice cracking on Lake Erie. Dr. Wrinklesides would decide I was undergoing several types of trauma.

He peered into my eyes for long, uncomfortable moments, and I couldn't help worrying that he was planning to report the bruise, maybe exaggerating it in the process, to Uncle Allen.

I must have appeared as distressed as Dr. Wrinklesides believed I was. He gave me an encouraging smile. "Time heals," he boomed.

I wanted to skulk away with my face hidden, but I had to see who might have been eavesdropping on my conversation with Dr. Wrinklesides.

Three men sat in the waiting room. They could have been among the group who had witnessed my argument with Mike the day before, but they were unrecognizable, bundled in dark winter clothes with baseball caps pulled low over their eyes.

I fled out onto the streets of Elderberry Bay. In homes on both sides of the street, drapes had been pulled, keeping family warmth and light inside.

Behind me, a door slammed. Footsteps resounded on concrete. Someone was running from the doctor's office.

Toward me.

10

For what seemed like a lifetime, but couldn't have been more than a second, I froze. Maybe I could beat my pursuer to the nearest house, but I wouldn't blame the homeowners if they kept their doors closed against impetuous strangers in the dark. I'd seen Susannah in a home down the block, too far away to reach before the person chasing me caught up.

Maybe I could dodge whoever it was and return to Dr. Wrinklesides's office. Fists clenched inside my mittens, I whirled to face my pursuer.

It was Dr. Eaversleigh.

I must have looked very fierce. She stopped running, well beyond my reach. I casually stuck my hands in my pockets.

"Are you all right?" she asked.

I caught my breath. "Sure."

Despite her wild sprint, she didn't seem the least bit winded. "You looked unhappy

134

when you left," she hinted. "And you're not registered with us as a patient. I wanted to make sure you were okay."

I couldn't help smiling. "If this is the way you're going to run your practice, you won't be able to spend much time in your office."

She grinned. "Run would be the word for it, wouldn't it? Listen, don't be worried. Dr. Wrinklesides might not seem like any doctor you've ever met, but he's a legend, always high on lists of the best doctors in Pennsylvania. Everyone sang his praises in med school. He knows what he's doing. I'm really excited about being the first doctor ever invited into his practice."

"How long have you worked with him?"

"Since Monday. I'll be here whenever you need me. Dr. Wrinklesides will be, too.

"Isn't he a little . . . past retirement age?"

She hugged her coat around her. "Retirement is not in his vocabulary. Being a doctor is his whole life. That and opera." She cocked her head as if she could hear him singing. "I'd better get back." With a cheery wave, she ran toward the clinic.

On Cayuga Avenue, Pier 42 was filled with light and laughter. At the foot of Lake Street, lake and sky merged at the horizon, a vast and awesome space that rested my eyes and calmed some of my anxieties. I turned toward home. The new restaurant and the papered-over store beside it were dark. Lights were still on in Naomi's apartment above Batty About Quilts.

A couple of black pickup trucks were parked in front of The Ironmonger. Could one of them have been the one Uncle Allen and I had seen last night? Between advertisements in Sam's windows, I made out old-timers clustered around the stove.

Had Sam heard anything that had gone on in my backyard last night or early this morning? As far as I could tell, he lived above the hardware store. When I first moved in, I had peeked through my cedar hedges into his backyard and had not seen a door to his basement, so I didn't think his apartment was below his shop like mine was, and Mike's attacker could not have come from or fled to Sam's basement.

Beyond In Stitches, the General Store was similar to The Ironmonger, with an apartment above it, and as far as I'd seen through my hedges, no basement apartment or exit, either. I didn't know anything about the store's young owners except their names, Luther and Jacoba, and that they had opened their store only days before I moved to Elderberry Bay. I still had the big-city habit of shopping for groceries in larger municipalities, a habit I had to change.

Immediately.

The store was still open. I went in.

Jacoba wore a long, old-fashioned dress in a pale blue geometric print. With her straight blond hair and clear complexion, she looked about sixteen. Someone was hammering in the apartment upstairs.

I plunked a newspaper on the counter. "I hope my dogs don't make too much noise."

Her smile was shy but sweet. "I hardly ever hear them."

"Did you hear anything unusual early this morning, before the police siren? If I can call it a siren . . ."

I detected a hint of amusement on her solemn face. "I don't think so."

"Did you hear the ATV?"

She tilted her head. "Was that what woke us up? Then I heard Uncle Allen's siren and figured he was looking after everything. I went back to sleep."

I handed her a bill. "Are ATVs a frequent problem down there on the trail?"

"I've never seen or heard them." She gave me my change. "We have no complaints. We like it here in Elderberry Bay." She gestured at the newspaper in my hand. "Whenever you need anything, come back. We're renovating, so excuse the mess."

The store was neat and clean, and the fruits and vegetables looked fresh and unblemished for mid-February. Promising that I'd shop there again, I said good-bye and went outside.

The pickup trucks were gone from the street in front of The Ironmonger. Sam's buddies must have driven off. I deposited the newspaper on my front porch and went on to The Ironmonger, which was even dimmer than it had been a few minutes before. Sam appeared to be alone inside. He was probably about to turn out the last light for the evening.

It would be rude to barge in on him now.

If I found out that anyone had asked for a padlock like mine, I'd be able to give Uncle Allen the name of someone who could have unlocked my gate, someone who could have let Mike into my yard, someone who could have murdered him . . .

Sam's door wasn't locked.

Ever the gracious shopkeeper, Sam welcomed me. "What can I do ya for?" His teasing tone showed that he knew he'd skewed his syntax. "Those padlocks still working for you?"

Thank you for the opening, Sam. "Do you have any more sets that match those two, so I can buy another padlock without having

138

to carry another key?" Weak, but it might do. I held my breath, watching him.

"Did you throw away your packages?"

"I'm afraid so. Do you remember the four digit number that was on those packages?" What I actually wanted to know was who might have memorized the four digits and bought a padlock like mine.

He frowned, tapped his fingers on the counter, rubbed his eyes, and came up with, "I think it had threes and sixes in it. And maybe sevens and twos."

That left a few possibilities. And didn't answer the questions in my hidden agenda. "Do you think anyone who helped you sort through those packages would remember?"

He opened a drawer, placed packaged padlocks on the counter, and conveniently asked me one of the questions I wanted to ask him. "Do you remember who all was here last evening?"

"The mailman and the mayor. I didn't know the other men."

Sam didn't take that hint, just kept hauling out those packages.

I prompted, "Your regulars, maybe? Are the same men here every evening?"

"Pretty much." In the semidarkness, his eyes seemed to twinkle, but maybe I only saw reflections from his stove's dying fire.

139

"I'm not sure those guys remember their own names from one day to the next." He pushed plastic-wrapped packages around on his counter like toy cars. "They wouldn't remember sorting through these, never mind a number." He scratched his head. "Sometimes they don't remember when to go home."

Was he saying I should leave, too? I took another stab at my ill-planned interrogation. "Did anyone else buy padlocks after I did?" I felt myself blush. Padlocks, maybe he'd focus on padlocks, not keys, and wouldn't guess where I was heading with my questions — who else could have a key to my padlocks?

No such luck. "Your gates were locked when Mike was found, weren't they." It wasn't a question, and he said it gently. Just the same, I became acutely aware of the distance to the front door. A hardware store was, by definition, full of potential weapons that Sam the ironmonger would undoubtedly be skilled at wielding.

Courage, I told myself. Sam was at least eighty, and always kind and polite. He grabbed an armload of packages, carried them to the table where his friends had sorted through them, and dumped them on it.

I answered, "Yes, my gates were locked, so of course Uncle Allen thinks I let Mike into my yard. I didn't, and I didn't know Mike was there until the dogs barked and we went outside to investigate. Somebody besides me has a key."

"And Uncle Allen suspects you of murder." Again, it wasn't a question. He came back to the counter for another load of padlocks.

I nodded, probably looking as wretched as I felt. I picked up the remaining packages and added them to the pile on the table beside the potbellied stove.

Sam frowned at the jumble of packaged locks as if something puzzled him. "Don't you worry. No one could possibly believe that of you. Uncle Allen should be sitting around the stove here with the other old fogies instead of running around in that silly car of his playing cops and robbers, and I don't mind if you tell him I said so. I've told him myself, often enough." He spread his hands in a gesture of helplessness. "I wish I could say someone came in here wanting a padlock to match yours, but no one has. Still —" He broke off and walked back to his cash register. Tilting his head, he squinted at the table in front of the potbellied stove. "Weren't there more packages of those things last evening?"

"I bought two."

"Even so." Fingers tight together, he polished his counter with the flat of his hand. "I wish I could remember for sure."

So did I. "Did you hear or see anyone last night, like after midnight?"

"Nope. I wear earplugs to bed so my snoring won't wake me up."

Thanking him for his help, I started toward the door.

Sam called me back. "There were other people in the store besides you and my regulars, and any of them could have memorized that number and bought a matching set somewhere else."

"How close are other hardware stores?"

"Nearly every small village has one. Bigger ones, too."

Not exactly the helpful reply I'd been hoping for.

"Clay Fraser was here," he said. "Betcha he's in and out of hardware stores and the like all the time, being a contractor and all."

Betcha he was. And betcha I didn't want Clay to turn out to be a murderer. I needed him to build a dog pen and renovate Blueberry Cottage, and . . . maybe . . . No. I'd already decided that love at first sight should apply only to my wonderful store

142

and delightful dogs. Not to a man.

"And those three girls, you know, the ones with the fabric stores and whatnot." He nodded toward the shops across the street. "Not the young blonde. I don't think she was here."

No, Haylee hadn't followed Clay and me into The Ironmonger last evening, but Edna, Opal, and Naomi, who would be girls to Sam, had. They weren't murderers, either. None of them would let the others do anything outrageous.

"Mike's cousin was here," I said. "The guy in the bee-stinger stocking cap."

Sam laughed. "Smythe Castor. He's too much, that one. Always marched to a different beat, you know what I mean? Ever since he was a boy, everybody teased him, but did he care? Nope, it's like he flaunts being unique, wearing funny hats and the like. No one can get a rise out of that guy. Betcha when his bees sting he doesn't feel it. Not him. Not that guy."

Wasn't that the kind of person who could snap when least expected? My heart rate quickened. Maybe I'd found my villain.

"He's coming back from Erie on Friday," Sam said. "You can talk to him then. He'll likely drop in here."

"Erie?" Maybe I'd lost my villain.

"Yep. When he left here, he was headed straight for some conference. What was it called, now?"

"The Honey Makers' Conference?"

"Yep, that's it. He's been gone ever since."

Dejected, I tried one last question. "Do you know anyone around here who drives a black pickup truck?"

I could see him struggling not to laugh. "Just about everyone. It's easier to think of who doesn't. That contractor guy, Clay Fraser, for one, with his red truck. And Dawn Langford drives a red Valiant. I sold it to her. Sure do miss it." He looked me straight in the eye. "I stopped driving ten years ago. If I can't walk where I need to go, I can always find some kind soul to take me."

Babbling that he could always count on me for a ride, I said my good-byes and went home, where I set the alarm for eleven forty-five and took a much-needed nap.

At five minutes to midnight, the dogs and I, all of us yawning, left In Stitches. Haylee's shop was dark. Wearing all black, she slipped out her front door and joined us. We didn't talk until we were in the car and I had steered quietly away from the shops on Lake Street.

Haylee directed me south of the village.

144

"What did you learn tonight?"

"Uncle Allen hasn't even called the state police for help," I reported, disgusted. "And Dr. Wrinklesides doesn't hear well, so Uncle Allen could have made up Mike's last words."

"No wonder he keeps changing them."

"My neighbors at the General Store didn't hear anything, except maybe that noisy ATV, before Uncle Allen's siren. Sam didn't hear anything." I drove and drove. "How far away is it?" I asked.

"About ten miles from Elderberry Bay."

"How could the zoning commissioner have lived so far away?"

"Elderberry Bay is the closest village, so our political boundaries include his farm and all the others out this way."

"And Uncle Allen's jurisdiction stretches all the way out here?"

"It should. There's Mike's driveway."

I slowed.

Haylee leaned forward. "I don't see any police tape or vehicles, but keep going." She had me drive down a dirt road running along the east side of his acreage. "Let's make certain no one's parked on the track cutting in from this road, either."

No one was. I stopped the car. "Shall we go back to the driveway?"

"Can you drive on this track without getting stuck?"

"Probably, since the ground is frozen. My tires shouldn't leave prints, either." I eased the car onto the track. The dogs must have sensed my nervous excitement. They sat up on the backseat and panted.

I found a place to park out of sight of the road.

Haylee told me, "Mike said people use this spot as a lovers' lane. He liked to hide in the woods and scare them by firing a rifle at the trees above them."

"I wonder if he ever 'accidentally' hit one of their cars."

"I wouldn't be surprised."

We got out and leashed the dogs. Haylee shined a pocket-sized flashlight at the ground. Dogs straining at their leashes, we followed the trail. It emerged from the woods, then ran between the woods and a south-facing hill where tiny grapevines inched toward wires strung between posts. Mike's straggling, struggling vineyard.

The trail branched off, part of it staying alongside the vineyard. Haylee pointed at the section that turned into the woods. "We're getting close," she whispered.

The woods ended close to Mike's back porch. She snapped off her light.

There was no sign of yellow police tape. And Mike's back door was standing wide open.

11

I whispered, "Let's go home." The dogs didn't bark or growl, but anyone inside Mike's house might hear their panting or the jingling of their collars and tags.

Haylee leaned forward in that stubborn stance I remembered from when we went to our office after midnight to sort through Jasper's files. "Let's watch and listen."

We did, for agonizing minutes. The dogs lay down as if planning to snooze. Holding up a hand to signal we should stay behind, Haylee left us. Tally wanted to go with her, but I kept a firm grip on his leash. Bent over out of sight of windows, Haylee crept to the front of the house, turned the corner, and disappeared. Tally whimpered. I knelt and hugged both dogs.

Haylee reappeared around the other side of the house, ran back to us, and spoke in a normal voice. "There's no sign of anyone or any vehicles in his driveway, either, except

Mike's truck."

"Maybe we should call Uncle Allen."

"To do what?"

I gestured at the back door. "Check out why this door is open."

"And how would we explain seeing it?"
She had me.

"I'm going in," she said. "You and the dogs can warn me if . . ." Without waiting for my reply, she was gone, through that open doorway. I had dressed warmly, but shivered, anyway.

She was back in minutes. She held up her hands. "I kept my gloves on and didn't move a thing. But someone has obviously searched the place."

"Uncle Allen?"

"This is more like a ransacking. But guess what?"

I was afraid she'd say she'd found a body. "What?" I faltered.

"Whoever was searching seemed most interested in Mike's filing cabinet. Follow the money! That's something we can do."
She didn't have to crow about it. "Let's go."

I wanted to take the dogs inside with us but didn't know what sort of ruckus they might cause. I tied them to a clothes pole and followed Haylee inside. Despite the open door, the house was warm. The furnace fan whined like it was straining to keep up with the cold air blowing in the back door.

Old bank books were heaped on the rug in Mike's office. Haylee laid the flashlight on the edge of Mike's desk chair. We sat on the floor next to it. Clumsy with our gloves on, straining to see in the gloom, we paged through bank books.

I found a deposit for almost two hundred thousand dollars about a year ago. Pulse pounding, I showed it to Haylee. "What crop might he have been selling in December?"

"Maybe he was paid late for it, whatever it was. But I got the definite impression he hadn't harvested anything for ten or so years, since he decided to switch to growing grapes."

"An inheritance?" I guessed.

"Maybe."

We checked more bank books. Most of the time, Mike's income had been small, a few deposits here and there, none of them very large. Outside, my dogs grunted and play-growled while their collars clinked and clashed. They were having one of their usual tussles. I went out to be sure they weren't tangled in their leashes. They were fine. I patted them and told them we'd be finished soon and to lie still and stay. They flopped down, panting, tongues lolling, tired and happy, so I reluctantly went back into Mike's silent house.

"Pay dirt," Haylee exclaimed. "Well, sort of. Ten years before that big deposit you found, Mike made an earlier one, about a hundred thousand dollars. In December, also."

We could find only two years of banking history before that. Those years, he had made more or less regular deposits during the harvest season and had not deposited much during the rest of the year. "Typical for farming," Haylee said.

"When did his parents die?" I asked.

She gazed off into the distance. "They died in a plane crash on their way home from a vacation, shortly before these bank books started, about two years before that first large deposit. Those amounts could have been from inheritances, if the wills took a long time to settle."

"Did he have other property that he might have sold?"

"Not that I know of, and if he had information like that, it's gone." She picked up a folder labeled *Deeds*. It was empty. So was one called *Sales*.

I flipped through one of the recent bank

books. "Uncle Allen said he had debts and mortgages, but I don't see any regular repayments, do you?"

Haylee pondered another bank book. "None. Do you suppose he received government grants or subsidies?"

Maybe that explained the two large deposits.

Outside, Tally whimpered, the sound he made when he was separated from me for too long. I heard a vehicle out on the highway. "We'd better go," I urged.

Haylee jumped up. "I don't want to be found in this mess."

We carefully tiptoed over scattered papers and outside to the dogs, waiting where I'd told them to. Of course they had to announce to the entire countryside that we were with them again.

I shushed them, detached their leashes from Mike's clothes pole, and we all hurried back through the woodland trail. I half expected to find Uncle Allen, perhaps accompanied by the entire Erie detachment of the Pennsylvania State Police, waiting for us beside my car. No one was there.

We scrambled into the car. I sped down Mike's lane, back to the dirt road, and finally back to Shore Road. Haylee reminded me, "We solved a crime before with the help of financial records. We can do it again."

I pointed out, "But that crime *was* a financial one . . ."

She grinned. "Yeah, and we investigated the criminal and the extent of his crimes that time, not the victim."

"It complicates things, doesn't it, not knowing who the villain is?"

"Sure does."

I parked the car where it had been before the night's excursion. Silently, we tiptoed up the hill to our shops and waved good-bye to each other.

Back in our apartment, exhaustion carried me off while the dogs were still stomping their beds into nests.

When we went out to the front yard in the morning, I was careful not to peer under bushes. If the unlucky person who spotted a murder victim was going to be accused of doing the foul deed, I would have to work hard at never finding another one.

For all I knew, though, victims could be piling up in my backyard, giving a whole new meaning to the words "crime scene" on the yellow plastic tape woven through my fence.

I took the dogs inside, closed them into the apartment, and set out cookies and cider. The phone rang. I pounced on it. "I've got good news for you," Trooper Smallwood said in her gentle, girlish voice. "We've convinced Detective DeGlazier to accept our assistance."

Uncle Allen was a detective? Trooper Smallwood took my address and ended the call.

To inspire potential customers, I had embroidered lots of garments to wear in my store. Today's was a fleece vest featuring an embroidered spray of elderberries in honor of Elderberry Bay. The morning's students admired the design, one of my computerized originals, of course. They practically jumped up and down with excitement when I showed them the range of commercial designs they could try during the lesson, and if they ever wanted to, could buy. Several had great difficulty deciding whether to embroider something cute for a grandchild or sophisticated for themselves. Many personalized their motifs with initials or names.

While they worked, I was gratified to see several investigators, wearing baggy coveralls over their clothing, in my backyard with Uncle Allen.

I told my students to create a sewing project using the designs they'd stitched and to bring their work to the next day's class. In hopes of encouraging more of them to purchase embroidery machines, I handed out a list of websites where they could shop for more designs, including mine, of course, plus a few others offering free designs. I also asked them to bring fleece scarves to tomorrow's class, and we'd embellish them with embroidery.

Rosemary clapped her hands. "We'll make the scarves ourselves."

Discussing their projects, they trooped off to Pier 42. I took the dogs outside for a leashed romp through the front yard, then we went downstairs to the kitchen, where we ate lunch and I listened for my chimes.

The afternoon class went even better than the morning's. The woman who had bought a sewing machine on Tuesday gleefully purchased the embroidery attachment for it. The desire to compete flared in several pairs of eyes, and I saw more sales in my immediate future.

A uniformed state trooper strode past my front door toward The Ironmonger. Without slowing, she seemed to take in every detail of In Stitches, inside and out. I waved, but she kept moving.

The Threadville tour bus wasn't scheduled to leave for an hour after the afternoon class ended, and its passengers shopped while they waited. I sat down at my computer and loaded the design I'd made showing the man in the camouflage jacket and orange neon hat disappearing between trees. For the stumpwork look I wanted to achieve, I created steps in the software similar to the process of appliquéing with an embroidery machine.

I kept having to stop my work on the design for the best of reasons — customers. Chattering, they bought stabilizer, felt, and more thread than they could possibly use in a year. Whenever they didn't need me, I went back to my embroidery.

I filled a bobbin with dark nylon lingerie thread and inserted it. I had learned through trial and horrendous error to try out new designs before stitching them on expensive fabrics. Like every fabriholic, I had a stash that kept growing no matter how many projects I concocted that might contribute to using it up. Working and living across the street from Haylee's aptly named store didn't help. I unearthed a large scrap similar to the linen I planned to use for the commissioned wall hanging. I tightened the remnant with stabilizer in my largest hoop, one I could actually jump through, and fastened the hoop to the embroidery machine.

My first instruction to the embroidery machine had it baste around the shape of the man and several trees near him. The machine stopped, leaving stitches that showed me where the puffy foam was supposed to go. I placed gray foam on the hooped linen and restarted the machine. It obediently tacked the foam down, perforated around the edges of the man and the trees, and stopped again for me to tear off excess foam.

Now I was ready to stitch the actual design. As always, I took the thread colors I needed from my sales display. Since I never put partially used spools back where customers might accidentally purchase them, my personal supply kept growing.

I threaded the design's first color, olive green, and started the embroidery machine. First, it stitched the underlay, a simple pattern that held the fabric in place and prevented it from being distorted by the smaller, denser stitches of the actual design. Then it did the fun part, machine embroidery stitches more intricate than anything our great grandmothers ever dreamed of. It stopped for me to change colors, then punched away at the design again. The picture began to come alive, raised portions and all.

Another group of women crowded into the store, too, women who obviously hadn't been taking Threadville courses. Their clothing lacked pintucks, ruffles, ruching, faggoting, quilting, and other decorative touches. They grabbed things from one corner of the store, dropped them in another, muttered to each other, and eyed me with speculation. Susannah and Georgina lived nearby and could shop any time, so they hadn't stayed around with the out-of-town students, or I'd have asked them who these women were.

Every time my computer monitor went to sleep, another of the strangers jiggled my mouse to display the design I'd begun stitching. It was easy to understand why. Watching the embroidery machine match the design on the computer screen was almost magical. I could hardly wait for Clay to build the dog pen at the top of the stairs, though. My computer would be safer inside a pen where curious people couldn't accidentally erase files. To be safe, I made backup copies of the design.

"Miss, can you help me?" A stocky older woman yanked a spool of gold metallic thread from the display. "What's this for?"

Her eyes and skin tone matched her gray hair and her salt-stained snowmobile suit, which she must have borrowed from a taller person. The pant legs nearly tripped her, and one sleeve threatened to devour the expensive spool of thread in her hand.

"Decorating. Embroidering."

She snorted. "Doesn't look practical."

I said in my nicest support-the-other-Threadville-retailers voice, "You'll find practical sewing thread at The Stash across the street. And if you want quilting thread, try Batty About Quilts."

She picked up a spool of purple silk thread. "What's this for?"

Was she planning to go through the displays, spool by spool, with the same question? Before I could answer, the dogs let out a volley of barking near the apartment door. They sounded like they were in the shop instead of in the apartment where they belonged.

A woman in a black, down-filled jacket had unlatched my apartment door. Two inquisitive dog noses wedged themselves out.

Gasping, I sprinted toward my dogs.

The snoopy woman jumped away from the door and asked in a strained voice, "Restroom?" She kept her face averted, not

159

that I'd have been able to see much of it anyway. The fur-trimmed hood hid most of it.

Tails waving madly, Sally and Tally tore around the shop, making friends with surprised customers.

Too annoyed by the nosy woman's nerve to risk speaking and telling her what I really thought of her, I nodded toward the restroom door. Not only was it clearly marked, it was ajar and the light was on. No one could have missed it. Except, maybe, a woman hiding inside a parka with an enormous hood snugged around her face.

She shut herself into the restroom. I hoped she was as mortified as I would have been if *she* had caught me sneaking into *her* apartment. Police officers might have found the woman's actions interesting, if not suspicious. Beyond my front windows, laughing shoppers ran between The Stash, Tell a Yarn, Buttons and Bows, and Batty About Quilts.

No state troopers were in sight.

With help from my sisters-in-thread, I captured the wiggly dogs and put them on the landing at the top of the stairs. As I closed the door, Sally-Forth and Tally-Ho looked up at me with their sweet, sad amber eyes. "Sorry, guys," I said. This time, I

160

locked the door.

I returned to the thread display to continue my interrupted discussion with the woman in the snowmobile suit. She opened her fist and displayed a spool of pale green glow-in-the-dark thread. "I'm buying this."

I led her to the cash register. Slowly, she unzipped one of her snowmobile suit's pockets. She rattled change, then called toward the back of the store, "Rhonda!"

The woman in the parka and enormous hood emerged from the restroom. What had she been doing, pawing through cleaning supplies and toilet tissue in the cabinet under the sink?

The woman buying the thread asked her, "You have any money?"

Rhonda looked at the amount I'd rung up and shook her head. What I could see of her face was pinched and sour, as if her life was so unsatisfactory that she spent it with a permanently downturned mouth. Her complexion said she was in her twenties, but her expression was haggard enough for someone several times that age.

The older woman prompted, "You've got your charge card, haven't you?"

Rhonda looked even more miserable. "I . . ." She turned to the woman and hissed, "She'll see . . ." I wasn't able to hear

161

the rest through the matted faux fur.

The older woman threw her a scornful look. "I already said your name. She musta heard."

Without looking at me, Rhonda fumbled in her pocket and brought out crumpled bills. "Here, Aunt Betty."

Aunt Betty added enough change to buy the thread. Apparently, that entitled her to ask me questions. "How long did you know Mike Krawbach?"

I had to put a stop to this idea that Mike and I had been more than distant acquaintances. "I didn't, except as zoning commiss—"

Rhonda interrupted. "You're the one Mike Krawbach was visiting when he died."

The back of my neck burned. "He never visited me!"

Aunt Betty crowed, "Ha! We know he was in here. And in your backyard."

"Uninvited." Did I have to sound so adamant? True, I didn't want anyone believing I had any sort of relationship with Mike Krawbach, but I shouldn't be handing out motives for others to use against me.

Aunt Betty's mouth turned up in a cunning sneer. "Where did you live before you moved to Elderberry Bay?"

"New York."

She gestured at the boutiques across the street. "I hear you knew those women there. Are you related to them?"

"They're my friends," I said. "I only knew one of them before I moved here. Haylee, who owns The Stash."

Aunt Betty leaned toward me. "If anybody had it in for poor Mike, she did."

All Haylee had done was refuse a second date with the guy. Plus maybe regale several people with her tale about the long walk home in new heels. I backed away. "I've known Haylee for years. She would never kill anyone."

Aunt Betty and Rhonda twisted their mouths in scorn.

It was my turn to ask them questions. "Are you two related to Mike Krawbach?"

Blushing, Rhonda backed away and whispered, "No."

I heard creaking noises and soft footsteps behind me. My heart hammering, I turned around.

Locals watched from various places around the store, but the women I recognized as Threadville tourists formed a semicircle around my back. My sisters-in-thread didn't speak, but their glowers and folded arms should have intimidated Aunt Betty and Rhonda into purchasing expensive machines to make up for their false accusations.

Rhonda muttered, "You're not getting away with this."

Aunt Betty shoved the younger woman ahead of her toward the door.

"Don't forget to sign the guest book," I called in my most invitingly musical voice, the one that would alert people who knew me that I was in one of my more dangerous moods.

Aunt Betty's only response was to slam her palm against the door, setting the glass pieces of my wind chime crashing together like Mike Krawbach had on Tuesday.

The two women clambered into a pickup truck and drove away.

A black pickup truck.

Who were those two women, Mike's girlfriend and her aunt? Or Mike's attackers? The rest of the locals followed them out. Were they trying to protect someone?

All my life, I had dreamed of owning a shop like In Stitches. Now I wasn't so sure, especially about my cheery, cross-stitched *Welcome* sign.

I had moved to a village of amateur sleuths who thought that investigating a crime meant deciding who the villain should be, and then searching for "proof" to fit

164

their theory.

And I was their chosen villain.

Or, perhaps, their chosen victim.

12

Local women had snooped through my store and peeked down the stairway to my apartment. Now these self-appointed sleuths were probably running to Uncle Allen to reinforce his determination to blame me for the murder of Mike Krawbach.

I must have been frowning. The locals had left, but the Threadville tour ladies watched me with frank concern.

Rosemary fanned her face and gave me a supportive smile. "Weren't they a bunch of lovelies?"

A woman in a white fuzzy vest demanded, "Can't they make themselves decent coats?"

I covered a giggle with a fake cough. My students probably didn't notice. They went back to serious browsing and lived up to their reputation for stretching the Threadville tour past its scheduled departure time. I realized Rosemary was the bus driver when she rounded up tardy passengers. She was good-natured about it, probably because she wanted the extra shopping time, too. She bought umpteen more colors of felt. Threadville tourists knew how to have fun.

By quarter after five, everyone was gone, and I was alone with my dogs.

Not for long. Sally-Forth and Tally-Ho had only begun investigating our snowless front yard when my front gate's latch clinked and Uncle Allen led a tall, uniformed man toward me. He jerked a thumb over his shoulder toward the man. "This is Trooper Gartener."

I had never, during my two entire months in Pennsylvania, been pulled over for speeding or any other traffic violation, but even though this trooper wasn't wearing a Smokey the Bear hat, and his short black hair was bare to the February night, my knees quaked. He was big and obviously strong, with rugged features. He looked hardy and competent, like he'd keep a cool head in emergencies, and would probably rescue several people and their pets each week. I would not want to be on the wrong side of the law with him around, though. Hoping it wouldn't even cross his mind that I might be, I managed to smile and say hello, and I very carefully did not let my eyes stray to his left ring finger.

Gartener gave me a curt nod. His dark eyes penetrated straight through me.

Hardy, competent, and tough, yes. Also forbidding. I decided not to offer to shake hands with him. "Is Trooper Smallwood here?" I asked. She would be friendlier than these two.

Gartener could, apparently, speak. "She's around." He became silent again. I broke up the staring contest and pulled my inquisitive dogs away from the two men.

Uncle Allen demanded, "How well did you know Mike Krawbach?"

"Not at all," I answered. "You were there when I exchanged the most words with him." My fickle dogs wagged their plume-like tails.

Uncle Allen let them sniff his gloves. "What about later that night? Ever since he was knee high to a rutabaga, every female for miles around wanted to be close to him. You didn't invite him over, let him into your yard, then fight with him?"

Angered because Uncle Allen believed his bevy of amateur sleuths, I retorted, "I most certainly did not! Unless he willingly climbed over the fence with his murderer or a very strong person threw him over my

168

fence, someone had a key that opened my padlocks." I explained about the search in The Ironmonger for matching keys, and the very audible bandying about of the numbers printed on packages. "Have you checked alibis for Herb Gunthrie, Irv Oslington, Smythe Castor, and Clay Fraser?"

Uncle Allen snapped, "You do your work and we'll do ours."

Fine, but I might define my work differently than he would, especially if he neglected what I thought might be important facets of the investigation and ended up, maybe, arresting the wrong person. Me, for instance.

Gartener stood with his feet slightly apart and his hands behind his back. He seemed fixated on me. He was so stiff that I wondered if he wore bulletproof long johns in addition to his bulletproof vest. Bulletproof socks, too, maybe. Even his facial muscles barely moved. "We're checking into everything." His voice was surprisingly warm for a man who looked so cold.

Uncle Allen squinted at me. "You were first at the scene of the crime, and besides, you have a picture of him on your computer."

"No, I don't."

He started toward my front door. "Mind

if we look?"

I did mind. Shouldn't they get a search warrant? Gartener stared at me with that unnerving and unwavering gaze, and suddenly I saw how I must appear. Yes, I had phoned the state police wanting them to help our one and only policeman investigate Mike's murder. And yes, my motivation was to prevent Uncle Allen from arresting me.

But I had made the call because I was innocent. I wanted justice.

Gartener, however, apparently thought I'd phoned them because I was *guilty* and hoped to encourage the state police to yank Uncle Allen off my trail.

One look at Gartener, however, and anyone might quail. Maybe I should have left my fate in Uncle Allen's hands.

Meanwhile, I was blocking the local policeman and the trooper from entering my premises. Actually, I wasn't. Sally and Tally were. I appealed to the men's reason. "If some of the women who were in my store today told you I have Mike's picture on my computer monitor, they're wrong. The picture they saw was taken after Mike died. So unless you're hiding something, like he's not really dead, it can't be him."

Uncle Allen stepped forward, putting himself in danger of becoming incorporated in an original weaving made by my dogs and their crisscrossing leashes. "If you showed it to others, you might as well show it to us."

I gritted my teeth. "I didn't *show* it to anyone. They looked." I didn't add that fiddling with other people's computers was rude. Usually, I liked people to discover my embroidery designs in any way possible — they might want to buy them. Although certain this would not be the case with Uncle Allen and his new sidekick, I relented, shortened the dogs' leashes, and led the two men inside.

Uncle Allen looked from my monitor to the partially stitched design in the giant hoop, where the man in the woods was merely a blob of gray puffy foam. "Where's the picture of Mike?"

I pointed at my computer monitor and the photo showing a dead cornfield, a band of trees, lots of sky, and a camouflage shape and an orange patch — the hunting coat and neon hat — among the trees. "That's the photo those women saw. They were imagining things. I don't have any pictures of Mike. None. Not one." I showed him the time stamp saved with the file. "See? That proves the photo was taken after Mike died."

"That could have been altered," Gartener said.

I shot back, "It wasn't."

His face an alarming blotchy red, Uncle Allen glowered at me. He should have been enraged at his self-appointed sleuths, not at me, even if I had been brusque.

I glowered back. I wasn't thrilled with his would-be local assistants for leaving a mess, either. Spools of yellow and green silk embroidery thread were mixed among spools of red and blue. I rearranged them. "Can I use my backyard yet?

Gartener crossed his arms and stared at me.

Uncle Allen said, "That's what we came to tell you. You can go back in there. We're done. That canoe paddle is the only evidence we have, so far, besides your gas can —"

"I never saw that can before early Wednesday morning!"

He went on as if I hadn't spoken. "Your blood-soaked coat —"

"It only had a few drops on it." I placed the smallest wooden embroidery hoops where they belonged, in front of larger ones. To my annoyance, my fingers shook, rattling the hoops.

The good news was that Uncle Allen's

172

rage-fueled flush subsided. All I needed was the village's only law enforcement officer succumbing to a heart attack on my property. The bad news was that my shaking fingers caught Gartener's attention. "Your hands are bruised," he accused. "Like you were in a fight."

I held the backs of my hands out for their inspection. "I don't see any bruises." It was true.

"Turn them over."

I did. Heat rose through my scalp. The color of last night's slight bruise had deepened to twilight purple.

He pointed at it. "There."

Uncle Allen leaned in for a look.

"I fell," I said. "And if Dr. Wrinklesides reported my one tiny bruise, be certain to ask if anyone else came into his clinic with bruises, cuts, or scrapes, then go harass them, too."

Uncle Allen straightened his shoulders and pulled in his gut. Trooper Smallwood had called him a detective. Would Uncle Allen discard his usual bumbling, just-one-of-the-guys act and live up to his title because a state trooper was with him? "The evidence points to you. We've got the physical evidence I mentioned a few minutes ago. And we've also got the fact that Mike died in your yard, his last words, and your death threats."

Did he have to emphasize those last three words so heavily?

Gartener cleared his throat. "Actually, we have more than that."

I squealed, "You can't!" This was getting worse. "Tell me what this supposed evidence is."

Uncle Allen quickly looked up at Gartener as if he wanted to know, too, which made me wonder if the trooper was saying he had other evidence only to unnerve me. He was succeeding, and his continued silence didn't help.

The silence must have stretched too long for Uncle Allen, too. Turning to me, he ordered, "Don't go destroying more evidence because you're afraid we'll get a search warrant. We'll find it all, anyway." Or he'd send his unofficial assistants in their oversized snowmobile suits and hooded parkas. He stomped toward the door like he was headed off for a warrant to search my store and apartment. Let him. There was nothing to find.

"May I have the key to my cottage?" I asked.

His back to me, Uncle Allen dug around in pockets, then tossed a key onto my cutting table. Without another word, he slammed himself out.

Gartener stood ramrod stiff beside my front door, looking at me, waiting for me to say something.

"Please," I said, undoubtedly sounding desperate. "I didn't hurt Mike. Or anyone. Can't you see? The people who live around here are trying to frame me because I'm new. And whoever murdered Mike Krawbach is still free." Now I was slipping into hysteria. Desperation might have been more convincing.

Gartener gave me only the slightest nod. It was not reassuring. "Justice will be done." The flat way he said it, despite the made-for-radio voice, wasn't very reassuring, either.

After one last assessment from his almost black eyes, he left.

In stubborn anger, I balled my hands into fists. These investigators wouldn't find proof that I'd killed Mike. It didn't exist and never had.

Trooper Smallwood of the Pennsylvania State Police would talk some sense into them.

Meanwhile, Clay had wanted to know when we could go into Blueberry Cottage. I dialed his number.

"Is it okay if I come over now?" he asked.

"Sure." He must really want the job. *Badly enough to kill Mike and eliminate the barrier between the project and the requisite permits?*

No, I told myself. Clay had returned my lost dogs to me. Even the dogs thought he was certifiably nice. But they also liked Uncle Allen and had tolerated Trooper Gartener. Only Mike had made Tally growl.

I charged downstairs for a coat, then returned to In Stitches, where I watched through my front windows. When Clay's truck parked beside the curb, I ran outside to him.

My fences were still covered in yellow tape. We went down the slope to the apartment's outside door and let the dogs out. They were ecstatic at being reunited with their hero. After mad sprints around the yard with him and head-on collisions with each other, they were willing to enter Blueberry Cottage. Sally mouthed Clay's hand as if to make certain he would stay beside her. The investigators had relocked the door facing my apartment. I opened it, thrust my hand around the jamb, ran my fingers across the rough wooden wall, found a light switch, and turned it on. A chandelier constructed of a wagon wheel illuminated the cottage's great room.

The air inside the cottage seemed colder than outside, with an eerie calm that made me want to wrap myself in a few of Opal's afghans or Naomi's quilts.

"Great bones," Clay said. I assumed he was talking about the cottage. He snapped pictures and jotted notes on a pad of paper.

The cottage was not, perhaps, the gem he had expected. Years of carpeting and vinyl covered the floors. Layers of paint coated the walls.

In the great room, Clay checked under a corner of carpeting, then took out a pocket knife and scraped paint from a wall. He whistled. "You have a fortune in timber here."

I pictured the plank floors in my shop and the hardware store. "Walnut?"

"What I can see of the floor is bird's-eye maple. And the walls look like hickory."

Next to the great room, the kitchen appeared to have been redecorated about sixty years ago and not touched since. Clay said, "This is great. Lots of space to put in everything you might want, and we won't have to tear much out first."

I pointed at the antique kitchen sink, a deep, white porcelain one, complete with integral drain boards and shapely legs. "I'd like to keep the sink and decorate the new

177

kitchen to match it."

He agreed enthusiastically. "You couldn't buy anything like it today without taking out a second or third mortgage. You could sell it, but it goes with the carpenter gothic style of the outside of the cottage."

"And the inside is carpenter rustic?"

He smiled. "We'll fix that. We'll need to drywall the interior walls, for fire safety, but we can keep most of the look and feel of the place."

Accompanied by enthusiastic dogs, we peeked into the final room, the bathroom. The toilet slanted so steeply that anyone who attempted to sit on it would slide onto the floor.

Clay seemed to have trouble controlling a grin.

"It's okay, you can laugh," I told him. "I had nothing to do with that."

He let the grin out, a full-fledged smile. "Your bathroom could use some work." The laughter in his eyes made Blueberry Cottage feel less alien and frightening. "What's upstairs?"

I thought he was joking. "Upstairs?"

I didn't see the trap door in the beadboard ceiling until Clay, who had to be at least six-four, reached up, unfastened a hidden latch, and lowered a sturdy set of stairs.

The dogs scrambled upstairs. Clay and I followed in a slightly more sedate manner. The ceilings of the second story sloped almost to the floor. I could stand underneath the peak, where a partition divided the two rooms. Clay had to duck.

Now I understood why the cottage's proportions gave it the look of a full-sized Victorian house. The second-story windows, which until this evening I had believed were only for an unreachable attic, went all the way down to the floor.

Blueberry Cottage was livable for anyone under six feet tall, and being inside it was fun, like walking around in a dollhouse. The cottage was next to a river where renters could canoe or kayak, and only a short walk along a pleasant trail to a beautiful sandy beach, so I'd figured I'd have no problem finding tenants even though they would have to sleep on pull-out couches in the great room. But the cottage actually had two bedrooms. If I could find a family whose members were shorter than Clay, I could rent the place for more than I'd planned.

Renovating those extra two rooms would cost more. I'd have to inspire more people to buy sewing and embroidery machines. Not a bad challenge. The renovations would also take longer. I tried not to linger on visions of Clay working in the cottage in my backyard day after day, week after week . . .

Luckily, he seemed to have no inkling of my too-vivid imagination. He was uncovering an ash floor in one of the upstairs rooms and an American elm floor in the other.

"Different types of wood?" I asked him.

"This was one of the earlier Victorian buildings in Elderberry Bay. In those days, as in the days of the first settlers, it was common to use lumber from trees on the property. The owners must have had at least one large ash and one large elm." I knew from the grove of elms I'd loved in Manhattan's Central Park that American elms are nearly extinct, and Clay told me that invasive insects were threatening ash trees as well. Blueberry Cottage began to seem like a treasure.

Clay took pictures and wrote down measurements. "I'll bring you an estimate. The cottage is definitely worth repairing, and it will be great to see this wood stripped and brought back to life."

We went downstairs, and Clay tucked the staircase up into its niche, where it became almost invisible.

I asked, "Should we build permanent stairs?"

He considered the ceiling. "We could, but those stairs are close to code. They hinged the stairs and turned them into a sort of trap door so they could live downstairs and save on heating in the winter." He pointed at the fireplace in the great room. "Though they probably burned their own firewood originally, too. If you like, we can completely winterize the cottage and you can rent it year round. If we don't winterize it, being able to block off the upstairs would extend your rental season into spring and fall if your tenants didn't mind sleeping in the great room."

I'd have to think about it.

He must have noticed my frown. "I'll give you quotes both ways."

"Thank you." I was liking this man more and more every minute. To keep him from reading the excessive appreciation on my face, I spun on my heel and headed toward the Victorian sink we'd been admiring. It was underneath the window looking out on the spot where Mike died.

Clay joined me beside the sink. "This is in great condition."

"It is. On Monday, I was in here planning how the cottage might look eventually, and I scrubbed the sink. No scratches or chips." I ran my hands over the smooth porcelain.

There was something in the sink, down near the drain, that hadn't been there on Monday, the day before Mike was murdered.

A beetle in the middle of winter?

But it wasn't a bug. It was a button.

13

In Wednesday morning's blackest hours, I'd sensed that someone might have been inside Blueberry Cottage.

This evening was as dark and nearly as cold as it had been then. Gripping the hard, rounded edge of the old sink, I imagined the attacker creeping away from Mike the moment my dogs started barking. I imagined him breaking into my cottage with one swift kick at the front door. Tiptoeing across the uneven linoleum floor. Stationing himself by the window.

Watching me run down the hill behind my dogs. Concentrating on us so intently that he hadn't noticed a button falling off his jacket and sliding into the sink . . .

It was no more far-fetched than some of Uncle Allen's oddball theories.

Did the attacker think I had seen him and would be able to identify him? Would he be back?

A draft snaked around my ankles. Something whimpered and nudged my knee. Although I knew it had to be Sally or Tally, I jumped.

"Willow? Are you all right?"

I'd been contemplating the inside of a sink. What must Clay have thought?

I stammered, "Sure." I'd left my camera in its docking station in my shop. "Can you take a picture of this button?" It was probably one of the more peculiar favors anyone had ever asked of him.

He managed to act like I wasn't nearly as strange as I felt. Without laughing at me or running away, very far and very fast, he took photos.

"It's evidence," I wailed. "The investigators should have taken it. There could be fingerprints on it."

"Maybe they didn't notice it, on the dark lip of the drain like that."

Maybe the investigators mistook the button for a dead beetle like I had at first. It was an unusual button, possibly handmade, uneven around the edges and not quite round, like someone had sliced a branch about the diameter of a man's thumb and drilled two holes in the disc. Wisps of brown thread trailed from the holes. At first glance, I'd thought they were antennas.

Clay asked, "Who makes buttons from black walnut?"

"I'll ask Edna." I searched the counter and floor near the sink for other threads that may have come off when the button did.

I didn't see a thread, but I did find an aqua spot barely bigger than a nickel, and shaped sort of like Ohio. A trail of similar spots led to the riverside door. I followed the trail and touched the door. It creaked open. I usually kept it bolted.

Hackles rising, the dogs barked. I grabbed their collars and held on. If Uncle Allen and the investigators had missed the button and the faint trail of paint splotches, what other evidence might they have missed? Meanwhile, we'd been wandering through the scene, possibly contaminating it.

Clay strode across the room, examined the door, then turned to face me. A muscle twitched in his jaw. "Someone forced the door. The wood around the lock is splintered."

More evidence. I had to get the dogs out of here before they compromised it. We took them out through the great room and up to the apartment and shut them in.

Back at Blueberry Cottage, Clay offered to nail the door shut, but I wanted to check on what else the investigators had missed.

Or added. One of them could have lost the button. Another could have tracked paint around.

We checked the front porch, the one facing the river. My flashlight's beam picked out two more, slightly larger, paint spots between the door and the thick blob of aqua paint that someone had thrown on my porch about twenty-four hours before Mike died. There was also a spot of aqua on the door, down low, where someone had kicked it open. Mike's murderer, or an investigator?

It was easy to see where the sole of a boot had pulled an Ohio-shaped chunk of paint out of the thickest part of the paint blob. The paint must have been mostly dry when the boot landed on it. I could convince myself that I could detect a faint boot print on the surface of the paint, but I could also convince myself I was imagining it.

I told Clay, "I first noticed this paint on Tuesday. Someone must have thrown it here Monday night. Wouldn't it have frozen by now?"

"A water-based paint would have." He squatted down but didn't touch the paint splash. "Even without the odor, I can tell this is an oil-based paint. They don't cure or freeze in cold temperatures as quickly as water-based paints." He stood and tapped my shoulder, his touch so gentle I barely felt it. "Are you sure you're okay? You're shivering."

"I'm fine. I don't look forward to haggling with the state police about evidence they might have missed, though."

We climbed the hill to the gate near the street. Clay touched the yellow tape. "I guess it's just as well this stuff's still here, if the police have to come back. But it can't be good for business."

"It attracted crowds. Not the sort of crowds who buy much, though." I didn't add that the yellow tape and the rumors flying around the community had brought accusations of murder.

He tilted his head and raised an eyebrow, and I had to tamp down the urge to concoct tales of astounding woe. I managed what I hoped passed for a confident smile.

He glanced up at the mottled charcoal sky. "Judging from the way those clouds are rushing east, we may get snow. I hope it doesn't warm up too fast. Ice could jam the mouth of the river, and cause a flood."

"It won't."

"Hope not." He went out, waved, and strode to his truck. I locked the gate.

In my apartment, I had to calm the excited

187

dogs before I could phone Trooper Small-wood.

Her voice was more clipped than last time I heard it. "Sorry I didn't get to talk to you today," she said.

"I found something you missed —"

She interrupted me. "The team is very thorough."

I ignored her annoyed tone. "Somebody left a button at the scene. The killer's fingerprints could be on it."

"There were no buttons. They'd have noticed."

But they didn't. I let my silence say it for me.

After a few moments, she asked, "Did you touch or move it?"

"No."

"Good. Don't. Where was it in relationship to where the victim was?"

"Inside my rental cottage, in a sink underneath a window that overlooks where Mike died. The door near the river had been kicked in."

"That's strange," she said. "Both doors were fine when we were there."

"They looked fine to me, at first. But that one was only sort of wedged shut, not bolted, and wood near the latch was splintered. Also, someone tracked paint into that

188

cottage, from the porch to the sink where I found the button."

"Tracked paint? In winter?"

"It was very thick." I repeated what Clay said about oil-based paints not curing in cold temperatures. "The paint's not dry yet."

"Could you have been the one who tracked it around?"

"I was careful to step over it."

I could hear nails clicking on her receiver. "Tell you what — call Detective DeGlazier. He's the lead investigator, he lives close to you, and he can go to your place and see all this. I'll check with him to make sure he keeps the button in a safe place, and we'll swing by tomorrow to collect it and see this paint you say was tracked around."

After we said our good-byes, I frowned at the phone. When I'd talked to her before, she'd seemed more willing to help. What had happened? Did it have anything to do with the additional evidence that Trooper Gartener had said they'd found against me? How could I get her — or any of them, but she seemed the most reasonable — to tell me what the evidence was so I could refute it?

I phoned Uncle Allen.

A child answered.

I stammered out, "Unc . . . er . . . Detective DeGlazier?"

The child pelted away, shouting "Granddad! Some lady wants to talk to you!"

Several minutes passed before I heard the phone being manhandled again. I half expected the prattle of a three-year-old. Instead, a woman demanded, "Who's this?"

"I need to speak to Detective DeGlazier —"

"Who's this?" she repeated. Her caustic voice was familiar.

"Willow Vanderling."

She must have dropped the phone. The crash it made as it fell on a table, or more likely from the sound of it, on a snare drum, nearly deafened me. It could not have benefited the phone, either. "Aaaaaallen!" she shrieked. "It's that *murderer!*"

Great. He'd indoctrinated his entire family to believe in my guilt. He had probably spread his suspicions to the entire village and surrounding countryside, too. It was all I could do not to growl into the phone.

But as I replayed her voice, I began to wonder if she could be Aunt Betty, who had come to In Stitches with her friends and accusations.

Finally, Uncle Allen came to the phone. "What d'ya want?" I must have caught him

190

during dinner. Dishes clattered. I could hear him chewing. Maybe I should be glad, after all, that the phone crashing down onto the snare drum had temporarily impaired my hearing.

I said carefully, "The investigators missed some evidence in my cottage."

Uncle Allen spoke around food in his mouth. "That's impossible. What evidence?"

"Somebody tracked through wet paint on my porch, left a trace of paint on my door when he kicked it open —"

"Who'd have done that?"

"Whoever beat Mike up."

A woman shouted, "Aaaaaallen, your dinner's getting cold!"

"I've got to go," he said.

"Wait," I commanded. "Somebody lost a button. It fell into the cottage sink. The killer's fingerprints may be on it. I called the state police. Trooper Smallwood said you should get it and save it for her."

"We should get your prints, too." He said it in his gotcha voice, like he was tricking me into something, like confessing to murder.

"Of course, since they'll be on most of my things."

"Aaaaaallen!"

Uncle Allen grunted, "Button's probably

191

been there for years."

"It wasn't there on Monday. We're not talking about a minor crime." I was getting as hot under the collar as the woman who had cooked his dinner. "And Trooper Small-wood said —"

"If she wants it that badly, tell her to go get it herself."

Oh, great, now I was going to be in the middle of an argument between two different police forces. "Come get the key from me again, anytime."

"Aaaaaallen!"

"Yeah, yeah." I couldn't tell if he was dismissing me or his wife. He hung up.

The button might have to stay where it was until Trooper Smallwood came.

Maybe Edna would remember if anyone had bought black walnut buttons, either for a new garment or to replace lost buttons. The one in my sink was distinctive, very likely handmade, and should be easily recognizable.

I went upstairs. The boutiques and apartments belonging to Haylee, Opal, and Naomi were dark, but Buttons and Bows was brightly lit. I shut the dogs into the apartment, threw on a coat, and ran outside.

Clay had been right. The night had warmed, marginally, and fine snowflakes

192

haloed streetlights.

"Willow!" A man's voice. Stores were closed and no pedestrians were in sight. Who was calling me?

14

Sam leaned out his front door and beckoned with his whole arm, as if he needed help. "Willow!"

I ran to his front porch.

"I checked my inventory against my records," he said. "A padlock *has* gone missing, package and all."

Although Sam and I were sheltered by the porch roof, snow billowed like chiffon between us. "Who bought it?" A murderer, most likely.

Sam shook his head. "No one bought it, that's the thing. I keep records of what comes in and what goes out, and I should have one more padlock."

He trusted his bookkeeping more than I did. "Do you know when it went missing?"

"Had to be Tuesday. When you and I looked at the heap of packages last evening, it looked too small to me. We'd had them all out the night before, you know. I do remember how heavy things are, and how much space they take." He tightened his lips around his teeth as if to hold in a secret. "I asked around this evening, and Herb reminded me that Mike Krawbach was in The Ironmonger Tuesday evening while you were."

"No, he wasn't." Mike would have complained when Smythe Castor apologized on his behalf.

"Well, now, not in the store, exactly. He was in my basement, inspecting my electrical panel to see if I could upgrade."

I admitted, "I did see Mike walk past my store shortly after I left yours. I guessed he'd been snooping around my yard, but maybe he was coming from here." While in Sam's basement, had Mike heard and memorized the unique number matching my padlocks? "Did he buy a padlock?"

Sam brushed the toe of one shoe at the snow blowing onto his porch. "Mike came upstairs the moment you all left and was talking to the geezers, right where those packages of padlocks were, and he was playing with the packages, and . . ." Sam heaved a careworn sigh. "One of the fellows thinks Mike might have picked up one of those packages and . . ." He met my gaze. "Just sort of neglected to put it back. But I don't

195

know . . ."

Sam didn't want to accuse Mike of stealing, but it seemed exactly like something Mike would do. Mike must have been near the top of the basement stairs when the men were calling out the numbers, and heard them find two alike. He must have seen another package with that number printed on it, and pocketed the package. He could have let himself into my yard.

It still didn't explain why he'd been beaten with my canoe paddle. Or who had done it.

It also blew apart my theory that his killer had to have been one of the people I'd seen in Sam's store when I bought my padlocks. If Mike opened the gate, anyone could have followed him into my yard. And he or she wouldn't have needed a key to snap the padlock shut afterward.

Sam flicked snow from his shoulders. "Mike told me he would issue me a permit to upgrade my electrical service, and he seemed quite proud of himself, y'know, that way he had."

I did know. Mike had probably been congratulating himself for obtaining a key that would let him come and go from my yard. Had he been planning something in particular, or had he merely enjoyed owning keys to other folk's places? "You'd better go inside," I suggested.

"Yep, the snow's blowin' all over the place, isn't it now? Weather's warming up. Hope the river doesn't rise too much, but . . ." Shaking his head as if to ward off the future, he backed into his store and closed the door.

I crossed the street. Opening Edna's door set off a jaunty little tune.

Edna straightened from bending over an open carton. "Like my new doorbell? That's an old Vaudeville tune, about buttons and bows. You should update those boring chimes you have."

I should? "I like the frosted sea glass." The irregularly shaped glass pieces were pastel greens, blues, and turquoises.

Haylee waved at me from the top of a ladder propped against shelves of trims. "Clay made Willow's chimes, from driftwood and glass he found on the beach."

I pictured Clay, tan and barefoot on a beach at sunset, picking up pebbles and chunks of glass smoothed by water and sand . . .

An intriguing image, but the sights around me were intriguing, too. To my left, one wall featured buttons in a breathtaking array of color. The opposite wall displayed as large an assortment of ribbons, fringes, and braids as I'd seen anywhere, including those

197

wonderful stores that Haylee and I used to browse through in Manhattan's Fashion District.

Opal smothered me in a hug. She had crocheted her voluminous poncho in diagonal stripes of navy blue and hunter green. "That Vaudeville tune was actually 'Buttons and Beaux,' " she corrected Edna, spelling it to make sure I understood. "It was rather risqué, more about *un*buttoning than buttoning." She helped me disengage myself from her poncho.

Haylee grinned down at us. "Think about all those tiny buttons and the clumsy hands of the beaux. You can imagine the lyrics." Her black wool slacks and burgundy Chanel-style jacket were perfectly tailored. She had to have made them herself.

With a sniff, Edna lifted her chin. "I prefer to think it's B-O-W-S." She pointed at the carton at her feet. "We're rearranging my shelves to add my latest shipment. There's so much!"

Who wouldn't be thrilled after receiving several cartons of notions? Colorful lace, fringes, and ribbons spilled out. I wanted to sink my hands into the boxes, fling decorations all over Buttons and Bows, then grab my favorites, which would be most of them, and dash home to start creating . . . I wasn't sure what, but simply owning the trims while I designed the whatevers would be satisfying. On the other hand, after Edna added them to her color-coded shelves, it would be easy to saunter over here anytime and buy whatever I needed.

Yes, *needed.* Threadville was a great place to live and work.

Edna smoothed her vest. "I finished this today." She had woven the vest from lime, lemon, and pale orange grosgrain ribbons embellished with matching ribbon rosettes and tiny, sparkly buttons. A yellow turtle-neck and slacks completed the outfit.

"It's beautiful," I said. "You look like a dish of swirly citrus sherbet."

Edna's dark brown eyes glowed.

"Complete with a cherry on top," Haylee teased.

Edna patted her curls. "I just love this shade of red. So cheery in the middle of winter."

It was that. And exactly the color of maraschino cherries.

Naomi wore a navy and burgundy quilted vest with flower-bedecked unicorns appli-quéd over it. "You looked worried when you came in, Willow."

"Mainly puzzled. A wooden button ap-peared in the sink at Blueberry Cottage about the time Mike was beaten up." I described it and asked Edna if she remembered selling any like it.

She led me to one end of her floor-to-ceiling button display. "Did it match any of these?"

None of her many wooden buttons were quite like the one I'd found.

She suggested, "Maybe seeing it would jog my memory."

I agreed to take her to it when we finished restocking Buttons and Bows. Although Haylee already knew most of what I'd discovered in the past two days, I related Dawn's allegations about Mike's friends and fellow gang-members, Irv, Herb, and possibly Smythe and Clay. I told them about the trail of paint and yesterday's interview with Dr. Wrinklesides. "Everyone around here except us probably knows about his hearing. Uncle Allen could have made up Mike's so-called last words."

Haylee frowned down at me from the top of her ladder.

I gave her a reassuring smile. Telling her mothers about our midnight jaunt last night would only worry them, and we hadn't found much besides evidence that someone had searched Mike's house.

Lovingly, Edna unfolded tissue paper to

reveal ecru lace. "Uncle Allen is giving himself poetic license with Mike's last words."

Haylee's ladder shook.

Rushing to the ladder, Opal stumbled over the hems of her trousers.

I steadied her. Either she hadn't measured the pants she'd crocheted, navy blue to match half the stripes in her poncho, or the pants had an unfortunate tendency to grow. The scallops around the hems tangled with her crocheted slippers.

Edna dove behind her sales counter. "We should write this down." She emerged with a pen and a small black notebook. "We'll be scientific about suspects in Mike's murder. Who are they?"

"Besides us," Naomi said quickly, "since we know that none of us did it."

Opal moaned. "None of us has an alibi. We were all home alone, sleeping."

"I seem to be Uncle Allen's favorite suspect," I reminded them. "And the state trooper who came today seemed to agree with him."

Naomi clapped her hands over her mouth. "Oh, Willow, how could they?"

Haylee cast me a worried look. "Everyone in town knows I hated Mike."

Naomi reproved her. "Hate is a strong

word, dear."

Haylee shrugged. "Not when applied to Mike Krawbach."

Maybe I'd been wrong about being the prime suspect. Maybe Uncle Allen and the state police were stewing about whether to arrest Haylee or me, while letting the real murderer remain free. I couldn't let Haylee go to prison, either.

I told them about my original theory about the padlocks, and that Sam had dispelled it. Edna insisted that we still had to suspect all the younger men who were in the store at the time, since they may have been members of Mike's gang. She handed the notebook to me. She had written *Clay Fraser* at the top of her notebook's first page "You jot down our notes about our suspects, Willow. The rest of us know where all these trims go."

We didn't have any evidence against Clay, Herb, Irv, or Smythe, but I gave them each a page and wrote that they been members of Mike's gang of kids.

They clucked in dismay about Rhonda, Aunt Betty, and their friends snooping in my store. I started pages for Rhonda and Aunt Betty. I had no evidence that they had attacked Mike, either, except for their strange behavior earlier that day.

"And this Rhonda?" Haylee asked. "You said she acted like she could have been one of Mike's girlfriends. Maybe it was wishful thinking. Maybe she chased him to your backyard and lost her temper."

Edna arranged satin ribbon in rainbow order. "Willow said Rhonda looked mean." Edna wasn't done fingering suspects. "Dr. Wrinklesides was closest to Mike when he died. Maybe the good doctor slipped a syringe into Mike's veins. Something that shut down his heart."

Haylee asked, "Why would Dr. Wrinklesides beat Mike up, lock him in Willow's yard, and then murder him? That doesn't make sense."

Edna fixed Haylee with a stern glare. "The one life lesson we've tried to instill in you, Haylee, is that men often do *not* make sense."

"And Uncle Allen makes the least sense of all," I said. I told them about his reluctance to investigate the button and the trail of paint.

Edna crowed, "Aha! Uncle Allen was the attacker who tracked paint into your cottage and lost a button."

"I never noticed buttons like that on him," I said.

"Of course not," Edna said. "He lost it.

Next time you see him, check to see if he's missing a button."

Haylee giggled. "He's missing lots of things."

Naomi defended him. "Don't underestimate him. That bumbling could be an act."

Edna's eyes sparked with excitement. "Aha! He's trying to fool us into thinking he couldn't plan and carry out a murder. Start a page for him, Willow."

I already had. She dictated, "May have made up Mike's last words to throw suspicion from himself to us . . ."

Someone pounded on the door. I jumped. Edna's little "Buttons and Beaux" tune jingled.

15

Uncle Allen stomped into Buttons and Bows. Snow covered his coat as if he'd sewn it himself from white fleece.

I was about to drop Edna's notebook casually into the carton of satin ribbons. In one fluid movement, she grabbed the notebook from me, stretched the neck of her sweater, and shoved the notebook down her front. Her lack of subtlety, Opal's and Naomi's horrified expressions, and Haylee's stifled giggle should have been enough to make Uncle Allen subpoena the notebook.

Instead, he came toward me. "You said you would let me have the key of your cottage again. You weren't in your store. I can't get into your yard, either, unless I climb fences. Your gates are locked."

"Come on in out of the storm and warm up," Edna offered, staring pointedly at his coat bulging over his belly. The middle buttonhole showed through the snow. Was he missing a button, or had he simply not buttoned it? His other coat buttons were navy blue plastic, which didn't rule out the middle one having been wooden. I thought back to Tuesday afternoon, when Mike called Uncle Allen to my shop. If he'd sported a mismatched button, one of us or the Threadville tourists would have noticed.

Edna wiggled and pushed at the top of the notebook until her hand-woven vest helped hide the notebook's sharp corners and spiral binding.

Probably hoping to distract Uncle Allen from Edna's gyrations, Opal launched into an interrogation. "What's going on with that vacant store between The Ironmonger and the new restaurant?"

Uncle Allen appeared to avoid looking at our faces and the challenge he might see on them. Or maybe he was dazed by the variety of buttons beside him. "I don't know." He unbuttoned his coat. Slush slid to Edna's shiny floor.

He was definitely missing a button.

Opal raised one eyebrow, but went on smoothly with the subject she'd started. "Someone appears to be renovating that store. Trucks came and went all day yesterday and today."

"Men carried in lumber and tools," Naomi

added. "And light fixtures."

Edna's eyes opened wide, as if two million volts of electricity had zinged through her. Or maybe the notebook had poked her. "It's a marijuana grow-op! Did anyone notice a building permit?"

None of us had.

"I'll find out." Uncle Allen's grumble was not very convincing.

Edna crossed her arms over her strangely angular bodice. "You'd better investigate. It's got to be a grow-op or a meth lab."

Opal enunciated over the howling wind, "You should look into Mike's dealings with the drug underworld."

Uncle Allen tucked his thumbs into his belt like someone about to draw six-shooters from hip holsters. "Mike was the victim. Don't go blaming him."

Naomi wiggled her eyebrows toward Opal in a quelling manner. "She meant that Mike may have stumbled upon information, and those drug dealers had to prevent him from telling you."

Unappeased, Uncle Allen grunted and turned to me. "I'll have those keys now."

I strode toward the door. "I'll take you."

"I can let myself in and bring the keys back."

I wanted to make certain he found the

button and saw the paint spots. "It's okay," I said.

Haylee climbed down the clanking aluminum ladder. "I'll come, too."

Uncle Allen hitched up his pants. "I don't want anyone disturbing the evidence."

Edna must have realized it was her last chance to see the button before Uncle Allen took it away. She tugged on boots. "We won't do that."

Uncle Allen, Edna, Haylee, and I trooped out. Snow blinded us. Wind pushed us back toward Buttons and Bows. Leaning forward, choking to breathe, we struggled across the street to my relatively sheltered yard. Tally-Ho and Sally-Forth voiced their indignation inside my apartment while we sidestepped past it, down the snow-covered hill to Blueberry Cottage.

I unlocked the door and turned on the light. Uncle Allen backhanded the space between him and us with one gloved hand. "You ladies stay outside while I do a sweep." His flashlight hardly gave off any light, but it did show up cobwebs in corners, and I was tempted to offer him a broom for his sweep. I managed to restrain myself and was careful not to look at Haylee. It wouldn't take much to set both of us off into giggles.

Edna stepped over the threshold. "This is

lovely, Willow. It doesn't need anything except a little cleaning."

Haylee let out a few fake coughs.

"Allergic to cobwebs?" I asked with overdone politeness.

Haylee coughed harder. "Some *sweeping* would help."

I suffered from an instantaneous coughing fit, too.

Edna cast both of us a stern look. "And some twig furniture," she added brightly. "With its bark on. And you could whip up pretty cushions and curtains, Willow, and trim them with bows. It would be very cozy. With your views of the river, you could charge a good rent."

Uncle Allen disappeared into the kitchen. I clamped my lips together, and Haylee did an admirable job of laughing silently. Edna shook a finger at us, which set us off again. Finally more or less in control of ourselves and of each other, the three of us tiptoed through the great room and positioned ourselves behind the line where carpeting met linoleum.

I couldn't simply stand still, however. I strode into the kitchen and pointed down at the trail of aqua blotches. "When we're done in here, I'll show you similar spots outside on the front porch and door."

Edna squealed, "The aqua spots lead from the door to the sink! Look, Detective De-Glazier. Here's the button."

He aimed his light into the sink. "I see it." He cleared his throat and harrumphed as if trying to supply the plumbing noises that had been missing ever since the cottage's water was turned off.

"What a charming kitchen," Edna cooed. "All you have to do is paint the walls and install new appliances, and you'll be ready for tenants."

With a quick shake of her head, Haylee nudged her.

Uncle Allen untangled a plastic bag from a jacket pocket.

Raising and lowering her eyebrows, Edna asked me, "Do you have a *paper* bag or envelope?"

Uncle Allen used the plastic bag like a glove to pick up the button, then sealed it in the bag.

Edna peered into the bag. "I haven't ever sold any like that at Buttons and Bows, but it looks familiar. The murderer must have lost it here."

Uncle Allen focused on me. "Are you sure it didn't pop off your coat? After you unlocked your gate and let Mike into your yard so you could beat him up?"

It was all I could do not to stamp my boot down onto his. "I didn't let him in and I didn't beat him up! And you took the parka I wore that night. Check, and you'll see that it zips. It never had any buttons. And tonight, Sam told me that Mike might have stolen a padlock from the hardware store after I bought mine. Mike's key may have opened my gate. He could have let himself and his killer in. Did Mike have a key to my gate when he was found?"

Uncle Allen pointed at me. "Aha! You caught him trespassing and attacked him. And no, he didn't have your key. You're the one who has your keys."

"When I found him," I reminded the policeman, "he had already been attacked. I didn't touch him." I pointed at the gaping door. "Somebody broke in here, probably after attacking Mike, because he heard my dogs coming." I gestured at the sink. "He watched us and didn't notice losing a button." I tried not to stare at the spot on Uncle Allen's coat where a button should be.

Edna must have had the same problem. Her head bobbed around as if she were looking for a new subject. She pointed at the closed bathroom door. "What's in there, Willow?"

Uncle Allen opened the door and stuck his head around the jamb. "Oh."

Haylee took one look at the steep angle of the toilet, and the dam burst on her giggles.

For once, Edna seemed to be at a loss for words. Finally, she concluded, with a great show of confidence, "All this room needs is a new toilet. You never needed a building permit, Willow. You were only trying to be nice to Mike by asking him for one."

Behind Uncle Allen's back, Haylee conquered her giggles and elbowed Edna.

Uncle Allen turned around and frowned at us. "It's not the toilet. It's the floor. This whole building needs shoring up. She would need a permit for that. And she was being nice? Nearly everyone in Elderberry Bay heard her threaten to *kill* Mike. You call that nice?"

Edna reminded him, "Dust that button for fingerprints. And maybe there's DNA on it." She made a pouty face. "Except if the button is damp, it will decompose in that plastic bag."

Uncle Allen scoffed, "You watch too much TV."

Edna raised her little chin. "I used to be a chemist." She had a right to be proud. Together, she and her two best friends had juggled degrees, careers, raising Haylee, and perfecting the handcrafting of original and unique outfits.

I showed Uncle Allen the Ohio-shaped paint splotches on the front porch and door.

Predictably, he scoffed. "Someone could have made those tracks last summer."

"That paint appeared the day before Mike's attack."

My hot retort barely fazed him. "So? Maybe someone tracked it in after we were done here."

Or maybe one of the investigators tracked paint around. I didn't say it.

He concluded, "It might have nothing to do with Mike or his death."

I hated to admit it, but he could be right.

He took a deep breath, sniffing the air with something resembling satisfaction. "Snow's still coming down like a son of a gun. It keeps warming up like this, the river's gonna overrun its banks."

16

The river didn't look higher than it had earlier when Clay had made a similar comment, but Sam, who had lived next to the river for most of his eighty-something years, had also predicted possible flooding.

Silently, we trudged up the hill. Newly fallen snow had obliterated our footprints from only minutes before.

At the street, Uncle Allen headed for his cruiser, and the rest of us returned to Buttons and Bows. Naomi and Opal were tidying up the last of the cartons. Edna gazed around her glittering store. "Thanks, everyone!"

We all agreed that we loved getting the first look at Edna's new merchandise.

Opal asked, "Did you recognize the button, Edna?"

"It wasn't a type I've ever carried in my store, but it looked familiar."

Haylee laughed. "Lots of buttons are

round with holes."

Edna glared.

I said mildly, "Not many are sliced from black walnut branches."

It seemed impossible for Edna to be anything but cheerful for more than a half second. She thanked us all, and we said our good nights and left. Opal, Haylee, and Naomi appeared to be blown along the snowdrifted sidewalk toward their stores. I fought my way through blustering snow to let Sally-Forth and Tally-Ho out.

They were drenched by the time they tired of wrestling in the snow. I had embroidered their names and portraits on microfiber towels, tan to go with Tally's brindle and white coat, and red to go with Sally's gorgeous black and ermine fur. Tally wriggled when I dried him. Sally went all relaxed, like she never wanted the rubbing to end.

The dogs accompanied me upstairs to the shop, which the woodstove still kept toasty warm. I inspected the design I'd started on my practice remnant. I tried to tell myself it looked fine, but I had to admit that the stitches were too small and close together, creating a needle-breaking fabric with the approximate flexibility of plywood.

I went back to my embroidery software, fiddled with the photo, lowered the number of colors the design would use, and manually lengthened stitches.

I put stabilizer and another remnant from my stash into my largest machine embroidery hoop and began my second attempt. The improvements were just what it needed. The embroidery was neither puckered nor slack.

Now I could stitch the design on the homespun-weight unbleached linen I'd bought for the finished product. By the time my machine began the cornstalks in the foreground, I couldn't help smiling at how well the design was coming out, almost like a seventeenth-century tapestry. Okay, not really, since the camouflage and orange neon fabrics the man wore had not yet been invented. Maybe if I added one of Naomi's unicorns? Maybe not.

While my favorite embroidery machine worked faultlessly, stopping and beeping to remind me to change threads, I looked through my photos for one that would show off my version of stumpwork and inspire Threadville tourists. I chose one of the fishing hut and ATV on the icy lake at dawn. I fiddled with the photo, trying one more thing to perfect it, then another and another until I lost count.

Meanwhile, my embroidery machine completed the design of the man disappearing into the woods. I still had to create three-dimensional cornstalks and trees.

When I thought my frozen lake photo was ready to be converted to an embroidery design, my eyes were too bleary to focus. The dogs and I went down to our apartment.

In the morning, the wind had died down, snow was no longer falling, and the sky was the color of frozen fog. Blueberry Cottage was charming, a pale teal gingerbread house underneath heaps of frosting. I snapped pictures while the dogs played tag.

When Sally saw me with the embroidered doggie towels, she trotted inside, lay down, and gazed imperiously at me, making it perfectly clear that she was ready for more rubbing. Wagging his tail and bopping Sally with his nose, Tally had to wait for his turn, then he wanted to bite his towel. By the time the two dogs were dry, I'd worked up a sweat. I showered, dressed, and fixed a yummy omelet stuffed with shredded sharp cheddar. Sally and Tally made certain they got their share before I went upstairs to In Stitches and locked the dogs in the apartment.

Lake Street had become an enchanted land during the night. Snow carpeted roofs.

Tree branches resembled white lace. Evergreen boughs peeked out beneath soft white mounds. Lights inside the boutiques across the street made Threadville both cozy and inviting. I turned my cross-stitched sign from *Closed* to *Welcome.*

While the day's cider sent cinnamon and apple aromas around the shop, I cut a scarf from red fleece. One of the fun things about sewing with fleece was that it wouldn't unravel and didn't need hemming. I hooped it underneath water-soluble stabilizer, which would keep the stitches from burying themselves in the fluffy fabric. I loaded my weeping willow design into my software, saved a new copy of the design, and deleted the green parts, leaving only the bare tree trunk and branches. Imitating the scenery outside, I added dollops of snow to the weeping willow. Later, it would be fun to create spring and autumn versions of the design. I stitched my new winter willow design in charcoal and white on one end of the red scarf.

The embroidery machine finished. In the sudden quiet, I heard shouts and laughter. I'd been afraid that the Threadville tour bus wouldn't make it through the snow, but some of my students, along with village children who apparently had the day off school, whooped it up as they built a snow-man in my front yard. I pulled on boots, coat, and mittens and ran out to join them.

Rosemary helped another woman lift a bulky snowball onto the snowman's rounded shoulders. "Hi, Willow! We left early because of the snow on the roads, and got here long before classes. We didn't want to bother you folks, so we've been having a little fun."

The Threadville tourists and village children had erected a huge snowman in front of The Ironmonger. They'd built snowmen in front of The Stash, Tell a Yarn, Buttons and Bows, and Batty About Quilts. Snow-men decorated the front yards of the General Store, the vacant store that Edna suspected was a drug dealers' lair, and the uncompleted restaurant. On the corner, Pier 42 boasted two snowmen, one in the front yard, and one on the side patio. Sisters-in-thread knew how to have fun, and they made it contagious. I'd have to talk to Hay-lee and her mothers about planning and giving children's courses.

Finished with their outdoor sculptures, my students left the children to invent more fun for themselves, and trooped into In Stitches. Several of them wanted to stitch my winter willow design onto the scarves they'd made. I helped others create mono-grams, some with crests from a commercial design collection. The woman who had already bought an embroidery machine wanted to learn to use software to create her own designs.

"How about a snowman?" I suggested. I demonstrated creating three circles, big, big-ger and biggest, and filling them with fancy stitching. We added eyes, a mouth and three buttons. Other students finished their stitch-ing and gathered around to watch. Several muttered about needing embroidery ma-chines and software for creating original designs.

Soon, I should be able to afford Blueberry Cottage's renovations, downstairs *and* up-stairs . . .

After I showed them how rinsing the scarves in hot water made the water-soluble stabilizer disappear, it was lunch time. They hurried away, some of them wearing their new scarves, complete with basted-on stabi-lizer.

I leashed the dogs and took them and my newly embroidered scarf to the front yard. Laughing, a boy pulled a toboggan loaded with smaller children down the snowy street. A family of two parents and five children, all of them with smiles so wide their teeth must have been cold, schussed past on cross-country skis.

I expected to have trouble hanging on to two lunging dogs while tying the scarf around my snowman's neck, but my biggest problem turned out to be trying to force Sally and Tally close to the snowman. They planted their feet in the snow, barked, and refused to look directly at the scary white creature. "It's okay," I told them, giving the damp scarf a toss. It draped itself precariously around the snowman's neck. I considered it artistic.

The other four Threadville proprietors came outside, too, and added scarves to their snowmen. Haylee's was a length of bright blue and green cotton. Opal must have knit her scarf that morning, using heavy yarn and huge needles. Edna tied a jaunty rainbow of ribbons around her snowman's neck. Naomi, possibly with the help of this morning's students, had sewn a row of quilt squares into a scarf.

We shouted to each other in voices as cheerful as the day's sunshine. Wearing an orange ball cap and an olive green cardigan with leather elbow patches, Sam came out of the hardware store and stuck a length of copper tubing where his snowman's mouth should be. Sam called to me, "He's smoking a pipe."

In case my groan wasn't loud enough, I twisted my face in fake pain.

With a grin and a wave, Sam stumped inside.

Jacoba and Luther emerged from the General Store. Jacoba used strawberry whips to create a jolly smile for their snowman. Luther gave it a radish nose. Jacoba was covered in so many layers I couldn't be certain, but I suspected that, a year from now, the couple would be trundling a baby around in a sled. I called a greeting. They waved, but I couldn't hear what they said over the sound of the white truck roaring past.

It stopped in front of the vacant store.

As one, Haylee, Opal, Edna, and Naomi began walking toward the truck. The dogs and I started in the same direction on our side of the street. Sally and Tally pulled toward the curb, away from the snowmen.

A man climbed out of the truck. Edna demanded, "What's going on in that building?"

The guy brushed past us, stomped up the unshoveled walk, unlocked the building, and stalked inside.

"Friendly sort," snorted Edna.

"You'd think he'd have decorated his

222

snowman," Opal commented.

Haylee giggled. "Maybe that's what he's here to do."

I pointed dramatically at the papered-over windows. "Anybody see a building permit?"

"No," they chorused, and I sang it with them. Their adoption of me seemed to have taken.

Edna grabbed my arm. "Look what color they painted the door."

Aqua. Unless I was mistaken, it was the same shade as the paint someone had tossed onto my porch.

Naomi looked disappointed. "It's been that color since September."

"It still gives us an idea where the paint may have come from," I said consolingly. "I first saw it on my porch shortly before Mike was attacked. We can't say that the person who threw the paint killed Mike. Only that the person who tracked through it and kicked open my door may have."

Opal frowned at the snowy street. "Tonight's Friday, storytelling night at Tell a Yarn. My guest has a long drive. The tour bus made it from Erie this morning, so you all should come to storytelling, in case she can get through."

Edna toed at rivulets of water channeling their way through the snow in the gutters.

223

"The snow could melt by tonight."

They crossed to their side of the street. I tugged the dogs to my yard and peeked over my yellow-bedecked gate. Was it my imagination, or had the river begun climbing?

During my afternoon class, my beautiful sea glass wind chime jingled. Aunt Betty and Rhonda. Just what I needed, snoopy browsers who bought very little and were inordinately fond of accusing me of murder. "Welcome," I called out, the very vision of a hospitable boutique owner. "Terrible day out, isn't it?"

Aunt Betty shuffled toward the back of the store. She'd managed to roll up the legs of her snowmobile suit, revealing blue plaid lining, but the suit was soaked to the knees.

Rhonda flashed me a quick grimace that may have been a smile. Her hood was tied around her face, bunching her cheeks, forehead, and chin together.

All around us, machines stopped stitching, and my students raised their heads.

Aunt Betty scooped up an armload of Dawn's lovely placemats and napkins, then gestured for Rhonda to do the same. After a sidewise glance toward me, Rhonda picked up the rest. They dumped them on the counter beside the cash register. Aunt Betty put her fists near where the waist of her snowmobile suit would be if it had one. "Do I get a discount for buying them all?" she asked. "How about half price?"

Appalled, I shook my head. "The prices are already very low for hand-woven linens."

"Can't you give me something off?"

"Did I talk to you last night?" I asked.

She gave me a blank look. "About place-mats?"

"On the phone. Are you Detective De-Glazier's wife?"

"What business is that of yours?" A cunning look came into her eyes. "You'll give me a discount if I am?"

"Only if you aren't."

I didn't know that a face as doughy as hers could show surprise. Maybe she didn't understand that citizens weren't supposed to give favors to policemen and their families. Especially if they didn't want it brought up in court during murder trials . . .

It was difficult to stay optimistic when the local policeman and a pair of state troopers seemed determined to arrest me for murder.

Aunt Betty elbowed Rhonda. "She's paying for it."

Paying for what? I'd been so lost in my own thoughts that for a confused second, I thought she meant that Rhonda would be suitably punished for murdering Mike.

Then, inwardly shaking my head at the conclusion I'd drawn, I realized that Aunt Betty was talking about the *linens,* not about Mike's death.

Grabbing the edge of the counter, Rhonda managed to stay upright. "I am?" Her snarly voice came out sounding pitiful.

Aunt Betty elbowed her again. "It's an investment."

Reluctantly, Rhonda unzipped her parka pocket and handed me a charge card. Rhonda Dunkle, it said. Her black nail polish failed to cover the fleck of aqua paint on the cuticle of her right thumb.

How had Rhonda gotten aqua paint on her thumb? By opening a can and heaving paint onto my porch? Or by cleaning her shoe after Mike was murdered?

Both Aunt Betty's snowmobile suit and Rhonda's parka were done up with zippers and snaps. Neither garment had ever needed buttons.

I offered, "How about two percent off?" It would come out of my slim margin, but selling the entire lot at once would save time and paperwork.

Aunt Betty looked triumphant. "Done."

I bagged the purchases, then the two women scuttled outside with their treasures. What did Aunt Betty plan to do with those lovely linens, grace the DeGlazier dining table with a different color scheme every night for two weeks? Pad the snare drum so she wouldn't deafen callers when she dropped the phone on it?

Because of the roads, the tour bus left Threadville earlier than usual. I downloaded the artwork I'd created of the fishing hut and ATV to my embroidery machine. While it stitched, I played with ideas for embroidering over wires so I could create objects that would stand out from the background as in traditional stumpwork. The stitches would have to be very precise, or the needle would hit the wires and break, which could damage the sewing machine.

My front door opened.

A visit from Uncle Allen was becoming a nightly event. He reached into his pocket. For a search warrant? A legible copy of the Miranda warning?

"I have a ticket for you," he said.

They issued tickets for murder now, instead of arrests, trials, and prison terms?

That couldn't be right.

He must be talking about my car. Maybe it was in the snowplow's way, and Uncle Allen had kindly brought my parking ticket instead of leaving it on the windshield to sop up snow, swell to double its size, and shed its wording.

He plunked a small square of pink construction paper onto my counter. It did not look like a parking ticket. Lines had been drawn near the edges, showing where to bring down the paper cutter's blade.

Roast Beef Dinner, it said in big letters.

Uncle Allen said, "It's for a good cause. Tomorrow night. Your friends are going."

To collect evidence, no doubt . . . Maybe Edna would bring her notebook of clues. "Sure," I said. "I'll go." I paid him for the ticket and challenged, "Trooper Smallwood said that state police investigators would come today to look at the paint someone tracked around my cottage. No one showed up."

"I told them not to bother. That paint can't have a bearing on the case."

"Yes, it could! What if it does?"

My pleading was in vain. With a dismissive wave, he was out the door.

I read the ticket's fine print.

The roast beef dinner was to be hosted by the ATV club.

A good cause, Uncle Allen had said.

Uh-oh. The ATV club might consider bulldozing Blueberry Cottage a good cause. I was tempted to chase after Uncle Allen and demand my money back, but there was

228

no telling how much I might learn about Mike and his enemies at a dinner put on by his friends.

Uncle Allen's never-ending siren wailed off into the distance. I stood looking out the front door at snow melting. Suddenly, the solution to the stumpwork problem came to me. I wouldn't have to embroider over the wires. I could have my machine stitch the design first, and I could thread the wires through the stitches afterward. Usually, I liked to make the machine do as much as possible, but this more manual method might end up being faster.

That little success gave me the courage to phone the state police again and beg them to come see the paint. The dispatcher said that several troopers were in the area, some of them helping sort out weather-related collisions, but she'd send one as soon as possible.

While I waited, I again loaded my embroidery software into my computer. On its screen, I superimposed the photo of the man disappearing into the woods. I traced cornstalks in the foreground and a few of the trees in the background, then sent messages to the software to fill those areas with textured stitches. The final step for the software was to make the embroidery machine outline the tree and cornstalk designs with satin stitches. I adjusted the satin stitches until they were wide enough for me to thread thin wire through them. This was going to work . . .

Sally-Forth and Tally-Ho, however, did not have patience for creating embroidery methods. I took them to the backyard. The snow had gone from sticky to slushy. The dogs bolted uphill from the back door toward the street. Afraid that the gate might be open, I ran around the corner after them. The gate was closed, and someone was rattling it.

17

It wasn't the murderer returning to the scene of the crime. State Trooper Gartener was on the other side of my gate. "Your store's locked," he said.

That wasn't surprising, since it was closed for the night. I let him into the yard and put the dogs back into the apartment. They weren't keen on ending their evening so quickly, but after having been in a rescue facility for most of their lives, they never tried to rush past me when I shut doors in their endearing faces.

Gartener accompanied me down the hill to Blueberry Cottage. We could have used a sled. I took him around to the porch where the paint was, but of course the paint was now knee-deep under snow. "I guess we shouldn't shovel this snow," I said.

"Certainly not."

"Come inside, then." In the cottage's kitchen, I showed him where we'd found the button and the tracks leading from the door to the sink. I opened the riverside door and showed him the paint that must have come off a boot when someone kicked the door. I explained Clay's theory about the uncured paint.

Nodding, he wrote in his notebook, then examined the floor. "I'm afraid I'll have to send someone to remove part of your flooring," he said, sounding apologetic, as if he could empathize, after all.

"That's fine. I wasn't planning to keep that linoleum anyway."

He spoke into his radio. "As soon as you can free up some of those techies from the Krawbach place, send them to the Vanderling cottage. Tell them they're going to have to pry up some floorboards from the kitchen and the porch."

How gratifying. I might be losing some porch, but with it would go the ugly aqua paint. When Gartener ended his call, I said, "I guess you'll need my door, too."

He could actually grin. "Only the lower fourth of it."

"You might as well take it all, then."

"The guys will cover the holes with plywood. Come help me figure out how much of your porch floor they'll need to take."

He led me to the great room and out the

door we'd come in. I trailed after him, feeling like an obedient stray. I was tall, but he was taller. I tried walking as straight as he did, but it felt really stiff. Good thing he didn't have eyes in the back of his head. At least I hoped he didn't.

At the porch, he had me point out where the blob of paint was.

"Does the paint go all the way to the edge of the porch?" he asked.

"It's closer to the wall of the building."

With a bare index finger, he made a tiny indentation in the slush at the edge of the porch. "The rate that stuff's melting, it'll be gone before the techies get here."

Such abundant loquacity encouraged me to question him, for all the good it would do. "What was the other evidence you said you found?"

He stared at the river.

So much for conversing.

"Evidence?" he repeated after the silence threatened to collapse in on itself.

"Against me?" I could answer a question with a question, too.

"Besides . . . ?"

Great. Now he was putting me into the position of summarizing the clues implicating me. I grumbled, "The victim was found in my locked yard. My coat had a small blood smear. My canoe paddle was supposedly the murder weapon."

"And you threatened to kill the victim."

I waved my hand in a gesture of dismissal. "That's just one of those things people say without meaning it. I didn't. Mean it, I mean." Gartener tended to bring out the worst in my conversational abilities.

He pondered the ice floating down the river for what seemed like another hour or two.

I remained resolutely mute. I'd read about policemen. They created long silences to tempt the unwary into filling the empty air with confessions. But I had nothing to confess, so I simply watched the river and waited for him to speak. He'd have to, eventually. Or maybe he'd simply leave, and I could phone Trooper Smallwood and engage in a real conversation.

Finally, I broke down and filled the silence, as he probably knew I would. "You have to tell me what the rest of the evidence is. I should be allowed to defend myself."

"You may get your chance. We expect to wrap this case up in a couple of days."

"I didn't think they could match fingerprints on that button that fast." I could be sarcastic, too.

"That button may have nothing to do with

the case."

"If the fingerprints were mine, it wouldn't, since it was found on my property. But I never touched that button, and the fingerprints will be someone else's. Find the person who's missing that button, and you'll have a real suspect. Even," I asserted with no care for self-preservation, "if that person is a police officer."

The guy had a real poker face. "Who's this person who told you all about the drying rate of oil-based paint?"

"Clay Fraser of Fraser Construction."

That annoying state trooper got out his notebook and wrote in it. A reminder to re-interrogate Clay, probably. Great.

I told Gartener about the aqua paint I'd seen on Rhonda Dunkle's thumb. He wrote that down.

I added, "I've seen her in a black pickup truck that could be the one Uncle Allen and I saw after Mike's attack."

"Describe the truck you and Detective DeGlazier saw. Black, you said?"

"It was the middle of the night, so I couldn't be sure. Streetlights were on. It was definitely dark, but could have been dark blue or brown or . . ."

"Red?"

"Not bright red like Clay Fraser's truck."

And like my face suddenly became. "And it didn't have writing on the door. His does."

He had about a million other questions about the truck. Obviously, I had not been paying sufficient attention to subtle variations in truck styling.

"What about the truck's cab?" he asked. "Standard two-door, or extended?"

"I don't know, but nothing about it seemed unusual, other than it was going more slowly than most people might drive at that time of the morning. Maybe Unc . . . Detective DeGlazier could give a better description." I asked again, as reasonably as possible, "So now that you've seen and heard the additional evidence I've found, how about telling me what supposed new evidence you have against me? Does what I just showed you refute it?"

Gartener really seemed to have a fondness for staring at slabs of ice on a river. Finally, he said, "The button and the paint on your porch and on your friend's hand —"

I shot out a quick denial. "She's not my friend."

He went on as if I hadn't spoken. "— could have a bearing on the case, but none of it refutes our latest evidence against you."

"What *was* it?" Wind blew hair into my mouth. Frustrated, I wiped it away.

After another maddening spell of river watching, he said, "We found something else extremely interesting."

"What?"

"One of those little aluminum dog tags that vets hand out when dogs get rabies shots."

It was my turn to dole out the silent treatment. I was afraid to guess what he was talking about, or what it might have to do with me. My mind churned through possibilities.

"Strangely enough, when I contacted the vet who issued it, she said the tag belonged to one of your dogs," he added.

"I didn't know that one of the dogs lost a tag." The dogs had definitely had their ID tags when Clay brought them to me.

His voice hard, Gartener shot out, "What was your dog doing in Mike's backyard?"

Playing there when Haylee and I were snooping inside Mike's house. Good thing it was too dark for Trooper Gartener to see my flaming face. "Nothing," I managed. "Mike must have taken the tag when he opened my gate." I warmed to my lies. "Now we know for certain that he's the one who let the dogs escape. Maybe it was worse than that. Maybe he was trying to steal my dogs, and all he managed to grab was a rabies tag." Was I babbling?

"Though the ground was frozen in Kraw-bach's backyard, dog claws managed to penetrate it. Odd, isn't it? It looked like a couple of dogs had been fighting around Mike's clothes pole."

It wasn't hard to sound shocked. "He did steal them, then, and they got away." Had I told the police what time the dogs had gone missing? Had Clay told them when and where he picked them up? If so, Gartener would know I was lying. Barely breathing, I threw in the hard, cold truth. "I did not kill Mike Krawbach. We have to find out who did." I crossed my arms.

"You stay out of it," he ordered. "Leave the investigating to law enforcement."

I didn't say anything, but my thoughts seemed loud enough that even he might have heard them. *Not if law enforcement is trying to convict the wrong person. Like me . . .*

"Don't worry," he said. "We're checking everything."

"Good. Then you'll find the murderer." More likely, they'd take the easiest route, arrest me, and go home happy. I wasn't bitter, or anything. I asked, "Are we done here?"

"You are. I'll wait for the techs."

I didn't want to give him the key to Blueberry Cottage. I told him I'd lock it

238

later tonight after the techs were done, then tramped up the hill.

The first thing I did when I went inside was examine the dogs' collars. Sure enough, Sally didn't have her rabies tag. I should have checked more carefully around Mike's clothes pole before we fled his yard Wednesday night. Had we left any other evidence of our presence at Mike's?

The second thing I did was fill a mug with cider, heat it in the microwave, and carry it and a plate of cookies back down the hill.

Maybe Trooper Gartener's long johns weren't bulletproof, but they must have been waterproof. Or his uniform trousers were. He had brushed some of the slush off my porch stairs and was sitting, his chin in his hands and his elbows on the knees, on a wet step. He leaped up when I came around the corner of Blueberry Cottage. I had probably startled him.

I thrust the cider and cookies at him. "I thought you might get cold and hungry."

He took them from me and set them on the step. "The team should be here soon."

Why had I bothered? He would probably have the forensics lab test the cider and cookies for every toxin known to man before he tried them.

I went back to the apartment, locked the

239

door, called Haylee, and told her the police had found Sally's rabies tag and signs of the dogs' wrestling match at Mike's, and that I hoped Gartener believed my story that Mike had stolen the dogs and they got away.

"Maybe he did."

I pictured the unbending state trooper. "I doubt it. Anyway, last I knew, investigators are at Mike's place."

"I guess we'd better not go back there." She sounded disappointed, then perked up. "Until after the police are done, some time when there's no snow."

"And no mud," I added.

"The police may miss something. Like where Mike hid his key."

And, assuming we weren't locked in some dark dungeon somewhere, we could go back and find more clues to the identity of Mike's killer. "I like the way you think. See you at Opal's!"

While the dogs and I ate supper, a dark van appeared on the trail beside Blueberry Cottage. Someone set up a brace of temporary outdoor lighting. In the end, Mike might get his way. The tech guys looked about to dismantle Blueberry Cottage bit by bit.

I wasn't going to depress myself by watching them. Opal's storytelling event should cheer me up.

18

Lights were turned down to only a glimmer inside Tell a Yarn. The door was unlocked. I tiptoed inside and kicked off my boots. Opal's store was a treasure chest of jewel hues. Yarns of every shade were arranged in niches along both side walls. Opal had fat yarns, thin yarns, soft yarns, wools, acrylics, nylons, cottons. She also sold tapestry yarns for needlepoint and crewel work, and crochet cottons for bedspreads, lace, and tablecloths. She even sold small hanks of embroidery floss for those patient enough to embroider by hand.

Racks displayed knitting needles and crochet hooks in every size. She had oodles of pattern books for fabulous knitting and crocheting projects. Completed sweaters and blankets hung from the ceiling.

An urge to learn how to knit and crochet flared in my brain.

Touching yarn, I followed the sound of

voices to the back room, which doubled as Opal's dining room and her classroom, where her students knit, crocheted, and, I'd been told, gossiped around a gleaming mahogany dining table. Logs burning in the fireplace and an assortment of pillar candles provided the only lighting in the room, making it eerie with a campfire-like atmosphere.

Opal sat in one of her chairs at the table. "Come sit down, Willow. Sorry I can't get up." Lucy, a gray tabby cat, was draped around Opal's neck like a purring fur collar. Opal's knitting needles flashed and clacked around a mound of dark gray wool.

Naomi was between Opal and a woman who was about Haylee's and my age. Naomi stopped knitting and patted the woman's arm. "Willow, have you met Karen? She's Elderberry Bay's librarian."

"I've been meaning to drop in at the library," I admitted, "and get a library card."

Humor glinted from her dark eyes. "Let me guess. Every time you tried, we were closed."

I hung my head like a naughty schoolgirl. "I haven't tried often."

Karen's laugh reminded me of bells ringing. "I'm the librarian for five small libraries, each open about one day a week. You can find me at the Elderberry Bay Library

Wednesday evenings and Saturday afternoons."

"It's like a bookmobile," Opal quipped, "except that the books stay and the librarian is mobile."

Karen picked up a crochet hook and began working at a mint green baby sweater. "Some folks around here remember when Elderberry Bay was served by a bookmobile."

Edna bustled in from Opal's kitchen bearing a tray holding a teapot, mugs, a sugar bowl, and a creamer. "It's herbal," she said. "And won't keep us awake." The electric blue of her hair and the shiny silver sequins attached to her creamy vest might, however.

Haylee, in another of her classically tailored suits, this one navy, followed Edna with a plate of date and walnut bread, sliced and generously buttered.

Naomi carefully removed her jacket, allowing us to admire the way she'd made it by cutting a sweatshirt up the front and decorating it with quilt patches and appliqués. "Karen's a wonderful storyteller," she said.

Karen smiled at the cat, who was meowing and rubbing her face against Opal's. "I love telling stories, but I wouldn't foist them on the group every week. I like to hear

244

the others."

Opal lowered her knitting away from Lucy's paw. "Tonight's storyteller hasn't phoned. She should be here by now."

Bells near the front door rang. Boots landed on the floor.

Seconds later, Smythe Castor, beaming in his bee-stinger stocking cap, matching yellow and black striped socks, black jeans and turtleneck, and his bright yellow parka, carried a large cardboard box into the room. "Here, ladies. On a night like this, you might like a little bottled summer."

He presented each of us with a glass jar shaped like an old-fashioned domed beehive. "Lavender honey," he explained. "From my bees and my lavender."

"Lovely," Opal murmured, holding her jar up to the firelight.

"I bottled too much for the Honey Makers' Conference." He really was sweeter than his honey. Some folks might have pretended they'd made the treats just for us.

Haylee looked as worried as I felt. Did Smythe know about his cousin's death?

He removed his cap. "Sorry I'm late." His curly blond hair added to his angelic appearance. "The road from Erie is pretty bad."

245

Naomi's face lengthened with sympathy. "Smythe, I'm so sorry —"

He waved her condolences aside. "Not a problem. My pickup has winter tires and four-wheel drive. I didn't land in the ditch, but lots of other vehicles spun out."

Hoping the Threadville tour bus had made it home, I crossed my fingers and slid my hands under my thighs.

"No," Naomi began again, only to be interrupted by the jingling doorbell and more thumping feet.

In her snowmobile suit, Aunt Betty burst in. "Smythe Castor! Don't you ever answer your phone messages?" Rhonda, her hood tied around her face, hovered in the shadows behind Aunt Betty.

Smythe held his hands out, offering the newcomers jars of honey. "I haven't been home yet. I just got back to town in time for tonight's Tell a Yarn party."

They paid no attention to his hands. They stared at his face. Rhonda wore her usual vinegary expression, but Aunt Betty appeared to be struggling with emotion. Horror, maybe.

Opal stood up without disturbing the languid cat around her neck. "Welcome, ladies, to storytelling. We have it every Friday night at eight." She was adept at not quite pointing out that it was now about eight fifteen. "It was good of you to come out on a night like this. Grab a seat and a mug of chamomile tea and —"

Aunt Betty interrupted her. "We need to talk to Smythe." She pointed toward the front door. "Come outside where we can speak privately, Smythe."

His brow lowered and his lips thinned, but apparently he was used to having Aunt Betty order him around. He replaced the annoyed expression with a neutral one, put the honey that Rhonda and Aunt Betty had rejected into the carton, and shoved the carton toward Opal.

Aunt Betty marched him out of Opal's dining room and into the front sales area of Tell a Yarn.

Behind them, Rhonda whined, "We recognized your truck outside, Smythe. We've been trying for days to reach you."

We heard him shuffle into his boots. The front door slammed and everything became quiet except for Lucy's purring and the ticking of the antique clock on Opal's mantle.

Naomi covered her mouth. "The poor boy." She sighed between her fingers. "He doesn't know yet. About his cousin."

Edna raked her fingers through her sapphire blue curls. "Those two women wouldn't be my first choice for bringing bad news."

Opal stroked Lucy. "They did seem eager to impart it, didn't they?"

Karen twisted a ring on her right hand. "I hope he takes it okay."

"Who are those women?" Haylee asked, staring at me like she'd already guessed.

"They're the two women I told you about who were" — I didn't want to say snooping — "*shopping* at In Stitches yesterday. They came back today. Have they visited you, too?"

"I've never seen them before," Edna stated categorically, and the others said they hadn't, either.

Apparently, Rhonda's and Aunt Betty's sleuthing for Uncle Allen only involved checking up on me. Interesting. Alarming, too.

Karen took a measuring tape from her bag and straightened it against a tiny sleeve. "The older one comes to the library. She's Betty DeGlazier. Ever since she married Uncle Allen, she's been called Aunt Betty."

So it *was* her I'd talked to on the phone.

Edna had strung substantial glass beads onto her yarn and was knitting a bead into nearly every stitch, which would make the resulting garment weigh a ton. Beads trailed

248

down her yarn, clinking together. She turned to Karen. "Who's that other woman who was in here with Aunt Betty?" She drew her lips down in an excellent imitation of Rhonda's snarl. "You know, Smiley." She must have hoped to hear Karen laugh again.

It worked. Karen's laugh really did sound like bells. "I don't know who Smiley was."

"Her charge card says Rhonda Dunkle," I contributed.

"Dunkle," Karen repeated. "She doesn't have a library card."

Opal jockeyed a slice of buttered nut bread around dangling kitty paws. "Then she's definitely beyond the pale." Ignoring Lucy's vigorous licking of a buttery paw, she turned serious. "Locals, including Uncle Allen, seem to think Willow did Mike in."

Karen flashed me a look of sympathy from under her lashes. "Don't let Uncle Allen frighten you."

I waved my hand in front of my face. "He doesn't. I've already decided that if he succeeds in sending me to prison, I'll do my time embroidering flowers on my fellow prisoners' uniforms."

Naomi gasped. "Don't even think that way, Willow!"

"He can't believe you're a murderer," Karen agreed. "That's preposterous. There can't be many people around here who are nutty enough to believe that."

Only the entire DeGlazier family, who had run Elderberry Bay for generations, and their friends. And, although I didn't want to admit it, possibly at least one state trooper.

Edna beamed expectant brown eyes at Karen and smiled encouragingly. "Do you have any idea who might have killed Mike? You must know nearly everyone around here." Any minute now, she'd bring out her notebook of clues.

"Karen knows everyone who *reads*," Opal commented darkly. "She won't know murderers and nutty locals. Did Mike visit the library often?"

Karen shook her curls. "Never, while I've been librarian. I've heard about him. He had lots of enemies," Karen said. "Since it looks like our storyteller's not going to make it, shall I tell you a story?"

We all said yes.

"Once upon a time . . ." She pitched her voice to a spooky octave that made me shiver. "Like about last winter, there was a fisherman we'll call Pete."

If my ears could have swiveled toward Karen, they would have. Clay had said that Uncle Allen's brother, Pete DeGlazier, had obtained a permit from Mike Krawbach to erect a gazebo on the flood plain.

Karen looked at each of us in turn, an experienced storyteller making eye contact with her audience. "He had a fishing hut out on the ice. He filled it with all the latest fish-finding technology and stocked it with food and beer and a heater to keep them from freezing. He put in a generator and a ginormous flat-screen TV. The lumber in that hut would have been enough to build a garage. Pete and his buddies had a great time out there in that ice mansion. Last winter was long and cold, and it seemed it could never end. But as April neared, other fishermen hauled their huts off the ice. Not Pete. He hired an enterprising young man we'll call Mike —"

Edna clapped a hand over her mouth. "Uh-oh."

Karen flashed her a smile. "It's only a story, remember."

Edna nodded obediently. Haylee's and Opal's mouths developed identical twitches.

Karen continued, "Mike had a brand-new, powerful snowmobile. He offered to drag the hut and all of its contents ashore. The lazy fisherman agreed. Now here's the strange part. Mike and his snowmobile were seen on the ice near that fishing palace, but Pete never received his belongings. The ice

251

melted almost overnight. Some folks swore that the hut was gone several hours before the ice broke up. No one could prove it."

Bells jingled faintly in the front room. Smythe returning after hearing about his cousin?

"Come in," Opal called. No answer.

Haylee and I raced to the front of the store. Nobody.

I opened the door. Boot prints, sloppy wet in the slush, led from the front door to a dark pickup truck pulling away from the curb. The truck roared away into the night.

"Smythe's?" I guessed.

Haylee backed into the store. "No. His is the color of honey."

That figured. I wouldn't have been surprised, though, if she'd told me it was yellow and black striped.

I followed her inside. She turned on a bank of lights. Our boots lay where we'd kicked them off.

Beside them, two very wet spots showed where slush had melted from someone's boots while he or she stood in the darkened yarn shop.

Listening, no doubt, to our every word.

19

Who had been eavesdropping on us? Trooper Gartener?

One of Uncle Allen's many amateur sleuths?

A dark pickup truck. I shuddered. Mike's murderer? We had mentioned Uncle Allen's belief that I might be guilty of Mike's murder, but we hadn't said anything that would make a murderer want to silence us, had we?

I followed Haylee past all those lovely yarns to the dining room.

The mothers waggled their eyebrows, and I could have sworn that Edna wiggled her ears. Even the cat's green eyes broadcast hints and suggestions.

Haylee only shrugged. "No one was there."

Karen transferred her questioning gaze from Haylee's face to mine.

I attempted to look innocent.

Haylee must have given her mothers wordless signals about waiting for Karen to leave before discussing what we'd discovered. Naomi yawned. Edna yawned. Opal made a show of hiding a yawn.

Karen yawned, commented that she was pooped, and left.

Edna asked, "What was it you and Willow didn't want Karen to know, Haylee?"

Haylee told them, "When we heard the door close, someone was leaving, not arriving. Someone had been hanging around, listening to us."

Edna put her fists on her hips. "Aunt Betty or Rhonda must have stayed behind after they dragged Smythe out. Nasty, nasty women!"

"Or they let someone in," Haylee suggested. "Whoever it was drove off in a black pickup truck. Didn't you and Uncle Allen see one shortly after Mike was attacked, Willow?"

"Yes."

Edna wailed, "Almost everyone around here drives black pickups. They probably buy identical trucks so they can commit crimes and be mistaken for someone else."

Opal said, "The murderer might have come here tonight to find out how much we know."

Edna retorted, "We don't know anything."

Haylee giggled.

Edna corrected herself. "Anything about the *murder*."

"Maybe we'll learn more tomorrow night," Opal said. "At the roast beef dinner. I'll drive. Meet at the parking lot at quarter to six?"

"How about in my shop," Edna said. "We can cut through it to the parking lot."

We all agreed, but I noticed that Edna seemed too excited about the opportunity to question Mike's buddies from the ATV club.

I reminded her, "Anyone who has murdered once may murder again, especially if he senses we're closing in on him. If he was spying on us this evening, he may have decided we know something incriminating about him, even though we don't."

Opal, Naomi, and Edna nodded, but they didn't make any verbal promises, and they avoided meeting either Haylee's or my gaze. Their studied lack of expression probably meant they were planning to delve into a dangerous murder investigation, no matter what Haylee and I said.

Haylee and I traded concerned looks. We would have to keep close track of The Three Weird Mothers.

The rest of us left Opal to close her shop. I waved to the others and crossed the icy street. Unfortunately, what looked like ice was nearly frozen water, higher than the tops of my boots. I sloshed down to my apartment and let the dogs out.

The dark van and brace of lights were gone, and plywood covered part of my porch and the doorway leading out to it. On the river, ice chunks ground ominously against each other.

I locked Blueberry cottage, brought the dogs inside, dried them, and went upstairs to work on my prototype stumpwork cornstalks and branches. The dogs curled up underneath the sewing machine while I worked. I burrowed my frozen feet underneath Sally. Her fur was damp, but she was a great little heater, anyway.

Since the cornstalks and branches would be three dimensional and would bend forward from the rest of the wall hanging, parts of the embroidery would show on both sides of the fabric. So, instead of using lingerie thread for the back of my machine embroidery, I filled bobbins with the colors of thread I was using for the top stitching: tan for the cornstalks, and gray for the trees. By the time I finished stitching the cornstalks and trees, it was late, even considering that, on Saturdays, the Threadville boutiques didn't open until ten. The dogs and I clumped downstairs to bed.

When I woke up, it was nearly fifty degrees outside, and ice seemed to be heaping itself higher and higher on the river. Cleaning Sally and Tally after their mud wrestling match was more fun than ever. They played tug of war with their towels. As soon as they were almost clean and almost calm, I took the day's cider up to the shop.

Most of the snow was gone from my front yard, and my poor snowman slumped forward, about to lose his head.

A bus rolled into town, and women smiled out at me through its windows. No classes were scheduled, but I didn't mind new busloads of tourists discovering Threadville. And it turned into a great day. One shopper was so excited by my demonstrations and samples that she pulled out a charge card and purchased a sewing and embroidery machine. By the time the last tour bus rumbled away, I had sold more supplies than I would have thought possible, even for a Saturday.

The evening was slightly above freezing. Instead of letting the dogs play in my muddy backyard, I walked them down the street. Although it was only dusk, lights were on in the vacant store. The windows were still papered over, and a new, darker square had appeared in front of the faded newspaper — a building permit, signed by Irv Oslington, mayor and acting zoning commissioner. Uncle Allen must have relayed Edna's hints about the lack of a building permit. I skimmed the notice. There was no proprietor's name.

My two energetic dogs pulled me home. I played with them and their squeaky porcupine until they flopped down for naps, then I changed for the roast beef dinner and teetered in my black high-heeled boots to Buttons and Bows.

As usual, Edna's display of trims and buttons caused me to mentally design about thirty-five new outfits for myself. None of them would compare to Edna's rhinestone-bedecked yellow velvet pants suit and the ribbon-trimmed coat that matched her pale green hair, however, which was probably a good thing.

Opal and Naomi arrived together. Turquoise crocheted pants peeked out beneath Opal's long coat, which, like her hat, was knit in an Aran pattern from thick, off-white wool. Naomi's quilted blue coat flapped open to reveal a pink sashiko-stitched jacket and matching pants, both crafted from heavy raw silk.

When Haylee rushed in, Opal scolded her for dressing too casually in jeans and a sweater.

"Opal, you knit this sweater for me." It was beautiful, red flecked with autumn colors.

Opal frowned at the sweater as if she'd never seen it before. "That must have been a very long time ago."

"About three months." Haylee giggled. "Definitely many sweaters ago, for you."

"The jeans fit you nicely," Naomi complimented her.

Edna, the shortest of us all, complained, "She's all legs." She led us out through her back display room. I sensed that I wasn't the only one longing to linger over designer zippers with crystals for teeth, scissors with pretty pastel flowers printed on their handles, and timesaving gadgets like bias tape makers, pocket forms, and loop turners that could transform a tunnel of cloth into a right-side-out strap in seconds.

Opal's car was in the parking lot behind the boutiques on that side of Lake Street. They had parking. I had a river and a view, a decent trade-off most of the time. "Haylee, Willow, and Naomi, you're the slimmest," Opal said. "You three sit in the backseat."

"I'm not fat," Edna protested. "They're too skinny."

Haylee folded her legs into the seat behind Edna's. "All five of us are just right."

"I'll take the middle," Naomi offered. "I'm shorter than you two."

I sat behind Opal. She drove a couple of miles south to the community center. Its vast lot was nearly filled with pickup trucks, SUVs, and vans. Opal had to park far from the building. As we stepped over half-frozen puddles, Haylee counted ATVs. Seventeen.

It wasn't only the puddles that slowed my steps. A murderer could be in the community hall.

Opal held her palm up as if to catch raindrops. "Mist," she concluded. "I hope it doesn't freeze on the windshield while we're in there."

Haylee pulled the community hall's door open. Warmth and chatter spilled out. We climbed a wide set of stairs to a folding table where a pair of scrubbed and smiling teen-aged girls took our tickets.

Next to them, Irv Oslington, in jeans, white shirt, bolo tie, and tight black suit jacket reached out to grab our hands and give them a hearty shake. He shoved a piece of paper at me. Mike Krawbach's charming smile beamed at me from the page.

Above his photo was a headline.

In Memoriam.

20

Someone had drawn stiff black curtains on the frame around Mike's face.

Beside me, Edna gasped. "I didn't dress for a memorial service!"

Haylee muttered, "Look around you."

Every man in the packed community hall wore jeans. Most wore plaid flannel shirts and baseball caps. A few, like Irv, had dug suit jackets and sports coats out of mothballs and pulled them over muscles made large by farming. Kids in jeans ran, laughed, and played tag between rows of tables and chairs. Most of the women were in jeans, too, making Haylee the most appropriately dressed of the five of us.

We took off our coats and shoved them onto hangers. In their pastels, Opal, Naomi, and Edna blossomed like a flower garden.

"Willow," Edna demanded, "why didn't you tell us it was a memorial service?"

"I didn't know."

"You dressed for it."

I'd worn all black — tall boots, tights, short skirt, and a sweater. Not a speck of embroidery, except for the wavy stripes crisscrossing my handbag. "Luck."

Luck, right. A memorial service for Mike Krawbach, when many of the villagers suspected me of his murder. I wanted to bolt from the community hall.

Edna gripped my elbow so tightly I feared my forearm might pop off. "Courage," she urged. "We're sure to learn something."

Like not to buy tickets from Uncle Allen.

We found seats at one of the tables closest to the door. Haylee sat beside me, with Opal, Naomi, and Edna across from us.

Irv Oslington vaulted onto the stage, tapped the mike, said, "Testing, testing," and raised both arms, palms toward the crowd, for silence.

Haylee and I and half the people in the hall faced the stage, but the other half sat with their backs to it. Turning their chairs around required untangling chair legs and then retangling them, along with sweater sleeves and purse straps. Gradually, the noises in the hall subsided. Pots and pans clanged in the kitchen, and the aromas of gravy and cooked onions and carrots promised more than a memorial service.

Irv announced, "The loss of a young life is always a sad occasion." Feedback screeched. Folks closest to the huge speakers covered their ears. Irv fiddled with the mike, then spoke again. "Tonight, we're celebrating the life of a fine young man." More feedback.

People yelled, "Move away from the mike!"

Irv's face became brilliant red, and I saw him as the easily angered teenager he must have been in Mike's gang. He told us what a perfect man Mike Krawbach had been. Hardworking. Upstanding. Devoted to friends.

That seemed to be the signal for friends to parade to the podium and deliver a similar speech. Even Uncle Allen, in full uniform and policeman's regalia, including holsters, nightstick, and handcuffs, gave his version of the evening's stock eulogy. Mike had apparently been a saint.

If we weren't fed soon, we might all reach sainthood earlier than expected.

Dr. Wrinklesides might not be a saint, but he looked particularly cherubic in a pink shirt and baby blue tie. He switched the mike off and sang. His deep, rich voice easily filled the hall. I wasn't sure if this dirge was the one he'd sung in my backyard after

Mike died, but it sent chills through me. The doctor could really sing. He kept it short, then flicked on the mike for the next man.

This guy looked like a slightly younger version of Uncle Allen, so it didn't surprise me when he introduced himself as Pete De-Glazier, Uncle Allen's brother, who had recently moved with his dear wife Mona to his beloved Elderberry Bay.

People clapped.

Haylee nudged me.

Mike had granted Pete DeGlazier a building permit for a gazebo close to the river. Was this the Pete in the story Karen had related about the lazy fisherman whose fishing palace, generator, TV, and cases of beer could have been stolen by Mike Krawbach?

Nodding his head up and down with every phrase he uttered, like he was encouraging us to agree with him, Pete told us how to buy raffle tickets for a brand-new ATV. We could also — nod, nod — drop pocket change into the humungous pickle jar on the table beside the podium. The night's proceeds would be donated to Mike's favorite causes. The crowd broke into loud applause, cheers, whistles. Boots pounded the floor.

I applauded politely even though I suspected Mike's favorite causes didn't involve rescuing puppies and hugging trees.

Sure enough, Pete added, "Members of the ATV club will continue to press for changes to the law until the sportsmen of this community can enjoy our beautiful little spot on this planet as much as everyone else can."

Although he kept nodding, he sounded angry, and I could have sworn he sent a spiteful glare to the back of the room where Opal, Edna, and Naomi glowed in their pastel finery.

"Smile," Haylee reminded me.

I obliged, but I wasn't about to contribute more than I already had to anyone's campaign to bulldoze Blueberry Cottage.

Luckily, Pete's presentation was the last one before the people nearest the stage were told they could line up at the buffet. Rumbling and squeaking, the corrugated door to the kitchen counter rolled up, miraculously revealing steaming chafing dishes.

When our table could finally join the lineup, I discovered that Karen the librarian had been at the table next to us. We chatted with her in shouts to make ourselves heard over the hall's clamor. The next thing I knew, Herb was standing beside me.

"Are you back for seconds already?" Karen hollered at him. She was probably thinking the same thing I was. How could we offer to help him carry his plate without insulting him? Or should we offer at all? His left arm was fine.

He said he'd only come over to keep us company. Smythe playfully shouldered him aside, and Edna, Opal, and Naomi backed up, obviously giving the young folks space to talk to each other. Smythe wasn't wearing his bee-stinger stocking cap and had used mousse or something in an attempt to tame his rowdy blond curls. Fortunately, he hadn't succeeded.

Karen asked him loudly if he really sang to his bees.

"I dance for them, too." He demonstrated a wild combination of foot stomping and arm flapping.

We laughed.

Herb leaned close and yelled into my ear, "Save a dance for me at the fish fry dinner dance tomorrow?"

Another dinner?

Herb pointed at flyers taped to the wall. Tomorrow night's fish fry dinner dance was sponsored by the nature club. Opal, Naomi, and Edna were ogling the flyers and sending Haylee and me pointed messages with their eyes.

"Okay," I said to Herb, nodding in case he couldn't hear me.

Probably content that Haylee and I had understood their latest nonverbal hints, Opal and her cohorts attempted to engage several older farmers in conversation. The men leaned away from them.

I couldn't come up with questions to ask Herb without sounding like I was accusing him of murder. Fortunately, I didn't have to try for long. Wails and howls burst from the sound system. A man in a western shirt and cowboy hat tamed the speakers, then announced that he was tonight's disk jockey.

Dance music boomed. Giving up on conversing, Herb and I moved closer to Haylee, Karen, and Smythe. Herb appeared to ask Haylee something. To save him a dance tomorrow night? Smythe crowded between them, shook his head, and took Haylee's arm. She looked surprised for a second, then nodded.

Herb moved to Karen and whispered in her ear. She smiled, showing her dimples. He gave her one of his big grins, twinkly eyes and all.

Everyone was pairing up with dates for tomorrow night except me. Although telling myself not to, I searched for Clay among seated diners. He would be head and shoulders above most of them. I didn't see him.

At the buffet counter, apron-garbed men and women teased each other as they filled plates and handed them to us. I hadn't needed to worry about getting enough to eat.

We said good-bye to Smythe, Herb, and Karen, and returned to our table with our overloaded plates. At least three hundred people were in the large room. Was a killer among them?

Across the table, Edna shouted questions to the woman next to her. The woman shouted back.

I hollered at the elderly man beside me, "How long have you lived in Elderberry Bay?"

He stabbed a fork into his baked potato. "Yes, very good."

"Is your wife one of the cooks?"

"Love beef and potatoes," he answered. "Always have."

Coming tonight had been a mistake. We wouldn't learn anything.

And tomorrow night's fish fry dinner dance might be as bad.

Edna caught my eye, mouthed an unintelligible phrase, and focused on something behind me. I turned to look. Ladies' room. When I faced her again, she was standing up. She covered her ears with her hands for a second, removed them, shook her head, and inched past Opal.

I poked a finger to my chest and mouthed, "Shall I come?"

She, Opal, and Naomi shook their heads. Edna held up one finger and pointed at herself, then at Naomi with two fingers, then at Haylee with three, me with four, and Opal with five.

Haylee translated. "We'll take turns. Edna first. Then Naomi, then me, then you, then Opal." Dramatically, she covered her ears and shook her head.

Okay, I got it. The room was too noisy with deafening music and hollering people. We would do our sleuthing, one by one, in the ladies' room.

What fun.

Edna marched off. The rest of us lined up at the dessert table. Colored lights flashed and strobed.

I centered one largish piece of vanilla fudge on my plate. I liked my sugar in one immense hit. Back at the table, I nibbled at the fudge and sternly told myself not to go back for more, no matter how yummy it was. Naomi and Haylee did their sleuthing stints in the restroom, and then it was my turn.

How was I supposed to find clues in a restroom? I pushed open the swinging door. After the dim lighting in the dining hall, I was blinded by bare fluorescent fixtures on the ceiling and hot pink paint on concrete walls and metal stalls. The door shut behind me, blocking out most of the racket from the dining hall.

No one was at the sinks, but boots showed underneath two of the stall doors. Probably the best way to stay in here long enough to eavesdrop was to take up residence in a stall.

I did, which left only one empty stall. If other women came in and had to wait, I'd give up my post. Actually, there were other reasons I wanted to leave. One was the buzz of the lights. Another was the mothbally room deodorizer.

The silence almost made me want to scream, *Please, somebody, confess to killing Mike so I can get back to my friends.* I dug around in my bag for pen and paper. If anyone in the ladies' room was going to confess, I would write it all down.

Finally one of the other women must have been similarly unable to stand the lack of conversation. She cleared her throat.

I held my pen at the ready.

"When's her baby due?" she asked.

"Not until August."

271

End of conversation. Nancy Drew would have had it easier. Someone would have written the murderer's name on the door.

Many messages had been scratched into the stall's paint, but none of the limericks, drawings, or phone numbers seemed to have a bearing on Mike's death.

The other two women washed their hands and left the ladies' room.

Ready to make my own escape, I stood up and poked my finger through the hole where the knob must have originally been. Just then, the ladies' room door opened. Music crashed into the room.

I backed up, plunked onto the toilet, and fished through my bag for the paper and pen.

The door to the ladies' room closed. Silence.

My fingers closed on the pen and paper. Was anyone in here with me? I bent forward and peeked out the hole in the latch. I saw only part of a sink. Cautiously, I exhaled my pent-up breath.

It was too soon to feel relief. Someone *had* entered the ladies' room. Stiletto heels banged on floor tiles. Toward my hideout.

I yanked the paper and pen out of my bag again.

"They have their nerve, coming to Mike's

wake," she announced in a thin, snarling whine.

I knew that voice. Rhonda.

21

Was Rhonda whining because Haylee, The Three Weird Mothers, and I had bought tickets for what she called "Mike's wake"?

"Yeah," another woman sobbed. "I can't believe we'll never see him again." It wasn't Aunt Betty. This woman had a younger, higher voice.

Rhonda's turn. "How could they have *done* this to us?"

"He was so great, so fun, so alive . . ."

"So gorgeous."

"He loved everything beautiful."

Mike? He hadn't loved Blueberry Cottage.

Rhonda sighed and went on, "Remember those jewelry boxes he made?" Her voice took on a gloating tone. "I think he only made those for his really special friends."

The other woman breathed, "Ahh, yes. Treasure chests, he called them. Mine has the cutest little —" She broke off.

Rhonda didn't say anything.

The other woman went on, "Remember all his other artwork? His woodcarvings?"

Had he made wooden buttons and given them away to all of his *really special* friends, too? Rhonda?

The other woman sobbed, "You just know he was about to settle down and make some woman very happy."

Rhonda paused before answering, "Yeah."

"When is Uncle Allen going to arrest his murderers?"

"It can't be too soon for me."

"I know someone whose brother's girlfriend works for the FBI or something."

The woman's voice got louder, as if she had turned away from the sinks and mirrors and was talking at the door of my stall. I wished I'd pulled my boots up where no one could see them. Now that I had something to take notes about, I didn't want to write for fear Rhonda and her friend would hear my scratchings and guess I was jotting down what they said. I should have chosen a stall with a complete latch, if one existed. Any moment, an eye would press itself against the hole in the door.

"If Uncle Allen and the state police don't arrest them soon," the woman continued, "I'll call my friend. The FBI will put them behind bars right away."

Rhonda's friend's voice became venomous. "If I could get my hands on Mike's murderer, like if she was in here, I'd make her sorry she ever laid eyes on him."

Did they hope to frighten me with their threats?

They were succeeding.

Had Rhonda or her friend been last night's intruder in Tell a Yarn?

"They're not getting away with it," Rhonda said. "Not if the respectable people in this village have anything to do with it."

The mothball fumes were going to make me sneeze. Pressing my index finger hard against my upper lip, I dropped my pen. It landed with a click that sounded like thunder, rolled under the door and into the main room, probably to Rhonda's feet.

Stiletto heels hammered into floor tiles again. The ladies' room door opened. The music reached new heights of throbbing. My head did, too. The door closed, shutting out the din from the main hall.

Listening to lights buzzing and faucets dripping, I waited for about half a minute, then fled.

When I returned to our table, Opal stood up. I shook my head at her. She firmed her lips and marched off, duty-bound to take her turn at sleuthing. I moved my chair so I could watch the ladies' room. I didn't recognize any of the women who went in and out.

I was about to fly to Opal's rescue when she emerged. Edna, Naomi, and Haylee gave her questioning looks. She shook her head, pointed toward the front door, and imitated someone shrugging into a coat. I was getting really good at understanding these women. Time to leave.

As we donned our coats, I eyed the hundreds of coats still in the coat rack. Was one of them missing one handmade wooden button? Checking all of them would be both time-consuming and extremely obvious. I followed the others outside.

Rain poured down. A cell phone pressed to his ear, Uncle Allen huddled against the wall underneath a porch light.

"You folks stay here," Opal offered. "I'll bring the car around."

"That's okay —" I started.

Edna held me back, rolling her eyes toward Uncle Allen. I nodded my understanding. While Opal fetched her car, the rest of us were to spy on him. Opal tore off into the rain. Standing very still, I tried to hear over rain pounding on the metal porch roof. Uncle Allen didn't appear to be speaking. Listening, maybe. His coat had a new button where one had been missing. The new one was plastic, not wood, and almost matched the other buttons. He beckoned to us.

Uh-oh. Rhonda's friend's brother's girl-friend had arranged for the FBI to arrest us already?

He spoke directly to me. "Ice on the river's breaking up. That cottage of yours is likely to flood." His eyes brightened. "Or get washed away. And you won't get permission to build a new one on a flood plain." He raised his forefinger toward the porch roof, and, presumably, toward the sky spewing water over everything. "Couldn't be a better tribute to Mike."

I opened my mouth to retort that no one could steal the land beneath the cottage from me.

Edna forced herself between Uncle Allen and me. "Did you get fingerprints from that button?"

He frowned. "They couldn't find even a partial. But they did discover that the button matched the buttons on Mike's coat. *Two* of them were missing, not just one." He eyed us suspiciously.

"Aha!" Edna said. "You find Mike's other missing button, and you'll find a killer."

Uncle Allen said what I was thinking.

"Not necessarily." He narrowed his eyes at her. "You have more buttons than anyone else for miles around."

I was going to have to keep Edna out of jail, too?

Opal's car pulled up beside the porch steps. Naomi grabbed Edna's arm. "C'mon. We're late."

"For what?" Edna asked, for once not cluing in to hints from her friends.

Haylee answered, "Beauty sleep."

Edna made a rude snorting noise, but she came along.

The puddles in the parking lot had grown and deepened. Was Blueberry Cottage really in danger?

Edna hadn't missed everything. As soon as we were all in the car, she asked, "What's up?"

Naomi leaned forward on her tenuous perch between Haylee and me. "Sandbags. We all have fabrics we can spare. And more than enough sewing machines to go around. We'll make sandbags, fill them at the beach, and place them around Willow's cottage."

"Don't be silly," I said. "The river must have flooded lots of times during the past eighty years. That cottage stood its ground."

Haylee peeked around Naomi at me. "Never argue with The Three Weird Mothers. It would be like arguing with the river. If they decide to do something, they're going to do it, no matter what."

"They haven't decided," I countered. "And they're not about to. We'd be up all night, and Sundays are busy in Threadville."

"Yes, we have decided," Edna declared. "Haven't we, girls."

Opal's windshield wipers zipped back and forth, with limited success. She strained forward. "We can sew all night."

"We've done it lots of times," Naomi agreed. "We love sewing."

"Not *sand*bags," I scoffed. "Where's the fun in that?"

"Where's the fun in watching your darling little cottage drift down the river?" Edna asked sweetly. "I'm sure we all have fabrics in our stashes that we'd be glad to donate. These will be the prettiest sandbags ever."

"The river may not flood," I tried.

Opal slowed through a puddle covering most of the road. "That's optimistic."

My next ploy was changing the subject. I told them about my experience in the ladies' room and the threats that Rhonda and her friend had aimed at my stall door.

Haylee said, "After you went in there, Rhonda and an equally mean-looking woman talked and gestured for a long time outside the room before they followed you in."

Edna chirped, "They must have been plotting what to say for your benefit. Uttering threats is against the law. You should report them."

Haylee gurgled with laughter. "How are we going to explain to Uncle Allen about snooping on other women in the john?"

Edna got all huffy. "We wouldn't need to. It's none of his business. Or the state police's, either."

After Opal parked behind Tell a Yarn, the other four women insisted on coming to my yard to assess the river. They didn't want to track through my store, so I unlocked the gate, and we slipped and slid down the mud-slicked hill.

Uncle Allen hadn't lied. The river looked to be about two feet above its normal level, and mini icebergs battered against one another in the rushing water.

I wanted my friends to get some sleep. "It's not that bad," I said. "The river's still almost a foot below the trail." *But at this rate . . .*

Opal clucked with disapproval. "It's best to be prepared. Now, how shall we do this? We'll want to be together while we sew."

Haylee wiped wet hair out of her eyes. "I

have the biggest shop, and lots of unsold fabrics that I need to get rid of. Plus my classroom has enough sewing machines, so you won't have to bring your own. Or scissors or thread. Just come as soon as you're ready."

"It's after nine," I pointed out.

Naomi patted my arm. "We can get lots done and still have time to sleep."

Make, fill, and pile sandbags in only a few hours?

But Haylee was right. There was no arguing with The Three Weird Mothers. Totally determined, they marched up the hill and out through my gate. I locked it behind them, then supervised the dogs' outing, as short and mudless as possible. When they were inside and reasonably clean and dry, I hauled a surprisingly large number of remnants from my stash.

I kissed the dogs good night, then carried the fabrics up to my shop, where I turned on lights and collected the partially used spools of embroidery thread I'd been accumulating, all different colors. Embroidery thread wasn't as strong as sewing thread, but the stitching had to hold for only a couple of days. And I'd be contributing something to the enterprise besides labor.

Through a blur of rain pattering on my

282

front windows, I made out brightly lit windows across the street in The Stash. The sandbag seamstresses must be gathering.

A gust of wind blew the front door open. Last I knew, that door had been shut. And locked.

22

My heart rate doubled. I knew I had locked the front door when I'd left for the roast beef dinner.

Glancing nervously outside in case someone was on my porch, I made my way to the open door. The glass section of the door was unbroken, but the metal framing it and the jamb were both dented near the latch. The deadbolt wouldn't keep the door closed, let alone locked.

Quickly, I checked my display of sewing and embroidery machines. None were missing. The storeroom where I kept new machines was locked. I looked inside, anyway. Everything seemed fine.

I dialed Uncle Allen. He was probably in the community hall again, contributing to Mike's favorite causes. I left him a message, adding, "I'll be across the street at The Stash."

I phoned Clay. He answered on the first

ring. "Willow!" He sounded glad to hear my voice, and despite being stressed, I smiled.

I told him about my door and asked him if he could fix it. My breathless request sounded needy. I backtracked. "I'm not sure when Uncle Allen will get here, and he should see the damage first."

"I'll come over now, anyway. Are Sally and Tally okay?"

"They were shut in the apartment while I was gone and were their usual selves when I returned, like they hadn't noticed anything unusual. As far as I can tell, nothing's missing. I'm going to close the front door as best I can and go over to Haylee's to work on a . . ." I didn't want to tell him about the sandbags. He might think I was asking him for yet more help. "A sewing project."

Clay promised to meet me at Haylee's.

I went outside, pulled the door shut, and wedged a fold of cardboard into it to keep it in place. Hugging my armload of sewing things, I dashed through pouring rain to The Stash. For once ignoring all the beautiful spring fabrics Haylee had for sale, I jogged toward her classroom, only to be stopped by a horrible ripping sound and an evil cackle.

I almost dropped all my remnants and

spools in the doorway. Haylee, Opal, Naomi, and Edna all wore wigs. Long, straight black hair. Witches' wigs.

"I love this," Edna crowed, ripping about eighteen inches of yellow calico from its bolt. She and her two best friends cackled. Haylee merely rolled her eyes and shook her head.

I couldn't help giggling. "Double, double, toil and trouble?"

Edna let out another huge cackle. "Take this strip and fold it double." She tossed the folded fabric onto a table with others like it, except that some were purple gingham and some were garish Halloween prints.

I envied Haylee that big classroom. Four tables faced each other in a square, with at least one sewing machine or serger on each table, and room for more. Haylee was at a serger, while Naomi and Opal sat at sewing machines. They quickly stitched down the open side of the folded fabrics, then across the bottom. They didn't turn the bags, since it wouldn't matter if the seam allowances showed. They did, however, make certain that the brightest colors would be on the outside.

"Sewing machine or serger?" Haylee asked me. Her black wig was slightly askew.

"Sewing machine. I wouldn't know what

to do if a serger needed new thread."

Haylee laughed triumphantly. "You need to come to my classes."

"And maybe buy a serger from you, too," I said.

Haylee finished another bag. "That'd be nice."

I let go of my multihued embroidery threads. "I brought these. Help yourselves."

Everyone oohed.

I sat down and began stitching. Someone stomped into Haylee's front room and hollered, "Miss Vanderling!" Uncle Allen. The other four women gasped and whipped off their wigs. Since when did their clowning embarrass them? Haylee, Opal, and Naomi sat on their wigs. Edna looked wildly around, then dropped hers behind long rolls of fabric leaning into a corner. "Miss?" she repeated in a loud and quivering whisper. "Is he here to arrest you?" Her pale green curls had been smashed by the wig.

I held up a placating palm. "It's okay. Someone broke into In Stitches while we were at dinner. I'll explain later." I dashed away from sympathetic groans and startled questions.

I joined a very soggy Uncle Allen beside Haylee's door. From behind us came a loud *riiiiiip.* Uncle Allen swiveled to gaze suspiciously toward Haylee's classroom. "What was that?"

Fortunately, no one cackled. "Fabric ripping."

"I thought they were sewing."

"They are."

"First they sew, then they tear it apart?"

"No, first we rip, then we sew."

He opened the door. "I'll never understand women. Show me this supposed break-in."

Supposed? It was very real. *Stay calm, Willow,* I reminded myself, *don't let him push your buttons.*

The pouring rain seemed to push his. He cursed when we crossed the street. On my front porch, he demanded peevishly, "You went off and left your door hanging open like this?"

"No." I picked up the fold of cardboard. "I wedged it shut, but the wind must have blown it open again." Water dripped down the back of my neck. "Somebody broke in." I led him inside and turned on the lights.

"How'd you know that?

"See the pry marks?"

"You didn't forget your key and have to break in to your own place?"

"Of course not. All of my doors have deadbolts. I can't lock them without keys."

I held them up and jingled them to show that I hadn't lost them, either.

"Anything missing?"

It was hard to spot something that should be in a well-stocked store but wasn't. Scissors? Gold embroidery thread? "Not that I know of."

Clay's truck eased into a puddle beside the curb.

Uncle Allen looked outside. "There's your culprit. He was in and out of this store all the time it was being renovated."

That was hardly surprising, since he'd been the one doing the renovating. Still, I knew not to rule out potential suspects without proof, a lesson Uncle Allen did not seem to have learned.

He persisted. "He may have kept a key to your place. He wasn't at that dinner, was he?"

"I didn't see him. If he had a key, he wouldn't have had to break in."

Ignoring my extremely valid point, Uncle Allen blustered on. "Well, what's he doing here at this hour?"

"I asked him to come fix this after you have a look at it."

"Hmmmph. I thought he was hoping to be clobbered with a canoe paddle."

If I'd had a canoe paddle right then, Uncle

Allen might have gotten the brunt of it.

Clay bounded up onto my porch. "Are you okay, Willow?"

Oh no, not his usual question again. What must he think of me, that I was always in one form of distress or another? "I'm fine."

Uncle Allen pointed at my front door. "I say it was like that."

"It was *not* like that," Clay ground out. "I installed it. And last time I was here, it was intact." He gave Uncle Allen a challenging look. "Have you photographed the damage?"

Grudgingly, Uncle Allen dug a notebook from a pocket. He circled his pen over it, then began writing.

Clay snapped photos with his digital camera. He glanced at me over Uncle Allen's bent head. "For your insurance company."

Pictures. Good idea. I had left my camera in its docking station next to my computer. I ran to the back of the shop.

My camera wasn't there. It wasn't anywhere.

Searching for other newly emptied spaces, I walked back to the men. "They took my camera."

Uncle Allen slipped a new page of his notebook out from the rubber band he kept around the unused part. "Was it expensive?"

"Not very."

"Had to be kids." Uncle Allen peered toward the back of the store. "You've got ridiculously expensive sewing machines, here, right?"

"They are expensive." And worth every penny.

"So a real thief would take those, not a cheap camera."

I wanted to stamp my foot. "Maybe Mike's murderer broke in."

Apparently, it didn't sound quite believable to Uncle Allen. "For a camera? Besides, you went off across the street and left your store unlocked after you called me. Anyone could have wandered in and lifted that camera."

Clay glowered at him. "The reason someone broke in, or whether the camera was taken by that person or by one of those hundreds of pedestrians out there in the rain" — he gestured at the desolately empty streets, then continued — "doesn't matter. What matters is that Willow could be in danger."

I appreciated his empathy but was less sure about the chills the idea gave me. A stranger had broken in and snooped through my possessions. A stranger had broken into

Blueberry Cottage, too. And probably into Mike's house. And someone had hidden in Tell a Yarn last night, listening to everything we said. And the person who had done all this could be a murderer, biding his time until he caught one of us alone.

Uncle Allen waved his hand in a dismissive gesture. "Just kids. Making mischief. We'll catch 'em, give 'em a good talking to."

"And get my camera back."

"Yeah, yeah." He headed out onto the porch. "If we can." He didn't sound very optimistic about it.

Leaving Clay to figure out how to repair my door, I accompanied Uncle Allen to his cruiser. I asked, "Does Elderberry Bay have sandbags I can use to keep my cottage from flooding?"

He made a call on his cell phone. "Irv, we got any sandbags to put along the river?" He shook his head as if Irv could see him. "Pete's place?" He sounded as amazed as I'd ever heard him sound. "Whatever for?" He listened, then said, "We got places downriver, lower elevations, that're gonna flood long before that." Then he said, "Yeah" about a dozen times, interspersed with "I know," and "You're tellin' me." He pocketed the phone. "The village doesn't have many sandbags, and they're already in

292

use where they're needed more."

To protect a gazebo, I suspected. Upriver, at a higher elevation.

He opened his cruiser door. "Now, you scoot inside outta this rain."

I was drenched, anyway. Muttering, "I didn't know you cared," I splashed back to my porch.

Clay ran his fingers over dents in the door jamb. "Someone used a crowbar."

"Great. All Uncle Allen has to do is drive around looking for a gang of kids carrying crowbars."

Clay brushed a lock of damp hair from his forehead. "I'll see what I can do to force the metal back into place so it will lock until I can bring a replacement."

"Do you mind if I go back to Haylee's while you work on it?" I twisted my hands behind my back. "Those women are helping me with something, and I should be there."

"I don't mind, as long as you trust me alone in your store."

"Of course I do." I didn't tell him Uncle Allen's suspicions about him and my break-in.

Clay probably guessed, but all he said was, "There's a dinner dance tomorrow at the community hall."

I stepped away from him. "A fish fry. In the middle of winter! Haylee, Opal, Naomi, and Edna and I are all going. Elderberry Bay seems to have lots of dinners." I was babbling, and my fingers were still behind my back, pinching each other. "Tonight's roast beef dinner included a memorial service for Mike Krawbach."

That didn't seem to surprise Clay. Maybe he'd known, and that's why he hadn't attended. "Save me a dance tomorrow night?" he asked.

Hadn't Herb used the same words? My face hadn't heated then. Now, it did. "Sure," I managed.

"I'll come over to Haylee's and tell you when I'm done so you can lock up again."

"Okay." I would have to keep him from seeing what we were making. He might offer to stay up all night to help, too, another person's sleepless night to chalk up to my account. As I attempted to skirt puddles covering most of the street, I realized that even if Clay recognized that we were making a gazillion bags, he might not figure out their purpose.

During my absence, which hadn't seemed very long, the women had sewn an incredible number of bags. I had to admit that it was fun using a new and different sewing machine, even for something as mindless as stitching bags. Besides, I enjoyed the warm camaraderie of sewing with other seamstresses.

Edna's curls were beginning to recover from their flattening when Clay called me from the front door. I ran to him, and we hopscotched around puddles to my door. I locked it. We both tested it. The door and the jamb were pockmarked and scratched, but the lock held.

I started across my porch toward the street again.

"You're not done at Haylee's?" Clay asked.

"Some people like to sew all night."

He pulled his collar up around his neck. "I'll watch until you're safely inside, then. See you tomorrow night."

I fled across the riverlike street. "Sew all night," I muttered. "What a strange thing to say. What must he think?" Inside Haylee's front door, I turned around.

Clay waved, got into his truck, and drove away.

I kicked off my boots and strode to Haylee's classroom.

Four witches looked up from their tearing and their sewing. They all wore black wigs, tall black conical hats, and long black plastic capes over matching skirts. Their faces were dark green.

23

I spluttered, "Did I interrupt a convening of the coven?"

The short witch, not surprisingly, spoke with Edna's birdlike voice. "We've made hundreds of bags."

"Dozens," the tall, thin witch replied. Haylee.

The Naomi-sized witch mediated in her sweet, kind voice. "Lots. Now we're ready to go to the beach and fill them."

"Why the witch costumes?" I asked.

"There's a full moon tonight," Edna said.

"There are clouds. It's raining," I objected. "And Shakespeare's weird sisters went to the *heath,* not to the beach."

Opal fluttered her fingers downward. "Rain. These plastic skirts and capes and hats will keep us dry."

And the wigs would do what?

"And we needed black clothing so we won't be seen in the dark." Edna shook her head, rattling her witchy rain gear. "I don't own those depressing dark colors you young people like."

Naomi pointed from the jar of green stuff in her hand to her face. Her facial masque? "And this will help keep us from being recognized."

"*I* recognized you."

"But, Willow," Opal explained, "you knew we were here. No one will expect to see us on the beach at midnight during a rainstorm."

"And if anyone *does* see you," I retorted, "they'll pay no attention, and go about their business." Very quickly. "Why don't you want to be recognized?"

Opal explained, "Removing sand from the beach is illegal."

"This is an emergency," I reminded them. "Who's going to complain?"

"Don't argue," Haylee advised.

She was right. We could have been at the beach filling sandbags if I hadn't been wasting precious time questioning The Three Weird Mothers, who seemed determined to live up to Haylee's nickname for them.

Opal advanced on me with a witch costume and a wig, and Naomi headed toward me with that jar.

I backed away. "Let them recognize me.

It's my property we're saving."

Naomi had the clincher. "Sorry, Willow. If they recognize you, they'll know who the rest of us are."

Five women doing strange things in Elderberry Bay during torrential rains in February? Right, no one would ever guess our identity, the Threadville storekeepers, the newcomers in town, already suspected of everything from murder to . . . to . . . digging in the sand at midnight.

A few minutes later, my face was green and I was wearing a witch costume and a wig, and we were clutching tall witch hats on our laps in Naomi's SUV. Naomi parked at the foot of Lake Street next to the beach. We clambered out and plunked our hats onto our heads. To my surprise, the brim actually did shelter my face from the rain.

Using the SUV as cover, both from prying eyes and from rain slanting in from the north, Haylee and I shoveled sand into bags that Opal and Naomi held open for us. We'd made the bags small on purpose, and we filled them only halfway, but they each seemed to weigh about a million pounds. We rotated shoveling, holding bags open, and loading them into the SUV. Since we would need the extra fabric at the tops of the bags so we could manhandle them out

299

of the SUV, we didn't tuck the tops in, and propped the bags upright against each other. It was just as well we hadn't taken time to turn the colorful bags. Seam allowances along the bottom and sides resembled fringed ruffles. They were kind of pretty. Cute, anyway.

The rear of Naomi's SUV sagged. Afraid that the front wheels of the all-wheel-drive vehicle would lose traction or the suspension would give out, we stopped piling sandbags into the vehicle, and Naomi, Edna, and I got in. Naomi drove to the trail, the one I didn't want motorized vehicles using.

How ironic. I joked, "Sometimes, I wish I had an ATV."

"They're allowed on the trail during emergencies," Edna reminded me sternly. "If we had one, of course we could use it."

Naomi pulled into the wide spot where Uncle Allen had turned his cruiser after Mike died. Edna and I got out and directed her as she backed her SUV close to Blueberry Cottage.

The river was still below the bank, but it had crept up since we'd begun making sandbags, and, if anything, the rain was coming down harder. Slabs of ice reared up on edge, making room for more.

We lifted sandbags out of the SUV, tucked their tops in, and laid them flat on the ground along my fence. Naomi and Edna wore leather gloves. My mittens felt clammy and clumsy, so I took them off. Usually, I loved the feel of fabric, but not when it was cold, wet, and gritty. I moved as quickly as I could, hoping to keep my hands from turning into sandy popsicles.

We ended up with one row, about a fifth of the way along the fence. It was paltry and dispiriting, but Naomi and Edna were not discouraged. They hopped into Naomi's SUV like they weren't nearly fifty years old and wearing stiff and crackling plastic witch costumes.

At the beach, Opal and Haylee had continued filling bags. We'd barely begun loading them into the SUV when, above the pounding rain and gusting wind, we heard Uncle Allen's plaintive siren. Was he really driving around all night looking for teenagers with crowbars?

"Quick," Edna yelled, slamming the rear hatch, "climb into the car and act like we just got here!"

By the time we scrambled into the SUV, retrieved the hats we had inadvertently knocked off, arranged ourselves primly with our hats on our knees, and closed the doors,

Uncle Allen was beside us, shining his feeble flashlight at our windows. He circled the SUV.

"Oh, no," Naomi whispered. "We left incriminating evidence outside — those shovels."

So we had.

Haylee giggled. "Who will he think we were burying?"

The others shushed her, but I couldn't help giggling, too. "I hope he doesn't trip over the shovels or fall into any of the holes we dug."

Uncle Allen had to choose that moment to fall heavily against the window, which flattened his face like in a cartoon.

Naomi moaned. "Oh, the poor thing."

Haylee shuddered with laughter. "Willow, watch what you foresee when wearing that outfit."

Covering my mouth, in horror, not amusement, I told myself that my witch outfit had not given me any unexpected powers.

Uncle Allen tapped on the passenger window. The wind carried his words away, but the meaning was obvious. Open up.

Naomi gasped, obviously flustered. "I can't lower the windows without turning the key in the ignition. If I do that, I might accidentally start the engine, and he'll think

302

we're making our getaway. He might shoot!"

"And I can't open this door," Edna said. "It's propping him up. I'll knock him down."

So I was the one, sitting behind Edna, who had to climb out of the car onto the damp sand. I barely avoided disappearing into a hole, myself.

Disappearing might have been a good idea under the circumstances.

Uncle Allen shouted, "Hands up!"

I complied, even though I had a witch hat in one hand and a bunch of unfilled bags in the other.

"Empty your hands," he ordered. I let the bags fall and plunked the hat onto my head before raising my trembling hands again. This was it? The moment he had chosen to arrest me for Mike's murder?

"What are you doing here?" he bellowed. "The beach is closed after dark."

The other four women surrounded me, all with witch hats on their heads and their hands in the air.

Taking in the sight of five green-faced witches, Uncle Allen seemed at a loss for words. Finally, he managed, "What is going on?"

"Just out for a drive and we stopped here because it's so pretty," Edna sang out, all innocence.

Uncle Allen demanded, "What're you up to?"

"It's raining," Edna explained patiently, pointing upward with her index fingers. "These are our rain capes and hats."

Uncle Allen scowled, either with suspicion or because freezing rain was cascading all over him. Too bad we didn't have a spare witch costume. He could have used it. "Why'd you paint camouflage on your faces?"

The downpour had streaked the other women's faces. My hastily applied masque probably hadn't fared any better.

Edna lowered a hand and wagged a finger at him. "Never question a woman about her beauty secrets."

Uncle Allen had the good sense not to respond to that. He probed his light at our shovels, the holes we'd dug, and the bags I'd dropped. "Whoever's car this is, open up. I want to see inside."

Edna piped up, "Show us your search warrant."

"Don't need one. I've got probable cause. Sober people don't act like you bunch."

Edna persisted. "Then give us all Breathalyzer tests."

Naomi stepped forward. "Only me. This

is my SUV and I'm the driver."

"I'm not thinkin' of alcohol," Uncle Allen said. "Whatever you five are on, it's gotta be illegal. Let me see inside or I'm hauling you all in."

In? Tiny Elderberry Bay couldn't possibly have its own jail. I supposed Uncle Allen could haul us home to Aunt Betty, which might be worse than prison. Embroidering orange jumpsuits might be one thing. Embroidering bulky snowmobile suits? No thanks.

We must have looked doubtful. Uncle Allen filled us in. "The state police will gladly lock you up. Now, are you going to open your trunk, or do I have to do it for you?"

Opal asked in a nice, reasonable tone, "Can we put our hands down?"

He rolled his eyes. We took that as a yes, and he didn't complain. When I wasn't waving my arms above my head, the cape kept rain off much better.

Naomi opened the back hatch. The light came on, showing about a dozen plump bags standing against each other.

Uncle Allen stuck his hand into one. "Sand?"

Despite her witch costume and makeup, Edna managed to look earnest. "As you

305

pointed out earlier, the river's about to flood Willow's sweet little cottage and destroy any evidence you might want to go back and find."

Nice, Edna, I thought admiringly.

Uncle Allen didn't buy it. "We're *done* with the crime scene investigation."

I'd heard that one before. And had found more evidence afterward.

Uncle Allen widened his stance, placing one foot precariously near the rim of another hole in the sand. "I'm gonna have to ticket you all for stealing sand from the public beach, and you're gonna have to dump this all back where it came from."

"We're only borrowing it," Edna said. "When the river goes down, we'll bring the sand back."

He objected. "The river might carry your sandbags away. What then?"

Edna had an answer for everything. "The river will deliver the sand back to the beach."

Well, maybe.

Naomi placed a gently quelling hand on Edna's wrist. "We'll return the sand when the danger of flooding is over. Meanwhile, how about calling the state police and asking them to send troopers to help us?"

I began making plans to sneak off, wash

my face, and replace the witch costume with a rain jacket.

Uncle Allen, however, seemed to lose his enthusiasm for involving the state police. He growled, "Make sure you put it all back when you're done with it, and don't leave craters for people to fall into. Someone could break a leg." Avoiding the holes we'd already dug, he shuffled to his cruiser and drove off into the storm.

Opal began filling more bags. "That man can find more ways to waste our time!"

Naomi's SUV was almost loaded for the second time when a set of headlights appeared on the road leading down toward the beach. And toward us.

Uncle Allen with five sets of handcuffs?

A bright red pickup truck with white lettering on the passenger door stopped beside Naomi's SUV.

Great. Here was Clay, the heartthrobbiest of Elderberry Bay's heartthrobs. And I was not only wearing a witch costume, but my face was streaked in hideous green goop.

Maybe he wouldn't recognize me.

Fat chance.

He climbed out of his truck. Mouth twitching as if he wanted to laugh, he called out, "There you are, Willow. I was looking for you."

"You found her!" Edna called out happily, shredding any hope that Clay wouldn't notice me in the midst of this quirky coven.

He gestured to the back of his truck. "I brought a shovel and a load of old sacks to fill with sand."

I could think of nothing to say.

Edna, down on her knees holding bags open for Opal, had no such problem. "How did you know we were making and filling sandbags?"

"I didn't," he said. "I was afraid that Willow's cottage would be the first place to flood." He turned around. Another set of headlights appeared on the hill above us, and another. Grinning, he faced us. "And I made a couple of calls."

Smythe arrived in his honey-colored pickup truck, and Herb pulled up in a black one. All of Elderberry Bay's heartthrobs at once.

All of them experiencing the pleasure of seeing Haylee and me at our drenched worst.

All of them helping, too — a lot. The men wore work gloves. Clay glanced from the other women's sopping leather gloves to my bare hands. The next thing I knew, he brought dry work gloves from his truck. "Here, wear these."

"I'll get them wet, inside and out," I warned.

"Doesn't matter. Put them on."

I did. They were too big, but their warmth was a nice change.

Before long, we filled every sandbag we had and loaded them into the pickup trucks. Slowly, we convoyed to Blueberry Cottage, where we unloaded the sandbags. Clay, Smythe, and Herb worked tirelessly and barely seemed fazed by the tonnage of sand they moved. Despite babying his right arm and relying mostly on his left, Herb accomplished as much as any of the rest of us. The men joked, too, and kept our spirits high. Best of all, none of them said anything disparaging about the way we were dressed or the green stuff dribbling from our faces.

Noticing Edna nudging Opal when Smythe and Haylee traded smiles, I carefully avoided looking at any of the heart-throbby men for more than a second.

When we were done, we had one long line of sandbags, piled two high, along my fence. We had worked for hours, and our little barricade would provide, maybe, five additional inches of protection.

"Let's go make more bags!" Edna hollered in glee.

I slapped at the air in front of me with

both hands, still encased in Clay's work gloves. "No. The rain has let up, and the temperature has gone down. Water on the ground will freeze. It will stop draining into the river." It sounded good, anyway. "We all have to work at our regular jobs tomorrow. Let's call it a night."

The others protested, but I insisted. They finally agreed when I said, without really knowing, that the river seemed to have slowed its rise.

I stayed beside my sandbags while the three pickup trucks and the SUV drove slowly away. When they were out of sight, I stepped over the row of sandbags, unlocked my gate, and went up to my apartment. The dogs barked at the sound of my key in the lock and barked even harder when they saw me. When I spoke, Sally and Tally tilted their heads comically, first one way, and then the other. They must have decided that the motley green face belonged to a friend, after all.

I hoped that whoever had provided the plastic skirt and cape didn't want them back. The excited dogs finished what the night's shoveling and hauling had started, and the outfit was suitable only for a witch's ragbag. But the hat could see service another day, and as soon as the wig finished dripping, it would be good as new. Well, almost.

Haylee called. It must be important for her to phone me at such a late hour.

Apparently, it was. "Willow, do you have a date for tomorrow's . . . I mean tonight's Fish Fry Dinner Dance?" I heard suppressed excitement in her voice.

"No, do you?"

"Yes."

"Let me guess. Smythe?"

"Yes." The smile came through her voice. "How'd you know?"

"It's obvious. Your mothers noticed."

She groaned. "I was afraid of that. And they're coming to the dance. I'll have to behave."

"I thought you were just looking," I teased.

"I am. But he sort of *told* me I was going with him." She giggled. "I didn't want to hurt his feelings."

How like her. "He seems very nice."

"With my luck, though, he'll turn out to be a murderer." She didn't sound worried. With a happy laugh and a promise to see me at the dance, she hung up. I bit my lip. Haylee had dated our boss, the embezzler, in NYC. Jasper was now behind bars. Her next foray into the dating world had been with the bad-tempered Mike. He'd been

311

murdered. Her recent record with men hadn't exactly been stellar.

Seeing my face in the mirror, I remembered Clay, Herb, and Smythe smiling at me while we worked, and I didn't know whether to laugh or cry. Crying seemed like a more reasonable option, but wouldn't improve my looks any, so I set to work with water. Then soap and water. Then cold cream. Then more soap and water. What was that green glop, anyway? Wouldn't masque have washed off, maybe even in the rain? Some of this stuff had, but the most yellow of the pigments stuck stubbornly to my skin. Very attractive. I kept scrubbing.

When my face was passable, I dropped into bed.

Nightmares about floods awakened me before dawn.

The dogs and I went outside. The wind had died and a few tentative snowflakes drifted down.

The river had risen.

It surrounded the bases of trees with swirling, growling ice. Water snaked across the hiking trail. If the river came up two more inches, it would breach our lovingly assembled earthworks.

24

Jamming my fists into my coat pockets, I blinked down at muddy water inching toward the colorful row of sandbags. It seemed that the river was still rising, and all our middle-of-the-night efforts had been in vain. I could make and fill more sandbags, but in only a couple of hours, In Stitches would open, and I'd need to be inside, waiting on customers.

I had to face it. A few more sandbags would not divert a flood from Blueberry Cottage.

I raised my chin and stared across jostling ice floes to the silent forest on the far bank. Some of those trees had been there for years and would continue to thrive and grow, come ice or high water.

Blueberry Cottage, too. I hadn't believed Mike when he said that ice had pushed my cottage toward the river, but now I pictured ice-laden water pouring into my yard and

313

surrounding the cottage. In its natural downhill flow, it would carry everything, including Blueberry Cottage, wherever it wanted. It could have pushed it toward the river.

The dogs discovered that, by pawing at thin ice on puddles, they could break through and enjoy long, noisy drinks. Splashing around, they churned up mud, then wrestled in this latest water feature. I finally coaxed them up to the apartment. At the rate they were going through their personalized towels, I would need to embroider more. That thought made me feel a little better.

After my shower, breakfast, and coffee, I was almost ready to tackle the day, even if the day included ice dislodging Blueberry Cottage and the river carrying it to the lake to join possibly fictitious ice-fishing palaces in the depths.

I went upstairs to my shop, lit the woodstove, and set a pot of cider on it. As the spicy aromas warmed the atmosphere, I fingered bolts of linen I'd hoped to sell. The cloth was expensive, but losing Blueberry Cottage would be even more expensive. I was about to rip into a bolt of midweight linen when the phone rang.

"I found more fabrics we can use for

sandbags," Haylee said. "And Naomi, Opal, and Edna are all in their own shops, making sandbags while they wait for today's customers. Want me to bring you a bolt or two?"

"I'll be right over." I thanked her and ran outside. Brushing past piqué, seersucker, and chambray, I jogged toward a sewing machine humming in Haylee's classroom.

She had already completed a dozen new sandbags. She pointed to a corner. "Why not start with that roll of plaid? No one bought even a quarter yard of it."

The metallic gold and red in the plaid could have made it Christmassy, but the orange and black gave it a Halloween look. The fuchsia simply clashed. "Why did you buy it?" And more importantly why had she kept it?

"Online, it didn't look so bad. Now, I order a swatch before committing to an entire bolt. I'm glad we have the perfect use for it. How's the water level this morning? Dropping?"

I tried to smile, but the corners of my mouth drooped. "I'm not sure. It rose during the night, but maybe it's about to go down. I'll go rip and sew this. Thanks! I owe you."

"No, you don't. The denizens of Threadville swim or sink together, and you're helping draw textile tourists to town. Besides, you're my best friend. You'd do the same for me and you know it." She rubbed at her face. "Naomi's going to help me remove the rest of this makeup later."

"How come her masque is so hard to remove?" I asked.

When Haylee stopped laughing, she told me we hadn't been wearing Naomi's expensive facial masque. "She had us put on theatrical makeup left over from Halloween. We probably all have green and yellow splotches on our faces this morning."

"Yours are hardly noticeable," I consoled her. "I used soap and water and cold cream."

"You didn't get it all off, either." Her wicked grin said she was teasing. At least I hoped she was.

I thanked her for the fabric and dashed back to In Stitches.

A hundred sandbags would raise our impromptu dam approximately two inches. I ripped twenty strips from the gaudy plaid, sat at my fastest machine, and stitched. Sea glass tinkled, and the day's first browsers shuffled in — Rhonda and Aunt Betty. They didn't seem interested in anything besides the view out my rear windows. Keeping an eye on them, I continued making bags.

Loud rumbling out on Lake Street made us all turn around. A large yellow earth mover rolled toward the beach.

"What the . . . ?" Aunt Betty asked.

"Call your husband," Rhonda urged in nasal excitement. "Someone's probably breaking a law."

They went back to looking out my windows and guessing how soon my cottage would drift off down the river.

"A day or two," Aunt Betty said.

Rhonda snorted breathily, her version of laughter. "Tonight."

What encouraging visitors. I bent my head over my sewing machine and stitched.

A bus stopped in front of the store. Its doors opened, and women I recognized as our usual Threadville tourists disembarked. On a Sunday?

Men came out of the bus, too, and shuffled their feet on the sidewalk as if they couldn't figure out what to do next.

The Threadville tourists were not as reticent. Carrying grocery bags overflowing with remnants, women trotted into In Stitches. My Elderberry Bay students, Susannah and Georgina, came in with them. "Willow," Susannah shouted. "We're here to make sandbags for you, and some of the ladies from Erie brought their husbands along to fill them."

Overwhelmed, I went to help with their coats. "How did you know?" I asked.

Georgina shrugged out of her lovely handmade fleece-lined jacket. She was dressed all in apricot. "We guessed you might be in trouble, so we started a chain of phone calls, and here we are. We went through our stashes and brought stuff we'd never use."

Women from the village and women from Erie had been phoning each other and sorting through stashes at a hideously early hour. For me. I couldn't speak.

Susannah clutched the bag of scraps to her chest. "It's a great way to discover we're running out of fabrics —"

Grinning fiendishly, Georgina finished Susannah's sentence. "— And need to buy more."

Susannah agreed. "We can never let our stashes get *too* low. You never know when a rainy day might come."

I didn't have enough sewing machines, so I sent several women across the street to The Stash. Considering that these helpful women were gearing themselves up to buy new fabrics, I didn't think Haylee would mind.

Rosemary came up onto my porch, opened the front door, and beckoned me closer so she could keep her boots on. She was wearing the scarf she'd embroidered in my class on Friday. "I'll bus the men, shovels, and empty bags to the beach. We'll fill the bags. Can I drive my bus on that trail behind your place?"

I explained that I wouldn't let her endanger herself and her bus on the submerged trail. "We'll have to carry the bags down from my front gate," I decided, not wanting to force all these good people, many of whom were probably grandparents, to do all that hauling and carrying.

I should have known that Rosemary would be optimistic. Smiling, she drove off with her passengers and cargo.

Seconds later, Clay and Smythe appeared in their pickup trucks. Not caring if my face was green or purple or red plaid, I ran out to the sidewalk to thank them again for last night's work. They opened their tailgates and unloaded wheelbarrows.

"We can't drive on the trail," Clay explained. "We'll leave these in your yard and go down to the beach to fill sandbags."

I told them about the men already down there planning to bring sandbags back on the Threadville tour bus.

Smythe tossed me one of his sweet smiles. "Loading our pickup trucks will be easier." Pulling his yellow and black bee-stinger stocking cap over his curls, he got into his truck and tore off toward the beach. He was enjoying this. I supposed that running a lavender farm could get lonely during the winter when his bees must be sound asleep.

Clay asked me if I was all right.

Either that was the only thing he could ever think of saying to me, or Haylee hadn't been teasing about the vestiges of makeup on my face. "Sure, but please be careful, Clay. If it's too dangerous, please don't go anywhere near that river. And stop others, too. Blueberry Cottage isn't worth risking lives for."

Susannah thrust an armload of empty bags at him. He accepted the bags, gave her a huge smile, then strode to his truck and drove off toward the beach.

I was curious about Aunt Betty's and Rhonda's reactions to the way our fellow villagers were helping me, but Aunt Betty and Rhonda had disappeared. They probably hated being around cheerful people and had marched outside in hopes of seeing ice crunch Blueberry Cottage into matchsticks.

The Threadville tourists and local women

in my shop had a great morning gossiping, sewing bags, helping themselves to cider and cookies, taking empty bags and treats to whichever of the workers appeared at the front door, and watching Clay and Smythe roll wheelbarrows of sandbags down the hill.

I felt like I should feed lunch to all these volunteers, but they took turns going off to Pier 42, and Susannah brought lunch back for me. Sisters-in-thread were some of the most wonderful people I'd ever met.

While they sewed, I took the two dogs out into the backyard. I kept them leashed since both gates were open. Planting his work boots carefully, Herb strained to prevent a wheelbarrow full of sandbags from flying down the hill on its own.

Sally and Tally backed away from him. Because of the wheelbarrow? Or because of something that they knew or guessed about him?

No one could maneuver a wheelbarrow full of sandbags down a steep, rutted hill if both of his arms weren't strong, and Herb was using his right arm just as well as his left.

Odd and potentially suspicious, but Herb had been really helpful during the past eighteen hours. He couldn't be a murderer. Still, I chewed on my bottom lip as I took the dogs inside and dried them.

At five, Rosemary apologized because she had to round up her passengers and take them home. "We added a second line of sandbags behind the first to shore it up, and both rows are mostly five sandbags high." She clasped her hands above her head in victory. "That should do it. Three layers of sandbags are still above the water. Someone should take a picture. That's the most beautiful levee I've ever seen."

If these volunteers hadn't shown up, the swollen river would be licking at Blueberry Cottage's foundation. I thanked everyone. There was no way to pay them back.

Rosemary placed a hand reverently over her heart. "That Fraser Construction guy. What a gem. Not only is he about the best-looking creature to ever walk this earth, he worked as hard as anyone out there, and one of his employees is down at the mouth of the river with a backhoe, breaking up the ice jam."

I felt myself flush. All this for me?

After everyone left, I scrubbed at Naomi's persistent theatrical makeup.

The phone rang.

"Sorry, Willow, something's come up." Clay sounded formal.

I had to be smart-alecky. "The river?"

A smile warmed his voice. "That, too. I'm afraid I may not make it to the dinner dance tonight. You won't need to save me a dance after all."

Suddenly, I didn't want to go, either. I tried to thank him for all he had done to save my cottage.

"No problem. The village hired me to break up the ice at the end of the river. Irv was out there helping, and Uncle Allen even pitched in for a while. But more ice keeps floating downriver."

Was Clay planning to work all evening on flood control? I picked at a fingernail. "Don't miss the party tonight just because of my cottage. There's really nothing else anyone can do."

"I'm not. The river has supposedly crested, and the temperature's supposed to stay below freezing for the next few days. We may get a reprieve."

For now. We couldn't do this every time we had a thaw, though.

Clay hung up. I was tired and out of sorts, and again considered staying home from the dinner dance.

But I was also hungry. And my friends and I planned to do more sleuthing. Getting ready, I chose a black miniskirt with a V-necked blouse that seemed too dressy for day but would be fine for evening. Especially if I had even the teeniest hope of seeing, as Rosemary had aptly described him, the best-looking creature to have walked this earth.

Haylee was going to the dance with Smythe, and in our flurry of activity, the rest of us hadn't arranged a carpool. I slithered down icy sidewalks to my car and drove by myself to the community center.

The parking lot wasn't nearly as crowded as it had been the night before. In his honey-colored pickup truck, Smythe followed me into the lot and parked beside me. Haylee smiled at me from his passenger seat. We all got out, and he offered her one arm and me the other. Laughing, we maneuvered over icy patches to the hall, where we joined Herb and Karen at a table. Two couples and me. Nothing like being the fifth wheel. I glanced around. No Clay.

Edna bounced, birdlike, into the hall and turned to Naomi and Opal, who followed her at a more sedate pace. She pointed at our table, then all three women choose a table across the room. Either they planned to question the people at their table about Mike's murder, or they decided to let the young folks have some time alone.

I had fun despite my lack of a date. There

were no eulogies for Mike or anyone else. The Lake Erie yellow perch and French fries were freshly cooked and delicious, the coleslaw was crunchy, and that delicious vanilla fudge was back. The music wasn't deafening. I could hear my tablemates, and Smythe kept us laughing.

After everyone had gone back for all the seconds and thirds they could eat, a woman climbed to the stage. Shaking her head like she hoped no one would take her suggestions, she announced a nature hike at six on Tuesday morning, and everybody was welcome whether they belonged to the nature club or not. She was president. "But you'll need reservations," she cautioned us.

I sat back, stretched my legs out, and folded my arms. I *had* reservations, many of them, about nature hikes in cold weather, especially at dawn.

She added that we could make our reservations tonight, in the back of the hall.

Across the room, Edna leaned forward, cocked her head, and nodded encouragingly at me. Oh no. She expected us all to go traipsing about at that ungodly hour.

I said to Haylee with as much enthusiasm as I could muster, "Let's go on the nature hike."

She looked pained. "Six in the morning?"

"It would be good for us." Without moving my head, I flicked my gaze toward Edna.

Haylee got the hint. "Okay, let's go sign up."

Smythe closed his hand around hers. "Glad you're coming. The walk is on my farm, and I'm serving toast and honey afterward."

Karen and Herb decided to go, too. At the table where we could add our names to the list of participants, someone referred to the president of the nature club as Mona. At last night's roast beef dinner, Pete De-Glazier had mentioned a wife named Mona. How many Monas could there possibly be in a village the size of Elderberry Bay?

The volume of the music rose a few notches, and the dancing began. Herb and Smythe made certain I had a couple of dances with each of them. After seeing Herb handle that unwieldy wheelbarrow, I wasn't surprised that his right arm was strong enough to hold me so tightly that I kept stepping on his feet. He laughed every time, like I was doing it on purpose to be cute, but I felt inept and clumsy. Being taller than he was didn't help my mood, either.

I danced with Sam the ironmonger. I danced with men I didn't know. I danced with Dr. Wrinklesides. "I'm glad to see you're getting out," he shouted. "Best thing to help you get over your ailments!"

I tried to convey that I hadn't suffered any sort of trauma.

"See? Time heals everything." He looked closely at my hand. "Even that bruise is gone." Dancers around us stared. He was the best dancer of the evening, and he seemed to make it his business to dance with every woman in the community center. When he passed me with Edna in his arms, he was singing along with the music. No one seemed to mind, since his singing was much better than the recorded musician's.

I danced and joked and talked and sipped at wine, but the evening passed, and Clay didn't show up. Firmly telling myself that I didn't care and therefore couldn't be the least bit disappointed, I left when Haylee and Smythe did.

Smythe tucked his bare hands into the pockets of his yellow parka and exaggerated a shiver. "It's even colder than last week."

Clay had been right. The river should stop rising.

The heater in my car kicked in about the time I turned onto Lake Street.

At the same time, a different sort of heater came on inside my brain.

A red pickup truck with white lettering on

the door pulled away from the curb next to
In Stitches and sped away into the night.
  Clay's truck.

25

My first instinct was to press down on my gas pedal and follow Clay. Maybe he'd been looking for me. On the other hand, he could be trying to avoid me.

I parked. Remaining in my car, I peered through the windows of In Stitches. The shop looked fine, with a small light in the back casting a warm glow over the tempting array of merchandise.

In Stitches. My home. My dream. Despite my love for it all, the cold night wasn't the only thing causing my sudden fit of trembling.

What had Clay been doing? He'd known I'd be out. He hadn't attended last night's roast beef dinner, either, and during that party, someone had broken into my shop.

As Uncle Allen had pointed out, Clay had renovated my place and might still have a key. After Clay finished replacing my door, I would learn how to change the lock. Haylee would help me, even if she didn't know how, either.

Smythe's pickup truck came down Lake Street and parked behind me. If Haylee saw me brooding inside my car, she'd be worried. I got out.

Haylee and Smythe were quick. In seconds, they were beside me on the sidewalk.

"Is anything wrong, Willow?" Smythe asked. Why did the nicest men in town always ask me that question? Haylee looked concerned, too.

I tried to arrange my face into a confident smile. "Nothing, but after last night's break-in . . ." I trailed off, letting them fill in the rest for themselves.

"We'll go in with you," Haylee offered. "And make sure everything's okay."

Inside the shop, I did a quick survey. Nothing seemed to have been disturbed.

On the other side of my apartment door, Tally whined and Sally barked. I let them into the shop. Although obviously glad to see us, they pushed past us. Looking for Clay? *Had* he been inside while I was at the dinner dance? The dogs snuffled up and down aisles.

"So, everything's fine here, Willow?" Smythe asked.

I brushed hair from my eyes. "Yes. It was

silly of me to think I'd have break-ins two nights in a row."

He shook his head. "It wasn't silly." He turned to Haylee. "Shall we go?"

"Go ahead," she said, giving him a sweet smile, taking his arm and leading him toward the door in a way that made it impossible for him to say no. "I have" — she paused for a second — "sewing questions for Willow."

She was the expert when it came to sewing. But Smythe included me in his sunny good-byes. "See you both Tuesday morning at my place." Whistling, he strode off toward his truck.

The moment he pulled away, Haylee locked the door and turned to face me, arms folded, eyebrows lowered. "Okay, spill. What happened?"

I walked my fingers across the top of a bolt of homespun linen. "Clay was in his truck outside my store when I arrived. I couldn't tell if he saw me, but he drove off quickly, and I didn't get to ask him what he wanted."

"Maybe he was looking for you."

I gave her a wan smile. "Maybe. How was your evening? I didn't mean to cut it short."

"We had a great time, but . . . sometimes, it's easiest if there's no question of inviting him — any date, that is, especially a first date — up to my apartment afterward." She glanced outside and threw me a grin. "He's gone. Don't let Clay worry you, Willow. He's not a killer."

I hunched into myself. "That's what I think, too, mainly because I don't want him to be one. But that makes my logic and sleuthing ability too much like Uncle Allen's. I have to be more objective." I plucked a teensy wisp of thread from the floor. "Something's been nagging at me since Mike's murder, since the evening before it, actually. Someone opened my gate and let my dogs out. I suspected Mike."

"Makes sense," she said.

"Yes, but Clay brought them back. What if Clay let them out and only pretended to rescue them?"

"That's silly, Willow. Why would he do that?"

I didn't have an answer to that, objective or otherwise.

"You can't distrust everybody in Elderberry Bay," she said. She must have had a *great* evening with Smythe. Hadn't she and her mothers and I been warning each other not to trust anyone? "I think your dogs want something."

They were racing up and down the stairs

to and from the apartment.

Haylee came out to the backyard with us. The dogs ran down the hill and barked at the levee of sandbags, which to them must have resembled a huge snake.

I shined my light at the flood. It had threatened the top of the sandbags all day. Surprised and excited, I said, "The water's gone down, maybe a whole inch."

"Time to celebrate!"

"You and your mothers were right," I admitted. "I tried to talk you out of making those sandbags. But they really did keep the flood out of my cottage."

"I'm right about Clay, too." I let her out through the front gate.

Despite what Haylee said, though, I was determined to be cautious around Clay.

That determination lasted until the next morning, Monday, the day all Threadville shops were closed. I took the last load of cinnamon cookies out of the oven and went up to the shop to embroider the rest of the cornstalks for my wall hanging. Someone tapped at In Stitches' front door. Jumping, I turned around.

Holding a tool box in one hand and a level in the other, Clay was looking in through the glass. Did I detect a certain wariness in the set of his shoulders and the thinning of his mouth as I walked toward him, or was he only imitating my expression? Trying to look as if I wasn't the type to go around murdering men in and around Elderberry Bay, I opened the door.

Clay must have decided I wouldn't murder all of them, or at least not him. He came inside.

The dogs went wild. He put his tools down, crouched, and let them slobber all over him. "Sorry I didn't make it last night."

"I saw you leave here when I was arriving home after the dance." I meant it as a question, but it came out as an accusation.

Rubbing Sally's ears, he didn't look up at me. "After your break-in the night before, I wanted to keep an eye on all the Threadville shops." He spoke slowly, like maybe he was making it up or had seen my car turn onto Lake Street, memorized an excuse, and then had trouble reciting it. "Threadville has become an important part of the local economy. I sat outside in my truck all evening. Nobody came near any of your shops." He scratched Tally-Ho's chest.

I would have preferred to dance with him. Only one dance, the one I'd been promised. All I said was, "Thanks. You didn't need to." It came out brusquely. "Like some coffee?"

"I'd love it."

I herded the dogs into the apartment with me so he could leave the front door open while he carried materials in from his truck. As I brewed coffee and heaped fragrant cookies onto a plate, I heard Clay's footsteps crossing the floor above me. My new caution forced me to consider that he might be snooping through embroidery hoops and bolts of stabilizer.

On the other hand, if he hadn't murdered Mike, he might think that I had.

We were in for a fun day.

I put a carafe of coffee, two mugs, and the cookies on the tray. Negotiating the stairs while balancing the tray and keeping it out of reach of two inquisitive doggie noses was a challenge. At the top of the stairs, I scrabbled at the knob with my elbow. Clay must have been waiting on the other side. He opened the door. Wriggling, Sally and Tally danced around him.

I set the tray down and poured two mugs of coffee. "Do you need help carrying things from your truck?"

"I've got everything I need, thanks."

I offered the plate of cookies.

One corner of his mouth quirked up. "Except these." My two cute little traitors sat at his feet and gazed adoringly up at

335

him. And at what he was eating.

I left the apartment door open so the dogs could be with Clay and me, but I locked the front door in case embroidery-crazed fabriholics should come wandering through Threadville and inadvertently let my pups escape.

Using sharp appliqué scissors, I carefully cut out the cornstalks and trees I'd embroidered Friday night. It was sort of like making paper dolls when I was a kid, drawing them and their clothing, then cutting them out. Clay whistled, measured, and sawed through oak. The combined scents of fresh sawdust, cinnamon cookies, and wood smoke took me back to a contented time in my childhood before my mother went into politics and my father shut himself into his workshop.

I couldn't help thinking that Clay was kind and gentle, not a killer. *Be careful,* I reminded myself. *Objectivity is a virtue.*

I threaded wire through the satin stitches outlining the cutout trees and cornstalks. I tried various ways of bending the wires until the cornstalks and tree trunks looked almost real. I fastened them to the wall hanging. With the tan cornstalks in the foreground, and the embossed hiker and trees in the background, the whole thing came across as a whimsical celebration of seventeenth-century stumpwork tapestries. I grinned.

Clay admired my handiwork and impressed me by understanding the amount of creativity that had gone into it. But then, he was creative himself. That was my totally objective judgment.

He was doing another spectacular job with his carpentry. An Arts and Crafts–style oak railing formed two sides of the pen, while walls formed the other two. The apartment door opened into the pen. He was building a neat gate that would be barely noticeable because of its similarity to the railing but would allow me easy access to the dogs and the apartment.

Although Naomi could have given me pointers about perfectly binding the edges of my wall hanging, I managed a neat binding. Sally-Forth helped by rolling onto the foot pedal and starting the sewing machine when I least expected it. Pulling my fingers away from the wildly stitching needle, I gained a sudden appreciation for the phrase "in the *nick* of time."

At lunchtime, Clay came downstairs and helped prepare hamburgers with all the fixings. He liked them, especially the buns. "I cheated," I confessed. "My bread maker makes the dough, and I shape and bake it."

We polished off every crumb, then accompanied Sally and Tally to the backyard. The river had gone down another couple of inches. I held my arms out triumphantly toward the river as if inviting it in now that it wasn't likely to accept my offer. "We did it!" Yipping, the dogs dashed around us in tight circles.

Inside again, Clay began fitting the gate to the dog pen. I arranged tissue-paper padding around the three-dimensional trees and cornstalks on my wall hanging and carefully packed it in a carton. Leaving Clay and the dogs to each others' company, I walked around the corner to the post office. A few days ago, the weather had felt too cold. Now I wanted the below-freezing temperatures to last a nice long time, then warm up very, very gradually. The river needed to recede a lot before the next thaw.

The tiny post office was empty except for the postmistress, a woman about my age. Her nametag said Petal. Auburn curls fluffed out around her face like a flower around its center, and her eyes were a soft violet blue. Even her voice reminded me of flowers. "Willow Vanderling," she read from my return address. Her mouth round, her eyes wide, she beckoned me closer. "Don't let them pin Mike Krawbach's murder on

338

you. That guy had plenty of enemies long before you moved to Elderberry Bay."

Putting on my most confiding expression, I asked in a hushed voice, "Do you have any idea who might have wanted to kill him?" I held my breath.

Her soft violet eyes hardened. "I hate to say anything against a colleague." She leaned closer. "You know Herb, our mailman?"

Herb. The thought of such a nice person being a murderer sickened me, but I nodded, encouraging her to continue.

She murmured, "He and Mike were friends. Herb wasn't always a postman. He used to drive those big eighteen-wheelers all over the country. He loved it. But he had to quit doing that and start working here when Mike hurt him."

I couldn't help gasping. "*Mike* hurt Herb?"

She whispered, "Herb told me in confidence that Mike told him to drive a big farm tractor across a slope at Mike's vineyard. Afterward, Herb thought Mike had purposely deflated the tires on the downhill side as a prank, and selected Herb as his victim. Mike actually laughed at Herb for coming down so far in the world that he had to drive our cute little post office vehicle instead of the big rigs." She looked at me sternly as if to make certain I understood the extent of Mike's villainy.

Biting my lower lip, I nodded.

She went on, "But . . . if you ask me, Herb's arm has improved a lot more than he wants anyone to know. Maybe he's still collecting disability? When he doesn't know I'm watching, he acts like nothing's wrong —"

A door slammed in the back of the post office. "Hi, Petal!" It was Herb.

Drawing her finger across her lips in a zipping motion, she backed away from me.

I gave her a terse nod. I'd noticed that Herb was stronger than he let on, too.

Strong enough to beat Mike up?

Herb sailed into view, saw me, and stuck his hands into the front pockets of his jeans. "Willow, what brings you here?"

"A package." Brilliant answer. I pasted on a smile. "The river's going down. Thanks for your help."

"No problem." He sauntered into a back room where I could no longer see him.

Waving good-bye to Petal, I left.

I stopped walking when I caught sight of the building that Edna had guessed was a meth lab or marijuana grow-op.

The old aqua wooden front door had been replaced by a gleaming glass one, and the building's windows were no longer papered over. They were clean, with furnishings tastefully arranged behind them. A rocking chair and knitting basket made a vignette in the window to the right of the door, while a garden table set in springtime pastels adorned the left window. Above it all, a shiny new sign said *Country Chic.*

I crossed the street for a closer look. Beyond the window displays, I made out wicker furniture, vases, *objets d'art,* throw pillows, and, against the back wall, shelves of fabric.

Fabric?

A new Threadville shop in Elderberry Bay? Why had its owners kept it a secret from the other Threadville retailers?

The door was locked. A sign in its glass announced: *Gala Opening, Everyone Invited.*

Five to seven o'clock. Tonight. Nothing like short notice. The other Threadville boutiques were closed today, and none of the regular tourists would know about the gala in time to attend.

Behind me, a woman called in a voice sharpened by anger or annoyance, "We're not open yet."

I turned to see who didn't want me snooping around the new store. It was Mona De-Glazier, Uncle Allen's sister-in-law, the woman leading a nature hike on Smythe's farm in the morning. The president of the nature club wore a genuine mink coat, though the irony seemed to escape her. She eyed my burgundy wool jacket with its subtle tone-on-tone embroidery. "Oh. You're that girl with the little sewing business."

I stifled a smug smile. Compared to Mona, I might be considered a girl, but my shop wasn't exactly little. Was she going to put me down whenever she got the chance? This could be fun.

Her mouth widened abruptly and narrowed again, a twitch more than a smile. "Well, you might as well come to our gala tonight." She shook her head again. "Tell your friends." She frowned toward the other side of the street where The Stash, Tell a Yarn, Buttons and Bows, and Batty About Quilts were. She bustled past me.

"Thank you," I said in my most gracious and un-girl-like voice. "We'd love to come."

Her back to me, she unlocked her door and mumbled something that sounded like "great," but with a sarcastic lilt. She was sure to be a supportive addition to the Threadville community.

26

Intent on delivering Mona's half-hearted invitation, I dashed across the street to Batty About Quilts. The front room was breath-taking, a gallery of amazing quilts on white walls. Some of the quilts were carefully crafted scenes, collages cut from new fabric. Others featured keepsake photos printed on cloth. Some were today's version of crazy quilts, every square inch embellished with embroidery, ribbons, buttons, and appli-qués. A few of the quilts might eventually become coverlets on beds, but I would be afraid to put them where dogs might deco-rate them with muddy paw prints.

"Naomi?"

"Willow! Come on back and see what I just finished setting up."

I kicked off my boots and padded into the next room, where Naomi sold everything that went into making quilts.

Her fabrics were neatly arranged by color

and size of print. I couldn't help running my fingers over them. Only one hundred percent cotton felt like this, a sensuous combination of crispness and softness. I saw myself piecing lovely shades together. With original embroidered motifs on every patch.

Naomi showed me a quilting frame with a long-armed sewing machine attached to it.

"Wow," I said reverently. "That's enormous."

"It will stitch queen-sized quilts. I already have orders for people wanting me to do the fancy stitching over the quilts they've made."

"So you get to keep this baby?" I asked.

She stroked the machine. "Until a newer model comes out. Then I'll sell this one."

We smiled happily at each other. Owning a Threadville store was even more fun than I'd guessed. Despite visions of always being able to play with the newest, most exciting machines, I remembered why I'd come to visit her. "The store across the street is having an opening gala tonight, from five to seven. Mona DeGlazier seems to own it."

Naomi hurried to her window. "A home décor shop!" Her forehead puckered. "And she never said a word to any of us, never introduced herself. She could have asked our advice, like about what sells in Threadville and what doesn't."

I pictured those bolts of fabric in the back of Mona's store. "Or what we carry so she wouldn't duplicate it."

Naomi stood taller and tugged at her patchwork vest. She had appliquéd adorable fuzzy poodles on every square. "Obviously, we have to go to this gala. We can do some more sleuthing and see if we can figure out for once and for all who killed Mike."

I headed for the door. "I'll tell the others. Have fun with that quilting machine." As if she wouldn't.

Opening Edna's door set off the little "Buttons and Beaux" tune. I didn't know how she kept those shelves of trims and buttons so pleasingly neat. I was sure she'd added a new collection of patterned twill tapes since I'd last looked. She popped out of her back room. "Willow! Can you join the rest of us for dinner here tonight at seven?"

I smiled at her enthusiasm. "I'd love to. Maybe we should all go somewhere else first." I told her about Country Chic's opening gala.

She beamed. "How nice of the villagers to provide us with gatherings every night where we can search for clues."

After cautioning her again about being

345

careful, I jogged next door.

Opal was arranging her latest creations for the next day's Threadville tourists to admire. Fingering an angora scarf in shades of blue that made me long to luxuriate on Mediterranean beaches, I relayed Mona's halfhearted invitation. Meanwhile, Lucy purred and wound around my ankles.

Opal clapped her hands. "I wonder what I should wear . . ."

I picked up the cat. "You have over three hours to whip up something." Lucy's purr revved to a rumble, vibrating her warm little body. Her fur felt like silk against my cheek.

Opal pulled a fluffy tangerine-hued ball from one of her diamond-shaped niches. "I was wondering how to justify knitting some of this for myself." The ball had to be yarn but was fuzzy enough to pass for another cat.

When I left, Opal was humming and carrying an armload of tangerine yarn toward her homey dining room, and Lucy was following her, tail straight up. Anticipating, no doubt, a long cuddle in Opal's lap. And attacking the fuzzy yarn.

Haylee was in her classroom. With practiced ease, she was tailoring a spring outfit.

I told her the plans the rest of us had made for this evening.

She squeezed her face between her palms like a woebegone waif. "Dinners, dances, the gala, supper at Edna's tonight, and that nature hike before sunrise tomorrow morning!"

"At Smythe's," I reminded her. "He is a sweetheart."

"Yes, and so's Clay. What are you doing racing around Threadville when he's working in your shop?"

"Running errands. Oh, and by the way, I asked him what he was doing in front of my shop last night. He claimed he was watching all of our shops."

"Then that's what he was doing."

I stomped my foot. "Well, he didn't have to. He should have come to the dance and . . . joined the fun."

"Trust Clay, Willow. I still think you two make the perfect pair."

"Perfect shmerfect. But maybe I'd better go back before my dogs decide to go home with him."

"Your dogs love him, Willow. You should, too."

I reeled as if from dizziness. "Now you're really getting ahead of things. Must have been last night's date."

"Ha." She ducked her head and guided fabric underneath the presser foot of a whirring sewing machine.

I ran outside and across the street. All the lights were on inside my store, illuminating my gorgeous merchandise and an equally gorgeous man working in the back corner. Clay lifted his head and smiled when I walked in. He was staining the dog pen. The dogs were nowhere in sight. "I hope you don't mind," he said, "I closed them in your apartment so I wouldn't stain them, too."

I didn't mind, but apparently they did. They whimpered in protest.

Clay finished staining, then rubbed the wood until it glowed.

I thanked him. As always, he'd done a magnificent job.

He packed his tools. "Be careful until Mike's murderer is caught, Willow," he warned. "Don't go anywhere alone."

I decided not to tell him that as soon as he left, I was going to drive out to Dawn's place to pay her for the linens I'd sold and pick up any new pieces she might have. She didn't scare me. She was afraid of everything. Even my dogs in the car would freak her out.

Clay drove away. I ran down to my apartment and took my dogs out the back so they wouldn't rub against their new pen's stain, then up through the side yard to the street.

Caterers were carrying covered trays into Country Chic. Tonight's party might yield more than sleuthing.

Dawn's farm was on Shore Road, east of Elderberry Bay, the same direction I'd gone early Wednesday morning after Mike's death. Had it really been only five days ago? Checking addresses on mailboxes, I drove slowly, enjoying glimpses of the ice-laden lake on my left and the woods on my right. I passed the little forest where I'd taken the evocative snapshot of the man disappearing into the woods. Dawn's house, a sweet gray cottage with white shutters, wasn't far beyond that.

Two mailboxes stood in front of it — Dawn's, and one for the house across the road. The other mailbox said Herb Gunthrie. Herb's house was tiny, with a pickup truck in the driveway.

Saturday night, I'd noticed, though it hadn't really registered, that Herb drove a black pickup.

Could it have been the truck Uncle Allen and I had seen turn onto Cayuga Avenue shortly before Mike succumbed to his injuries? Did Herb attack Mike, drive home, then, pumped with adrenaline, go for a walk in the woods?

I knocked on Dawn's front door. No

answer. A beautifully maintained old barn was behind her house. Remembering my promise to Clay not to be alone, I returned to the car and leashed the dogs, then walked them across Dawn's frozen yard.

Fragrant wood smoke downdrafted from a chimney on one end of the barn. I knocked on a normal-sized door on the side of the barn. "Dawn?" I called. "It's Willow."

She opened the door a crack. Her gray hair stood out in wisps around her head as if she'd run out to the barn the second she got out of bed. "Oh, it *is* you," she gasped like someone calming down from an enormous fright. "Come in and bring the puppies with you." She bent to let them sniff her fingers. "Hello there, you two darlings." She wasn't afraid of everything, then.

I gave her the check I'd written. "All of your placemats and napkins sold." Several looms were behind her in the toasty warm barn-turned-studio.

"That's odd."

"No it's not. Your work is very attractive."

She waved one hand in front of her face. "No, I mean someone called me, a woman with a low, hoarse voice like she was talking through burlap. She offered to buy everything I made. She wouldn't tell me who she was, so I turned her down."

"It wasn't me," I said quickly. "Mona De-Glazier is opening a home décor shop in that store next to The Ironmonger. Maybe she called you."

She looked perplexed. "Mona De-Glazier?"

"Pete DeGlazier's wife."

With a little gasp, she staggered backward. I hoped she wasn't about to swoon again. "*Pete* DeGlazier?" She shook her head as if clearing cobwebs. "He must have remarried. Into money, sounds like, if his wife has the wherewithal to open a store." Dawn probably hadn't talked to anyone since Wednesday morning, when she'd told me about Mike's gang, and now she was making up for her silence. "Years ago, Pete lost his farm and moved away. Not surprising he lost it, either. He was the laziest farmer around. Left crops to rot on the ground while he . . . I don't know. Drank, I guess."

"I hear they bought a Victorian mansion upriver from the village."

Judging from her bug-eyed expression, that astounded her.

On a loom beside me, a bedspread in a colonial pattern and shades of indigo and ivory was almost finished. I stroked the homey cloth. "Beautiful. Do you have a buyer for this?"

"A museum shop. I sell most of my work through mail order."

A smaller loom was set up for placemats and napkins, while a gorgeous chenille scarf in spring greens and pastels reminding me of daffodils, hyacinths, and lilacs was materializing on an even narrower loom.

She handed me a bag of placemats and napkins she'd finished. I suggested, "You might want to sell your things through Mona's new store, Country Chic, instead."

"No, not to a DeGlazier. Never." Her hands shook.

Time for a new subject. "Has Herb always lived across the road?"

"Only since his injury. That place is always being rented to someone new. A man named Foster inherited it. His great-great-granddaddy was one of the first settlers around Elderberry Bay. Everyone calls it the old Foster place, but no Foster's lived there for years."

"And Foster owns that field and woods immediately east of the house Herb rents?" The woods where I'd seen a man the morning Mike died.

"I own that. My farm straddles the road. The old Foster place is smack dab in middle of my farm. I've offered good prices for it. Foster refuses to sell."

Had she been planning to buy the land with the proceeds of weaving that she seemed to undervalue?

She tilted her head toward Herb's place. "Uncle Allen asked me where I was Tuesday night and Wednesday morning. I was here. I don't sleep well. Every time I looked outside that night, Herb's truck was in his driveway. Uncle Allen seemed pleased that I provided Herb with an alibi. He said that Herb told him my lights went on and off all night. Then he acted like that proved *I'd* been coming and going all night. He can't have it both ways. Either I was here all night, providing Herb with an alibi, or I wasn't here, and Herb doesn't have an alibi. That ornery policeman twists everything to suit himself." Her face paled to gray. She backed to her largest loom and plunked down onto the bench.

I decided to stop agitating her or she'd never weave another row. As I turned away with her linens and my dogs, I heard her throw the shuttle, then smack the beater against the bedspread. Maybe I could come back some time and learn more about weaving. Threadville tourists would probably love to add the skill to their many ways of creating textiles. Could Dawn come out of her shell enough to teach them?

Driving back to the village, I wondered what it had been like for her, living all alone on those bluffs above the lake where bullies like Mike Krawbach made frightening her a sport.

Mike and some of the other people around here.

Including Irv, Herb, and perhaps Smythe and Clay.

27

Back in my apartment, I opened my closet and stared at the clothes hanging in it. How dressy would Mona's party be? I finally chose black silk slacks and a black top I'd embroidered with colorful butterflies. Not owning a mink coat, I had to make do with my wool jacket.

Mona met me at the door. The velvet of her crystal-bedecked gown was stretched to its limits, riding up in unflattering ripples. She showed me where to hang my coat. "So glad you could make it." She shook her head. "Your friend is here."

Apparently, Mona meant Opal. In the short time since I had joked with Opal about whipping up an outfit for tonight, she had knit a long caftan from the fuzzy tangerine yarn. Wearing it over red hand-knit slacks and a pale yellow sweater, she resembled a sunset. She beckoned me to a buffet table. "Look at these hors d'oeuvres!"

"Tempting," I agreed. "Let's explore the store and put ourselves as far as possible from them."

A man turned around and bumped into me. "Hi!" He nodded encouragingly. "I'm Pete DeGlazier. Welcome to Mona's and my boutique, the latest on the Threadville tour."

I carefully kept my jaw from dropping. The latest on the Threadville tour? Would our usual Threadville tourists agree? Nearly everything in Country Chic was finished and decorated, with no scope for the creative touches that Threadville tourists loved to add. What would draw them to this store more than once? I asked, "Will you teach courses?"

"My wife will offer tips on interior decorating." Nod, nod. "You'll be glad to know and to tell your customers" — nod, nod, smile — "that we also provide custom upholstery and window treatments. White wine?"

I nodded back at him. White appeared to be the only choice, which was probably just as well in a store stocked with furniture upholstered in pale fabrics.

As soon as my wine was safely in my glass, I gravitated toward the fabrics in the back of the store. They were stylish and upscale, with prices to match. Who would actually do the upholstery and create the window treatments? Not, I guessed, the famously lazy Pete. Mona? Or would the work be done offsite by someone else?

Haylee found me contemplating amazingly realistic faux suede that we could sew — and embroider — if we used needles made specifically for leather. Like me, she couldn't help touching the material. She wore a tailored black suit and high-necked white blouse. Her blond hair was pinned up. Near the front door, Edna and Naomi accepted wine from Pete. Edna's hair was brown tonight, a color I'd never seen on her before, and her outfit was quite tame, although I suspected that what looked like a plain brown jacket from across the room was not plain at all. Beside her, Naomi wore a long skirt and matching jacket, both quilted in patches of black and white in a pattern resembling flying geese. Mona could learn a few things about how clothes should fit from the other Threadville boutique owners.

Hatless again, Smythe arrived and made a beeline for Haylee.

Herb brushed past the other two and zeroed in on me. "What was Petal saying about me in the post office today?"

What a strange greeting.

Pondering an answer, I sipped at my wine. "That you work very hard. But, of course, I already knew that." I tried to give him a charming smile that wouldn't signal my suspicion that he might have murdered Mike. "I couldn't have saved my cottage without your help." I felt myself flush. Whoever killed Mike Krawbach had been very instrumental in saving my cottage, either from being burned down that night, or from being bulldozed later if it survived the fire.

The store became crowded and noisy. Herb stepped closer. "I saw you visiting my neighbor today." He showed his teeth in what was probably supposed to be a grin. "The old bit . . . witch."

So Mike's gang members were every bit as fond of Dawn as she was of them. Shouldn't they have outgrown their childish animosities? Herb was Dawn's neighbor. Maybe she'd done something recently to bring about his caustic reaction. I answered his implied question. "I sell her weavings in my shop. Don't you like her?"

Herb put his face almost in mine. Maybe he didn't want to shout to make himself heard in that crowd, but his invasion of my personal space felt threatening. "All my life, she's blamed my friends and me for things we didn't do. Whenever anything happened, she was on the phone to the police."

Pursuing that line of questioning might make it dangerously clear to him that, alibi or no alibi, he was among my lists of suspects. I asked, "Where's Karen?"

He shrugged. "I don't know. Was she supposed to be here?" He kept moving closer to me, and I kept edging backward. If I was going to be cornered in one part of the store, I should have stationed myself closer to the buffet table.

A huge hand fell on my shoulder and a familiar voice bellowed, "Hello there, young lady! I see you're feeling better."

Dr. Wrinklesides.

Certain I couldn't yell loudly enough to make him hear me, I smiled.

He pushed a huge plate overflowing with food toward me. "You could use some fattening up. Help yourself."

Choosing a cube of cheddar, I looked for Herb. He was gone. Avoiding the good doctor? Maybe I should, too, if he wanted to fatten me up. "Are you singing tonight?" I shouted at Dr. Wrinklesides.

His blue eyes sparkled. "If enough people ask me to."

I pointed a finger to my chest, then held it up. "Here's one."

"It's not over until the fat man sings." Laughing, he pushed away through the crowd, giving hearty greetings and snacks to everyone.

Someone tugged at my sleeve. "Willow," Edna squeaked. "Come see what I found." I'd guessed correctly that her brown jacket wasn't plain. She'd woven it from brown satin ribbons, and had sewn tiny dark red, gold, and amber beads at each intersection of the ribbons.

I followed her past vases of silk flowers to a table of linens. "These look like Dawn's," I began. I touched a placemat. "They *are* Dawn's, the very ones I had in my store." I checked the prices. Twice what I'd been asking.

Aunt Betty had bought the lot from me and resold them to Mona and Pete. No wonder Aunt Betty told Rhonda she was making an investment. If the weavings sold at these prices, Rhonda could earn a lot.

From now on, I would charge only a little less than Mona and Pete were asking for Dawn's linens, and Dawn could have the extra profit.

Speak of the devil, I thought, catching sight of Aunt Betty. For once, she wasn't covered by an oversized snowmobile suit. Her shapeless denim dress showed off impressive biceps. She had combed her hair and smeared lipstick near her mouth. Where was Rhonda?

Edging around the crowded room, I stumbled over a love seat upholstered in tapestry featuring roosters and hens. *Fowl furniture,* I said to myself, rubbing my bruised shin and wishing I could have shared the dopey pun with someone.

A coat was thrown over the loveseat. Not thrown, actually, neatly tucked inside out so that any spills would fall on the satin lining instead of on the fur.

The only mark on the lining, so far, was a monogram, the type woven into ribbon squares, with a large initial in the middle and two smaller initials flanking the large one. The first initial was M, for Mona. The large initial was an F, not a D, and the third initial was a B. Mona must have bought — or been given — the coat before she married Pete DeGlazier, which gave credence to Dawn's theory that Pete, too lazy to farm, had married money. Too lazy to retrieve his fishing hut from the lake, too, no doubt.

I made it to the buffet and filled a plate. Herb, Haylee, and Smythe joined me. We made small talk about food until Haylee glanced toward the door. Opal and Edna were leaving, and Naomi wasn't far behind.

Haylee and I made our excuses, too.

"See you tomorrow morning at my place," Smythe said, sending Haylee a smile that should have warmed her to the toes.

"I'll be there, too," Herb reminded us.

Great. But I would heed Clay's warning and not be alone. Haylee and her guardian mothers were coming, too. We would protect each other.

"Stop in often," Mona said with a phony smile and a shake of her head when Haylee and I put on our coats.

It was dark outside. Haylee ran across the street toward The Stash. I hurried to my side yard, reached over my gate, unlocked it, and made my way down the hill to the back door. The wheelbarrows the men had used yesterday to transport sandbags had made grooves that were, for now, immortalized in frozen mud.

Not bothering to change out of my dressy outfit, I let the dogs race around while I checked on the river. It had definitely gone down, depositing debris on the trail outside my fence. But one of those branches was too boxy. I unlocked the gate, made certain the dogs stayed in the yard, tiptoed onto the icy trail, and grabbed the rectangular thing.

It was a small wooden chest, banded in

362

brass and in excellent condition as far as I could tell. I coaxed the dogs inside and gave the box a shower to wash off some of the mud it had gained on its voyage down the river. The wood grain varied from very dark to very light, exactly like the black walnut of the floor in my shop. I turned the chest over. On the bottom, someone had carved a message, very neatly.

TO SKIPPY WITH ALL MY LOVE MK

Rhonda and her friend had sighed over the beautiful jewelry boxes that Mike had made. MK had to be Mike Krawbach, but who was Skippy?

"Do you know?" I asked my dogs. They barely opened their eyes.

The box wasn't hard to open. It was empty. If I scrubbed the rest of the mud from it, I would probably discover it was new. It wasn't banged-up or dented.

How had it ended up in the river?

Leaving it to dry, I filled a tin with cookies and went upstairs through In Stitches and out to the street.

Apparently, the gala was winding down. A group of men had migrated from Country Chic to the sidewalk in front of The Iron-

363

monger.

I stopped walking with one foot on the curb and the other on the street.

Irv, Smythe, and Herb, all possibly members of Mike's gang when they were teenagers, were among the large group of men outside Sam's. Mike's old buddies. Had Mike threatened to expose one of them for something they did years ago?

The men's laughter grated, like they were having a laugh at someone's expense. They turned and stared at me.

Smythe was the only one smiling.

28

Dr. Wrinklesides drove past in a black SUV. Apparently, he recognized me underneath the streetlight. He tooted his horn, lowered his window, and called out, "The fat man sang!"

I made an exaggeratedly sad face to show I was sorry I'd missed it, then ran across the street to Buttons and Bows. Haylee met me at the door. The lights inside Edna's notions boutique had been dimmed, but ribbons and buttons glimmered in stray beams from Mona's brightly lit shop kitty-corner across the street. Haylee preceded me through Edna's back room and up the stairs. At the top, Haylee turned around, obviously to see my face. Her eyes danced with mischief.

My tin of cookies nearly slid out of my hands. Entering Edna's living room was like walking into a lemon. Pale yellow was everywhere. Floors, walls, furniture, and window coverings. And Edna had been creative with her notions. Cording, braid, and fringes embellished upholstery and cushions. Grommets and tiny silver medallions decorated blinds and matching drapes. The rug was bound with tape in shades of lemon and lime. Even the picture frames were covered in crystals, gilt, and sequins. As I took it all in, I realized I shouldn't have termed them picture frames. There was no artwork, only mirrors in the frames. Beveled mirrors, convex mirrors, small mirrors, huge mirrors. Blinding mirrors.

Naomi, Edna, and Opal rushed into the living room. Opal hugged me. I couldn't see the stitches in the caftan she'd knit because the yarn was so fuzzy, but my fingers accidentally poked through holes. She must have used very large needles. "You look like you've solved Mike's murder, Willow," she said.

Actually, I was in awe of my surroundings, so maybe it was just as well that she misread my expression. I told them about the jewelry box I'd found and the inscription carved on it. They were disappointed that it hadn't been filled with jewels. On the other hand, if it had, it might have sunk and I never would have found it.

Haylee laughed. "Mike made furniture for

his dog?"

Naomi asked, "Did he have a dog?"

Haylee shook her head. "I don't think so."

"Who lives upriver from you, Willow?" Opal asked.

I hadn't lived in the area long enough to know. "Pete and Mona DeGlazier. And Clay's building new houses." I frowned at the sheer number of possibilities.

"Lots of people," Haylee said

"How about Mike Krawbach?" Opal prodded.

Haylee shook her head. "His vineyard is . . . wasn't near the river."

I could have attested to that, but I said nothing.

Edna's dining room matched the living room, all pale yellow, except that the table was covered by a deep green tablecloth edged in green and gold. Linen napkins, rolled up and tied in satin ribbons, matched the tablecloth. The plates were lemon yellow, and so were the wine glasses. Two bottles of red wine were open and breathing.

Edna's kitchen was also pale yellow. She had even found drawer and door pulls made of yellow porcelain. Below the counter, they were shaped like bows. Above the counter, they were shaped like buttons, complete with porcelain thread.

I peeked out between pastel yellow curtains. Aunt Betty had joined the group in front of The Ironmonger. I told the others about the investment she and Rhonda had made, buying low from me and selling high to Mona and Pete.

Edna lifted the cover from her slow cooker. Boeuf bourguignon? She sniffed. With a satisfied smile, she concluded, "Aunt Betty even looks like a murderer."

Haylee tamed a grin. "And how does a murderer look?"

Edna lowered her eyebrows, wrinkled her nose, and showed her teeth. "Evil."

I giggled. No matter how hard she tried, birdlike little Edna could never look ferocious.

Still attempting to snarl, she added, "Aunt Betty got that look from her years of evil deeds." She drained homemade noodles. Where had she found time to make all this?

Haylee tossed shredded red cabbage with a dressing containing aromatic, freshly toasted sesame seeds. "And her motive for murder was?"

Opal dished up roasted eggplant, onions, and peppers. "We don't know her motive, but why has she been helping her husband collect evidence against Willow?" Without waiting for us to answer, she continued, "She can't let Uncle Allen guess that *she* committed the murder."

Edna picked up a bowl of stew. "Don't forget Rhonda and her fleck of aqua paint. And her threats against Willow in the ladies' room." She jingled into the dining room in orange felt slippers that she must have crafted herself. She'd sewn tiny bells all over them.

We followed, all bringing dishes of food. I laughed off Rhonda's and her friend's threats, even though they had frightened me at the time. I reminded everyone, "Rhonda also tried to sneak into my apartment."

Edna dimmed lights and lit candles. "I'm guessing that after Mike gave Rhonda one of those jewelry boxes, he spurned her. Who could blame him? Now she regrets killing him, since she lost her only shot at capturing a man. And Aunt Betty guesses the truth and is trying to protect her. Maybe Uncle Allen is trying to protect her, too. These people! Banding together against outsiders. Against us."

I could only hope that the state police weren't about to join that band.

We sat at Edna's dining table and toasted each other with the wine. Edna flapped her napkin into her lap. "I noticed the pretty white placemats in your apartment Wednesday morning, Willow, when Uncle Allen interrogated us. I hope you have some dark linens."

I loved new projects. "I'll make some." Or I'd embroider Dawn's. I mentally kicked myself. No. I would not destroy the simplicity of Dawn's hand-woven placemats. I'd make new ones, using the nice, heavy linen I carried in my shop or the scrumptious cottons Haylee offered in The Stash. "Why should I have dark linens?" My apartment was mostly white, with coral and sage accents, nothing dark. Branching out into other colors wouldn't exactly hurt me, though, especially if it meant creating and embroidering new soft furnishings.

Naomi poured burgundy into our glasses. "We all love red wine. And we spill."

Maybe I would make my new placemats and napkins from a synthetic that might release red wine stains more easily than cotton or linen, and I'd embroider them with dark red thread.

Watching my face, Naomi giggled. Was she already tipsy, or had my thoughts been transparent, and funny, besides?

Haylee rolled her eyes. "These three sometimes forget they're no longer eight years old."

Naomi raised her glass. "I'll drink to that."

"Forever young," Opal said, clinking her glass against Naomi's.

Sort of like Mike Krawbach, I thought, with an involuntary pang of sympathy for a man I hadn't liked, a man who would never have the chance to grow old. Who had wanted him to cease to exist?

Edna took a bite of her stew, then jumped up, raced to a pale yellow side table, grabbed her notebook, and rejoined us. "Uncle Allen wants to solve the case quickly, so he's fallen into the trap of believing his friends and relatives but not us."

Haylee suggested, "His brother, Pete DeGlazier, could be the Pete in Karen's story about the lazy fisherman."

I tasted Edna's delicious boeuf bourguignon. "Dawn said that Pete DeGlazier was a lazy farmer —"

Edna bobbed her head up and down. "Goes with being a lazy fisherman!"

I finished, "And lost his first farm and his first wife due to his laziness. And maybe drinking. Now, he's married to Mona, who has opened a shop and also wears a full-length mink coat."

Opal turned her yellow goblet around, as if studying the way it gave her wine those brassy orange tones. "A mink coat? And she's president of the nature club?"

Edna stabbed a finger down onto one page. "Irv," she announced. "I don't trust Irv. He gave sandbags to Pete DeGlazier when he should have given them to Willow."

"And Pete is Uncle Allen's brother," I added. "Irv could have been trying to get on the good side of the law after all those years of lawlessness in Mike's gang."

"Irv has a short fuse," Haylee contributed. "Remember Mike's memorial service, when the sound system kept giving him problems, and people yelled at him to move back?"

Opal answered, "He got really annoyed, really fast."

"I learned more about another former gang member today — Herb," I told them. "Petal, our postmistress, seems afraid of him. She told me that Herb believes that, for a prank, Mike caused the tractor Herb was driving in Mike's vineyard to roll over. Mike deflated the tires on one side of his tractor and then ordered Herb to drive the tractor across a slope."

"Awful," said Opal.

"Despicable," Naomi added.

Haylee scowled. "Some prank. Not funny. But I can easily believe Mike would do something like that."

Edna hopped up. "That's it! Herb has to be the one who killed Mike. We discounted him because we didn't think he was strong enough, but the way he heaved those sandbags around . . ." She plopped into her seat and paged through her notebook. "Herb could have been *killed* when Mike's tractor toppled over on him. His anger probably simmered and simmered."

Naomi covered her mouth with her hand and closed her eyes for a second. "I'd hate to think of Herb as a murderer. I'd hate to think of anyone . . ." Her voice trailed off, and her eyes became shiny like she was about to cry. She whispered, "But someone is a murderer. Very likely someone we know."

Naomi was usually the one who patted arms. This time, I patted hers. "At the gala, Herb didn't seem to care where Karen was, though he took her to the dinner dance."

Haylee giggled. "Maybe the evening didn't go well for him."

Her mothers studied her face, probably wondering how her evening had gone with Smythe.

I quickly brought the subject back to suspects. Specifically Herb. "He was avoiding Dr. Wrinklesides, like maybe he was hiding a new injury from him. Or a lack of an old one. He asked me what Petal said about him at the post office — naturally I didn't tell him about her accusations — and he doesn't like Dawn, either. He claimed she kept calling the police on him and his friends."

"Not surprising," Haylee commented. "If they did all the things she said they did."

I held up a cautionary finger. "However, Dawn reported to Uncle Allen that Herb's truck was in his driveway all night when Mike died. So although Dawn and Herb don't like each other, Dawn gave Herb an alibi."

Opal asked sensibly, "What was Dawn doing up all night watching Herb's driveway?"

"Insomnia," I answered.

"Right," Edna chimed in. "Insomniacs say they never sleep. Never? Herb could have gone out that night long enough to attack Mike, and she slept through it. Some alibi."

I added, "And Herb claimed that Dawn's light kept going on and off that night, implying that she went out in the middle of the night to attack Mike."

Haylee burst out laughing. "Imagine both of them peering out at each other's houses all night! It sounds like neither one of them can be trusted to know what really happened. Didn't Herb sign up for tomorrow's hike?"

I twisted my napkin in my lap. "Yes. With Karen." I felt sorry for her. "We'll have to watch them. She may not know to be cautious around him."

Haylee put on a carefree smile. "Or she does, and that's why yesterday's date didn't go well for Herb. Lucky thing Smythe's main crop is lavender. No one can hide in tufts of lavender, even in the full bloom of summer. No murderer will suddenly jump out at us." She raised her arms in the air. "Boo!"

Naomi squinted with worry. "We're supposedly hiking in Smythe's woodlot. Trees and things like that." She shuddered.

Haylee waved that aside. "It's winter. No leaves on the trees. We'll easily keep track of each other."

"Shall we all go together in the morning?" Opal asked.

Haylee shook her head. "Don't anyone wait for me, in case I sleep late. I'll go in my own car and catch up."

Opal frowned at her. "And you'll drive carefully."

"Of course," Haylee said.

"I'd better go in my own car, too," I said. "So if the hike drags along, I can take off

375

early and have time to walk the dogs before opening my shop. Otherwise, they'll have to suffer through a very long morning."

Opal, Naomi, and Edna reluctantly agreed that we would be safe in our own cars. They were going together in Edna's car. Opal raised her glass in a toast to a safe and worthwhile nature hike. By worthwhile, I didn't think she meant we'd be learning about nature. Human nature, maybe.

Edna paged through her notebook. "I want you to know that our suspicions about Herb fill the most pages in my notebook. We'll have to be especially careful around him."

"Around *all* of them," I amended.

29

After I went home and let the dogs out, I phoned Trooper Smallwood. She wasn't available, so against my better judgment, I asked for Trooper Gartener.

"What's up?" he asked. What a talker.

"Someone here in Elderberry Bay had a real grudge against Mike Krawbach."

Gartener responded with his usual silence.

I summed up the allegations Petal had made about Mike harming Herb.

Another long silence. Then, "Did you witness this yourself — the tractor rolling, tires deflated, everything you just told me?"

"No, but —" I barreled on without thinking. "Did *you* witness *me* threatening to kill Mike?"

I immediately wanted to take my words back.

"I believe that Detective DeGlazier did. Am I right?"

"No, he only heard about it. As I told you

before, it wasn't a real threat."

"As I told *you* before, we're checking everything. If we arrested on hearsay and incomplete evidence, the wrong person could be behind bars."

Like me. I guessed I was supposed to thank him. I said good-bye and told myself not to call the state police again unless I had concrete evidence. Like a confession. Written, signed, and witnessed.

When the alarm went off the next morning, I wanted to go back to sleep, but my friends and I had promised to look after each other during the nature hike, and I wouldn't dream of endangering the others by not showing up. I dressed in warm layers. I would have liked to take my camera, but the police had not recovered it.

My dogs, with their enthusiasm for chasing anything that moved, probably wouldn't be welcome on a nature hike. I let them have a quick run around the yard, then put them in the apartment. Stars twinkled in the predawn sky.

The beginning of the route to Smythe's farm followed the same roads I'd taken the day before. Dawn's house was dark. A light burned in Herb's, and his truck wasn't in his driveway. Stars dimmed and disappeared as the sky paled. A mile farther on, I turned inland and drove to the sign announcing *Hap-Bee Hap-Bee Lavender Farm.* Hand-painted bees, apparently drunk with happiness or lavender pollen, swirled around the letters.

Cold magnified the crunch of my tires on Smythe's long and winding gravel driveway. When I rounded the last curve, my headlights picked out a slew of black pickups. It was almost enough to make me flee, but Smythe's honey-colored pickup and Haylee's and Edna's sedans were there. I turned my car around so I'd have no problem leaving in time to take the dogs out before work, and parked on frozen ground beside the driveway.

I pulled my collar up and jogged toward Smythe's brightly lit, screened porch.

Through the screens, I recognized Haylee, Opal, Naomi, Edna, Herb, Karen, Irv, Pete DeGlazier, Jacoba and Luther from the General Store, and Smythe wearing his bright yellow parka and bee-stinger cap. I didn't know several people clustered around a woman whose back was toward me. She wore a black puffy parka with a fur-lined hood hiding her face. Rhonda?

I climbed the wooden steps to Smythe's porch. They creaked with cold. Herb opened the screen door for me. Its hinges screeched.

"So glad you could make it, Willow," Opal called, waving.

The woman in the black parka faced us. Mona DeGlazier. Of course she'd wear fur. "We can't wait for any *more* laggards." Shaking her head, she shot me an irritated look, like I was a foot-dragging kindergartner. "We have to start out."

She herded us all off the porch and away from the driveway, then paused to allow Smythe to catch up. She looked annoyed at having to ask him for directions, and even more annoyed when, beaming, he handed each of us a map showing his farm and trails running through it. He must have drawn the original — cute bees like the ones on his sign decorated the upper edges. He'd drawn bouquets of lavender and pumpkins on the sides, and bunches of grapes and shocks of wheat on the bottom margins. Always on the lookout for designs to interpret in embroidery, I carefully folded my copy into a pocket.

A car door slammed, and I thought Mona might have apoplexy at the sight of more laggards. Aunt Betty in her snowmobile suit and Rhonda in a parka similar to Mona's ambled toward the group.

Mona led us across the corner of a field where last summer's cornstalks waved their tattered flags. The broken cornstalks reminded me of the wall hanging I'd mailed yesterday. If my client didn't love it, I'd be happy to take it back. But I knew she'd like it. Who wouldn't?

I tripped over a frozen, lumpy furrow. Smythe grabbed my elbow and kept me on my feet. I thanked him. "I thought you grew lavender."

He grinned down at me. "I do, lots of it, but in some of my fields, like this one, I alternate between corn and soy. And sometimes pumpkins."

"The really big ones?"

His eyes twinkled. "I'll plant a patch of those this spring. You can have the biggest one you can carry."

"Like I can carry a three-hundred-pound pumpkin."

Mona halted with her back to a forest. "Smythe, don't you maintain a trail into your woodlot?"

He politely showed her the trail without pointing out that she was merely five feet from it. With Pete beside her, she marched along the wide pathway that Smythe had obviously kept neatly cut.

Haylee, Naomi, Opal, Edna, and I walked together, chatting about the difficulties of getting up so early.

Mona stopped and raised a hand. "We must *all* be silent." Her head wobbled back and forth. "To best experience the wildlife." If the wildlife had any sense, they'd be cuddled into warm nests and dens.

We managed to stop chatting, but our boots were not exactly quiet. We bumbled along, tripping over roots and halting whenever Mona lifted her binoculars and scanned trees. "Woodpeckers have been here," she stated once. Apparently, *her* voice wouldn't frighten the wildlife.

Smythe hiked behind Mona and Pete. Haylee caught up with him. Who could blame her? He was not only handsome and sweet, he drew cute bees and was fun to be with. And he had offered me a huge pumpkin. Knowing him, he would lend me his pickup truck and wheelbarrow to transport it. Opal and Naomi walked side by side behind Haylee and Smythe, and Edna and I followed them. Aunt Betty and Rhonda were close behind me, breathing loudly.

Mona stopped and pointed at the ground. "Coyote scat."

"Scat, coyote," Edna mumbled, which earned her a dirty look and another head shake from Mona.

I had something to worry about besides coyotes. We had expected to be in a forest of bare trunks and limbs where we could easily keep track of everyone, but the trail had entered a grove of evergreens, and Karen and Herb had fallen back where I couldn't see or hear them. Karen could be alone with a murderer. I whispered to Edna, "Karen must be somewhere behind us. With Herb."

Edna's eyes opened in frightened shock. "We'd better go back and find her."

"But what about Hay—"

"Naomi and Opal will stay with her."

I hoped Edna was right. We retraced our steps, passing hikers I didn't know, then Irv with a woman I'd seen at the roast beef dinner. Jacoba and Luther were behind them. Jacoba threw me a half smile.

Finally, Edna and I were alone with pine trees that whispered mournful secrets above our heads. Someone stumbled on the path behind us. I pivoted around.

Rhonda ducked behind a large pine. Somebody coughed and was shushed.

"We'll have to lose them," Edna murmured.

I wasn't sure how to go about that. If we stepped off the trail, we might lose ourselves and not be found until summer, except by those coyotes.

We found Herb and Karen standing apart,

like a couple in the midst of a quarrel, with their backs to us. Herb must have heard us. He turned around and asked cheerfully, "Going back already?"

That might have been nice, but we had to stick to this pair until they joined the rest of the crowd.

Edna, seldom at a loss for words, began talking about recognizing trees by their bark. Since the only tree I could identify, and not by the bark, was a weeping willow, which I suspected we weren't likely to find in the midst of a forest, I hoped she knew more about tree bark than I did. Or than Herb and Karen did. She adroitly herded them toward where we'd last seen our friends. We passed Rhonda, stooping to help Aunt Betty disentangle the tops of her clodhopper boots from her pant legs.

Finally, we emerged from the thick pines and caught up with the others in a more open section of the woods that had once been used for what farm woodlots were supposedly meant for — firewood. Stumps dotted the ground.

Mona darted angry looks at us as we joined the group circling her and a particularly large stump. "You may think that Smythe is a lazy woodsman," she said, "leaving all this brush about, but there's a method to his madness. Can anyone guess what it was?" She shook her head as if discouraging anyone to answer.

Nodding his head beside his wife, Pete looked totally unconcerned. Maybe he had no idea that half the village pictured him whenever they heard the word "lazy."

Smythe's face reddened. From the cold or from being called mad, I wasn't sure. He opened his mouth.

Mona forestalled him. "No, don't tell them, Smythe, let them guess why you didn't clean up the brush." With every phrase, she shook her head no, while her husband nodded his head yes.

Picturing their dinnertime conversations, I stifled a giggle.

Pete's cold blue eyes bored into me.

I finally came up with the pun I'd been wanting to make the entire time I'd been creating a version of machine stumpwork. "I'm stumped."

Rhonda and Aunt Betty tiptoed out of the woods and crept closer.

"Wildlife," Edna stated loudly.

Mona glared at Edna like she didn't want anyone, especially *laggards,* coming up with answers to her questions. "Habitat," Mona corrected Edna. "Wildlife needs habitat."

So did I. Preferably with central heating. I

mentally designed a coat for Pennsylvania winters. I'd make it hooded and ankle length, which would be nice and warm. And would also provide plenty of yardage to embroider. Right, I reminded myself, and then I'd really fit in with the most eccentric of the Threadville retailers and tourists.

Meanwhile, Mona presented us with an exciting, nature-inspired activity for a freezing winter morning. "I want you all to count the rings on this stump. As you can see, the tree was very old." She shook her head. "By counting the rings, one for each year, we can find out how old."

Opal and Naomi joined the group of hikers who were obediently bending over, pointing with mittened and gloved fingers, and muttering numbers under their breath.

"What kind of tree was it, Mona?" Edna asked. She looked innocent and curious, but I had a feeling she knew the answer and wanted to find out if Mona did. As far as I could tell, the fur around Mona's hood was fox, as real as the mink she'd worn yesterday. Were all naturalists this unnatural?

One thing I could say for Rhonda was that her fur did not appear to come from any animal. I didn't dare turn around to double check, though, for fear I would accidentally knock her down. On the other hand, if I knocked her down, she might learn to stay more than an inch away from me.

Mona blustered about the stump having weathered since the tree had been cut down.

Good excuse. *She* was the one who had suggested counting mostly invisible rings.

"I can tell you what kind of tree it was," Irv said. "Black walnut." He threw a challenging stare at Smythe.

Clutching at his back, one man straightened from his ring counting. "It was at least a hundred," he said.

I couldn't help a gasp. "What a pity, to cut down such an old tree!"

Smythe's cheeks became redder and his blue eyes watered. I immediately felt guilty for my outburst, and tried to tone it down. "I suppose trees die of old age, anyway, and the wood just rots away, so it's best to cut it down while it can still be used for firewood."

"Black walnut for firewood?" Irv's voice was full of scorn. "It's worth too much as fine lumber for furniture and such. No one would burn it up." Again, that wordless challenge aimed at Smythe.

I felt worse. Was selling lavender honey, plus a field of corn one year and soy the next, and maybe a few giant pumpkins, a reliable way of making a living? Maybe Smythe needed cash. If forced to choose between killing a tree or selling the farm to a stranger who might chop the trees down anyway, who wouldn't opt to save his farm?

Smythe twisted toward Haylee and cradled the tops of young shrubs between his work gloves. The shrubs had rooted themselves in a crumbling log. I was close enough to hear him murmur, "Forests regenerate themselves. Dead trees provide fertilizer for new plants."

The woman who had been with Irv at the roast beef dinner lifted a spray of bright pink and mauve plastic orchids to her nose as if enjoying their fragrance. Obviously, I didn't understand the finer details of nature hikes.

Hiding her face behind the artificial flowers, she drifted off the pathway, slipped between the lower branches of two massive pine trees, and disappeared.

Irv made an abrupt turn. Clenching his jaw and placing his feet carefully between twigs on the frozen ground, he dodged silently into the woods after her.

Edna and I looked at each other in dismay. Irv had been one of Mike's gang. We'd been focusing on Herb, but, like almost everyone on this hike, Irv could be a murderer.

30

With unnerving stealth, Irv disappeared into the woods behind the woman with the plastic orchids. Whoever she was, she could be in danger.

Edna nudged me. We ducked under pine branches. Aunt Betty and Rhonda stayed with me like I had them on leashes.

In a clearing, Irv and the woman he'd pursued stood side by side, holding hands and gazing downward. Her garish pink orchids stuck out of a rotting log, an incongruous sight in February. A candle burned next to the log. Quietly, the rest of the hikers filed into the frozen glade. Irv raised his head and launched into another eulogy about what a fine man Mike had been.

Another memorial service? What had we gotten ourselves into?

I'd become good at understanding my friends' wordless communication. Haylee, Opal, Naomi, and Edna were as thrilled about being tricked into yet another service for Mike as I was.

"My wife and I thought we should include a little tribute to Mike as part of this morning's events," Irv intoned. "In Mike's woods."

I thought we were in Smythe's woods. Smythe had drawn grapes on the lower corner of his map — to indicate Mike's vineyard? I didn't want to make crinkling sounds, so I didn't haul my map out of my pocket to check. Haylee had directed me to a different part of Mike's farm in the dark, and we'd made several false turns. Suddenly, part of the geography south of Elderberry Bay fell into place for me. Mike's house had to be near the south boundary of his farm, or vineyard, as he'd preferred to call it, and these woods had to be on the north boundary.

Irv corroborated it. "Mike's woodlot was next to the vineyard where he toiled so many years, trying to make an honest living for himself. And now he has been *mowed down*." Irv glared at me. "Unmercifully, at a terribly young age."

My heart beat so loudly I was sure everyone could hear it. Had Mike's buddies conspired to bring the village's newcomers to this lonely spot in Mike's woodlot so they could exact revenge for his death? I tensed, ready to grab my friends and flee. I felt their resolve to do the same thing shimmer through the air between us.

Mike's buddies did come precariously close to slaying us.

With their singing.

The hymn's first verse dove catastrophically into a minor key. The second shattered into dissonant wails with no recognizable tune. Where was Dr. Wrinklesides when we needed him?

Giggles were hard to control. Not only because of the singing, but because of the array of outerwear in that clearing — Aunt Betty in her reprehensible snowmobile suit, Rhonda in that ratty parka, Haylee and her mothers in their perfectly handcrafted coats, Mona in her fox-trimmed parka, Irv in a navy blue jacket with the plastic tie that had once held the price tag still sticking out of a seam, his wife in cashmere, Jacoba and Luther in bulky down-filled coats, and last but not least, Smythe in his bright yellow parka and bee-stinger stocking cap.

Fortunately, no one seemed to remember the words to the third verse, and they pulled their scarves up over their mouths like a bunch of bandits trying to figure out which bank to rob.

Or who to chase through Mike's forest.

I edged backward. Edna did, too.

So did Rhonda and Aunt Betty.

Mona and Pete charged past us toward the trail. Most of the group followed, but Haylee and Smythe hung back. Without even the smallest signal passing between us, Edna and I waited.

Haylee bent over and blew out the candle. Standing, she gave Smythe a defiant look. "I wouldn't want a fire in Mike's woods to spread to yours."

He thanked her and gave her shoulders a squeeze. Seeing Edna and me watching like old-timey chaperones, Haylee blushed, though she had to understand that we were only guarding each other as we'd promised.

Throwing the pair a bland smile, I offered an excuse, mainly for Smythe's benefit. "We were going to put that candle out if Haylee didn't." The snuffed wax smell lingered like an unwanted memory. After a last glance at the shrine with its dismal fake orchids, I followed Haylee, Smythe, and Edna out of Mike's woodlot and into Smythe's. Mona waited impatiently, as if we couldn't find our way back to Smythe's house, even with him along.

Leading us along the wide trail, Mona made sporadic comments about flora and fauna. "In the spring," she announced, shaking her head ominously, "these woods will be full of songbirds."

Maybe by spring, someone could coax me to go on another nature hike. Maybe, but I sincerely doubted it.

Walking beside my loyal protector, Edna, I pictured the antique black walnut floors in my shop and in The Ironmonger, the buttons Mike must have crafted from thin walnut branches, and the carved treasure chest that the flood had left behind. Who was I to criticize someone else for wanting to enjoy the beauty of black walnut? I hadn't meant to criticize Smythe, and had probably hurt his feelings.

Edna pulled at my sleeve. Haylee and Smythe had gone ahead, out of view, and Opal and Naomi were trying to forge past Mona and Pete, who were very neatly blocking their path.

I stopped. Rhonda crashed into my back. Ignoring her shrill swearing, I grabbed a pine bough. "Mona," I called. "Can you tell what kind of tree this is?" It looked exactly like every other pine tree around us.

My ploy worked. Mona and Pete came shaking and nodding back to us, allowing Opal and Naomi to rush off after Haylee and Smythe. "How many needles in a cluster?" Mona asked.

With Aunt Betty wheezing alarmingly close to my shoulder, I took time counting to give Opal and Naomi a chance to catch up with Haylee.

"Five needles," Edna answered for me.

"W-H-I-T-E," Mona spelled, shaking her head. "Five letters and five needles. It's a white pine."

I thanked her, and she rushed to the head of the line again, at least to the head of the line that we could see. Opal, Naomi, Haylee, and Smythe had to be way out in front.

Edna and I stuck to Herb and Karen along the trail through the woods, across a corner of the field, through a natural windbreak of bushy evergreens, and into Smythe's farmyard. We passed his barn and outbuildings, all recently painted and very neat. Padlocked, too, maybe to keep the latest generation of teen gangs out.

Irv positioned himself beside the straggling line of hikers and collected Smythe's maps. With an innocent smile, I kept my map hidden in my pocket. I would find out when Smythe's birthday was and I'd embroider a version of his map on a fabric card for him.

Aunt Betty and Rhonda straggled behind. They may have decided they didn't have to continue playing detective. Or they couldn't keep up.

We climbed onto Smythe's screened porch. He opened a door, showing off a spotless, warm, and inviting kitchen. He'd taken off the yellow parka and bee-stinger cap, and had donned a yellow and black striped apron. Behind him Haylee, Opal, and Naomi wore aprons identical to his. They all looked extremely proud of themselves.

"Come on in, everybody," Smythe called. "Coffee's on, and we'll have toast and honey."

He had rushed ahead to prepare breakfast. Apparently, Haylee, Opal, and Naomi had volunteered to help.

I hesitated. Smythe's breakfast sounded delicious.

"Are you coming in?" Edna asked me.

I shoved my coat sleeve back to catch a glimpse of my watch. It was nearly eight. "I need to get back to take my dogs out again before I open the shop so the poor babies won't have to wait until noon. You stay."

She made a show of eyeing the black pickup trucks parked along both sides of the winding driveway. I got the message. Anyone could be hiding behind or in one of them. "I'll walk you to your car," she muttered.

I whispered, "And who will escort you back to Smythe's house? The others are inside helping him."

She raised her chin. "I'll be fine."

I suggested in a quiet mumble, "Just watch from here until I get to my car."

She agreed.

I ran down Smythe's porch steps and jogged past Jacoba and Luther, who were sitting in one of the black pickups with its engine running. I got into my car and negotiated the driveway's curves.

Smythe's farm had to be about halfway between Shore Road and the next road, farther south, the one I thought passed Mike's driveway. I chose the way I knew.

I turned the corner onto Shore Road. A black pickup truck was behind me. I thought it might be Herb's, but it passed his place. Smoke drifted from the chimney on Dawn's barn.

I stepped on the gas. The truck sped up. I slowed down. It did, too. It never came close enough for me to see who was in it.

Was someone following me? Mike's murderer?

I told myself to calm down. Nearly everyone in this morning's group had arrived in

396

black pickups. It stood to reason that at least one other hiker besides me couldn't stay for Smythe's breakfast and would return to Elderberry Bay along Shore Road. Herb could be on his way to work. Or it could be Luther and Jacoba on their way back to open up the General Store.

The truck dropped back before I made the turn onto Lake Street. Nevertheless, I parked in front of In Stitches, ran inside, and locked the door.

In the apartment, Sally and Tally attempted to kiss my face without putting their paws on me. "Sorry I didn't take you along," I told them. "Mona wouldn't have liked you interfering with the wildlife, though you might have been more interested in coyote scat than the rest of us were." I opened the back door. Forgiving as always, the pups raced around until I called them in so I could make certain that In Stitches was ready for the Threadville tour bus and the day's lessons.

I'd swept the night before. My shop was spotless, but some of my smaller embroidery hoops were hidden behind larger ones again. I rearranged them on the counter. Nestled together, the laminated oak hoops made concentric circles like the rings of that stump this morning. My pun about being stumped had gone over like a . . . like a downed tree. Clay might have laughed.

Smythe was usually happy to joke around, but something had been bothering him. Probably Mona and her discouraging head shaking.

I booted up my computer to work on my next stumpwork project. I planned to puff up the ice fishing hut, the smoke coming out of its chimney, and the ATV parked on the lake. I would add several layers of foam to the foreground, too, and I would embroider copies of twisty, bare sumac trunks growing on the edge of the bluff above the lake, then wire them to bend forward from the picture. When it was done, I would display it where it might encourage my students to try new things. And to buy new sewing and embroidery machines.

As I hooped fabric and stabilizer and placed pieces of foam in the right places, all I could see was Smythe's distressed face when I blurted my feelings about killing an old tree.

Later, in his kitchen, he'd appeared happy and proud of his place. His farm was amazingly neat, and he obviously tried to keep it perfect. I saw again his recently painted barn and the sturdy outbuildings surrounding his farmyard.

I flung the back of my hand across my mouth.

All of his outbuildings had been padlocked. One of those locks had been shiny and new.

Wasn't that lock similar to the ones I'd bought the night before Mike died?

According to Sam the ironmonger, the old-timers had seen Mike pocket something that could have been a package containing one of those locks with a key matching mine. Where had that padlock ended up?

Smythe's farm?

31

I'd ruled Smythe out as Mike's murderer for three reasons. One, he was too sweet. Two, I hadn't figured out a motive for him. Three, he'd been in Erie when Mike was attacked.

Murderers could appear sweet, I knew.

Other people had stronger motives.

Herb was my prime suspect. Mike had caused him injury and pain. Herb had loved driving big rigs. Now all he could do was putt around in a cute post office vehicle.

Pete DeGlazier's motive was a little more nebulous. Maybe Mike had stolen Pete's fishing hut and everything in it.

Irv had been Mike's friend when they were boys, committing minor crimes together, maybe. Had Mike threatened to reveal things about Irv's past that could cause Irv to lose his job as mayor of Elderberry Bay?

If Smythe had been a regular in Mike's

gang, his motive could be similar to Irv's. Was it worth killing over, many years later?

Those huge amounts going into Mike's bank account — had Mike been successfully blackmailing someone? Smythe?

Smythe had seemed uncomfortable about the black walnut stump on his property, right next to Mike's woods. And Irv had goaded him about it. Smythe's face had become red, and he'd turned away. So we couldn't see his expression? Was it anger? At Irv or at Mike?

According to the women who threatened me in the ladies' room at the roast beef dinner, Mike had loved beautiful things made of wood. Mike had wanted to bulldoze Blueberry Cottage, which was built of irreplaceable hardwoods. Had he loved beautiful wood enough to condemn my cottage so he could take the lumber for his own projects?

Enough to steal a tree from Smythe? Many trees?

Lots of trees had been cut down in that section of Smythe's woodlot, and in Mike's woods next to it, but not in other parts of Smythe's forest where hardwoods grew. Had Mike logged his own forest and part of Smythe's, fooled the timber company into believing he owned it all, and pocketed the proceeds? There had been about ten years between the two huge deposits in Mike's bank account. The timing seemed odd for blackmail, but not impossible. Timber probably couldn't be harvested that often if the woods were totally cut down each time, but in Smythe's woodlot, only selected trees had been felled, including an enormous black walnut that might have netted tens of thousands of dollars by itself.

And Smythe, reputedly as sweet as his honey, may have said nothing about the theft. Not then.

There was a fly in the honey. Smythe had left for the Honey Makers' Conference the evening before Mike died, and hadn't returned until Friday. I'd assumed he'd done the obvious thing and stayed in Erie all that time.

That had been a silly, unthinking conclusion, the sort Uncle Allen might jump to. In fact, Uncle Allen had jumped to it. Surely, I could reason better than that.

Smythe could have waited until Wednesday morning to leave for Erie, he might have never gone to the conference, or maybe he left Erie during the night and made it back to the hotel before the conference's first morning meetings. It would have been daring, though. His amber truck would be recognizable among all the black ones in and around Elderberry Bay.

Maybe he borrowed someone's black pickup truck. Mike's? Or he'd come with Mike on Mike's ATV, and walked home, shortening his time away from the conference by cutting through Dawn's farm.

I needed to take another look at the photo I'd taken last Wednesday morning of the man in the orange hat disappearing into the woods. The only hat I'd ever seen on Smythe was his whimsical yellow and black striped stocking cap, but that didn't mean he couldn't have worn an orange one, especially if he didn't want to be recognized. Had I taken a photo of a killer walking home after beating Mike?

I discovered another fly in the honey. I realized with a shock that all of the photographs I'd taken that morning were missing. Someone had deleted them.

There was no reason to do that unless the killer feared that my photos could provide evidence against him. It was a stretch. When I'd photographed the man, he'd been almost ten miles from the scene of the crime, and Mike had been dead for almost three hours. *Long enough for someone to walk that distance . . .*

But if the killer knew he was the person

I'd photographed, it wouldn't have seemed like a stretch to him. He could be afraid that my evidence might point straight to him.

And he could have easily heard about the photographs I'd taken. The local amateur sleuths had snooped around my computer and informed Uncle Allen, and probably everyone else in Elderberry Bay, that I had a picture of *Mike,* but when I took the photo that was now missing, Mike was already dead.

If the man in the photo was a murderer, he might fear that, sooner or later, someone would examine that photo and discover the time and date the picture was taken. They would know that the man in the photo couldn't be Mike.

To prevent anyone from identifying him and figuring out that he had been fleeing the scene of the crime, the killer could have stolen my camera, turned on my computer, and erased all of my photographic evidence.

All?

He wouldn't have known to search through my embroidery portfolio. Trembling, I loaded my embroidery software.

Sure enough, I'd saved the best photo where only an embroiderer would look.

The man was taller than Herb or Irv. As

tall as Pete or Smythe.

Or Clay.

The break-in had occurred while I was at the roast beef dinner, which Clay hadn't attended. But Clay couldn't be a murderer, I told myself, repeating Haylee's confident assertion from the night before.

Smythe had attended the roast beef dinner. I'd seen him when we were lining up for food, but not before or after. He could have arrived at the dinner late or departed early, could have broken into my shop, stolen my camera, and deleted my photos. I didn't want Smythe to be a murderer, either, but I'd seen that shiny padlock hanging from one of his sheds.

In hopes of figuring out for sure who the man was, I enlarged the photo on my screen. The resolution wasn't great, but I could make out a bit of yellow and maybe some black on the man's right hand.

Could that be one of Smythe's hand-knit yellow and black striped gloves? I hadn't seen those gloves since before Mike's death. Smythe had been bare handed or wearing work gloves ever since. He had worn the hat and socks that matched the gloves, however.

Although I couldn't positively identify the man in the photo, I renamed it and saved copies in unrelated files. To be extra safe, I also saved a copy to a thumb drive and jammed the tiny drive deep into the front pocket of my jeans.

Haylee, Opal, Naomi, and Edna were with Smythe. None of them believed Smythe could be a murderer. What if Haylee's mothers decided to leave the young lovebirds alone?

Dialing Haylee on my cell phone, I rushed to my front windows. *Closed* signs were still displayed in all of the Threadville boutiques across the street.

Haylee didn't answer. I texted her to return to her shop as soon as possible. If she was too busy to answer her phone, would she look at her messages?

I didn't take time to power off my computer. I closed the dogs into their pen, ran out the front door, locked it, and dashed to my car.

A black pickup truck was parked in front of the General Store.

I pressed down on the gas pedal and careened around Cayuga Avenue. I zigzagged through village streets to Shore Road. No one was following me.

I accelerated. To the speed limit. Above it.

Dawn's farm looked the same as it had a half hour earlier, and so did Herb's house. No vehicles in their driveways.

406

I barreled onto Smythe's road, then zoomed to the *Hap-Bee Hap-Bee* sign that marked the end of his driveway, and turned in.

The driveway curved. Curved again. Smythe's house came into sight.

All of the vehicles, including Edna's and Haylee's, that had been parked in front of it were gone. No pickup trucks.

Not even Smythe's.

Haylee and her mothers must have driven home the other way, and we had passed each other on roads a mile apart. They were probably warmly ensconced in their boutiques, ready for the day's students and shoppers. I didn't have to rescue anyone, after all.

I didn't want Smythe to be a murderer. I much preferred Irv, Pete, or possibly Herb. And maybe one of them was.

A potential method of ruling out Smythe dangled with other keys from my car's ignition. I parked the car, grabbed my keys, and tiptoed around behind Smythe's house. If he showed up, I'd say I was hunting for . . . a lost glove. I thrust one of my gloves into the pocket with Smythe's map and dashed to the shed that was locked with a gleaming new padlock.

The key went easily into the lock. It turned.

The padlock popped open.

32

My throat dry, I stared at the padlock in my hand. Smythe had a key that would open my locks. He could have beaten Mike, dragged him into my backyard, and fled, locking the gate behind him.

Smythe, sweeter than his honey. A murderer?

Out on the road, brakes squealed.

Tires crunched on the gravel in Smythe's driveway.

My car was in plain view. If anyone came around the corner of Smythe's house, he'd see me.

I had to get out of sight quickly. There was only one place to hide, and it was right in front of me.

I yanked the padlock off the door, pocketed it and my keys, pulled the shed's extra-wide door open, slipped into the shed, and closed the door. I let go of the door. It inched open by itself. I yanked it shut.

Maybe someone had driven to Hap-Bee Hap-Bee Lavender Farm hoping to see Smythe, would realize he wasn't here, and go away.

The vehicle's engine turned off.

A door slammed, a *thunk* of metal on metal. My ungloved hand cramped on the icy door handle. If the new arrival was Smythe, and he was a murderer . . .

Would he recognize my car in front of his house? Someone clomped up the porch steps. The screen door screeched. My teeth chattered. I huddled my chin into my scarf.

I was nicely hidden in Smythe's shed, but if whoever it was came out to look for me, they might notice that the shed door wasn't completely closed and the padlock was missing.

Being discovered skulking in a shed could be a bit embarrassing. If a murderer was doing the discovering, however . . .

My left arm tense across my chest, I grabbed the door handle with my gloved hand and thrust my bare right fist into my pocket. By the time my eyes adjusted to the dim shed, my hands were warm enough to dial Uncle Allen on my cell phone.

"Come out to Smythe Castor's farm," I whispered.

"Why?" He sounded sleepier than usual.

I didn't want to explain. I needed to listen for sounds from Smythe's house. "I'll show you when you get here," I whispered.

With a grumpy grunt, he disconnected.

I shoved my phone into my pocket and let my gaze drift around the inside of the shed.

What I saw turned my bones to ice.

A camouflage jacket and an orange ball cap hung on a hook near the door. The cap had been professionally embroidered. Under purple grapes were the words *Krawbach Vineyard*. Mike's cap? A scrunched up pair of yellow and black striped gloves lay on the dirt floor. Why would Smythe lock his coat, gloves, and Mike's hat in his shed? Was he hiding evidence until he figured out how and where to destroy it? Again, it seemed like a farfetched theory, but a murderer might only be thinking of ways of saving his own skin, and would destroy or hide every bit of evidence anyone might ever pin on him.

If he found me here, he would know that I knew, and he'd put me where only the coyotes would find me. I didn't dare run to my car. He would see me from his windows and catch me before I could reach it.

I sagged backward, nearly letting go of the door. Reflexes jerked my bare hand out of my pocket. I caught my balance against smooth metal.

A lawn tractor.

A key was in the ignition.

I saw it as a sign.

I peeked outside. No one. My car was on the other side of Smythe's house, and the newcomer's vehicle must be, also. I couldn't see it. The screen door hadn't screeched again. The person had to be inside the house, and he had to be Smythe. With any luck, he wouldn't hear the noise I hoped to make.

Smythe's tractor started with a deafening, and very satisfying, roar.

I put it into gear and accelerated into the shed door. It swung open on its hinges. Giddy with success and dread, I steered the lawn tractor out of the shed, through a gap in the evergreen windbreak surrounding Smythe's farmyard, and into the cornfield.

I had driven lawn tractors in spring, summer, and fall when I was a girl living at home with my parents, but I had never driven one in winter, much less on frozen furrows. Riding the thing was bone- and teeth-jarring. Aiming the wheels as best I could into furrows, I gunned the motor. The lawn tractor sprang forward. Trust Smythe to buy a really fast one.

Not fast enough.

I looked over my shoulder at the expanse of cornfield I'd already crossed.

A man wearing a bright yellow parka and a yellow and black striped stocking cap dashed out through the gap in the wind-break. Arms flailing above his head, he sprinted into the cornfield.

I needed to get to a road where I could urge the lawn tractor to its top speed. The relatively smooth road leading to Shore Road was just beyond a line of trees. The field had been plowed parallel with the road. I hauled at the steering wheel. Crossing the furrows was like sewing sideways on wide-wale corduroy, though, and I nearly beached the tractor on ridges.

I hauled at the steering wheel again and took a gentler angle across the field. The tractor moved marginally faster, but I would have to drive it farther on bumpy ground to reach the road.

At the edge of the field, I squeezed the tractor between spindly trees. Luckily, there was no fence.

There was, however, a ditch. A deep one.

Picturing myself flying over the steering wheel or rolling the tractor, I drove straight down into the ditch. The tractor bottomed out, and crawled, much too slowly, up onto the road.

Letting out a triumphant whoop, I glanced back. Smythe had closed some of the distance between us, but I was now driving faster than any man could run.

Jolting along with my teeth bared to the wind, I was about to freeze.

Jolting. Uh-oh.

The road wasn't that uneven.

A flat tire or two? Like a bicycle racer, I bent low to improve my aerodynamics. Nothing, not even speeding along on the rims with sparks flying, was going to keep me from driving all the way home.

Nothing.

Except Uncle Allen in his cruiser.

The tractor was so noisy that I hadn't noticed the cruiser's siren or horn. The cruiser cut in front of me.

I had never been happier to see Uncle Allen. He had taken me seriously enough to break speed limits. I pulled onto the shoulder and climbed off the tractor, which, now that no one was on the seat, promptly shut itself off. The right front tire was as flat as freshly ironed damask.

Hands on holsters, Uncle Allen swaggered to me. "Get back on that thing."

I could barely hear him. As usual, he hadn't shut off his siren, and the ever-persistent horn had not quite worn itself out yet. *Hoot, bloop, hoot, bloop.*

"Uncle Allen —"

He chopped the air with one gloved hand. "Driver's license?"

"It's in my car. This," I explained, "is a lawn tractor. The reason I called —"

"You were driving it on the road."

"Yes, but —"

"And it has no license for on-road travel." He was really fond of his gotcha look.

"No, but —"

"I'm gonna have to ticket you."

"Fine, but do it later, please. I called because I've discovered that Smythe —"

Uncle Allen gazed at something behind me. Between the police car's barnyard noises, I heard footsteps, running on pavement. Close.

Smythe called out, "Willow, whatever are you doing riding around on my lawn tractor in the middle of winter?" He arrived, panting, beside me.

"She stole your tractor?" Uncle Allen asked with more drama than was absolutely necessary.

I edged out of Smythe's reach. "I had to escape!" I didn't mean to shout, it just sort of came out that way. Besides, I had to make myself heard over the cruiser's horn and siren.

"From what?" they asked in unison.

"From Smythe. Uncle Allen, that's what I was trying to tell you. I've found evidence that Smythe murdered Mike."

"I did not," Smythe said.

At the same time, Uncle Allen announced. "That's impossible."

Hoot, bloop, hoot, bloop.

I pulled Smythe's padlock, with my keys dangling from it, out of my pocket. "This was on Smythe's shed. My key opens it. Therefore, his key opens the padlocks on my gates, which explains how Mike ended up locked inside my yard." There. Perfectly indisputable logic. I tightened my frozen fingers around the lock, ready to plunge it back into my pocket if Smythe or Uncle Allen reached for it.

Uncle Allen's eyebrows came down toward each other over his nose. Had he finally started to believe me?

"I never saw that padlock before in my life," Smythe said in his most honeylike voice.

And that was when I was sure that dear, sweet Smythe had murdered his cousin. Why else would he lie about the padlock?

I was also sure that I had made a colossal error. By removing the padlock and bringing it with me, I had destroyed my own

416

credibility, not to mention a crucial piece of evidence. I leveled a gaze at Smythe. "I'm disappointed in you. You and I both know you're lying." When had I begun channeling my long-ago kindergarten teacher?

"And I'm disappointed in you," Smythe countered. "For taking my lawn tractor without asking. I'd have given you a ride."

Hoot, bloop, hoot, bloop.

Uncle Allen reached for my elbow. "You're coming with me."

He carried two guns and a billy club. "I'll come," I agreed. "But I only borrowed the tractor."

Uncle Allen grunted. "You only *borrowed* the sand, too."

I resisted the urge to point out that just because I hadn't yet put it back didn't mean I wasn't going to.

I pointed at Smythe with the top of my head. "Bring him, too. I have more proof in my store. A photo of him the morning Mike died." I didn't mention the embroidered cap, camouflage coat, and wadded gloves for fear that Smythe would hide them before Uncle Allen could see them.

"Impossible," Smythe said.

"No it's not," I argued. "You didn't manage to destroy all of my photos when you stole my camera."

Smythe turned his most innocent look on Uncle Allen. "She's not making sense."

Uncle Allen said, "We're not going to argue about this out here in the cold. Both of you, get into my cruiser, and we'll go see this photo she claims to have."

Maybe I was making a teeny bit of progress with the stubborn policeman.

Smythe turned away. "I'll just take my lawn tractor home and follow you in my truck."

I cried out, "Don't let him!"

Hoot, bloop, hoot, bloop.

Uncle Allen fixed Smythe with a sterner stare than I thought he could give a local. "No one's going to bother that tractor. Just bring the key and come along. We'll get this all straightened out, then I'll drive you home."

I hoped that after I made my case, *I* would be the one catching a ride to Smythe's farm to retrieve my car, but I figured this was not the time to suggest it. If these two men had their way, Uncle Allen would deposit me in jail. Maybe Troopers Smallwood and Gartener would pay social visits from time to time.

Uncle Allen let me ride in the front seat and put Smythe in the back, probably out of chivalry.

We didn't go anywhere.

33

The siren hooted and the horn blooped, but apparently, the cruiser's engine had the right to remain silent.

Uncle Allen and Smythe got out and lifted the hood. Uncle Allen asked me to try starting the car.

So there I was, pressing the gas pedal and turning the key in the ignition of a police cruiser while a murderer and the man who wanted to put me in jail for the murder stood in front of me.

Maybe I was lucky the cruiser didn't start.

I slid out in time to hear Smythe offer, "I'll go back for my truck."

"My car's at his place, too," I told Uncle Allen, hoping he wouldn't haul me off to jail for, if nothing else, taking a lawn tractor without permission. I needed a chance to show off my evidence, first. "His pickup truck only has two seats, but all three of us will fit in my car for the ride to my store.

You can't stand here, Detective DeGlazier. It's too cold. We'll have to walk back to Smythe's together."

Rescue came in the form of a *deus ex machina*. The god was Rosemary, and the machine was the Threadville tour bus. I flagged them down.

Rosemary opened the door. "Willow, what are you doing out here?"

Hoot, bloop, hoot, bloop.

"Do you have room for us? Our vehicles don't seem to be working."

Rosemary cast a puzzled glance at the listing lawn tractor and moaning cruiser, but she had the good sense not to ask questions. "Hop in!"

Smythe made one last try. "I'll go back for my truck."

To my surprise, Uncle Allen told him he might as well come with us and get it over with. They stood back and let me climb aboard, then actually followed me.

Students near the back of the bus flapped their homework at me. "Willow!" Catching myself against seats as the bus bumped along, I made my way down the aisle. I plunked down beside the window in the next to last row of seats.

Uncle Allen and Smythe rode in front, close to Rosemary. They didn't appear to be enjoying themselves nearly as much as I was. Maybe no one was giving them embroidery to admire.

Rosemary turned onto Shore Road and picked up speed. Just outside Elderberry Bay, she pulled out to pass a red pickup truck that was driving too slowly to suit her. I opened the window. We barreled past Clay. His eyes opened wide. He couldn't be used to seeing me sticking my face out a bus window and screaming his name while urging him forward with a furiously waving arm.

The women on the back bench turned around, knelt on the seat, and beckoned to him. Settling again like a bunch of happy hens, they reported, "He's coming."

Clay would help, but I needed to recruit other sympathetic witnesses for my showdown with Smythe. I asked the woman behind me, the two women in front of me, and my seatmate to run across the street as soon as we arrived in Threadville, and to bring Haylee, Opal, Edna, and Naomi to In Stitches. I also had them spread the word that everyone on the bus was to gather at In Stitches for an important meeting before the morning's classes.

We rounded the corner near the post office. A portly man in a long black coat strode along the sidewalk. Dr. Wrinklesides, another possible supporter. I threw the window open again. "Come to my shop!"

He gazed for a startled second at me, then raised a thumb in the air. He probably thought I was undergoing a new sort of trauma. Or that I needed his services as a coroner's assistant again.

With any luck, it wouldn't come to that.

Before Rosemary pulled up in front of In Stitches, I made certain I was between Smythe and the door of the bus. This was not the time to allow him to escape. I jumped out of the bus, then turned around and gave Uncle Allen a hand. He escorted Smythe and me to the front porch of In Stitches. Women streamed out of the bus. My four messengers dashed across the street toward The Stash, Tell a Yarn, Buttons and Bows, and Batty About Quilts. The rest of the women joined us on the porch.

Clay parked at the curb. He and Dr. Wrinklesides, still carrying his package, climbed out of the pickup and walked toward us. Both of them watched me carefully, no doubt wondering what symptom I might display next.

I attempted a reassuring smile, but my entire body seemed to lack stabilizer. I unlocked my front door and let Uncle Allen and Smythe in first. From their pen, Sally and Tally yipped.

Clay gave my elbow a quick pat, then strode to the back of the store, went into the pen, squatted, and hugged the two wriggling dogs.

Rehearsing what I was going to say, I joined Clay and the dogs in the pen. My computer hummed on the desk beside me.

Haylee, her mother, and her mother's lifelong friends ran into the store. All four of them bit their lips, probably imitating my thin-as-thread smile.

I hated to hurt Haylee. With a deep breath, I raised my chin and announced loudly, "This morning at Smythe's farm, I discovered that Smythe had a padlock matching the ones on my gates."

Naomi and Opal steadied each other. Edna's mouth pruned up like she'd expected an orange and gotten a lemon. She thumbed through the notebook where she'd written clues about our suspects.

Haylee crossed her arms.

I waved Uncle Allen and Smythe closer but made them stay outside the pen, on the other side of the railing. Uncle Allen's lower lip jutted out with belligerence. Smythe was casual and relaxed, his hands in his pockets.

The store had quieted. This time, I didn't

have to raise my voice. "Several hours after Mike died, I drove out into the countryside to take pictures." I jiggled my mouse until the picture became clear. "This photo shows a man cutting across Dawn Langford's fields into the woods on a route that would take him directly to Smythe's farm. I believe it's Smythe."

Uncle Allen put a hand up like he was stopping traffic in an intersection. "That's Mike. Everyone says so." Everyone? Aunt Betty and Rhonda and their friends.

Smythe scratched the back of his neck. "It's not me."

"It's Mike," Rhonda snarled. Where had she come from?

Aunt Betty, too. "He's tall, like Mike," she commented. "But like Smythe, too."

I nearly fainted. I didn't expect any sort of help from her. I enlarged the photo to show the man's right hand. "Look closely and you'll see a tiny bit of yellow and black glove."

Opal gasped. "Smythe bought his yellow and black hat, socks, and gloves at my store."

Uncle Allen hitched at his belt. "Doesn't prove a thing. The person in the picture could be anyone. Every hunter in the state owns a coat and cap like that."

I squared my shoulders. "This morning in Smythe's shed, I saw his yellow and black striped gloves with a camouflage coat and a neon orange cap. A bunch of grapes and the words *Krawbach Vineyard* were embroidered on the cap." My turn to dish out a gotcha look.

It didn't bother Uncle Allen. "Mike gave those hats to everyone. Besides, Smythe said he never saw that padlock you claim was his."

From the back of the crowd, Sam the ironmonger piped up, "Mike may have stolen a padlock from me. He could have given it to . . . someone else."

Beside him, Pete DeGlazier nodded three times. "Mike and Smythe were thick as thieves."

Mona shook her head.

Irv edged around Jacoba and Luther. My store was becoming quite crowded. "More like thick as *arsonists*."

Smythe rubbed at his chin, then thrust both hands into the pockets of his jeans again. "Mike was the arsonist, but he always had a way of proving that Herb or I did it."

"That's right," Herb shouted. "We were always Mike's fall guys."

I tried to put sympathy and understanding into my voice. "The night Mike died, someone emptied a gas can around my cottage, the one Mike wanted to bulldoze. Maybe Mike brought someone he could blame another arson on. Maybe that person was angry at Mike for the theft of timber, including a very old and valuable black walnut tree."

Irv jeered, "You loved the tree house we built in that old tree, didn't you, Smythe? Did you still go up there to daydream, right until the time Mike had it cut down? Did Mike steal trees from you?"

I asked Smythe, "Why didn't you report Mike for stealing your timber? It had to be worth a lot." Mentally subtracting the amount of Mike's first large unexplained bank deposit from the amount of second, I came up with a ballpark figure. "Like maybe over a hundred thousand dollars."

Smythe tore off his stocking cap. "Yes, I did suspect that Mike had some of my trees cut down and sold the timber, but I didn't need the money, and he did. He had a hard time making a go of everything, especially after my aunt and uncle died. Our farms were originally one, owned by our great grandparents. I didn't want to confront him about it until, well, maybe until he brought it up and, I don't know" — Smythe shrugged — "confessed and paid me back on his own." He shoved the cap into a pocket of his yellow parka and folded his arms. "But none of this *matters*. I was in Erie the night Mike died. I didn't know anything about it until Friday night when Aunt Betty and Rhonda told me." A muscle twitched in his jaw.

I turned to Uncle Allen. "Subpoena the hotel's surveillance tapes. You may see Smythe's truck arriving early Wednesday morning."

34

It was a shot in the dark, but it found its mark.

Smythe lowered his head, backed away, and bumped into my cutting table. "You don't have to subpoena the hotel's surveillance tapes, Uncle Allen. I did leave the hotel Tuesday night and return early Wednesday morning. And I did come to Willow's place with Mike on Tuesday night." If Smythe hadn't clutched the table with one white-knuckled hand, he might have crumpled to the floor.

Keeping my eyes on him, I backed to the phone, called the state police, and asked them to send reinforcements. To my amazement, Uncle Allen didn't stop me, and after I hung up, he reminded me, "It could take a half hour for them to get here."

Naomi stepped forward, her narrow shoulders fragile, her head up. "What happened, Smythe?" she asked in her usual sweet and gentle tones.

Smythe rubbed his forehead, then pinched the top of his nose between thumb and finger. "Last Tuesday evening, after I talked to you ladies, I started toward Erie. Mike passed me in his pickup and waved at me to pull off." Smythe caught his breath with a gulp. "He said we were going to torch Willow's cottage —"

I interrupted him. "Who's 'we'?"

Smythe looked surprised I would ask that. "Mike and I. He told me to check into my hotel in Erie, then come back to, as he called it, get in on the fun, because the conference would give me a perfect alibi." Drooping against my table, Smythe studied the backs of his hands. "I knew Mike. He would find a way to blame me, but I agreed to go with him." As if afraid to let me see the entreaty on his face, he looked past me toward my back window. "I had a good reason. I was going to stop him from burning Willow's cottage down."

I closed my eyes, swayed involuntarily, and opened them again. If Smythe was to be believed, I owed him for saving Blueberry Cottage.

I said quietly, "So you were the one who broke into my store, stole my camera, and erased photographs from my computer."

He started to shake his head, then gave me a rueful smile. "I'm sorry, Willow. I heard about the photos you had on your computer, and I figured out that the one they were talking about, supposedly of Mike, was of me. Sooner or later, someone would recognize me, even though I wasn't wearing my usual hat and coat, and they'd jump to the wrong conclusion about where I was when Mike was attacked. But I didn't kill him, didn't touch him, and didn't want any evidence around that might make it look like I did. I was going to return your camera to you."

"With the pictures erased?" I asked.

He gave a dejected little nod.

If Smythe had worn his usual cap, I'd have known right away who he was. If he hadn't been wearing a bright orange cap, though, I might not have stopped to take pictures. I asked him, "Why did you wear a cap from Mike's vineyard on your long walk home?"

"I forgot and left my hat in my hotel room that night. Mike gave me his."

"And he wore . . . ?" I asked.

"He didn't wear one. He was being macho."

That was easy enough to believe. He hadn't worn one earlier that day, either. "How did you end up with a padlock matching mine?"

Smythe toed at the grain of my walnut floor. "Mike brought it in a package with a key that would open your gates. After he unlocked your gate, he told me to hang on to his lock and keys for him. He gave me the packaging, too. I was going to give it all back, but I . . . kind of left your place in a hurry that night, Willow. After I heard he died, I didn't see the point in returning them."

"And the lock turned out to be very handy when you got home, didn't it," I challenged. "You could lock your hat, coat, and gloves in your shed. Maybe you were afraid they had blood on them."

He gaped at me. "They reeked of gasoline. I didn't want them stinking up my house. I hung them in the shed to air out."

"And you *locked* the shed," I repeated.

He pulled his stocking cap out of his pocket and shoved it onto his curls, covering his eyes for a second before rolling up the bottom edge. "That was later. I'd seen some kids hanging around." His gaze didn't meet mine.

More likely, he locked the clothing in the shed after he heard about the photo the local sleuths had seen on my computer.

Edna flipped a page in her notebook. "You

drove to Erie that night, checked in at the hotel, then drove back. Where did you park your truck, and how did you get to Willow's?"

Smythe steadied himself against the table. "I left my truck at Mike's. I rode behind him on his ATV."

I burst out, "Why did he drive that? It made a racket and woke me up."

Herb answered for Smythe. "Mike liked being noticed, and he probably wanted to prove you couldn't keep ATVs off the trail."

"Mike was a daredevil," Irv said. "He wouldn't have minded if you caught him. He'd have charmed you into helping him burn down your own shed."

"Cottage," I corrected automatically. "And nothing would have made me destroy it."

Smythe looked more hangdog than my enthusiastic dogs ever could. "Mike brought his ATV so we could avoid roads when we made our getaway. He said we would never get caught."

Threadville tourists gasped. My sisters-in-thread.

Naomi extended both hands, palms up, toward Smythe. "How did you stop Mike from torching Willow's cottage, Smythe?"

Smythe rubbed the back of his hand

across his eyes. "Mike had brought along a can of gasoline. He told me to douse Willow's cottage while he broke into her lean-to. I dumped the gas out of the can, safely far from Willow's cottage." Smyth's yellow parka seemed to deflate. "Mike came out of Willow's lean-to. He was carrying her paddle like a weapon. He charged me and swung it, like my head was a baseball and the paddle was a bat."

Naomi's hands flew to her cheeks. "Smythe, how perfectly terrible! What did you do?" Although she resembled a kindly aunt, she was as good as any policeman about questioning her suspect.

"The only thing possible. I ducked, ran out the gate we'd left open, and escaped. I didn't understand what it had all been about at first, but I've thought about it ever since. Mike had known Willow's canoe paddle was in her lean-to and broke in specifically to get it. He had planned all along to knock me out, set fire to the cottage, and leave me for Willow to find."

The shop was silent except for several audible intakes of breath.

"My so-called perfect alibi wouldn't matter," Smythe went on. "Everyone would believe that I had burned down Willow's cottage, and that she'd attacked me because

434

of it. The key that opened her gate would have been in my pocket."

All very plausible, except for one detail. I asked, "When you escaped, why didn't Mike follow you on his ATV? That doesn't sound like him."

Smythe admitted, "I expected him to. I cut through backyards, first the General Store's, then around behind others until I was out of town. I didn't hear the ATV, or anything besides my own boots hitting the ground and my breathing."

With Clay at my back like a coiled spring, I bravely left the dog pen and stood up to Smythe. "Why would Mike go to so much trouble to burn down my cottage and hurt you in the process?"

Smythe hauled in one harsh breath, then another. "You stood up to him in public. He always bragged that he didn't get mad, he got even. And that's how he lived his life. I was the most available scapegoat. He thought he could tempt me with my 'perfect' alibi."

Sally and Tally whined. Clay pulled them closer.

Haylee's face could have been carved from wood. "Mike hated you, Smythe. He set you up."

Irv growled, "Mike wasn't that smart.

435

Smythe's making it up to save his skin."

Smythe flushed but didn't take his eyes off Haylee. "Mike certainly didn't set me up to *murder* him. I don't know who attacked him after I left. All I know is Mike liked to watch buildings burn but didn't want to be blamed."

Haylee interrupted him, speaking more harshly than ever. "He could only blame you if you didn't stand up for yourself."

Smythe bowed his head. "True, but —" He didn't have to say the rest. Mike had probably cowed him all his life.

Edna had a different interpretation. "He could have blamed you if he hurt you so badly you *couldn't* stand up for yourself."

Naomi asked gently, "Did you have to defend yourself from him, Smythe?"

"No!" I'd never seen Smythe this assertive before. "I told you. I left."

Edna turned pages in her notebook. She cast a condemning glower toward Herb. "Okay, Smythe, if you didn't hit Mike with that canoe paddle, who did?"

"I don't know."

The trouble was, I believed him, and I'd learned to read Haylee and The Three Weird Mothers. They believed him, too.

I'd built up a case against a person who might prove to be innocent. I was worse than Uncle Allen and the state troopers, who had not yet accused anyone, including me, of murdering Mike. I felt sick.

Edna asked, "Smythe, did you see or hear anyone else in Willow's yard or cottage that night?"

"No," he answered. "I was too busy running away."

Irv let out a scornful laugh. "Smythe was always good at running away."

"What about vehicles?" I asked, remembering the dark pickup truck that Uncle Allen and I had seen.

Smythe closed his eyes as if trying to bring back that night. "I heard something with noisy snow tires roaring down Lake Street shortly after Mike shut off his ATV."

Uncle Allen and I looked at each other. When I'd tried to describe the truck to Trooper Gartener, I'd forgotten that the sound of the truck's tires on pavement had seemed loud considering that the truck had only been creeping along.

From Uncle Allen's expression, he was remembering the same thing. "Could you tell which direction it was going?"

Smythe studied his fists. "So many things happened at once. It sounded like it was heading toward the beach. But I think it stopped before it got there."

Uncle Allen and I gave each other a slow, measuring assessment. Were we drawing the same conclusions? The truck could have parked at the end of the trail, and Mike's murderer could have approached on foot.

But how would the killer have known what was going on? Had Mike arranged for someone besides Smythe to help burn down my cottage? Someone who may have been the actual killer?

I went through the exact order of what I remembered from that night. The ATV had awakened me. The dogs had barked. I'd still been trying to wake up enough to sort it all out when the ATV's engine shut off. I'd hidden my head, first under my duvet and then under my pillow, trying to go back to sleep, but the dogs had continued their fussing and barking. I'd given up sleeping after what seemed like ten minutes but may have been as little as five, then had taken another few minutes to dress before I let the dogs out.

Everything that Smythe had described could have happened during the ten or so minutes from when Mike shut off his ATV to when the dogs and I made it outside. Mike could have unlocked the gate and brought the gas can into my yard. Smythe could have dumped out the gas while Mike broke into my lean-to and got my canoe paddle. If they'd raised their voices when Mike swung the paddle at Smythe, I hadn't heard them over the dogs' racket.

The timing worked. Smythe could have been telling the truth. The killer could have parked the truck with the noisy snow tires on Lake Street and come along the trail on foot. He could have spied on Mike and Smythe, could have seen Smythe run away, and could have been certain that Smythe didn't know he was there. This third person could have attacked Mike, only to be interrupted by my dogs racing down the hill and barking.

Desperate for a place to hide, the attacker must have broken into Blueberry Cottage and watched to see what we did. The moment we ran back up the hill, he'd have had at least five more minutes while I phoned for help and let Dr. Wrinklesides into the yard. He could have rushed out of Blueberry Cottage and finished his attack. That explained why my canoe paddle had suddenly appeared next to Mike. Then the attacker would have had time to run to his truck, hop in, and be at the intersection of Lake and Cayuga at about the moment that Uncle Allen arrived in my front yard.

What were the odds that the truck Uncle

Allen and I saw had nothing to do with the case?

Smythe had reported that Mike had said "we" were going to burn down my cottage, and Smythe had assumed that by "we," Mike meant the two of them. But what if someone else was involved and Mike hadn't told Smythe?

I asked, "Smythe, when you heard the truck with the snow tires stop nearby, did either you or Mike consider leaving before someone caught you in my yard?"

Smythe bit his lip. "I did urge him to leave. But he just said something like 'the more the merrier.' "

Rhonda's mouth curved up in a fond smile. "That would be like him."

Yes, I thought. *Especially if he'd known all along that a third person was coming.*

I stepped closer to Smythe. "Was Mike the usual instigator for his arsons?"

He looked bewildered. "Usually."

"Tell me exactly what he said when he pulled you off the highway to get him to join you."

"He said" — Smythe scrunched up his face and closed his eyes — "we were going to burn down your cottage, and it was his job to bring the gasoline because he would be coming on his ATV and it wouldn't stink up anyone's truck." He opened his eyes, apparently waiting for my reaction.

I suggested, "And you thought he meant your truck or his truck?"

Smythe nodded.

"Could he have been talking about a third truck? Someone else's, someone who had assigned him the job of bringing the gasoline? Someone who conveniently arrived after you were supposed to have been knocked out? Maybe someone who set the whole thing up because he had a serious grudge against Mike, and no one would think of blaming him for Mike's death because you or I would be the obvious suspect?"

The speed of Smythe's nodding accelerated, and he began looking relieved. "Yes," he said. "Yes to all of it."

I glanced at Uncle Allen. "So now maybe we're looking for a dark pickup truck with snow tires. Maybe belonging to someone who was capable of ordering Mike around." *Unlike Smythe.*

I scanned faces in the crowd for anyone who appeared nervous. Aunt Betty thrust her many chins forward. "I drive a black pickup with snow tires, but I wasn't out that night. I was home with Uncle Allen, as he well knows."

Herb's gaze didn't meet mine. Like nearly everyone else, Herb drove a black pickup. He lived out in the country, and probably had snow tires, too.

Trying to make it look accidental, I backed into a display of threads, jostling about a zillion spools out onto the floor. As I'd hoped, people scrambled to pick them up and give them back to me. Sally and Tally barked their pleasure at seeing humans involved in something resembling the games they liked to play.

Acting like a flustered shopkeeper, I asked Herb to check underneath my cutting table in case any spools rolled under there. With a smiling salute, he got down on his hands and knees. Smythe and Irv joined him. Their hands patted the floor. Spools clicked and clattered as they rolled away from the men.

The soles of Herb's and Smythe's boots had a little mud in the treads.

The sole of one of Irv's boots had a little mud in the treads, too, next to an aqua outline so broken up that it looked more like thread than paint. Most of the paint must have rubbed off, but it was obvious that it had originally been one solid blotch, roughly the shape of Ohio.

35

Herb and Smythe stood and handed me spools of thread.

I thanked them, set the spools on the counter, and whipped Smythe's map from my pocket. In the brightly lit store, I saw things I hadn't noticed in the cold dawn.

Boundary lines and names.

The upper two-thirds of the map showed Smythe's farm and was labeled with his last name, Castor. The bottom third was divided roughly in half, with grapes on the section labeled Krawbach, and sheaves of wheat on the section labeled Oslington, Irv's last name. The woodlot covered the area where the three farms met. The main feature in the Oslington section of the woodlot was a drawing of a gigantic tree with every child's dream tree house perched among the branches. That must have been the tree house that Irv had said Smythe loved.

I'd figured out the motive but had assigned it to the wrong person. That valuable tree must have belonged to Irv, and Mike had sold that tree and probably a few others of Irv's to a logging company.

But why would Irv kill him over that? Why not report the theft and let the authorities deal with Mike?

Had Mike known something that Irv couldn't let the rest of the world know, something that could end Irv's career, perhaps land him in jail?

Pete DeGlazier was staring at me. He couldn't help nodding. Maybe Mike and Irv had worked together to steal Pete's fishing hut and equipment and sell them. Or they had pulled other similar "pranks" together.

Irv was still under the cutting table, presumably collecting spools.

I grabbed Uncle Allen's arm and pointed at the sole of Irv's boot. Uncle Allen bent over. Slowly, he rose, and I saw understanding in his eyes, along with apology and a great deal of hurt. He was going to have to arrest the mayor of Elderberry Bay. When Mike and Irv were teens, Uncle Allen had done all he could to keep the boys out of trouble. And now one of them had murdered the other. I wondered if Uncle Allen had always been afraid of just such an outcome. Maybe after the younger men outgrew their teens, Uncle Allen had relaxed, but the animosities between the two men had continued to fester . . .

Irv crawled out from under the table and handed me a spool of thread as red as his face.

"Irv," Uncle Allen said gently, "give me your boots."

Irv rolled his eyes as if to say that Uncle Allen had finally lost it, but he sat on the floor and dragged off his boots, one by one, and set them where Uncle Allen could reach them.

Irv had been underneath that table for a longer time than the other two men, but had come up with only one spool of thread. What had he been doing? I squatted to peer underneath the lowest shelf.

A wooden button lay near one of the table legs. I had vacuumed carefully the night before. I jumped up. "Detective DeGlazier, look at what appeared just now underneath my table."

With much creaking, he flattened himself to look. His voice came out muffled. "Get me a bag, Miss Vanderling."

Edna leaned forward as if she could see through the table. "A paper bag, Willow. What's under there?"

"The only thing I saw," Herb said, "was that spool of red thread Irv gave Willow."

"Me, too," Smythe agreed.

Still sitting on the floor, Irv said nothing.

I handed Uncle Allen a paper bag. He surfaced and held it open for me to see inside. The button was black walnut, almost identical to the one I'd found in the sink of Blueberry Cottage. Frayed brown threads trailed from the button's two holes. I called to Clay, "Come see this."

He peeked into the bag. "The grain is similar to the one we found in your cottage, isn't it?"

Edna squeezed in for a look. "The forensics lab will be able to tell if it was cut from the same piece of wood as the button you found and the buttons still on Mike's coat."

Irv's face reddened even more. He rose from the floor and towered over Uncle Allen. "I gather that one of Mike's buttons was found in Willow's cottage and now this one was in her shop. Shouldn't that be enough for you to arrest her for Mike's murder?"

I shot back, "Those buttons were deliberately placed on my property." I pointed at the bag in Uncle Allen's hand. "That one was put there only moments ago. While *you* were under the table."

Irv seemed totally unrattled. "Smythe must have planted it."

Uncle Allen glowered at Irv. "You were the last one to come up from underneath that table."

Irv pointed at me. "No, she was."

Actually, Uncle Allen was. He asked Irv, "When did you last wear these boots?"

"How am I supposed to remember that? I wear them around the farm, and on days like this morning, hiking in the cold."

I asked Uncle Allen, "Do you think we saw *Irv's* pickup driving slowly through the village the morning Mike died?"

"Can't rule it out," Uncle Allen said. "Especially if the print of Irv's boot matches the one the state police carried off with your porch floorboards. They'll check for Mike's blood in Irv's pickup, also, transferred from Irv's clothes."

Irv's wife's face froze in a deer-in-the-headlights stare.

"Do you know something about the outfit he wore that morning?" I asked her. "The jacket he has on today looks brand new." The plastic tie that must have held the price tag still stuck out like a needle from the side seam.

"No," she answered.

"Don't be an accessory after the fact,"

Edna warned her. "The forensics lab will test everything. If the paint on your husband's shoe matches the paint found at the scene . . ."

Irv's wife snapped, "I can't be expected to keep track of every item of my husband's clothing."

She had a point, but I had a feeling she was lying and had told the investigators her husband was home all night Tuesday night, when he hadn't been.

Edna bobbed her head. "It will all come out in court."

Opal asked Irv's wife, "Did Irv perhaps dig a hole since last Wednesday morning and bury his clothes?"

Irv looked at Opal with a superior sneer. "The ground's frozen. It didn't thaw that much during the rain we had Saturday night."

Opal went on as if he hadn't spoken, "Or build any fires?"

Irv's wife's voice was so quiet we could barely hear it. "He burned the trash on Wednesday, just like he always does."

Irv snapped, "Shut up, Skippy."

Skippy.

Maybe Irv had another motive for killing Mike besides the theft of valuable timber. I turned to Uncle Allen. "I have something else to show you. Don't go away."

I dashed downstairs. Outside, a normal police siren sounded. I ran back upstairs with the chest that the flood had brought me.

State Trooper Gartener and the petite blonde I'd seen on Lake Street who must be Trooper Smallwood were standing just inside the door, looking perplexed by the large and noisy gathering in my shop.

Before I could turn the box over to display the inscription, Rhonda burst through the crowd and ran toward me. "How did you get my jewelry box? Did Mike make you one, too?" She reached for it. "Or did you steal mine?"

"It came down the river with other flotsam. I washed off some of the mud, but didn't quite get it all." I held it so everyone in the room could see the carving on the bottom.

His face now verging on purple, Irv snarled, "Mike only started making those a couple of years ago. And we've been married for how long, Skippy? A lot longer than that. I couldn't believe it when I found that in Mike's workshop after Smythe killed him." He took a step toward her, but Smythe held him back.

Haylee and I traded glances. Now we

knew who had searched Mike's house before we got there.

Skippy gasped. "That's not mine. I never saw it before. Me and Mike?" Her shudder looked real. "Never! I have no idea why he would have such a thing in his workshop. He never gave it to me."

Irv must have jumped to the conclusion that crossed my mind. *Maybe Mike had been planning to give it to Skippy and hadn't done it yet.*

The female trooper said, "The deceased had a whole shop full of those boxes when we searched his place, didn't he?" Trooper Smallwood's voice was as soft and sweet as it had been over the phone.

Stern as ever, Gartener didn't look at her. "I've been going through photos of all of them, figuring out the inscriptions. A whole bunch of women's names. Skippy was definitely not among them."

Skippy repeated, "I never saw it before in my life."

Looking up at Gartener beneath fluttering eyelashes, Rhonda reached for the box again. "If it's like mine, it has a secret compartment."

What a show-off.

Gartener came close to Rhonda. She looked about to swoon. He asked her, "How did you get aqua paint on your thumb?"

She hid her hand behind her back like a stubborn child.

Gartner just stared at her, like he had all day for her confession.

Finally, she admitted in a small voice, "I wanted to see if the paint on the porch of Willow's cottage was dry. I did it after you took the crime scene tape down. I swear."

Aunt Betty pulled Rhonda farther from Gartener. "I was with her. We'd heard about the paint and were just checking."

They'd heard about the paint from her husband, no doubt. And were snooping on me. They must have climbed my fence to get in. If the occasion had been less serious, I might have laughed.

Gently, Gartener removed the box from my hands and set it on the table in front of Rhonda. "Does this one have a secret compartment?"

She tossed her head, which didn't do anything to show off her hair, since her hood had matted it rather drastically. "Probably not. Mike said mine was special."

It took both troopers, under the supervision of Rhonda, to discover that the box did have a false bottom. They lifted it out, along with a bunch of sodden papers.

Trooper Gartener put on white cotton

gloves and moved the pages, one by one, into another pile. I saw the word "deed" on one.

And the name of a logging company on another. I quickly looked at the bottom of a column of figures, and saw an amount close to two hundred thousand dollars, and even closer to the amount I'd seen listed in Mike's bank account. I didn't dare mention that I'd seen Mike's bank books. The investigators would surely notice without my help that the figures and the timing matched.

One of them seemed to. "Huh," the garrulous Trooper Gartener said.

Trooper Smallwood moved closer to Gartener. "These could have come from those empty files we found in the deceased's house."

I carefully did not look at Haylee. We'd seen empty files marked *Deeds* and *Sales.*

Smallwood eyed Irv. "Someone broke into that house before we arrived. You've already admitted you found the wooden box on the deceased's premises. It's easy to believe that you were the one who put these papers into the box."

Irv quickly denied it. "I've never seen those papers before. I didn't know the box had a secret compartment."

Smallwood clicked a fingernail down on the table next to the wet pages. "There must be something in here that someone didn't want anyone else to see. I have a feeling that when we read these papers, we'll have a pretty good guess about who might have hidden them in the box and dumped it."

Trooper Gartener grunted and began one of his long, dark-eyed stares at me.

I did my best to look completely innocent, but all I could think of was the rabies tag he'd found in Mike's yard, evidence that my dogs and I had done some illicit sleuthing.

"You'll have to show us later, Miss Vanderling," he said calmly in that deep, warm voice, "where you found this box."

"On the riverbank," I answered. "In front of Blueberry Cottage."

"Any idea how the box, and its contents, got into the river?"

"Somebody must have thrown it into the river thinking it would sink or be washed out into the lake."

"Who would do that?"

I answered his question with a question. "Someone who didn't want the world to find out about grudges he held against the deceased?" I stared directly at Irv. "You said Mike wasn't smart enough to set Smythe

453

up to burn down my cottage and injure Smythe so that I'd be blamed for everything. Who did come up with the scheme? Smythe?"

Irv lifted his chin. "Are you kidding? Smythe?"

And yet Irv had said Smythe was making it all up . . .

Herb called out, "Irv's the smart one in the bunch, at least to hear him talk."

Skippy defended her husband. "He is smart. He's our mayor, after all. None of the rest of you could do that job, not even Mike."

Irv growled again, "Shut up, Skippy."

But Skippy wouldn't be quiet. "Did it never occur to you that Mike might have carved that inscription just to make trouble between you and me?" Huge tears welled from her eyes.

Naomi, Opal, and Edna flurried to console her.

Uncle Allen took Irv's arm and summarized the evidence we'd collected about Irv, the paint on his boots, the possibility that his boots would match the print found in the paint, the noisy snow tires, the theory I'd come up with earlier about the theft of the timber, and this latest evidence that Irv might have believed something was going on between his wife and Mike. And to top it all off, the evidence the police hoped to find when they read the papers they'd discovered in the box.

Herb called out, "Mike got the last laugh, Irv. Even after his death, he proved you aren't as smart as you like to think."

That must have been too much for Irv. "He's the one who ended up dead." He glared at me. "It would have all worked out fine if she hadn't stuck her nose in where it didn't belong. She humiliated Mike in front of the whole town. He couldn't have that. I told him so. I told him he had to get even. Didn't take much convincing, either. He wanted to take her down a peg or two. Her and all her weird, crafty friends over there." He gestured at Haylee and her mothers. "I told him to bring Smythe along so we could leave him behind to take the blame, like we used to do as kids."

Irv had orchestrated Tuesday night's entire fiasco and had involved Mike. But all along, he'd had an agenda he'd hidden from Mike. Even before he'd found the box with the name Skippy carved on it, Irv must have harbored suspicions about Mike and his wife, suspicions that, judging by Skippy's behavior, could have been false, could have been fostered by Mike for the "fun" of making Irv angry. And Irv had been ready to be angry. He had to have known that Mike had stolen the timber from him, including the beloved old tree and its nostalgic tree house.

Mike had been too arrogant to realize that Irv's plan was really for Mike to end up dead, and for Smythe or me to be blamed.

Irv had succeeded in killing Mike and had nearly succeeded in sending Smythe or me to jail for the crime.

Uncle Allen relinquished Irv to the state troopers. "You'll need to question him further, impound his truck, and search his premises, especially where he burns his trash. You'll also need to Mirandize him. I'll come along to help as soon as I get a ride back to my cruiser and, um, get it started."

Trooper Gartener drilled into him with his policeman eyes. I winced on Uncle Allen's behalf and offered Gartener a half smile. He gave me the barest hint of an unsmiling nod. From that taciturn man, it nearly amounted to a declaration of friendship.

The two state troopers escorted Irv, in his stocking feet, toward the door. As they passed Haylee, something jingled near Trooper Gartener's boot. He bent over, picked the object up, and handed it to Haylee, saying very courteously, "Ma'am, I think you dropped something."

Haylee's eyes went wide, and she started to shake her head, then closed her fist on the thing, and thanked him. I tried to catch her eye, but she seemed to be avoiding looking anywhere near me.

The troopers went outside and helped Irv into a sparkling, new cruiser.

I had one more question for Smythe. "Did you hide inside Opal's store Friday night, eavesdropping on our storytelling?" I was fairly sure he hadn't, unless he'd borrowed a black pickup truck.

Smythe tilted his head as if confused. "I came straight inside the moment I arrived and gave you honey, remember? Then I left with Rhonda and Aunt Betty."

A dawning softness on Rhonda's face said that Smythe had a chance with her, now that Mike was gone. "That's right, he went out with us."

Smythe looked away from her. He was probably considering confessing to Mike's murder and asking for a sentence that would end only after Rhonda found herself a different man.

"Did you let someone into Tell a Yarn when you went out the door?" I persisted.

Aunt Betty put her hands on her hips and stared at her husband.

Uncle Allen cleared his throat and shuffled his boots.

Hugging her notebook, Edna advanced on him. "No search warrant?"

Uncle Allen looked up without seeming to focus on anyone. "I had a murder to investigate," he growled.

Aunt Betty tripped over her snowmobile suit pant legs in her rush to her husband. "I'll take you to your car and jump-start it for you again." She placed her fists on her hips. "You've been saying for years that you'd retire after you solved a big case. Now's your chance."

Uncle Allen squinched up his mouth. "Maybe."

Dr. Wrinklesides boomed, "Think about it, Uncle Allen!"

Uncle Allen boomed back, "Are *you* going to retire anytime soon?"

Dr. Wrinklesides laughed. "Can't. Too many patients."

Uncle Allen retorted, "And I've got too many criminals."

Uh-oh.

Uncle Allen looked his wife up and down. "If I retire, I won't be able to wear my uniform jacket anymore, and I'll need my snowmobile suit back."

"What will I wear?" Aunt Betty asked. "I

don't have anything else as comfortable or warm."

Rosemary had the answer for that. "Haylee gives classes where you'll learn to make scrumptious coats. Naomi can help you quilt them, and Edna and Willow will help you embellish them."

"Speaking of which," Opal said, "we'd better go." She and Naomi and Edna led their students outside.

Belting out an aria, Dr. Wrinklesides carried his package down the street. Luther, Jacoba, Herb, Rhonda, Aunt Betty, and Uncle Allen left.

Twisting his hat between his hands, Smythe came to me, with Haylee beside him. Haylee opened a drawer in my cutting table and thrust something jingly inside. I caught only a glimpse of the object, but it looked a lot like Sally's lost rabies tag. With a conspiratorial grin, Haylee shut the drawer.

I was stunned. Gartener should have passed that "evidence" to the rest of the crime investigators. Why hadn't he? Because he wanted to confront me with it first to see what I said, and I had come across as totally innocent? How had I managed that?

I realized Smythe was talking. "Sorry to have caused you so much trouble, Willow.

I'll bring your camera back."

I said, "You didn't cause me nearly as much trouble as I caused you just now with my false accusations. I didn't want to believe you were a murderer, couldn't believe it, really, but I kept finding all these clues that pointed to you. I'm really sorry, Smythe."

He looked down at his hat. "Don't be. If I'd confessed my part in Mike's scheme from the beginning like I should have, the false accusation would have come from Uncle Allen, and I'd be in jail for Mike's murder now, but thanks to you, I'm free. Except for —" He made one of his funny faces. "I think they can charge me with . . . something."

Haylee touched his arm. "They won't." Throwing me a smile that said she would have done the exact same thing if I'd been the one hanging around someone she suspected of murder, she headed for the door. Smythe and her students followed her.

Clay gave the dogs good-bye pats and climbed over the railing. This morning, for once, he hadn't asked me what was wrong the moment he arrived, but he had to have realized something had been terribly wrong when our bus sped past him, and he had, as always, come to my rescue.

"Thanks, Clay," I said, knowing it was inadequate.

"Anytime."

"I guess we won't be able to renovate Blueberry Cottage until we can get permits," I began. With Irv in custody, who could act as zoning commissioner?

"We'll figure it out." He nodded toward the Threadville tourists preparing for this morning's embroidery lesson. "It looks like you have work to do. Talk to you later."

Haylee had known me for years and obviously understood why I had accused Smythe. If she'd suspected I was dating a murderer, she'd have exposed him for what he was. Smythe, who was entirely too trusting, seemed to have forgiven me, too. Someday, maybe, I could forgive myself.

But what about Smythe's friend, Clay? He was kind and helpful like Smythe, but not as trusting, which was probably a good thing — he wasn't likely to get into the sort of predicament that Smythe had gotten himself into. Clay and I might get to know each other — and to trust each other — one of these days, maybe when we renovated my cottage together. It was something to look forward to . . .

Susannah broke into my daydreams. "What are we doing today, Willow?"

"Stumpwork."

My students cheered.

I grinned. I loved my embroidery boutique, and I loved Threadville.

WILLOW'S EMBROIDERED CELL PHONE CASE

Whether you own an embroidery machine or not, you can use basic thread art techniques to embroider and embellish your sewing crafts. Naturally, I would like you to come to my sewing and embroidery machine boutique, In Stitches, in Threadville, where you can browse and join our classes. Meanwhile, here are instructions for a simple project you can do with any sewing machine that sews a satin stitch (zigzag stitches sewn tightly together), followed by instructions for those of you who already own embroidery machines.

MATERIALS EVERYONE WILL NEED, WHETHER YOU OWN AN EMBROIDERY MACHINE OR NOT

Embroidery hoop to fit your embroidery machine, or if you don't have an embroidery machine, any embroidery hoop about ten inches in diameter

2 squares of felt in color(s) of your choice and large enough for a couple of inches to stick out all around the hoop

1 square of heavy stabilizer or 2 squares of midweight stabilizer, the same approximate size as the felt

Embroidery thread

Nylon lingerie thread

(Optional) button, snap, ribbon, or hook-and-loop closing

INSTRUCTIONS FOR THOSE OF YOU STILL DECIDING WHICH EMBROIDERY MACHINE TO BUY

1. Lower or remove the teeth ("feed dogs") that move your fabric for everyday stitching.★
2. Fill the bobbin with nylon lingerie thread and place it in your machine.
3. Install a special spring-loaded embroidery presser foot.★
4. On 1 square of felt, draw around the sides and lower edge of your cell phone, making a U shape that's

★ If you can't remove or lower your feed dogs and/or don't have a choice of presser feet, straight and zigzag stitches in a variety of colors can make interesting plaid or striped effects.

about a quarter inch larger on all three sides than your phone. Inside the U, draw the design that you will stitch over (also known as freehand thread art). Simple sketches are best at first.

5. Place this square of felt on top of the stabilizer in the hoop. Tighten the hoop, being careful not to tear the felt or stabilizer.

6. Slide the hooped felt under your presser foot and lower your presser foot. Holding the hoop with both hands, start your machine stitching. Guide the stitches along the design you've drawn, changing the top thread color whenever it suits you. Go wild!

7. Fill a bobbin with embroidery thread that goes nicely with your felt and with the design you've stitched. Place the new bobbin in your machine.

8. Keep the felt that you just decorated in the hoop. You don't have to insert the second piece of felt into the hoop. Instead, pin it to the back of the first piece. The stabilizer will be sandwiched between the two pieces of felt. Without stitching inside your

U shape, baste the layers together. Remove the pins.

9. Carefully stitch a line of straight stitching to follow the U shape you drew. Leave the top unsewn. Your two pieces of felt are now sewn together, with your design on the front.

10. Carefully satin stitch over your straight stitching.

11. Remove the felt from the hoop. Carefully cut around the outside of the satin stitching without snipping stitches. The top can be cut straight across, or you can leave envelope-like flaps and add a fastener of your choice.

12. Last but not least — send me Willow@ThreadvilleMysteries.com a photo of your project that I can display along with your name on my website gallery. Extra points if you incorporate stumpwork using the method I described in the preceding pages of this book!

INSTRUCTIONS FOR THOSE OF YOU WHO ALREADY OWN AN EMBROIDERY MACHINE

Follow steps 1–5 above.

6. Fasten the hoop to the embroidery machine. Stitch a design in the center of the felt. You can purchase a commercial embroidery design, create your own, or download one of my free original designs from www.ThreadvilleMysteries.com.
7. Fill a bobbin with embroidery thread that goes nicely with your felt and with the design you've stitched. Place the new bobbin in your machine.
8. If you don't have embroidery software, remove the hoop from the embroidery machine, but keep the project in the hoop. Using your sewing machine, follow steps 8–12 above.

   If you do have embroidery software, keep the project in the hoop and keep the hoop in your embroidery machine. Slide the second square of felt underneath your hoop. You don't need to insert it in the hoop. Instead, stitching around the inner edges of the hoop and away from the design you stitched, machine-baste (a simple procedure for those who already own embroidery software) the second piece of felt to the first piece. The stabilizer will be sandwiched between the two pieces of felt.

9. Use your embroidery software to create a new design of a simple straight-stitched U that is about a quarter inch larger than the lower 3 sides of your phone and will surround the design you already stitched with the design centered.

10. Create a satin-stitched outline over the first line of stitches. Send the design (straight stitches covered by satin stitches) to the embroidery machine. Stitch.

To finish, follow steps 11–12 above.

THREAD ART TIPS

Thread Art Tips for everyone, whether you own an embroidery machine or not. (Be sure to read the instructions that came with your machines.)

NEEDLES

Use the correct needle: Embroidery needles will keep embroidery thread from tangling or breaking. Metallic threads require needles designed specifically for them. If sewing on leather or leather-like fabrics, use needles created for leather.

Never use a dull needle. The rule of thumb is to replace it after four hours of sewing, but if it becomes dull, nicked, or bent, replace it immediately.

THREAD

Can you ever have too many colors? Thread tends to dry and become brittle with age, so to prevent breakage, use it freely and buy new spools often (like whenever you see another color you just have to have . . .).

STABILIZER

Never stint on stabilizer. If you don't use enough, your design may pucker.

HOOPING

When tightening your hoop, don't distort your fabric.

Happy hooping it up and embroidering!

WILLOW